Ellie Darkins spent her formative years devouring romance novels and, after completing her English degree, decided to make a living from her love of books. As a writer and editor, she finds her work now entails dreaming up romantic proposals, hot dates with alpha males and trips to the past with dashing heroes. When she's not working she can usually be found running around after her toddler, volunteering at her local library, or escaping all of the above with a good book and a vanilla latte.

Kathy Douglass came by her love of reading naturally—both of her parents were readers. She would finish one book and pick up another. Then she attended law school and traded romances for legal opinions. After the birth of her two children, her love of reading turned into a love of writing. Kathy now spends her days writing the small-town contemporary novels she enjoys reading.

Also by Ellie Darkins

Frozen Heart, Melting Kiss
Bound by a Baby Bump
Newborn on Her Doorstep
Holiday with the Mystery Italian
Falling for the Rebel Princess
Conveniently Engaged to the Boss
Surprise Baby for the Heir
Falling Again for Her Island Fling
Reunited by the Tycoon's Twins
Snowbound at the Manor

Also by Kathy Douglass

How to Steal the Lawman's Heart
The Waitress's Secret
The Rancher and the City Girl
Winning Charlotte Back
The Rancher's Return
The City Girl's Homecoming
The Maverick's Baby Arrangement

Discover more at millsandboon.co.uk

FROM BEST FRIEND TO FIANCÉE

ELLIE DARKINS

REDEMPTION ON RIVERS RANCH

KATHY DOUGLASS

MILLS & BOON

First Published in Great Britain 2021
by Mills & Boon, an imprint of HarperCollins*Publishers* Ltd
1 London Bridge Street, London, SE1 9GF

www.harpercollins.co.uk

HarperCollins*Publishers*
1st Floor, Watermarque Building,
Ringsend Road, Dublin 4, Ireland

From Best Friend to Fiancée © 2021 Ellie Darkins
Redemption on Rivers Ranch © 2021 Kathleen Gregory

ISBN: 978-0-263-29979-3

0521

MIX
Paper from
responsible sources
FSC™ C007454

This book is produced from independently certified FSC™ paper to ensure responsible forest management.

For more information visit: www.harpercollins.co.uk/green

Printed and bound in Spain
by CPI, Barcelona

FROM BEST FRIEND TO FIANCÉE

ELLIE DARKINS

This is for everyone who has called, texted, tweeted, messaged, sent cards, sent flowers, and delivered milk to my door. This year has been a test of endurance for us all, but I've never felt more loved or supported by friends, family and complete strangers. Thank you all.

CHAPTER ONE

'WHO KNEW THAT you were such a stud?' Lara said, eyeing Jannes over the top of the magazine.

'You know there's not a truthful word in the whole article, don't you?' her best friend replied with an eye roll and a withering look. He pulled the magazine back from her and pushed her towards one of the food stalls at Broadway Market. They'd met at the corner opposite London Fields, the same as they did every weekend he was in London, catching up on everything they'd been up to in the weeks that he'd been in Harbourside, the coastal town where his yacht club was located, or away sailing. That was the price you paid for your best friend being a professional athlete, she supposed. If he was going to keep winning these round-the-world races and breaking records left, right and centre, she was going to miss him while he was doing it.

But at least she got to see his face in the papers while he was away. Even if he wasn't very happy about it. She smirked at Jannes. 'At least they spelt your name right.'

He groaned. 'This isn't funny, Lara. All the sponsors we were lining up for the next transatlantic record attempt are freaking out. If they drop me because of this, then my plans will be down the toilet.'

She gave his arm a comforting squeeze and then bought him dhal and samosas from one of the stalls at Broadway Market, and crossed back over the road to eat in the park, spreading out her jacket on the grass as a makeshift picnic blanket. It felt like months since she had had the sun on her face. The winter had been long and hard, with an epic blizzard thrown in for good measure. But this morning she had woken up to spring. Her coat cupboard was still scattered with hats and scarves, but she'd left the house in just a sweater and a light jacket for the first time since September. London was glorious like this, and the whole of Hackney seemed to have a smile on their face.

She knew that her social feeds were going to be flooded with sunshiny pictures and iced coffees and spring flowers, and could hardly wait to launch her own spring theme. She made a mental note to take some pictures in the park before they headed back to her apartment. As an influencer, half her life was lived online, and the other half was spent studying for her MBA and launching her consultancy business, to help others achieve the success that she had found in building her little online community.

She took one look at Jannes, though, and stopped grinning. 'I'm sorry, Jannes. I don't know why they would make stuff up like this.'

He shook his head, looking again at the magazine. 'I went on, like, four dates this year. None of which went particularly well. And they've gathered every pa-

parazzi photo that can possibly make me look like I'm with a girl and made me look like some sort of Casanova. I sneeze in a woman's general direction and all of a sudden I'm cheating with her on my other nonexistent girlfriend.'

He said that as if she wasn't hyperaware of every date he had been on. As if she hadn't hung off his every word and nearly killed herself feigning nonchalance every time he had mentioned another woman's name. Really, sometimes it was exhausting loving Jannes as a friend the way she did, and him being beautiful, the way that he was. And knowing that under different circumstances—if she were someone different, someone less broken—that this could really be…something. But she was broken. And she wasn't someone different. And if she and Jannes tried turning this friendship into anything more then she knew that she would hurt him and lose him, and she just couldn't risk that. So she changed the subject, as she always did. Lightened the tone and tried to pretend that it didn't hurt. You'd think after three years of this, it would be easier.

'Or, you know,' she said, aiming light and hoping that her voice didn't shake. 'You've got your arm around a girl wearing a bikini…'

He hit her playfully on the arm with the magazine and she figured she'd got away with it. 'Oh, my God, I'd gone for a swim!' he protested. 'This is what I'm talking about. She slipped and I caught her. I probably saved her a concussion, but according to this we had a torrid three-day affair.' His voice sounded a little strained, and he was avoiding eye contact. Was he embarrassed about the picture? she wondered. Or was he in tune with her on this, as he was on just about anything else? Did he feel them drawing together every time that she did? Was he fighting as hard as she was?

'She does look a little dazed,' Lara observed, looking at the girl in the photo and accidentally dripping raita on her face.

Jannes shoved her with his foot. 'You're meant to be on my side.'

'Of course I'm on your side,' she told him gently. 'Tell me what I can do to help.'

'How are you with crisis PR?' he asked, a note of tension in his voice that she couldn't account for.

Lara smiled, after just a fraction of a hesitation. 'I don't know. I've never tried it, but I'll probably be excellent. What are you thinking?'

He shifted a little uncomfortably. 'Well, I had an idea. It was something my grandmother said, actually. The thing is, I have an awards thing in a couple of weeks, and it could be a good chance to present a new image. And I thought if you came with me, it might… change the narrative.'

'Explain,' Lara said, creasing her forehead as she listened to him.

'Well, people know that we're friends. We've been photographed together before. If we went together, and made it look like we were together, it would make me seem more…settled. Less…'

'Man slutty?'

He barked a laugh—she loved that. Loved that she could take him by surprise and make him lose control for a second. 'Well. Yes. You have this thing that makes people love you. I could do with a pinch of that.'

She frowned, thinking. 'I don't know, Jannes. It feels a little…weird. You're my best friend, and nothing more, and we've always been very clear about that. With each other. With everyone else. I'm worried that if we start bending the truth about that, there'll be a grey area, you know?'

'I know,' he said. 'And I agree. You know how much you mean to me, and I don't want to do anything that would risk that. But… Lara, I cannot lose this sponsorship. If I don't attempt the speed record this year— I don't know if I'll be able to do it again. And I can't think of another way to turn things around as quickly. And we know what we are, right? We know where we stand. That doesn't change.'

She thought about what he'd said while she ate. 'Why don't you take your grandmother?' she asked at last, thinking aloud, avoiding the proposal he'd put to her until she had thought about it some more. Maybe there was some other way out of this that didn't involve her examining her feelings for him quite so closely.

'You think I could trust Mormor near a TV camera?' Jannes said with a laugh. 'She'd be rampaging on my behalf. It was her idea that I ask you.'

Lara nodded. 'That's a good point. I love it when Mormor rampages.'

'Which is why it always terrifies me when you two are in a room together.'

She should agree to it, of course. She shouldn't even have to think about it. Jannes was one of her closest friends and, much as she would do just about anything to help him if he was in trouble, this was just…a little close to the bone. Because she was pretty sure that Jannes had been as determined as she had over the years to ensure that their friendship had never been in danger of being mistaken for more. And they'd never spoken about it, but she was pretty sure it was a battle that was being fought by both of them.

Jannes was a great guy. Certainly the best one that she knew. And Lara had a thing about nice guys—she didn't date them. What was the point when they got attached and she got attached and then they both got hurt? It hadn't taken her long into her twenties for her to realise that she was really bad at relationships. She'd freaked out the few times that things had been going well, and it had become clear that she wasn't cut out for making things serious.

Looking back, she knew exactly what the problem was—there was something wrong with her. When her father had walked out on her—for the other family he'd kept hidden from her her whole life—something inside her had broken. She wasn't sure what part it was, but somewhere along the line between dating and liking and loving, something was just…off. She was off. She tried to love and she couldn't, so she pushed boys away before she could hurt them. She wouldn't hurt Jannes. It was just unthinkable. Which was why she'd been keeping him firmly in the safe zone since the day that she had met him.

But he needed her, and she'd never been able to resist it when Jannes needed her. Eventually, she gave him her answer.

'Fine, I'll be your plus one,' she said. 'And I'll pretend to be your girlfriend. But we don't let this change anything between us, right? Everything stays the same. I don't want things to be confusing—I love you and you know that, but as friends and nothing more. I don't want anything to change.'

He nodded firmly, which gave her a little bit of confidence that this was all going to be fine, even if her gut was telling her something different. 'I know; I understand and I feel the same. This is all just for show. It doesn't change anything.'

'Good.' She let out a breath, let the tension drain from her shoulders. And then an idea struck.

'Hey, you know it's Pip's wedding next weekend? Will you come with me? If we're going to pretend to date, it'd be weird if you didn't, right?' If they were doing it once, what harm could it do to make it twice?

Her sister—her half-sister—had sent the invitation months ago, and she hadn't been able to say no, not when Pip had uninvited their father so that Lara wouldn't have to see him. She'd ignored the event in her calendar, hoping that something would come up that would mean she could get out of going. But nothing had and she'd been dreading it, but this could be perfect. She took a deep breath. 'I can't not go and I'm dreading it. I was going to just tough it out but… I'm wavering. So just do me a favour and hold my hand for a few hours?' He'd just told her that he wanted her to do practically the same thing for him, so it could hardly be a big deal.

'You know you could just find a nice boy to take you?' Jannes said at last.

Lara rolled her eyes. 'Ew, no thanks.'

Jannes laughed. 'Did you say *ew*? Are you twelve?'

'No, I'm thirty-one, very busy running a business where I'm expected to be available twenty-four-seven and can't be arsed filtering through all the douchebags in London to find the one decent guy left. So you'll have to do.' Which were all perfectly valid reasons for her not to date. And all true. But Jannes didn't need to know that they weren't the whole truth. That she didn't see the point in dating, when everything always ended in tears. And she didn't like doing that to people, least of all someone who she actually liked.

Jannes smiled, so broadly that it almost annoyed her. 'Ah, so you're going to convince me with flattery.'

'I'd ask Jess—' great friend, but also newly married '—but she's up in Yorkshire being deliciously loved-up with Rufus. For once you're not on a boat somewhere, you just asked me for a massive favour and I promise to buy you loads of booze if you say yes.'

He caved. 'Fine. Yes. You're very persuasive. But I don't get why you're dreading it,' he added, because he knew nothing about anything.

'You've never been a single woman in your thirties, have you, Jannes?' Lara said, giving him the most con-descending look that she could muster. 'I can't be doing with everyone asking me when I'm going to find a nice young man and settle down.'

She felt a release of tension that she hadn't known she was carrying when Jannes agreed to go with her. At a regular party, she would show up solo without giving it a second thought. But this was family, and her family was...complicated. Her half-sister was getting married, and had invited Lara to the big day. And when she said invited, she actually meant insisted, tearfully, on how much she wanted Lara to be there, and when she'd said that she wasn't sure it was a good idea...

That was when Pip, and her mother, and Lara's mother to boot, had suggested that maybe she needed to see someone about her issues with her family. That perhaps they could go to therapy. Family therapy, all of them together, and maybe even ask her father to go along too. She was practically sick at the thought. She had to do a better job of holding it together around them, or she was going to be subjected to that torture. Because how could she say no to Pip or her family, when they had taken her in when her world was falling apart?

She had no choice but to go to this wedding and convince them all that she was perfectly fine. There was no way that she was going to choose to do that either sober or alone.

'Fine, I'll come,' Jannes said, giving her a smile that crinkled his eyes. 'But are you sure that the whole pretending to be your boyfriend thing is necessary? I could come just as your friend. I mean, the best man might be hot. I don't want to cramp your style.'

'If he is, I'll drop you in a heartbeat, don't worry,' Lara said with a smile. 'It's just so that I don't have to spend the whole day defending my single lifestyle. You know they're all going to be talking behind my back anyway.'

He gave her one of those sympathetic looks that she hated. 'Jannes. Cut it out.'

It was only because he looked suitably remorseful that she decided at the last minute not to throw the chickpea she'd been threatening him with. 'Thank you,' she said. 'It'll be very romantic. Kidding,' she added, swatting him in the chest when his face went kind of grey. 'I'm kidding. Don't freak out.'

'I didn't freak out,' Jannes said, pulling himself up a little straighter.

Lara snorted. 'You so did. And one of these days we're going to talk about your rampant fear of commitment. But not until I'm done with you.'

'It's hard to know if that's a threat or not,' he said, narrowing his eyes.

'It's absolutely a threat.'

'Fine, we'll deal with my commitment issues when you're ready to talk about yours too.'

Pfft. What was the point of having a fake boyfriend instead of a real one if it didn't get you out of talking about your commitment issues? Besides, those commitment issues had been doing them both a favour ever since they'd met. You didn't meet a man as pretty as Jannes—and if anyone doubted a man could be pretty, she'd simply produce him as evidence—without being ever so slightly tempted to know what it would be like to get naked and sweaty with him, just the once. Besides, he was a nice boy, and she was a disaster with nice boys. She wasn't consigning Jannes to the 'do not drunk dial' group in her phone over a couple of nights of fun and then a major freak-out on her part. Or his, for that matter.

It wasn't worth losing him over an orgasm or two. However tempting he looked.

She could manage those all by herself.

No, she'd learned just not to think of him like that. It hadn't been easy at first, what with the cheekbones and the muscles. The lithe hips and blond hair and the general wholesome Swedishness of him. But Lara was more than just her libido. And Jannes was more to her than just a pretty face.

They were just doing each other a favour, Jannes told himself sternly. There was absolutely no reason to feel hesitant about agreeing to keep Lara company at her sister's wedding and then take her as his plus one to an awards ceremony. They had eaten dinner together plenty of times. Been out drinking. Dancing together. This wouldn't be any different really.

And they'd both been very clear that this didn't change anything between them. They had been friends for three years and never even set a toe over the line between friendship and something more. Because Lara was special and he was a mess, and she deserved so much more than that.

He hadn't always felt this way about relationships. There'd been a time in his early twenties that he'd wanted it all. Someone to love. To settle down. And every time that he'd tried, the fear had started to creep in. The closer he got to someone, the darker the shadow hanging over him, waiting for the moment that they'd inevitably leave him.

He at least had the advantage of knowing what he was afraid of. He'd been left behind so many times that the scars that it had caused were etched deep into his soul. Every time he'd watched his parents drive away from his boarding school, the wound had gone a little deeper, past the point where it physically hurt to the place where it broke down who he was.

That feeling when they'd walked out of the door and he'd watched their car drive away was something he'd sworn he wasn't going to allow to happen again. And the safest way to ensure that he didn't have to watch anyone leave? He didn't exactly need a degree in psychology to see the connection with a career that kept him constantly on the move. He'd taken up sailing at boarding school; it needed enough concentration that he couldn't think about much else while he was out on the water. And schoolboy competitions had led to life as a professional competitive yachtsman.

Maybe that was where the playboy image had come from. The few attempts that he'd made at relationships had fizzled out over the months that he'd been away sailing. The people he'd been with hadn't liked being left any more than he had, and he hadn't liked the thought that he had been hurting someone as much as he had been hurt. So it had made sense to stop trying to make relationships work. There had been a few short-term things over the years, when he'd been in one place long enough to see someone for more than a night or two. But knowing a relationship wouldn't last put a dampener on things, stopping them from ever really taking off.

And when it came to Lara, there was just no way that he could start something with her, knowing how it would end. Knowing that he would hurt her. Which was why it was so important that if they were going to do this thing, they were completely open with one another. There wasn't room in this for misunderstandings. They had to trust one another.

'There's something we should talk about,' he said, wondering whether she could hear his doubt in his voice. He had planned to bring this up nearer the time, but if they were going to go to Pip's wedding next weekend, they were going to have to do this now.

'Everyone knows that we're friends. We've been photographed plenty of times before; it never stopped me dating other people. If we want people to believe that things are different now, that we're together, then we're going to have to look as if we're…together.'

'Meaning?'

'Well, we should probably agree to some of the details before the wedding,' Jannes said, 'if we're telling people that I'm your boyfriend. Get our stories straight. Agree to our ground rules.'

'For goodness sake, Jannes. We don't need a contract. I'm not going to make you sleep with me!' Lara said with a laugh.

He frowned before he could catch himself. He hadn't thought for a second that she would, but was the prospect really so appalling? He certainly didn't think so. In fact, if Lara wasn't one of his best friends, he'd find the thought of it rather…appealing. But she was one of his best friends. She was one of the people that he liked best in the world, and that meant that he wasn't willing to risk having her in his life over something physical and meaningless. They were more than that.

'I know that,' he said. 'That's not what I meant at all.'

She laughed, and he wondered whether he was blushing. He felt as if he was probably blushing. 'Ha, well, I guess dating me is going to be full of surprises.'

He shook his head. 'I'm not sure I'm able to…' How were they meant to have a serious conversation when she was so…disarming? He needed to tiptoe through this, and she was forcing him to leap.

'You wanted to get our stories straight,' Lara said, changing the subject. 'How complicated are you expecting our origin story to be?'

He shrugged, going with it, because what else could he do in the face of Lara's enthusiasm? He'd never been able to resist. 'I don't know. Not complicated, but if someone asks us where we went on our first date and we don't know, then the gig is going to be up.'

'Fine.' Lara crossed her legs and rested her elbows on her knees, leaning closer to him and fixing him with a mischievous look. 'Where do you want me to take you on our imaginary first date? Knock yourself out. Choose something fancy—I'm buying.'

He raised one eyebrow. 'So generous.'

'Well, I like to treat you like a princess,' she said, lifting one corner of her lips in a smile. 'You deserve it, baby.'

'Baby?' He gave her a strong look, trying not to laugh.

'Babe?' she suggested.

He shook his head. 'Absolutely not.'

'Darling? Sweetheart? Cutie pie?'

He was in so much trouble.

She turned and pressed an impulsive kiss on his cheek and he just knew that that smirk on her face was because he was blushing.

'So. There are other things that we need to talk about if our story is that we're together now. Not just friends. Like kissing,' he said, blurting the words out as he rubbed at his cheek, his fingers catching where her lip balm had left a shimmer of stickiness. 'We might have to do that. Would it look weird if we didn't?'

'It might do,' she agreed. 'If you need the story in the press to be that we're together now, they're going to want the pictures to go with it.'

He nodded slowly. That was what he had been thinking too. But kissing Lara… That would… It wouldn't just be a kiss. Would it? With his best friend? Maybe it could be. Maybe he was making all this just too damn complicated. They had just said that this wouldn't change anything about who they were to each other, after all. If the kissing wasn't real, it shouldn't be a big deal. 'Do you think we should…practice?' he asked.

She narrowed her eyes at him. 'How complicated do you normally make it?'

He pulled her to her feet, took a step towards her, bringing his body right in front of her so she had to tilt her head back to look him in the eye.

'Depends on the occasion. And who I'm kissing. But the last thing we want is a picture of us that makes it obvious we're faking this. If we feel awkward just talking about it between ourselves, how's that going to come across to anyone else?'

'That's a fair point,' she said, not moving any closer. 'So…' she said, hesitating slightly. Up this close, standing like this, she felt less like laughing. This was serious. Suddenly, as Jannes's tongue moistened his lower lip, she felt her teeth close around her own. She wasn't sure this was a good idea. Was equally sure that it didn't matter because she was going to do it anyway.

This was Jannes. Lovely, safe Jannes. Who would never hurt her, who couldn't hurt her, because they both knew exactly what this was: fake. And she couldn't hurt him, because faking this was his idea.

'All right, then,' she said, eyes fixed on his mouth, noticing for the first time how the light caught at the top of his cupid's bow, the touch of shadow below the fullness of his bottom lip.

He tucked her hair behind her ear, a light, friendly touch. Something that wouldn't ordinarily make her pulse stutter, make her draw in a breath and hold it, not sure when she'd get a chance for another. His fingers lingered behind the curve of her ear, hit a sensitive spot that made her bite down harder on her lip.

This was nothing. It was friendly. They were friends and this was a friendly kiss. Not even that. Just a practice run at a friendly kiss.

Until his hand threaded in her hair, tightening at

the nape, and she found herself swaying into him. She put a hand out to steady herself—felt considerably less steady when it landed on Jannes's hip. She held on, fingers curling round the jut of his hipbone, and let her eyes leave his mouth to flick up to his eyes. His lids were half-lowered, long blond lashes catching sunlight, glinting gold at the tips. Pupils blown wide, deep blue irises barely visible.

'Jannes…' She had just managed the word when his head lowered, eyes sweeping shut, tongue darting to moisten his lips one more time.

For a second she couldn't move, could only absorb the soft drag of his lips over hers, until instinct took over and she started to move against him.

Her other hand found his waist and she lifted to her tiptoes, hands anchored on Jannes, using him to push herself closer, higher.

Her tongue flickered out, tasting his bottom lip, just as Jannes's hand in her hair tilted her, changing the angle so their noses brushed together. So that when he bowed his body closer to hers, her head tipped back and her mouth opened, deepening the kiss and letting out a low moan as his tongue stroked along hers, hot and confident in her mouth.

His other arm was a vice in the small of her back, pinning her to his body with the strength of muscles built and honed as a professional athlete.

This was a *kiss*.

Her brain scrambled to catch up while her body took liberties. One hand in Jannes's hair now, slipping through her fingers where he'd let it grow longer. Fingers digging into his hip. Legs tangling with the scratch of denim of his jeans. Belly pressed to the hardness of his belt buckle, his...

She pulled away suddenly, Jannes's hand still in her hair, his arm still solid against her waist. His cheeks were flushed, his lips red, swollen, bitten, and his eyes still closed as he pulled in a shuddering breath.

CHAPTER TWO

'Now aren't you glad that didn't happen at a family event?' Lara asked, laughing shakily. They could joke about this. They *should* joke about this. It wasn't serious. It wasn't *real*.

He glanced around them. Somehow, life in the park hadn't ceased to exist just because they'd been...swept away. 'This is very public.'

'Safer, I think. Imagine if we'd been...' Alone. She could imagine it. Was imagining it right now in fact. And frightening herself knowing where it could have ended up if they hadn't come to their senses.

It was just the shock, the novelty of it that had made it so explosive, she told herself. And now they had it out of their system, knew what to expect, they'd be better prepared next time. Would guard against getting carried away.

'So.' She uncurled her fingers from his hip, leaned back against the arm clasped at her waist. 'Now we have a first kiss story.'

'Yeah, I suppose we didn't need to get too creative after all.'

'We tell people…friends, feelings for one another, kiss in the park. Here we are.'

'That sounds plausible,' he said, with an expression that it didn't seem safe to interpret just yet. Of course it sounded plausible: if she wasn't so scared of hurting him, of being hurt in return, that was the reality they would be living right now. But she couldn't lose him, so they both pretended that it hadn't meant a thing to either of them. At least, she thought he was pretending.

'Should we walk?' Lara said, taking a deliberate step away from him, needing this friendship back on familiar ground before one of them said something that they couldn't take back. 'I could do with a coffee.'

'Good idea,' Jannes said, avoiding eye contact.

They turned back towards the park, followed a path past squealing toddlers on the playground, a group of teenagers gathered around a speaker, dodged pairs of runners sweating in the late spring warmth. She startled when she felt Jannes's fingers thread through hers and she looked up at him, surprised.

'What's this?' she asked, lifting their linked fingers with trepidation. Was he…did he think that kiss was real? That it had changed something between them? Because she thought that they had been clear. If she wanted to know why he was holding her hand, she could just ask.

'Practice,' he said, and shrugged as they let their hands drop.

'You need to practice holding hands?' she asked, forcing a laugh, trying to make light of this. 'How long *has* it been since you last dated properly, more than a first date?'

She thought back, tried to remember the last time he'd introduced her to a girl. More than a year ago, at least.

'I need to practice holding hands with *you*,' he clarified. 'Need to make it look like we do this all the time. Not like we're—'

'We're walking through the park to get coffee,' she cut in on a nervous laugh, not wanting to hear the end of that sentence. 'We *do* do this all the time.'

Jannes shrugged. 'I don't want to walk in there unprepared.'

'Fine,' she said, sighing. 'You're right. If you want to practice, we can practice. Now, do you need to practice my coffee order? Because I'm hot and this shady bench is looking very tempting. It's still five minutes to the coffee stand.'

'Fine,' Jannes said, and she knew his expressions well enough to recognise relief when she saw it. 'You sunbathe, I'll get the coffee.'

That was…intense.

Jannes stalked off towards the coffee stand, walking faster now that he didn't have to slow for Lara's shorter frame.

He had meant it to be a quick peck on the lips, to prove to himself if no one else that he and Lara were good enough friends to fake being an item without things becoming weird. He hadn't been prepared for the chain reaction that the merest brush of her lips against his had triggered. He hadn't been thinking at all when he'd pinned her body flush against his. When he'd arched into the kiss, wanting to be closer, to lift her higher, to bring every inch of her body into contact with his own. It had taken every gram of strength that he'd had to pull away from her, to remind himself that the reason he'd been resisting her since the day that he'd met her was because he didn't want to hurt her. Because she deserved better than that.

Jesus, it had been a while. Perhaps he could pretend that that was why he had felt so desperate for her. Far from having a girl in every port, the last year he'd been…circumspect. Aware that every date he had would inevitably end up in the tabloids or going viral. A version of his life gaining traction that he just didn't recognise. He hadn't left a string of broken hearts in his wake, regardless of what the papers wrote. It was the opposite, in fact. He'd avoided getting involved past a first date, knowing that he would only hurt someone if he let himself get closer.

The holding hands—where had that come from? He'd given Lara a convenient excuse to cover up the fact that he'd done it without thinking. The kiss had broken through all the defences that he'd constructed, and he'd just acted on instinct. Forgot, for a moment, that he had to resist taking what he wanted. His skin had wanted hers and he'd reached for her before his brain had caught up with what his body was doing.

He reached the stall and ordered their coffees, realising after he'd done it that he hadn't even had to think about what she wanted. He couldn't remember the last time he'd been with a girl long enough to know her coffee order. But this was different. Lara wasn't a girlfriend. She was a friend. A good friend. Probably the best one he'd had, in fact. It was perfectly understandable that he knew what coffee she liked. He spent more time with her than just about anyone else.

And now he had kissed her and his head had exploded and all these years of keeping their relationship carefully platonic had gone up in smoke.

It was friendly, he told himself again. They were kissing and pretending to date because that was what a good friend did when they were asked.

He walked back towards where he had left Lara on the bench and found her stretched out, thumbs tapping at her phone, face screwed up with concentration. He stood and watched her for a moment. She looked focused. No hint that she shared in the roiling anxiety he'd been fighting since their kiss. He was making a big deal out of nothing. To her, it had clearly been what they'd intended: a practice kiss between friends. No feelings involved. She knew the score, and he did too.

CHAPTER THREE

'WOW, YOU LOOK…'

Lara stood by the door of her apartment, eyebrow raised as Jannes looked her up and down, waiting for him to finish his sentence. They really needed to get on their way to the wedding, but there was no way she was leaving until she had heard what Jannes thought.

'…nice,' he finished, and she rolled her eyes.

Nice was the worst of all the compliments. She kind of wished that she'd not let him finish now.

'You too,' she replied with a smirk. 'Shall we go?'

Normally she would have invited him in. Let him lean his long limbs against the kitchen counter while she darted between her bedroom and bathroom, posting pictures of her getting ready, gathering up last-minute bits for her handbag, forgetting her credit card and having to run back for her lipstick.

She was nervous about seeing her family, wanted to get it over and done with. That was what she told herself as she hustled Jannes out of the door. Nothing to do with not trusting herself to be alone in her apartment with him after that kiss. Everything would go back to normal after tonight. They would put this behind them and get back to slobbing around in lounge pants and watching bad TV together at the weekends. Back to maintaining their friendship over video calls while he went from training camp to training camp, around the world solo and back again.

Soon, she'd be able to look at him and find him *nice* again. The way that she had before that kiss. Because, right now, nice didn't seem to be doing him justice, and she wasn't sure what could have changed that other than the kiss that they'd shared.

The suit helped of course. Cut close to his shoulders, the waist and hips slender enough to make her jealous, but which she knew now were hardened muscle underneath. His shirt was pale blue, just enough of a hint of colour to do something to his eyes that made them hard to look away from. That made his skin and his hair glow. Really, sometimes it was very hard being his friend.

She fluffed up her hair and locked the door behind her, checking her lift sharing app to make sure that the driver had found her apartment building. Or to give her eyes somewhere to look that wasn't at Jannes.

'So, anything I need to know before we go in there?' Jannes asked in the car on the way to the ceremony at the groom's parents' manor out in the home counties.

'Oh, you know…the usual: my jackass of a father. Secret second daughter—i.e. me—taken into the bosom of the "official" family when her mum received an eviction notice from the flat that she thought she owned and all was discovered. Step-family determined to make up for his shortcomings by being obsessively kind. Pip, the only child who always dreamed of having a sister, suddenly finding she had one all along and determined to love me.'

Jannes was silent for a second as she collected herself. 'Will he be there?' he asked, his voice so gentle it threatened to spark tears.

'Nope. Haven't seen him for years. He sees some of the family but I've always managed to dodge him. Pip didn't invite him; she knew I wouldn't come if she did.' And she wouldn't care if she never saw him again. Which was convenient, really, considering that he seemed to feel the same way about her. 'His mother will be. My grandmother, I suppose. Hard to think of her like that though when I spent most of my life being told that she was dead.'

Jannes reached for her hand and squeezed it. She pulled it away before she could do something stupid like turn her palm to his and lace their fingers together. 'I'm sorry today will be hard for you. I think you're really brave for doing this.'

'Brave. Stupid. What's the difference?' She forced a smile to her face, but knew that Jannes wouldn't be fooled.

'You're a good sister, putting yourself through it for Pip. You must really care about her.'

Lara shrugged, shifting her hand out of reach just as he reached for it. 'They took us in. Kicked him out. I owe them.'

Jannes nodded in agreement. Squeezed her hand again.

The car slammed to a halt outside the gates to Pip's fiancé's family home, stopping her from doing anything stupid. 'You sure you want to do this?' he asked as she reached for the door handle.

She forced a smile. 'Nope, but we're going to anyway.'

'That's my girl.'

CHAPTER FOUR

HIS GIRL.

Well, it was true enough for the next few hours, Jannes supposed, walking through the grounds with Lara's hand in his. He'd half expected that they'd be hidden away in a corner, being unobtrusive, avoiding notice. He wasn't sure why he would think that when three years of friendship with Lara had yet to produce a problem that she didn't think was best tackled head-on with the volume turned up. She marched straight to her grandmother and kissed her dryly on the cheek before introducing him.

'Elaine, this is my boyfriend, Jannes.'

Warm hands clasped his as a kiss was pressed to his cheek.

'I was just saying that it was about time you settled down,' Lara's grandmother said. 'Now you two, come and sit by me and fill me in on your news.'

'Ah—' Jannes said.

At the same time Lara replied, 'We're just going to grab a drink before Pip arrives. But we'll definitely catch up with you later.'

And then he was kissed by a series of aunts and cousins and assorted other strangers before being pushed into a chair near to the front of the assembled rows in the largest marquee and the chatter dropped to a hushed whisper.

'You doing okay?' he asked.

She gave him a tight smile, and then Pip arrived, floating down the aisle in a powder-puff-pink dress. But Jannes's eyes snapped back to Pip's fiancé as he watched her, dumbstruck, grinning dopily. His expression—as if he couldn't believe his luck—didn't change the whole time they were exchanging their vows. It was a good look on him, Jannes decided, slightly envious of the satisfied glow that emanated from the happy couple.

He risked a glance across at Lara, who was watching the proceedings with a fixed smile in place. He linked her fingers with his, trying not to notice how natural that had started to feel. They had done it only a few times since that first time in the park, but it just felt…right. This was why they had been so careful before—because they had both known that the attraction was there, because they both knew that this could be something more if they wanted it to be. And because he knew how much he didn't want that to happen. He didn't want to get closer to Lara, only to be afraid that she would leave him. He didn't want to hurt her, pulling away because of that fear. Being just friends was safer for both of them.

It was easy to see now that they had breached the buffer that had always been between them. How they had always been careful to avoid the accidental touches that sent sparks flying between them. Because now they had crossed that divide and seen—felt—what things were like on the other side, it was hard to remember how it had felt to *not* know. Harder to think about how they were meant to get back to a place where they were ignorant of this. And when he thought about that kiss…

Well, mostly, he just *didn't* think about that kiss, because, well, when he started it was too hard to stop. He'd have a flashback while he was waiting for pasta to cook and find himself half an hour later, staring at a glutinous mass of overcooked starch and wonder how he could lose time thinking about a simple kiss. A kiss that wasn't even supposed to be the real thing. But had nonetheless shaken him to his bones in a way that no other kiss seemed to have ever managed.

Speaking of kisses, the happy couple were now locking lips while somehow simultaneously giggling, and then passing back along the aisle, and he realised he'd missed the last ten minutes and the ceremony was over.

Lara let out a long breath that made him wonder when she'd last inhaled, and he reached an arm around her shoulder in a way that he had meant to be friendly. But he hadn't been counting on the effect of the bare skin of his forearm—he'd rolled his sleeves up in the sweltering garden outside, and Lara had taken her jacket off—against the warm skin of Lara's shoulders. Her jumpsuit had a complicated criss-cross of straps spanning her shoulder blades, revealing golden skin down to the small of her back. Which had never really been a part of the human body that had interested him before, but that he was finding hard to resist. Lara sat stiffly beside him, not leaning into him, and that should have been fine. This whole day was about Lara and if what she needed was this inch of clear space between his ribs and hers, then that was fine. That was what they were doing. It was completely out of order for him to be disappointed that she had passed up the opportunity to lean into him, just because he was curious about how good that might feel.

This wasn't about feeling. It was about appearances. And if an arm around her shoulder was all the situation required then that was all they would do.

Lara gave herself a little shake and turned to him with a slightly more natural smile on her face.

'Bar?' she asked.

'Bar,' Jannes agreed, keeping his arm around her shoulders as they walked towards one of the smaller marquees—just for the sake of authenticity, of course.

'Just so I know,' Jannes asked, as she ordered a beer for him and a bottle of wine for herself, 'is the drinking going to be in any way in moderation? No judgement either way.'

'Absolutely not,' Lara said, pouring herself a large glass and tucking the bottle under her arm as they went to find a seat outside. 'I'm counting on you to make sure I get home later without making too much of a tit of myself.'

'Babysitting duty. Got it.'

She frowned at that. 'Less babysitter. More…wingman.'

'Isn't a wingman meant to help you get laid?' he asked. 'That might undermine our story a little.'

She waved his concern away with a hand. 'You just have to help me find *you*, then. You're my hook-up.'

'I thought I was your boyfriend,' he said, laughing at how quickly Lara had got flushed and silly with the wine.

'Right. Otherwise known as a guaranteed hook-up.'

Jannes rolled his eyes. 'You're so romantic.'

'You're not with me for hearts and flowers. I don't really go in for that.'

'Oh, really?' He regarded her carefully, trying to keep his expression neutral. 'What am I with you for?'

'The wild sex and Instagram freebies.'

He felt his face warm and knew it must be flushing red. His only hope was that he had caught enough sun this summer that his tan would hide it a little.

'I've embarrassed you!' Lara said with a small squeal of delight and smacked a kiss on his cheek. 'That's adorable.'

'*Don't* call me adorable. You're insufferable.'

'I never said today was going to be easy.'

'You never told me that you were going to be the hardest part.' But he smiled, because even when she was being insufferable he had more fun with her than he knew how to have with anyone else.

'Sorry,' Lara said with a smile and a gulp of wine that suggested she wasn't, in the least.

'Here,' he said, handing her a glass of water, condensation beading the glass.

'Spoilsport,' she said with a frown. 'Some wingman you are.'

'I'm not slowing you down, *sötnos*. But you'll thank me for the hydration in the morning.'

'Fine.' She drank half the glass in one go, and he found himself unreasonably intrigued by the line of her neck as she tipped her head back to drink. 'And don't speak Swedish to me. You know I think you're cute when you do that.'

As she handed back the glass, cheers and applause rippled through the garden and he turned to see Pip and her husband in the doorway, fresh from having their photos taken and ready to party with their guests.

Pip made a beeline for Lara and wrapped her in a tight hug. He saw how Lara stiffened in the presence of her half-sister, and he slid his arm around her waist and squeezed gently, making sure Lara knew he was there for her if she needed him. He leaned in to kiss Pip on the cheek too—they had met a couple of times—and shook hands with the groom.

'Congratulations,' he said, covering for Lara's awkward silence. 'It was a lovely ceremony.'

'It was short,' Pip said with a laugh. 'I'm impatient, and it makes you popular with the guests. And we're not the only ones who need congratulating. It looks like you two have news for us too!' She looked pointedly at where Jannes's arm was still resting on Lara's hip. 'I always said there was something between you two. I'm glad you finally worked it out. We all wondered how long it would take you.'

'All?' Lara said, hiding a laugh. 'You should have said something. Maybe it wouldn't have taken us so long.' Jannes resisted the urge to roll his eyes. Lara couldn't resist the opportunity to tease, even when no one but the two of them were in on the joke.

'We're keeping you from your guests,' Jannes said tactfully as the conversation petered out and a crowd gathered around Pip and her new husband. 'I don't want to be accused of monopolising you.'

'You're right, but I'm going to want to hear all about it later,' Pip said with another hug for her sister. 'You guys look great together,' she said. Adding, 'Look after her. She's special,' with a mock stern look at Jannes before she turned away from the crush of well-wishers.

Jannes looked down at Lara and saw that the hand holding her wine was shaking slightly. Her shoulders were set in a stiff line, and the smile on her face was threatening to slide into a grimace.

'Hey,' Jannes said, turning Lara's face up to his and then wrapping her in a hug. 'You did well. Really well. Pip was so happy to see you here.' He held her tighter still, until he felt the shaking stop. 'Better?' he asked, looking down at the top of her head. Her forehead was pressed against his chest and, before he could think too hard about it, he dropped a kiss to her hair and brought up one hand to cup the nape of her neck.

He wasn't even sure that this was what she had meant, when she'd asked him to pretend to be her boyfriend. That was meant to be for show. To satisfy the curiosity of her family. But holding her like this—this wasn't for show. This was because she needed him, and when it came to Lara he didn't know how to say no to her. And now that the usual boundaries between them had been bulldozed by that kiss, here they were, in the middle of a family wedding, with her head on his chest and his fingers in her hair, learning the texture of it, the feel of it slipping through his fingers as she took a long shuddering breath.

When she looked up the strain had gone from her expression. Instead there was something there he recognised from that day in the park, right before they'd kissed. His hand was still tangled in her hair, hers still rested lightly on his hips. Looking into her eyes, he could see that she was thinking about it too, and when her tongue darted out to moisten parted lips he knew she was tempted. Or she was acting, playing a part. He was here to play a part too, and he leaned down to brush a gentle kiss to her lips.

'Lara!'

She broke away at the sound of her name and Jannes looked up to see Pip's mother and her new partner brandishing a bottle of champagne and a handful of glasses.

'We're so thrilled you're here,' Gloria, Pip's mother, said, kissing Lara on both cheeks and then leaning back to get a good look at her. 'You're looking incredible,' she said, and then glanced up at Jannes. 'And you must be Jannes. I've heard so much about you. Thank you for coming.'

'Thanks for having me,' he said, smiling and shaking hands and silently cursing that they'd been interrupted. And then wanted to kick himself for the selfish thought. He wasn't supposed to care whether or not he was kissing Lara. This was meant to be play-acting.

He reminded himself of that as he made small talk with Lara and her family, his hand resting on the small of her back, as if he wasn't thoroughly distracted by the thought of all that golden skin under the criss-crosses of her jumpsuit.

He was good. Oh, he was really good. She had to remind herself of that. Remind herself not to let herself get dizzy from the warm, lazy circles Jannes was rubbing at the small of her back. He was being supportive. And kind. And he was kissing her and touching her because that was exactly what she'd asked him to do—to pretend to be her boyfriend and to make it convincing… There was nothing personal in the feel of his skin on hers. Even in the way that his lips brushed hers.

Thank God they had talked about this. She didn't have to think about her feelings. About what feelings Jannes might or might not be having. Here, of all places, among these people, she needed that certainty. Having talked with Jannes beforehand about what they were doing, the fake boyfriend was the only solution.

She'd spent her childhood adoring someone who had lied to her every time he had opened his mouth and spoken to her. Every 'I love you' that had come from his lips was worthless. She wasn't going to spend her adulthood repeating those mistakes. And if that meant agreeing in advance that a relationship was a lie, rather than waiting and hoping and then just finding out later, then that was what she would do. What would Jannes think if she told him that? she wondered. If she confessed that she wanted him, but only if they were pretending. Would he settle for that? If that was all that she could give him?

She leaned into Jannes's side, breathing freely again as she watched her stepmother move away, making her way through the assembled guests, kissing cheeks and directing wait staff with trays of champagne and spreading her good mood throughout the crowds.

'You going to finish the bottle now?' Jannes asked, watching her watching Pip's mother and sensing her mood.

'Oh, yeah.'

'Then we should go and find you some carbs.'

He pulled on her hand and she thought he really might be the best man she knew. Which was precisely why she wanted him in her life permanently—which meant as a friend. Where he couldn't break her heart. Couldn't make her love him and then take it away again when she gave in and loved him back. She didn't want to lose him, which meant she was never going to hope for—want—more than she had now.

CHAPTER FIVE

'COME ON THEN, *sötnos*,' Jannes said, one arm around Lara's waist as he helped her from the taxi. 'Let's get you upstairs before you do something disgusting in this nice man's car.'

She laughed, as he knew she would.

'I told you: don't be all Swedish and charming. I'm too drunk not to find it adorable.'

He hoisted Lara against his side as he went through her bag looking for her keys, a job made somewhat more difficult by the fact that Lara kept sinking down, threatening to slip from his grasp every time he thought he had a hand on her keys.

'And I told you hours ago to stop calling me adorable. Here we go,' he said, wrapping her arms around his neck for extra safety as he finally got hold of the keys and opened the door to her apartment.

All in all, the day hadn't been too much of a disaster. Lara had managed to keep a smile on her face throughout the speeches, including the one that Gloria made in place of Pip and Lara's conspicuously absent father, and as the wine had made her looser and more morose, he had simply wedged her against him in the corner of the dance floor so it would look to anyone who took an interest that they were simply too besotted with one another to be dragged apart rather than the fact that by nine o'clock Lara could no longer stand unassisted. But she'd achieved the status of falling-over-drunk with more panache and style than he'd seen anyone manage before. And he was nothing if not impressed by her stamina.

He staggered through the door with one arm clamped around her waist, and it was more awkward to stoop than it was to simply straighten up and carry her, her toes just brushing the doorjamb as he manoeuvred them into her apartment. He shouldered open the bedroom door and dropped her on the bed, both of them letting out an undignified 'Oof!' as he dropped her. Good job no one was trying to impress anyone. If this had been a normal date…

He batted away her hands as she tried to unbuckle her sandals and pulled them off for her and then averted his eyes and escaped to the kitchen while Lara wrestled out of her jumpsuit. By the time he returned with a pint of water and a couple of paracetamols, Lara was in bed with her hair pulled into a messy bun and the lace-trimmed strap of a tank top slipping from her shoulder. He pulled the strap back into place and the duvet up higher, before handing her the pills and the water.

'You are the best boyfriend I've ever had,' she said as she took the pills from him, and he laughed. But she shoved his arm. 'Don't laugh. It's true. I owe you. You really took care of me tonight. You are an excellent friend and I love you.'

He bit down on his lip to stop himself laughing again—Lara was clearly not in the mood to find her drunken rambling amusing. He kissed her on the forehead with a murmured, 'Goodnight,' and grabbed a blanket from the bottom of the bed. With the amount of wine she'd put away tonight, she was going to be in no state to make the cup of coffee he knew she'd be gasping for the minute she woke up tomorrow, and he had no intention of losing that boyfriend of the year award he'd only just won.

He walked back through to the living room to the sound of Lara snoring and glanced at the notifications on his phone that he'd been ignoring all day. There was one from his manager, asking how many tickets he wanted for the awards show next week. He replied that he'd need a plus one, and could his manager sort out accommodation for them? If tonight had been a test of concept, he was pretty sure they'd passed, and one more fake date couldn't do any harm.

Today had been fun. It wasn't exactly hard to pretend to enjoy hanging out with his best friend. All they had to do was keep this up a little longer and he would be the reformed bad boy. Tamed by the sweetheart of the social media influencer world.

He lay back on the sofa cushions, pulling the throw blanket from Lara's bed over himself and falling, satisfied, into sleep.

She was dying. It was the only possible explanation for this experience in her mouth. It went beyond taste. It was…stale and…furry and…if she didn't think about something else right now she was going to throw up.

She looked round at the sound of a tap on the door and scrunched up her eyes at the sight of Jannes in the doorway. How did he look so fresh this early in the day? Bastard.

'Good morning, sunshine,' he said with a smirk that totally deserved the pillow that she launched at his head. 'Careful, that's your coffee you're spilling.'

'Oh, my God.' She scrambled upright, arms hooked around bent knees. 'Gimme. Please?' she added when all he did was raise an eyebrow at her.

'So, yesterday went well,' Jannes said, sitting on the edge of her bed and putting the coffees down on the bedside table.

'You'd have to tell me. Did I disgrace myself?'

'You were wonderful. You always are. Everybody loved you.'

'You're being very nice,' she said suspiciously, sniffing at her coffee and trying to decide whether her stomach could handle it yet.

'Yes, well, I'm still hoping for that second date. I told my manager I'm bringing a plus one to the awards. Is that still okay?'

'I don't know. Probably?' she said, leaning back on her pillows. 'Am I still drunk?'

'Possibly. You were far enough gone last night to agree to go to at least one more wedding and a christening this summer. I'm making you another coffee and a bacon sandwich. Then you're having a shower.'

'Ugh, why did I do that? Why did you let me do

that? And is that a hint?' she asked, trying to discreetly sniff herself.

'Nope, it's an order. You smell bad. And you agreed to those other events because you are a very good person.'

She collapsed back on the pillows, arm across her face. 'I take it back. You're the worst boyfriend ever.'

She let the water run over her head into her eyes, and by the time she was squeezing her hair dry with a towel she felt almost human again. Jannes was in the kitchen when she emerged, dressed in comfy cashmere pants and a sweater. She could smell bacon and coffee, and the toaster popped as she walked past it, making her jump.

'Tell me more about this awards thing,' she said, taking the coffee he held out to her.

'I'm presenting one of the awards,' Jannes said. 'All you need to do is show up, hold my hand. If anyone asks maybe tell them I'm the best boyfriend you've ever—'

'Worst boyfriend.'

'Best boyfriend you've ever had. I'm getting it embroidered on a pillow. Just stand with me for a few photos, look madly in love with me. Post them on your social media feeds so people get the general idea of how wonderful and dependable and not flaky I am.'

'And that's it,' she clarified. 'Just the awards ceremony and then we're done?'

'If you want it to be,' Jannes said, but a couple of fine lines appeared between his eyebrows. His thinking face. 'Or, if it goes well,' he went on, 'perhaps we carry on playing rent-a-date for each other. Like, at the other family events you agreed to yesterday? I can come to those, if you'd like, when I'm home. And you can come to work things with me. We have fun—you know I love hanging out with you. And, not to be too mercenary about it, but the longer this goes on, the better I look.'

It was her turn to frown, and she rubbed at her forehead, where the throbbing headache she'd woken up with was starting to ease. 'What happens when we don't want people to think we're together any more?'

'Then we gracefully part ways and decide that we were better off as friends. Behind closed doors, nothing has changed.'

Lara nodded, finishing one cup of coffee and pouring herself another. 'And are you sure...' How should she put this? '... I'm not going to be stepping on anyone's toes if we do this? I don't want to find myself as the other woman,' Lara said.

Jannes crossed his arms. 'Are you asking me if I'm seeing someone?'

'Seeing anyone, sleeping with anyone.' Lara waved a vague hand. 'Sending suggestive messages on dating apps to anyone. I mean, you can do what you want, but even if we're just pretending, I don't want it to ever look like we're cheating. At—'

'I'm not seeing anyone,' Jannes said, his expression hard. 'And I won't, as long as we're keeping this up. I wouldn't have agreed to yesterday if I was.'

She took a deep breath and passed him a knife as he reached for the butter. 'Okay. I knew that. I think I knew that. I just had to be sure.'

'It's fine.' He didn't look as if it was fine. And right here was the reason that she didn't date for real. Because she'd had to ask that question, even though she knew that she could trust Jannes. Even though she *knew* he'd never be any less than honest, she'd still had to ask the question. Because she'd *known* that she could trust her father too, and look where that had got them. She'd put that hurt look on Jannes's face, and she had no interest in doing it again. 'I understand why you had to ask,' he said, which didn't change the fact that he was hurt that she couldn't just trust him.

The ease that had been there between them when she'd woken up, when he really had been boyfriend of the year, and she'd been happy to let him, had disappeared. She'd pierced it with this reminder that she would never be able to trust, and that eventually that scar in her soul always ended up with her pushing away anyone who got too close. The closer she let Jannes get, the more she was going to hurt him eventually. She had to remember that.

'So what happens when you meet someone?' she asked, moving the focus of the conversation away from herself, making sure that their terms for this relationship were crystal clear. If they had everything on the table from the start, there was no way that this could become something that it shouldn't.

'What, before Saturday?' Jannes crossed his arms as he looked at her, and she could see him trying to understand the change in the atmosphere. '*If* I meet someone, or you do, we'll talk to each other and work something out. I won't hurt you, Lara. I won't ever hurt you.'

She nodded, took another sip of coffee. 'I know you won't. So how does this work? You'll pick me up?'

'It's in Liverpool. I have to be there early to go through the presenting stuff. I don't want you to have to sit around getting bored. I'll get them to arrange a car for you. Meet you there. Does that work for you?'

'Fine. Fine. I guess I'll see you there.'

CHAPTER SIX

IF THE BACK of Lara's wedding jumpsuit had been sent to test him, then surely this dress was going to end him. He was talking to his manager when she arrived. From the corner of his eye he had spotted long tanned legs, and it was only when his eyes had reached her face that he realised he was looking at Lara. He stopped talking abruptly, and when he heard his manager call his name for the third time he realised he'd been staring.

At the top, the dress was positively demure, cut high on the neck with sleeves past her wrist bones. Midnight-blue crystals covered her body, down over her hips to the top of her thighs, where the dress stopped abruptly, revealing those long soft thighs and the same strappy sandals he'd slipped from her ankles last Saturday night. She waved when she spotted him, and he forced his legs to move.

'Hey, you're here,' he said, leaning in to kiss her on the cheek, remembering at the last minute that she was meant to be his date. He kissed her on the lips, but pulled away before he could be tempted to turn it into anything more than the lightest peck, a mere brush of skin against hers, gone practically before it had started.

'You look beautiful,' he said, eyes fixed on her face now. Her eyes were wide, lined with smoky black and grey, with long, long lashes that fluttered when she blinked.

'You don't look too bad yourself,' she said, leaning back and tweaking the lapel of his dinner jacket. 'I always loved you in black tie.' He was just at the point where he was going to have to start untangling which parts of this were real and which were for show when his manager clapped him on the shoulder and held his hand out to shake with Lara.

'You must be Lara. Glad the car got you here okay.' He looked from Lara to Jannes with a smile on his face. 'Okay, I'm going to let you guys catch up. Jannes can show you to your table. Look forward to talking to you more later, Lara.'

Jannes looked her up and down again, trying to form just one coherent thought and turn it into words.

'You look amazing,' he said.

She laughed awkwardly. 'We did that bit already. What else have you got?'

'Um, let's find you a drink?'

'Ah, much better,' Lara said with a laugh. 'But let's make mine a sparkling water. If I'm the wingman tonight, I'm going to need to stay sober.'

'Of course, the squeaky-clean image I'm meant to be cultivating,' Jannes said. 'But you don't have to do or not do anything on my behalf. You're perfect as you are,' he said. 'Just be yourself.'

'Ah, there you go with the boyfriend of the year script again.' But her cheeks had pinkened. Yes. Right. Because they were faking this. He loved her—as a friend. His hormones were briefly confused by the fact that they had kissed. But they weren't doing any more than playing a part here—if he forgot that, Lara would end up getting hurt, and he wasn't prepared to risk that. 'You get the credit for briefing me in advance.' He guided her towards the bar with a hand on the small of her back.

'Well, if we're going to make it look realistic...'

Because this wasn't real, and he could never forget that he had good reasons for that. He had learned the hard way what happened when you cared more about someone than they cared back. He'd learned it when his parents had shipped him off to boarding school so that they could continue the travelling that they had put on hold when he had been born seven years earlier. He had spent his holidays with his *mormor*, his grandmother, in London. And saw his parents whenever their travel schedule allowed, which was something like twice a year by the time he was in his teens.

Which was why he could be sure that he could commit to this fakery with Lara. Even if he met someone who made him wonder if things could be different, he had long since given up acting on those feelings. What was the point when he already knew how it would end? So why hadn't he just said that to Lara? Because it just seemed sad, somehow, to admit that at the age of thirty he was so afraid of being left—or of hurting someone to stop that happening—that he never even started a relationship. This thing with Lara was nothing like that.

She couldn't leave him if it wasn't real, if they were only acting. He couldn't hurt her when they both knew that they were going to stop pretending just as soon as their arrangement was no longer convenient. He had to make sure he remembered that.

He showed Lara to their table as the ballroom started to fill with people, and he introduced her to his manager, agent and teammates. She saw the sidelong glances being thrown their way and wondered what they made of the situation. There was something about the knowing looks on his colleagues' faces that made her wonder if she was missing something.

The room hushed as the lights dimmed and the awards ceremony began.

Lara was hyperconscious, now that she was sitting next to Jannes, of just how much skin her dress left exposed. Because every time Jannes leaned in to whisper something about one of the nominees or winners, the soft fabric of his trousers brushed against her bare thigh and made her shiver in response. It was just an involuntary physical reaction, she told herself. A reflex. Practically a sneeze. It shouldn't make her think about his hands touching her there. She had to stop letting her brain do this to her. She was meant to be in charge here. And yet her body and her brain kept ganging up on her and trying to make her believe that indulging these fantasies about Jannes were a good idea. And if both her brain and her body were working against her, she didn't know which part of her was meant to fight these urges.

He was her friend. That was what made this whole

'date for a date' thing a good idea. Neither of them had unrealistic expectations of the other. Neither of them had to air their commitment issues, because it wasn't real. It was company and it was convenient and it didn't need any more consideration than that.

Jannes went and did his presentation thing: she clapped him enthusiastically as he took to the stage and received his kiss on the cheek when he returned with hardly a flutter where she shouldn't be fluttering.

In fact, she was just congratulating herself for how very responsible she was being when she realised she'd spaced out for a minute and missed something. Because on the big screen behind the stage was a picture of Jannes, soaking wet in a white dress shirt, and she couldn't be sure that she wasn't drooling a little. She snapped her mouth shut and smudged the corner of her lips with her finger, hoping it would look as if she was just fixing her lipstick.

She glanced across at Jannes and found him staring at her and thought that maybe she hadn't got away with it after all. She looked back at the screen and kind of wished she hadn't, because now Jannes was shirtless, still dripping wet, and more ripped than his narrow frame suggested. It didn't exactly hurt that he was hanging off the side of a racing yacht, in a photoshoot that made it look as if he was in the process of winning one of those trophies that took up an entire wall of his house.

She worked out what was going on before Jannes did, which was perfect, because it meant that she got to watch as realisation dawned and just the very tips of his ears went red as he was announced as the winner of the special achievement award. The assembled guests burst into applause and whoops of celebration as she pushed Jannes to his feet. She stood too, and gave him a little push towards the stage. He leaned forward and pressed a kiss to her lips and she didn't know whether it was because he was dazed or doing it for show or…she didn't know why else. He was just maintaining their story, keeping their pretence going. It wasn't real. It didn't mean anything. She had to remember that, because at this minute her feelings were all too real.

Jannes took to the stage to accept his award, and his eyes still had that wide, startled quality as he stepped up to the microphone. He thanked his manager and his agent, the award organisers. And then, after a split-second hesitation: 'And Lara, for everything she is to me.'

She stood staring at him, her face frozen in surprise. When he kissed her on the cheek and laced his fingers through hers as he came back to the table, her thoughts were too much in disarray to come up with a coherent question. Until she remembered that this was all for show. He was just sticking to their story, proving once again that he really was the best friend a woman could wish for—far too good to risk losing over something as superficial as how he looked in a wet shirt. She fixed a smile on her face and sat back beside Jannes, her hand still in his, aware of the photographer just to one side.

This was fine. This was simple. This was the reason she'd taken a fake date to Pip's wedding: because she was choosing a life where she didn't have to guess and second-guess people's feelings. Where she didn't have to worry about the fact that second-guessing people's feelings usually led to them getting hurt. She already knew that Jannes was faking his feelings for her, exactly as they had agreed. Which really should have made her feel better. Grounded. But somehow, just… didn't. She shook herself. It turned out that fake relationships were sometimes confusing, complicated, too. But still, compared to the real thing—she thought about the way her father had treated her, and her mother, and Pip's mother, and decided that a fake relationship was the lesser of two evils.

She stuck to Jannes's side as the party wound down, as he accepted congratulations and handshakes and slaps on the back from all directions. Lara felt a swell of pride seeing everything that Jannes had achieved. There was no denying that he deserved the award he'd been presented with that night.

He turned to her finally, when he'd shaken almost every hand in the room.

'Mr Henriksson, I can show you to your room if you're ready,' the hotel manager said, coming over to shake Jannes's hand. Lara wondered if he was glancing at his phone to ward off the awkwardness that had suddenly popped up between them at the mention of the hotel rooms arranged by the awards organisers. 'Congratulations on your award,' the hotel manager went on, beaming at them. 'We've upgraded you to our best suite.'

Lara was on the verge of asking about her own room when she remembered about their pretence. The whole point of her being there was to convince everyone that they were a couple. Separate rooms was going to undo all their hard work, so she squeezed Jannes's hand and followed the hotel manager to the lifts.

When they closed the door of their suite behind them, she looked up at Jannes and burst out laughing. What else could she do? This had started with her agreeing to pretend to be Jannes's girlfriend for a few hours and had so far escalated to a family wedding, a ballroom and now the honeymoon suite of a luxury hotel.

'Wow. This is…' Jannes started, before his voice trailed off. Lara glanced up at him and smiled at the pink flush of his freckled cheeks.

'Extravagant?' Lara suggested.

'That's one word for it,' Jannes said in a low voice that suggested there were several other words that he could think of.

She burst out laughing, because it was the only thing she could think of to break the tension.

'So,' Lara went on, when her laughter eventually petered out. 'Um…what do we do here?'

Jannes looked around him at the extravagant suite with its four-poster bed and freestanding copper bathtub. Lashings of rose petals and crystal and polished wood. 'Lara, I'm so sorry,' he said. 'It never occurred to me to say something about the sleeping arrangements—I should have checked.'

'Relax, Jannes. It's just one night,' Lara said, turning on the spot to take in the whole of the room. 'We don't need to turn this into a big deal.'

'You're right. I'll just sleep on the sofa,' Jannes offered.

She laughed. 'You're at least a foot longer than the sofa,' she pointed out. 'And it's velvet. You'll slip right off in your sleep. There's really no need. I'm sure I can be trusted to spend tonight in a king-size bed with you without trying to jump your bones.'

He laughed at that, but she could still hear the tension in his voice. No wonder, because jumping his bones was exactly what she wanted to do right now, and her and Jannes were good enough friends that she wouldn't be at all surprised if he knew it.

'It's not you I'm worried about,' she could have sworn she heard him murmur. No way was she calling him out on that—that would be *way* too dangerous. Better altogether just to ignore it.

'Come on, Jannes. We're friends. Let's not make a big deal out of this. It's not like there's any danger of something happening between us.'

Well, not now there wasn't. When she made it so clear that she wasn't interested. There had been times that evening when having Lara by his side had felt so right, so uncomplicated, that it made him start to question all the reasons why he was so sure that seeing if there might be something more than friendship there between them was a good idea. But there was no point letting his thoughts wander in that direction. Even if Lara did see him as more than a friend, he wasn't going to risk her walking away from him by suggesting that having her in his life as a friend didn't always feel quite…enough. And he wasn't going to risk losing her by letting them get closer, and then pushing her away. He couldn't lose her—it wasn't worth the risk.

'So,' he said, hand rubbing at the back of his neck.

'What do you want to do for the rest of the night? Are you tired? I'm still a bit wired from all…that.'

A knock at the door interrupted the awkward moment, and a hotel employee came in, pushing a cart with a bucket of champagne and two tall crystal glasses.

Lara thanked him and took out the card propped up against the ice bucket. Well, there were worse things than room service and a movie and free champagne.

'Telly in bed?' she suggested. 'And open this?'

'Absolutely,' Jannes said, holding up the glasses while she popped the cork.

She poured the champagne and then took a full glass, lifting it towards Jannes in a toast. 'To…us?' she suggested, hoping that Jannes could hear the heavy irony in her voice.

'To us,' he agreed with a smile, clinking their glasses together.

What did she want to do with Jannes in the honeymoon suite of a luxury hotel? Well, wasn't that the question. What she wanted to do and what was actually a good idea were at opposite ends of the spectrum. On the one hand, she had an evening's worth of inappropriate fantasies involving Jannes, a white shirt and a shower. On the other hand, acting out even one of those fantasies would turn this situation from complicated to…impossible. So that pretty much left them with the minibar and a movie.

She stalled in the bathroom, taking her time brushing her teeth and pulling on the shorts and crop top pyjamas she had packed when she'd thought that she'd have a bed to herself. Jannes slipped past her as she walked back into the bedroom and she was left watching his retreating back.

She climbed onto the bed, pulling a blanket around her shoulders and nudging the throw cushions in between the two firm duck-feather pillows.

'I can still sleep on the floor, you know,' Jannes said, leaning in the doorway of the bathroom, wearing just a T-shirt and boxers.

This wasn't a good idea at all. But saying so would only suggest to him that there was something other than friendship between them that made this a big deal.

'You're making a big deal out of nothing,' Lara told him, desperately trying to convince herself at the same time. She wasn't going to act on temptation—if she did she would end up hurting him, and that just wasn't acceptable. So instead she found the remote for the TV and grabbed some snacks from the minibar. If they were stuck in this awkward situation she was going to make the best of it. And champagne and snacks in bed definitely counted as the best of it.

She scrolled through the TV guide, looking for a movie, before stumbling on an episode of the dating show she was guiltily addicted to. She popped the lid to her Pringles and took a sip of champagne as the opening credits rolled.

'Budge up,' Jannes said, reaching for a handful of crisps. 'Hey, you're two episodes ahead of me. What did I miss?'

She froze with her crisp halfway to her mouth, her jaw hanging open.

'Seriously? You watch this? How did I not know that?'

'Don't judge,' he said with a little huff. 'You watch it too.'

'Yes, but you're—'

He raised an eyebrow. 'Careful there, do I hear some incoming sexism? *What* am I, exactly?'

'You're a relationship-phobe,' she said. 'And yet you want to watch members of the public falling in love?'

He snorted. 'They're hardly in love, most of them. And anyway, pot, kettle et cetera.' He waved a hand, which she assumed stood in for all her commitment issues. Well, those commitment issues were the only thing standing between him and getting hurt, so he probably should be a little kinder about them.

'We're not talking about me,' she reminded him. 'Oh, my God, this guy's my favourite,' she said, taking another sip of her champagne, hoping that it would dissolve the atmosphere that seemed to have suddenly thickened around them.

'You can't like him. He's an idiot. I forbid it.'

'Excuse me?' She widened her eyes, wondering if she was seeing him for the first time. 'You forbid it?'

'I'm your boyfriend now,' he said with a shrug, his eyes never leaving the TV. 'That means I can forbid things. At the very least I can forbid you from talking about other guys that you fancy when we're in bed together.'

She shoved him with her shoulder. 'No wonder you're single, thinking that you get to go around forbidding things. The women of the yachting world have had a lucky escape. Anyway, we're not in bed. We're on the bed.'

'Oh, yes, of course. That's a very important distinction.'

She rolled her eyes. '*In* bed and *on* bed are worlds apart. Everybody knows that.'

'Well, I don't know that. I'm not an expert, but I am fairly sure you're not meant to talk to me about other guys.'

'Jealous?' she asked, wondering why she felt a twist of nervous anticipation in her belly as she waited for his answer.

'Not at all,' Jannes said at last, leaning back on the pillow with his eyes safely back on the screen. 'I don't need to be. I know he's not your type.'

She laughed and elbowed him in the ribs. 'Oh, really? And what's my type?'

'You know. Tall, blond, sporty. Swedish, preferably.' The corners of his lips turned up infinitesimally, so no one but her would have been able to tell that he was joking.

She jabbed him with her elbow. 'Ugh. Stop talking, I can't hear the TV.' But he swiped her back with a cushion, catching her just as she was taking a sip of champagne and spilling the whole lot down her pyjama top.

'Argh,' she cried, kneeling up and brushing off the front of her crop top. 'I'm soaked! You did that on purpose!'

'I didn't—I'm sorry!'

She dived into the bathroom—leaving Jannes looking crestfallen on the bed—and rinsed out her top, before hanging it in the shower to drip dry. It was only once the emergency was dealt with that she realised she was wearing not much more than a slightly damp bralette underneath. And now she was in her underwear, in a hotel room with Jannes, and had no idea where she was going to find something dry to wear.

Jannes appeared at the bathroom door, his eyes fixed firmly on the floor. 'Everything okay?' he asked. 'Could it be rescued?'

'No harm done,' she said, crossing her arms over her chest, and then spotting the towelling robes on the back of the door. Jannes's eyes grew wide as she came towards him, and then a look of relief washed over his features as she grabbed the robe and tied it firmly around her waist.

'Do you want me to get you something from your case?' he asked her, his ears slightly pink, giving him away.

'I didn't bring a spare,' she said. 'Wasn't anticipating pyjama disasters.' But they would have to do something, because it was hard enough ignoring these feelings for Jannes that were only growing stronger. Spending the night with him in only her underwear would be unbearable.

'Want to borrow a T-shirt?' Jannes asked, and she could have kissed him with gratitude, if that wouldn't have made things infinitely more complicated. She took half a second to think about how intimate it was, borrowing his clothes to sleep in. But if the alternative was this flimsy underwear, she didn't really have much of a choice.

'Thanks, yeah, that'd be great.'

CHAPTER SEVEN

LARA WOKE TO the smell of oranges—the smell of Jannes, his shower gel or his laundry powder, she'd never been able to work out exactly what—and a complete lack of feeling in her left arm. She opened her eyes a crack before squeezing them back shut. She couldn't be responsible for what she did when she was sleeping, she told herself. Except she might have been dreaming about Jannes—things were a little hazy—so that did make her kind of culpable if she'd somehow started acting out her fantasies. But that wasn't important now.

What was important was extracting herself from this situation without waking him. She took an inventory of body parts. Her left arm was trapped under his chest, hence the lack of feeling. Her right had fallen into the notch of his waist. Her left leg was tucked in behind his knees, but her right was clamped between hard thighs. She tried an experimental pull, but Jannes's legs tightened around hers and he pulled her closer with the arm trapped beneath his body. He smelled of oranges, and the soft hair at the nape of his neck was tickling her face.

She had to get herself out of this before Jannes woke up. The last thing that this situation needed was for there to be two of them conscious of how unbelievably close and unbelievably hot this was. Because while this was one-sided it was something that she could undo. If they were both awake, both aware of how close they were to...to something stupid, then she wasn't sure if her self-control would hold and she wouldn't do something to embarrass herself—something that could break her heart and their friendship.

She took just half a moment to imagine a world where things were different. Where something deep inside herself hadn't broken when her father had left her. Where Jannes wasn't scarred by being left again and again by his parents. Where they were both whole and healthy and ready to trust. If she had been that person, if he had been that man, she knew that they would be happy. She knew that there was no one on the planet who was more perfect for her than Jannes was. But they weren't those people. And trying to make this friendship any more than it already was would result in both of them getting hurt. And losing Jannes from her life... Removing herself from the bed was the only safe course of action.

She withdrew the arm that was resting on top of Jannes's waist and laid it against his back, using it to gently push him away. If she could just free her leg, she could snatch her arm from underneath him and it wouldn't matter if that woke him because she had every intention of being out of the room before he even realised what was going on. But she couldn't take that approach with both arm and leg: too high risk. Too much of a chance of getting caught.

She tried easing away from him again, this time pushing gently at his shoulder as she tried to move her leg. But he just held on to her tighter, wrapping her trapped arm around his middle and scooting back closer to her. So he was a touchy-feely sleeper. She tried really hard not to file that fact away for future reference. She let her forehead rest against the nape of his neck as she took stock of her failure and reconsidered her tactics. When she moved away, he pulled her closer. So if she wanted to get out, she would have to get…closer? Oh, this was going to end in tears, she was sure of it.

She rested her arm back on his waist and tightened it experimentally. Jannes took a deep breath in and let it out as a long sigh. Interesting. She pressed her chest harder against his back, keeping her forehead close to the soft hair at the nape of his neck. She was never going to be able to eat an orange again after this. But the longer she held him, the more his grip on her relaxed. She just had to stick this out.

The next time he breathed out, she pressed herself against him again, trying hard not to notice the shift of his muscles under his shirt, the tensing of his abs as she pressed her hand against them. But the vice around her trapped thigh loosened, and slowly, slowly, she drew her leg back.

Jannes shifted restlessly when she finally got it free, and she tucked her cheek into the notch where his neck met his shoulder until his stirring stopped. This was torture. It was everything that she wanted, but knew that she couldn't have. If she had to design a torture for herself this would be it. Being so close to Jannes that she was practically inhaling him without being able to do anything—to keep them from both getting hurt. Worse—having to rely on her own slightly shaky self-control to keep them both in line.

She listened and waited as Jannes's breathing slowed and deepened. The soft hairs on his thigh tickled her sensitive skin and she bit her lip to stop herself sighing. She had to keep her eye on the prize here. And the prize was unquestionably extracting herself from this situation without doing something that couldn't be taken back. Without doing something that would lose her Jannes for ever.

But it was so tempting not to fight this. Just go back to sleep with her body smooshed up against Jannes's. To wait for them both to wake up like this and…allow the inevitable to happen.

But then what if she started to feel…*more* for Jannes? And he'd inevitably start to pull away—she'd seen him with girls before; she knew his MO too well to question what would happen. And she would be left, leaving her hurt and confused—and without her best friend there to help put her back together. She was smarter than that. Too smart to keep doing the same thing over and over and expecting different results.

She took a final deep breath, pulled her leg back and breathed a long sigh of relief. She'd done it, and Jannes hadn't even twitched. She was so close to being free from him.

Except she wasn't, was she? Because even when she

was out of his bed she was still in his life. She'd agreed to date him. To bring him to family parties, to show up on red carpets and photo calls with him. She could do that as a friend. As long as they were doing it in separate beds from now on.

She pulled her arm out from underneath him and rolled towards the edge of the bed, her eyes on Jannes to see if he would wake. Nothing. Not even a twitch. She let out her held breath in a rush and darted from the bedroom, knowing how dangerous it would be to stay.

Jannes woke to unfamiliar surroundings, unable to shake the feeling that he had lost something important. It was only as he clicked where he was—the honeymoon suite of the Liverpool hotel—that he realised what was missing: Lara. He sat up in bed, looking round until he heard movement in the next room and realised she must be up already. No wonder he'd slept in later than her. He'd been awake half the night, listening to her breathing beside him, fighting the urge to deconstruct their pillow barrier and pull her close.

She had fallen asleep while they were still bickering good-naturedly about the relative merits of the slime-balls on the dating show that they'd both admitted to liking. And then she'd snored on, oblivious to the fact that they were in bed together.

Had she felt awkward when she'd woken up this morning? Was that why she was in the next room instead of lounging in bed, taking advantage of the opportunity for a lazy Sunday morning? He swung himself out of bed and pulled on jeans from his bag. Lara was in the sitting room of their suite, coffee in hand as she listened to the radio, head tipped back against the sofa, eyes closed.

'You're still tired,' he said, leaning against the doorway and watching her. Her eyes snapped open and he thought for a second that she was going to spill her coffee, but somehow she managed to rescue it. 'Sorry, I didn't mean to startle you. Was I hogging the duvet?'

They could make light of this. They could pretend that they could share a bed without it meaning anything, as if they were the simply platonic friends that they had always told each other they were. He didn't know why he had brought up the subject of their sleeping arrangements at all when it was clearly so much simpler if they both pretended that they had never shared a bed, but it just felt like...something that needed acknowledging. It was too big to ignore.

She let her eyes drift back closed. 'It's fine. Just a late night. Wasn't expecting the raucous after-party.'

He laughed and crossed the room, prising her coffee cup from her hand. 'I'm just getting you a refill,' he said at her squawked protest. 'You should go back to bed for a bit,' he added, placing the coffee on the table beside her. 'Now that I'm up.'

'It's okay, I'm awake now. Won't be able to get back to sleep.'

He laughed again. 'Right. You look very awake.'

She opened one eye. 'Don't start. So what have you—?' she started to ask, when his phone started ringing.

He glanced at the screen. 'It's Mormor,' he said. 'I should get this.'

'Tell her I say hi,' Lara said with a smile of genuine affection, eyes drifting back closed.

'*Hej*, Mormor,' he said, answering the phone.

Lara listened to the sing-song of Jannes speaking Swedish. She'd picked up a few phrases over the course of her friendship with him, but nowhere near enough to follow when he was speaking rapid-fire to his grandmother. He was agitated, she realised. His smile was fixed in place and his tone was still cheerful. But somehow unnaturally so. She wished she knew what he was saying. And, for that matter, why she kept hearing her own name every time his eyes slid over to her.

He hung up the phone and then pinched the bridge of his nose, looking like a teenager who knew he was about to get into trouble with his parents. Or his stern Swedish grandmother.

'Jannes? What have you done?' she asked, not sure whether she was more amused or worried by the expression on his face.

'That was Mormor,' he said, his expression bleak.

'I know. What's wrong?'

'She saw us—pictures from last night.'

Lara shrugged. 'So what? I mean, I didn't think she would have seen them already, but pictures of us was kind of the point, right?'

'Apparently she follows you on Instagram. I thought I'd have a chance to talk to her before she found out.'

Lara nodded, still not quite seeing what the problem was. 'And *this*—' she gestured at him, his bleak expression and anxious posture '—is because she thinks we're together?'

He shook his head.

'Jannes, just tell me or I'm going to start panicking.'

'She summoned us for lunch,' he said in an ominous tone. 'Today.'

'Today? I was going to—I need to study.'

What she actually wanted to say was that she needed space. Distance. To catch her breath and try not to think about waking up stuck to Jannes like a barnacle. An impromptu lunch with his grandmother didn't exactly fit in to that plan.

'I tried to argue,' Jannes said, 'but she was…quite persistent. Apparently that's not the way she should find out that…'

'What?'

He frowned. 'It's hard to translate.'

'Try,' Lara said through gritted teeth, and Jannes shook his head, giving in.

'To find out that I've stopped being an idiot and…'

'And?'

'And finally seen what was staring me in the face all this time.'

Lara stared, not sure what to say. 'Jannes…'

'I know.'

She softened towards him, knowing how much his grandmother meant to him. 'You don't have to lie to your family just because I'm lying to mine. It's not as if Mormor is going to go to the papers. You can just tell her the truth.'

'I know. I know that. And I tried to explain that it's

not what it seems but… I don't know what happened… she somehow just refused to hear it.'

'Well, you can explain properly when you go to lunch.'

'*We're* going to lunch.'

Lara frowned at him. 'She's not *my* grandmother. She can't make me.'

'I'm sorry, are we back in the playground?' Jannes asked, clearly frustrated. 'Of course she can't make you. But she isn't going to believe me if I go on my own. She'll convince herself that I'm over-complicating things and I should settle down and produce offspring immediately. Trust me, she already laid the groundwork on the phone. If we're both there she can't insist that we're both wrong about whether we're together or not.'

She shook her head. How had she ever expected dating Jannes—even fake dating him—to be simple? 'You know this is ridiculous, don't you?' she said. 'I have other friends, Jannes, quite a few of them, and I've never had to go for Sunday lunch to convince any of their grandmothers that I'm not sleeping with them.'

He smiled, and somehow that felt like a victory. 'It's not my fault you've led such a sheltered life, is it?' he said.

She threw a cushion at him. 'God. Fine. I'll come. But only because your grandmother is absurd. I cannot believe I'm agreeing to this.'

He walked over, all fluid and graceful and disgustingly composed, and placed the cushion back beside her. 'You're the best,' he said, nudging her feet so she'd make room for him on the sofa. 'I told her we'd be leaving in an hour and would get a car straight to hers.'

She sat abruptly upright. 'Jesus, Jannes. An hour? Straight to hers? I've got to go home and change.'

'No, you don't.'

'I'm wearing your T-shirt. I *slept* in this T-shirt. It's hardly going to convince her that we're just good friends.'

He settled further into the corner of the sofa and took her coffee off her, stealing a sip before placing it on the end table. 'Well, you must have brought other clothes.'

'I brought *getting a cab back home* clothes. Not *going for lunch with your eccentric grandmother* clothes. Jannes, I can't—'

'Stop. You're perfect.'

He cut her off and she stared at him for a moment, not quite sure where her next thought was supposed to come from when her brain had just turned to mush in the space between one word and the next.

'I mean—I just meant—you'll be fine. Whatever you wear.'

'Fine?'

'Yeah.'

Cool, so they were just going to not talk about the perfect thing. That was a good idea. It was just a slip of the tongue. Or something you just say to a mate. They were on their way to go convince his *mormor*—the person he was closest to in the world—that they weren't really together. If she ever needed an ego check, well, there was one ready-made.

CHAPTER EIGHT

'I CAN'T BELIEVE I'm doing this in ratty old jeans,' Lara said as they climbed the stairs towards Mormor's apartment. She lived across two floors of an old town house in west London, with a view of the gated garden to the front through the big Georgian windows, and out to a little mews at the back, with Farrow & Ball painted doors and bay trees in tubs outside each house.

'Should I point out that I'm also wearing jeans?' Jannes asked. 'Or will that get me in trouble?'

Lara rolled her eyes. 'She dotes on you—you can wear what you like. I'm meant to be making a good impression.'

Or at least that was what it felt like. The whole thing had a decidedly *meet the parents* feel to it. Which was ridiculous, truly, because she had known Mormor for years and they were here to announce that they *weren't* a couple. But still.

'Mormor loves you,' Jannes said. 'You know that.'

Well, Lara certainly loved Mormor, that much was true. She was mischievous and sharp and wry. And Lara still hadn't quite got the knack of knowing if she was one hundred per cent joking or not at any time. But she still couldn't shake these nerves.

'Hmm, we'll see if she still feels that way about me when she finds out I'm not really making an honest man out of you.'

'She doesn't think that we're getting married. It's not that far out of hand.'

Lara shuddered at the thought of things between her and Jannes getting that far—the certainty that she would end up losing him if they did.

'Well, that's a relief at least.'

'Ready?' Jannes asked, and then knocked on the door. Lara set her shoulders, not sure why she felt as if she were going into battle.

'*Älskling!*' Mormor announced, throwing open the door. 'And you brought Lara with you. You're a good boy.'

She pinched his cheek and Lara smothered a laugh at the grimace on Jannes's face. 'You two have made an old woman very happy. I knew you couldn't be so stupid for ever. I can't believe it's taken you so long to work out that you're perfect for one another.'

Jannes threw Lara a look that was pure *I told you so* as they walked through the apartment to the elegant living room.

'Like I explained on the phone, Mormor,' Jannes said, his voice slow and deliberate. 'Lara and I are just friends. We were pretending to be a couple for…for a few reasons, but we're not really together.'

Mormor narrowed her eyes at him. 'I saw a picture

of you kissing her. Are you telling me you go around kissing women who are not your girlfriend?'

Well, that sent him a delightful shade of pink, Lara thought, watching him squirm with embarrassment.

'Like I keep saying, that wasn't real.'

'I imagined it? I didn't see you kiss? Are you trying to make me think I'm going senile?'

'No, of course not. We did kiss, but—'

'So you are friends who kiss sometimes. She is your girlfriend,' Mormor declared, as if that settled the matter. 'Now, Lara, I need you to tell me everything and explain in great detail because Jannes has told me nothing.' She tutted and Lara felt a lurch of dread in her stomach.

'Mormor,' Lara said as they followed Mormor through to the kitchen, watched her fill a coffee pot from the tap and add heaped scoops of coffee. 'I'm really not his girlfriend. I'm sorry if we've disappointed you.'

'Oh, you kids, always overcomplicating things.' Mormor threw her hands up in an expression of exasperation as she reached into a high cupboard for cups and saucers. 'Jannes. If I say she's your girlfriend, she's your girlfriend. Now, who is going to drink coffee with me?'

'Some help you were,' Jannes said under his breath as Mormor bustled around them, taking a tin of cinnamon buns from the cupboard and swearing colourfully when she couldn't find the milk jug.

'I told her!' Lara whispered back. 'It's not my fault she didn't want to listen.'

'No, you're right,' Jannes said, shaking his head,

the picture of dejection. 'It's my fault for yesterday. For thinking that something like this would be simple.'

She hated when Jannes looked dejected. It just made her want to comfort him. To make him feel better. In all sorts of ways that would lead to nothing but trouble for them both. So she kept things on track.

'It's your fault for thinking that you know better than Mormor whether I'm your girlfriend? I don't think you can really take the blame for that. So what do we do?' They threw a look over to Mormor, where she was arranging the coffee things on a silver tray on the kitchen island.

'We drink the coffee and eat the pastries, I suppose,' he said. 'Try and show her that she's made a mistake.'

Lara crossed her arms in front of her body. 'How do we prove that we're not together? It's not like we would be going at it on the kitchen counter either way.'

He spluttered in surprise and Lara laughed. 'Oh, close your mouth, Jannes,' she whispered. 'You're so easily shocked. It makes it impossible not to tease you. You're adorable.'

He threw a look to make sure Mormor wasn't listening and then crossed his arms and leaned back against the wall. 'Adorable?'

'You still have a problem with adorable?' Lara asked with a smile.

'It's not very manly.'

'Ah—' She laughed quietly '—and you want to impress me with your manliness?'

'Stop flirting, you two,' Mormor interrupted, lifting

up the tray with an ominous clinking of china. 'Anyone would think you are boyfriend and girlfriend.'

'We weren't flirting,' Jannes and Lara protested together.

'Right, and the Pope doesn't wear a hat,' Mormor said. 'Enough talking anyway. Jannes, I need your help in the kitchen. Lara, make yourself at home, my dear. I'll have your man back to you in a moment.'

'I'm not—'

'He's not—'

'How can you just refuse to believe two people who say they're not together?' Jannes asked in the car later, for what felt like the millionth time. He was pinching the bridge of his nose in that way he always did when he was tired, and it was reassuring to know that she wasn't the only one feeling the after-effects of their late-night *Love Island* binge. It had been gone two o'clock when she had finally given in to sleep.

'If anyone is up to the task it's Mormor. Do you think she really didn't believe us or was she just winding us up?'

'I don't know how you cannot believe it when you have the both of us there telling her we made the whole thing up.'

Lara nodded; she'd been thinking the same thing. 'So she's winding us up. Any idea why, other than to torture us?'

'Honestly, when it comes to Mormor it's anyone's guess. So…what do you think?'

'What do I think about what?'

Jannes gestured to her, and them himself. 'About this whole dating thing. Fake dating.'

'I don't really get where this is going, Jannes.'

'I was just wondering if it's something that you're still happy to continue,' he said, looking a little awkward. He looked it; she felt it. She wasn't sure that this was at all a good idea.

'Even after all this with Mormor?' she asked, going for the easy excuse, the one that didn't give away too much about what she felt.

'She's clearly going to believe whatever she wants, regardless of what we say or do,' Jannes said. 'So maybe we should just do what's best for us.'

She raised an eyebrow. 'And you're still sure that's pretending to date?'

'Well, you have all those family things that you were invited to at the wedding. The twins' christening is soon, isn't it? And the longer that we appear together the better it is for my chances of securing sponsorship. Just one appearance with you has generated more positive press than I've had in a year.'

'I'm pretty sure that was your doing, with the special achievement award,' Lara pointed out. He had earned that award, and she didn't want him thinking that his successes were down to anything but his own hard work. She couldn't take the claim for that.

'And I think it's because everyone adores you and they have to like me when I'm near you.'

She shook her head. 'So you're just using me for my adorability?'

'No, we're helping each other out. But I'm not going

to push you into anything you don't want to do. If it makes you uncomfortable, we won't do it. It's as simple as that. I don't want to do anything that risks our friendship.'

Their friendship. Which they had to protect at all costs, because if they lost sight of that at the wrong moment then she was sure that they would do something stupid that would mean that she lost him for ever. And then they would both end up hurt, and broken, and without their best friend there to hand out tissues and help pick up the pieces. She couldn't bear the thought of having to go through something like that without Jannes there in her corner. Or the thought of hurting Jannes, and then not being the one to hold him and help him heal.

'You *are* my friend, Jannes, and all the hand-holding and kissing and stuff, that's not important, is it? We know what we are to each other, and what we're not. And as long as we remember that then the other stuff doesn't matter. This just makes our lives a little easier, with no cost.'

'And when we're not in public then nothing changes,' Jannes assured her. 'We carry on as before. We're friends, Lara. Nothing's going to change that.'

Good, because she didn't want to back out of this now. Later that night, as they tucked into a takeaway, she thought again about the family events she'd agreed to go to, and how she couldn't even consider going without Jannes at her side. And it didn't cost her anything to show up to Jannes's events. It took dating completely off her radar, meant that she could concentrate on her work, her studying…and not on those commitment issues Jannes always seemed to want to make her talk about. It was hard not to think about those issues when she was with her family, faced with the evidence of how little she had meant to her father. How she had been a footnote to his real life. How easy she had been to hurt. How destructive following his desires had been for the two families that he'd destroyed.

With Jannes by her side, it had all felt…less bleak. She'd felt less disposable. Sure, it helped that no one was asking her about her love life any more, but it helped that he was simply there. Grounding her. Reminding her that she was present and she mattered.

'Okay,' she said at last. 'We'll keep things going a little longer. If you're sure you wouldn't rather be dating someone else for real.'

'I'm sure,' he told her, and she took comfort from the certainty in his voice.

'And are you sure you don't want to talk about that?' she pushed him. 'We're friends, Jannes. I don't like the thought that you're missing out on meeting someone for real because you're sitting through family parties with me.'

'I… I wouldn't be dating anyway,' he told her.

She tried to keep her voice light, as if the idea of talking with Jannes about his love life wasn't giving her butterflies. 'Oh?'

He shrugged. 'I haven't dated for a while. You hadn't noticed?'

Well, of course she'd *noticed*. She couldn't help but

notice that it had been over a year since she'd seen him with anyone else.

'I noticed. Why is that, though? You can't be short of offers.'

He picked up his chopsticks and dug them into his Pad Thai, not meeting her eyes. 'I just didn't see the point, after a while. I didn't want—don't want—anything serious, and after a while the casual thing gets repetitive, don't you think?'

Yeah, it did, which was precisely why she'd stopped doing it too. But she knew it was more than that. That he was scared of getting hurt. Of having someone walk away from him the way his parents had done, over and over again. She couldn't trust herself to never do that to him, never to hurt him, and that meant she had to hide what she really felt.

'You're not worried that I'm going to be getting in your way?' Jannes asked, with the honesty that she loved him for.

She shrugged. 'I'm not missing much. Not when I already know that it's not going anywhere—not when I'll freak out and leave as soon as the question of whether I can trust him comes up.' In the end she'd realised that it was far simpler not to get into something, rather than walking in while simultaneously checking for a secure exit. She would have thought that Jannes would have understood that better than anyone. But they'd never actually talked about this before.

'Why doesn't it ever work out?' he asked. 'Why don't you want it to?'

'Because I can't make it work,' Lara said, her voice

tightening slightly as she defended herself. She didn't expect this from Jannes. More than anyone, he was supposed to understand. 'Because, at the back of my mind, I'm always wondering if they're going home to someone else every time I say goodbye. It's just easier not to start something; isn't that basically what you just told me about why you don't date?'

'I don't know; it just seems…sadder when we're talking about you.'

'Ouch,' she said, leaning away from him.

'No—' he dropped his chopsticks and reached for her hand '—I don't mean that you're sad. I just don't like the idea that you've given up because you haven't found a guy who you know will treat you like you deserve. You're amazing and any guy should feel incredibly lucky to have you.'

She rolled her eyes at him. 'You're patronising me.' After all, it wasn't as if he was pushing for the chance to be with her for real. He was quite clear that faking it was all that was ever going to be on offer from him. Which was fine. Obviously.

'I'm sorry. That wasn't my intention,' he apologised, and then hesitated. 'This is all to do with your dad, right?' he asked.

It was as if he had thrown cold water over her, killing the conversation dead. 'Jannes. I really don't want to talk about my father with you. I'm happy fake dating and so are you. I won't grill you on your reasons; you don't grill me on mine. I thought that was the deal?'

'Okay, fine,' Jannes said at last. 'But if it's not working for you, you have to tell me and we just undo the whole arrangement. Okay?'

'Fine.'

She picked up her chopsticks, heaped more Pad Thai on her plate, and then chewed on a dumpling thoughtfully and sank back into the sofa cushions. 'So what do we do next?' she asked, trying to steer the conversation onto safer ground. 'Should we compare diaries? I've already had invitations for some of the family stuff you agreed to at Pip's wedding. It's only a month until the twins' christening.'

'Fine, yes, I suppose we should. I'll forward you details of a few things. The regatta in Harbourside is happening in a couple of weeks. I'll be there meeting with potential sponsors—it would be good if you could be there, help the image, you know, if you're there doing the girlfriend thing. And I think you'll enjoy it.'

She nodded. 'Okay. Regatta in a couple of weeks.'

'And of course I have a spare room at my place there so we don't have to repeat the *only one bed* incident.'

'I didn't realise it had been so traumatic for you,' she said with an exaggerated head-tilt. 'Poor little flower.'

He shoved her playfully with his foot. 'It wasn't traumatic; it just complicates things, doesn't it?'

CHAPTER NINE

LARA PUT ON a wide-brimmed sunhat as she stepped out of her car. With the air-con on all the way down from London, she hadn't realised how hot the day had become.

Jannes had warned her that he wouldn't be there when she arrived and so she followed the instructions he'd sent her to get into the key safe. She hadn't seen his Harbourside house before. He visited Mormor so often that he had a room there, and it made more sense for them to meet up in London and hang out at her place. Which meant that she had never seen a space that was entirely Jannes's. She couldn't help but be secretly pleased that he couldn't meet her until later. It gave her a chance to see his place without him in it. She wasn't sure why exactly that appealed so much: if there was something she wanted to know about him then she could just ask.

But this was different, she thought.

The hallway was bright and clean and sparse, with just a couple of pairs of shoes stored neatly by the door, a couple of jackets she recognised on the hooks. She dropped the key into a bowl on the shelf above the radiator and walked through to the kitchen. Ah, so here was Jannes. Glass doors covered the whole of the back of the house, offering unbroken views of the sea, all the way out to the horizon. A host of boats bobbed in the water, sails billowing in the breeze, and she wondered how often Jannes sat here, watching people out on the water. Every seat in the open-plan room—from the great big corner sofa to the pale wood chairs arranged around a circular table—faced towards the sea.

And there were touches of the ocean inside too: the woven blanket tossed haphazardly on the sofa, with a mix of blues and greens, aquas and azures, and sky and stormy grey. The artwork on the walls all captured a part of life on the shore or the sea: shells, and fishing boats, and always the rich blue-green of deep water.

She wandered along the bookshelves that held Jannes's trophies and, across the facing wall, the ones with actual books. She pulled a few out and looked at the titles, curious. There were books on travel and nature and woodwork. Sports biographies and sailing, and more sailing, of course.

She walked back through to the kitchen and found the coffee machine, made herself a double espresso and slid the glass doors open. A wide deck spanned the width of the house, with a glass barrier the only thing breaking the view from the deck to the sea. Lara sat on a wicker chair, eyes drawn to the white caps and sunlight glinting on the water and felt the stress and anxiety of her working week fall away. She could get used to this. Well, maybe she would, she considered, depending on how long she and Jannes kept up their pretence.

She watched the yachts out on the water and listened to the rattle of wires in masts from the marina. With every lungful of sea air, her body felt looser and heavier. If Jannes didn't call soon and let her know that his meeting was finished then she might decide that she was never leaving this deck.

As if on cue, her phone buzzed in her pocket. Jannes. She hit answer and tried to hide the smile in her voice.

'All done schmoozing?' she asked.

'For now. If you want to join me here, we can do some more together if you like. You know you're much more charming than I am.'

'Sure,' she said, stretching out in the chair. If she didn't move soon she would definitely fall asleep here. 'I need to earn my keep.'

She could practically hear his frown. 'You know that's not what I meant.'

'I know. I'm kidding.' It was adorable, how seriously he took her sometimes.

'I'll walk back up and meet you. Shouldn't take more than ten minutes if you're ready to head out.'

'I am, but there's no need to walk back up here. I'll mooch through the town and meet you at the yacht club,' she told him. She'd never visited Harbourside before, and wanted to explore in her own time.

She said goodbye, pulled the glass doors closed and gathered up her bag and her sunglasses and hat. Pocketing the key, she pulled the door closed behind her and followed Jannes's directions to the main street of the town. Bunting was strung between the shops, across the cobbled street, and the sun was fierce on the heads and shoulders of pinkened tourists.

Ahead of her, a toddler sat down abruptly, striped pinafore dress gathering around her chunky legs as she sobbed and declared she wouldn't walk another step. Lara gave the parents a smile as she passed the family, and stopped to look in the window of a boutique. There was vintage furniture, clothes and jewellery of all her Instagram dreams. She took a couple of photos through the window and made a mental note to stop in before she went back to London. The next window was filled with second-hand books, and if it wasn't for the knowledge that Jannes was waiting for her at the entrance of the marina she was in danger of losing the whole afternoon in the little row of independent shops that led down to the seafront.

She followed the sound of the music and found Jannes waiting for her by the entrance to the marina, ice cream melting down his wrist.

She laughed as he licked a trickle of cream that was making its way around the circle of his wrist bone. Laughter was definitely the right response to that, she told herself, eyes still fixed on his wrist. She definitely shouldn't offer to lick it off for him. She licked her lips involuntarily as he held the cone out to her.

'I got you ice cream. Probably should have waited until you were actually here.'

'You're sweet,' she said, reaching up to press a kiss

to his cheek, just a friendly thing to do, and took the ice cream from him.

'How are things going?' she asked as they walked down steps into the marina and along the row of yachts moored there. She tucked a free strand of hair behind her ear before it got stuck in the ice cream.

'Not bad,' Jannes said, slipping his hands in his pockets as they walked. His sunglasses hid his eyes, making it hard to read his expression. She was distracted, anyway, by the glint of sunlight on the pale hair on the back of his legs, bare skin between his shorts and his deck shoes.

'Lara?'

'Hmm, what was that?' She tried to cover her embarrassment, not sure how long she'd been distracted.

'Nothing—I just asked you if you found the house okay. I'm sorry I wasn't there when you arrived but they changed the meeting at the last minute.'

'Like I said on the phone, it was absolutely fine. And I love the house. You do know you might never get rid of me now? I think I could live here for ever.'

Even with the sunglasses on there was no hiding the flash of panic across Jannes's face. 'I was kidding, Jannes. I'm not really about to move in.'

'I didn't panic.'

'You look terrified.'

'It's fine.'

'I do know what we're doing here, and I know that moving in with you isn't a part of it. I just meant that I love the house. You need to stop freaking out every time that something I say makes you think I'm trying to trap you into committing to me. We're not even to-gether. I don't understand why you keep thinking I'm trying to make you do something you don't want to do. This was *your idea*.'

Because if he started to think that she might stay, then he had to be afraid that she might leave. It didn't make any sense, of course it didn't. He knew that they weren't really dating. Knew that her trip to his home was part of their charade and nothing more. But irrational fears were just that—irrational. And any time that he got the feeling that Lara might want to stay, might want to make this thing more than a fantasy, he got this feeling like a hook in his gut, a wrench, an inkling of what it might feel like when she would inevitably leave him, and he couldn't help but retreat.

He'd been here before. He knew he threw up these walls and barriers when he liked someone too much. It had destroyed relationships before, and he was deter-mined that this wasn't going to come between him and Lara. If he was willing to risk that, then he wouldn't be so sure that fake dating was the only romantic future that was available to them.

'Jannes!' he heard shouted by someone in the crowd of people outside the yacht club, and he turned to see his agent walking towards him. Lara slipped her hand into his. She didn't break her stride or even look up at him, just gave him this little show of togetherness as though it was nothing.

He had to keep his head on the job here, which was securing sponsorship for his next transatlantic race.

Otherwise, the three months he had pencilled in for the race next season started to stretch uncomfortably in front of him. Standing still always felt like this. He had learned as a kid that it was a lot less painful to tell himself that he was racing back to school for extra training than because it was better to walk away than be left somewhere. When he had signed up for every sports club and extracurricular activity, he had told himself that he was just a sporty kind of guy, not that he couldn't bear the thought of sitting with nothing but his own thoughts to distract him.

'Lara, lovely to see you again,' Chris, Jannes's agent, said, looking a little surprised to see her with him. Jannes rolled his eyes—was it so out of character that he turned up with the same girl twice? Okay, stupid question. But Chris was only giving him that look because of the bad press he'd been getting before this thing with Lara, and every word of those articles had been fictional. He had wanted to deny it publicly but, according to his manager, that would just add fuel to the fire, and now his career was at risk because his sponsors weren't happy. He loved his job, but it came with a cost—and this was it. He would be happy if he never had to take another meeting with a sponsor again. But, unless he happened to find a spare few million to fund his ocean-going lifestyle, he couldn't see that happening any time soon.

Chris dragged them over to meet Spencer, the representative from a new online bank who were looking to raise their profile with sponsorship, and within half a minute of him introducing Lara she had them charmed and eating out of her hand. It was always that way with her—she was so disarmingly friendly that it was impossible not to fall in love with her.

He remembered the first time he'd met her, at a party thrown by a sportswear brand. When she'd walked up to him with a tray of canapés she'd swiped from the wait staff, and had asked him if he was as bored as she was. She had suggested that they help out the servers to liven things up a bit. By the end of the night they'd been firm friends, and if he had known one thing it was that he wanted her in his life. Which put to bed any temptation he had felt to see if it could go further. Dating her would be a fast track to alienating her—he knew his limitations. He knew the damage that he carried around inside himself, and the harm that could do to others if they got too close. Hurting himself by taking a risk was unappealing. Hurting Lara was unthinkable.

He loved to watch her in action at events like this— her complete lack of social niceties, which translated into charm rather than rudeness. If anyone else said half the things that she did, they'd be met with stony silence. And yet Lara always managed to cultivate a circle of guffaws that followed her around a party. He could always locate her by listening for the most outraged laughter.

Spencer was not immune to her charms, it seemed. Lara was listening with rapt attention as he explained the features of his new banking app—a subject Jannes knew she wasn't the least bit interested in. And all the time that she was nodding along and asking probing questions, she never once let go of his hand. It shouldn't be the part of this that was holding his attention—and yet there was something about her warm palm pressing against his that had shut off key operating pathways in his brain.

He snapped back to attention when he heard mention of the transatlantic record attempt, and he looked from Spencer to Lara, trying to catch up with the conversation.

'Lara was just telling me your plans for next summer. You've got your eye on that speed record, eh?'

'Well, he's already the youngest to cross single-handed and the youngest to skipper a circumnavigation,' Lara said without hesitation. 'I keep telling him to leave some records for somebody else, but he doesn't listen to me.'

'Well, I like your ambition,' Spencer said. But Jannes was having difficulty looking away from Lara, or from ignoring the swelling in his chest he felt hearing her list his achievements. He hadn't known she'd been paying that much attention to what he'd been up to—they rarely spoke about work. 'And I know there's an issue with the press coverage. Sorry to bring it up—' he slid an apologetic look to Lara '—but you seem like a solid sort of chap to me.'

Which had to be entirely Lara's doing, Jannes knew, mainly because he had barely managed to get a word in the entire conversation.

'I'm not making any promises, of course,' Spencer went on. 'But I think that Chris and I have a lot to talk about.'

Jannes looked at Lara as Spencer walked away. 'How do you do that?' he asked her, mouth agape.

'What?' she asked with a bewildered smile.

'Charm people like that?' Jannes said. 'He would have given you anything you asked for.'

'I don't know.' She shrugged. 'I listen. I talk. I'm honest.'

It was more than that. There was just something about Lara that was so easy to fall in love with. In a friendly way, he reminded himself, spotting the way that his thoughts were heading. He had only fallen in love with her in a friendly way. 'You know,' he observed lightly, 'not everyone likes honesty.'

'They do with me,' Lara said with another smile, but narrowing her eyes at him.

'I know. I noticed that. I'm wondering how we bottle that and sell it so you can be my next sponsor.'

She laughed, and Jannes breathed a sigh of relief that they had swum out of deeper waters, for now, anyway.

'Well, if you figure it out, let me know. I think I could stand being a billionaire, as an entirely selfless act, of course. So, do you have any more meetings, or shall we go have fun?'

'Why does it always make me nervous when you say things like that?'

'Because of the high probability of me stealing a yacht?'

He shook his head. 'Oh, God, Lara, please don't steal a yacht. If you want one, there are half a dozen people here who would probably just give you one for free.'

'Should we try?' Her eyes lit up, and he couldn't resist teasing her.

'If you like. Do you get a lot of yachting opportunities in Hackney?'

'You're such a killjoy. And also annoyingly right,' she said. 'So maybe I should steal a really big yacht and just live in it here.'

Jannes shook his head. 'Come on,' he said, pulling her gently by the hand.

'Where are we going?'

'Window shopping.'

He led her down to the water, and along the jetty to where a long line of boats was moored, from the little dinghies the kids from the yacht club sailed to huge pleasure cruisers with their satellite masts, multiple decks and speedboats at the aft deck.

'What are we doing?' Lara asked again, grabbing hard onto his arm and nearly toppling them into the water as they stepped down onto the floating pontoon.

'Woah, you all right there?' he asked, grabbing her and pulling her towards him to steady her.

'Didn't realise I'd need my sea legs just yet,' she said, and they both laughed. But his laughter died quickly when he realised how close he had pulled her to stop her falling. They hadn't been this close since that night in Liverpool. He'd had to forcibly remove memories of it from his brain. How her high heels had tipped her forward so her hips had brushed his thighs, her breasts just barely touching his ribcage. The way she'd tilted her chin up so that she could meet his gaze, despite the difference in height between them.

He was forcibly reminded of standing not unlike this at Pip's wedding, with Lara's forehead resting against his chest and his hands in her hair. He reached for a strand of it now, tweaking the end of a curl where it tickled against his hand. This was where they always pulled away. Pretended that neither of them had noticed the sparks flying between them. He never asked if Lara had felt them too. That hadn't seemed necessary, considering he had no intention of acting on them. But now that they had blurred the lines between friendship and something more, it was hard not to wonder whether she felt the same. He could just ask her. He probably should just ask her—get it out in the open. Take the mystery and the danger out of it.

Except he wasn't sure that he wanted to talk about it. If it turned out he was imagining this—and he had no intention of acting on any of it—it would just be stirring things up for no reason. He just had to do what he always did when he had these thoughts—push them as deep down as possible and focus on something else.

'So you're in the market for a yacht,' he said, getting his mind out on the water, where it was safer.

'Absolutely.' She threaded her arm through his and looked at him conspiratorially as they walked. 'How do I do this? Do I just pick the biggest one?'

'That's one approach.' He rolled his eyes. 'Or, you know, you think about which features are most important to you and how each vessel measures up, and the environmental credentials of each company and—'

'Maybe one of the huge ones that has a little speedboat on the back. That seems practical. A boat for every mood. Or I could just pick the most expensive one. Or the cleanest or the shiniest. I like the idea of the cleanest one.'

'What if you liked one of the others better, though, and then we just took a pressure washer to it?'

Lara sighed melodramatically. 'Darling, you are making this far too complicated.'

A cannon sounded, marking the start of a race, but Lara startled, making the pontoon wobble again. Jannes pulled her tighter against him and wrapped an arm around her waist.

'Should we get you back on dry land?' he asked.

'That's an excellent idea. Window shopping makes me thirsty. And I'm pretty sure you owe me a G&T. Photos first, though,' she said, holding out her phone. 'You're an Instagram boyfriend now. Got to start acting like one.'

He took the phone from her and took a few pictures of her posing in front of the yachts, capturing her hair whipping in the wind and her shrieks of laughter as the pontoon wobbled and she nearly lost her footing again. She looked beautiful, of course. He wasn't sure there was anything even he could do to a camera that would prevent that.

'Really?' he asked, scrolling through the pictures so that she could see them. 'I still need to hear why it is I owe you a drink.'

'Well, I'm pretty sure I just locked in that sponsorship for you. And I drove all the way down here and was nearly lost at sea.'

He laughed. 'You're impossible.'

'It's why you love me.'

The worst thing about it was that she was right. He'd had to acknowledge to himself a long time ago that he loved her. Platonically, of course. Everybody loved their friends. And yes, the fact that he was wildly attracted to her could make that complicated—if he let it—so he just wouldn't. It was as simple as that. If he wanted her in his life, he had to make sure he kept things safe. And friendship was safe. Anything more intense risked both of them getting hurt. And he didn't want to hurt Lara any more than he could bear the thought of Lara realising he wasn't worth sticking around for and leaving.

He left Lara outside the yacht club, where she instantly entered into conversation with a couple who had crewed for him last year, and with whom she seemed to have struck up an instant friendship. When he returned, clutching two balloon glasses of gin and tonic, Lara was in hysterics, wiping her eyes, and looking instantly guilty when she spotted Jannes coming towards her.

'Why do I get the feeling you were talking about me?' he asked.

'They were just telling me what a tyrant you are.' Lara laughed. 'How have I never seen this side of you?'

He raised an eyebrow at the two crew.

'Tyrant seems a little harsh. I'm…competitive.'

They all fell into hysterical laughter again and he decided he'd rather not know the specifics of what had been said in his absence.

'Have you seen much of Harbourside?' one of them asked Lara, and she shook her head.

'So far just the yacht club and Jannes's place. I'm looking forward to exploring.'

'Well, if you ever want to get together… No, what am I saying? Of course you don't. Just call me in a year or two when you're out of the honeymoon phase.'

Jannes hadn't realised until he caught their pointed looks that his arm had sneaked back around Lara's waist, as if it always rested there. He met Lara's eyes and the expression there hit him somewhere in the gut, the top of his ears turning pink as he wondered whether his thoughts were as clear on his face as Lara's were on hers.

'You two are too cute,' one of the crew said. 'Don't let him get away.'

Lara nodded solemnly. 'He's a dictator but he's one of the benevolent ones.'

'Well, thank you for that resounding review,' Jannes said with a laugh, 'but I'm going to have to steal Lara away before you spill all my secrets.'

'Everyone is so nice,' Lara exclaimed as they walked back to his house that evening, the light fading from the sky and the sounds of the party still going on in the yacht club behind them.

'I've told you before,' Jannes said as they skirted round the side of his house and came straight out on to the deck behind, with its view of the stars reflecting on the water. 'You have that effect on people—they're never half so nice to me.'

'Because they're in awe of you.'

He scoffed, but she tugged on his hand to pull him closer.

'I'm serious,' she said, meeting his eyes and fixing him there with a look. 'They respect you, and it's obvious why. I like seeing you here, you know. You make sense here in a way you don't in London.'

He huffed out a half-laugh. 'You do know it's quite hard not to be offended by that, considering you have only ever seen me in London before today. Which basically means I have never made sense to you.'

Lara smiled. 'What can I say—you're an enigma. Very mysterious. Impossible to know what you're thinking.'

Her voice had started out jokey, playful, but fell towards the end as her gaze dropped to his mouth and stayed there.

'Do you really want to know what I'm thinking?' he said. 'You only have to ask.' But he wasn't sure that he wanted her to. He knew what he wanted the answer to be. He needed her to be sensible here, because he wasn't sure that he could count on himself to be. He was watching her mouth now, as intently as she had been watching his.

'Okay,' she said, her voice rough. 'What are you thinking about?'

'You.'

The word slipped out before he could stop it. The monosyllable the only sound he could manage amidst the cascade of malfunctions in his brain at the thought that she wasn't being careful with him.

'That's a coincidence,' Lara said, her voice dropping to something low and breathy and unfamiliar. 'I'm thinking about you too. Specifically, I'm thinking about kissing you. Does that freak you out?'

This was such a bad idea. This was everything that they had both been fighting for three years. Fighting harder than ever since that day in the park when they'd both discovered that the two of them together would be every bit as intensely perfect as he had always imagined it would be.

'Yes, it freaks me out,' he replied, too on edge to smile. But he was so tired of fighting something that he knew would feel so right. All his life, he had watched people walk away from him. He'd nursed those wounds through his whole childhood. And here was something *good*. Someone who loved him and had never walked away and had never hurt him. And he didn't know if he could trust yet that that would never change, but he couldn't carry on pretending that she wasn't everything to him.

'I don't think that you should let that stop you though,' he added at last, his gaze fixed on her.

'From thinking about it or doing it?' she asked.

'Either.'

She narrowed her eyes at him. 'We agreed that it would be a bad idea. It would complicate things.'

He nodded. They had, but he couldn't bring himself to care right at this minute. 'Things are already complicated,' he told her. 'I can't stop thinking about you. About us together. I've never felt like this before, and I don't know what to do with that. This whole thing is complicated and I don't have the answers.'

'You've been thinking about it too?'

He shook his head. 'Jesus, Lara. Only every second since that day in London Fields.'

'That does sound complicated.' She nodded thoughtfully, her eyes still fixed on his mouth, and he wondered if she was ever going to put him out of his misery.

And then, finally, after all the months and years of resisting this, he was done. He was out. He couldn't do it any longer. 'You're killing me here. Are you kissing me or not?'

Finally, she broke into a smile. 'Not, if you're not going to ask nicely,' she said, even as her hands landed on his waist.

He let out a growl of frustration, grabbed her by the hips and pulled her closer, tipping up her chin with one hand so that he didn't have to break eye contact. 'I can be nice.'

She nipped at his finger with her teeth. 'I've changed my mind. Nice is overrated.'

She pulled him down with a hand on the nape of his neck and rested their foreheads together for a breath, and then another.

He was braced for the feel of her, his body tense, but the kiss, when it came, was so gentle that he melted instantly. Her body sank into his as he wrapped both arms around her waist, pulling her up towards him so that he could chase her lips before they ghosted away.

He breathed in her scent as he gathered her close, nudging at her nose with his, tipping her face up so she could kiss him deeper. When she moaned into his mouth, he thought he might die. Or explode. Die then explode, explode then die. He didn't know or care. All he knew was that he wanted more. More of this. More of her. More of her lips hungry against his and her tongue flickering into his mouth. More of her arching back against the hard brace of his arms.

They had nowhere to hide this time. No excuses. No pretending that this was somehow for show, or for other people, or for whatever reason *not real*. This was just them, acting on the instincts they'd been fighting for years. Years. He pulled away abruptly. They'd fought this. For good reason.

'Freaking out?' Lara asked, and she was so out of breath it made him want to kiss her again.

Instead, he nodded. 'Yes. You?'

'Oh, yeah. Shall we make it hard to think again?'

He threaded his fingers in her hair and kissed her again, aware of nothing but the taste and the smell and the *feel* of her. Every fantasy of the last weeks…months, years, coming alive in his hands.

A boom overhead pulled them apart and he looked up to see a shower of colourful sparks falling to earth.

'Fireworks,' Lara breathed, looking up. 'Think the universe is trying to tell us something?'

'Just trying to tell us it's the last day of the regatta,' Jannes said, breathing heavily and looking for reason.

Lara slapped his chest gently. 'Killjoy.'

'Sorry,' he said, looking directly at her and meeting her gaze for the first time in this new world. 'We should probably talk about what just happened,' he went on, real life starting to creep in at the edges of whatever this thing was.

'I know. We should,' Lara said, holding his gaze

until another boom behind her made her jump. 'After the fireworks?'

He nodded and she turned in his arms, leaning back against him and watching the fireworks over the water, explosions in blue and green and red. In blinding white. He kissed the side of her neck, his fingertips exploring her collarbone, down the side of her arm, his hand circling her wrist and then back up to just behind her ear. Later, they would talk about this. They would remind each other about all the reasons they'd agreed that they didn't want to do this. All the ways that they could get hurt, and the reasons why they couldn't let that happen.

Later—tomorrow—they would talk themselves out of it. Undo this step and get their friendship back. But, for this moment, he didn't have to pretend not to want her. It was only in release that he realised how heavy this had been to carry. Only when he gave in that he could feel how hard he had been fighting. Only in kissing Lara—no tricks, no pretence—that he could feel how desperately right it was. Giving in was so much easier. It was as natural as breathing. His body welcomed it and his mind quieted at having her in his arms.

And while he was watching the fireworks he could just soak her in. Absorb how right this felt without worrying about the consequences. He squeezed tight around her waist—unwilling to waste a second of this time before they had to get back to real life.

Lara's hands covered his, fingers threading together to hold her even tighter, and her head fell back against his chest, giving him a clear view down her elegant neck, over flawless shoulders and collarbones, the freckled skin of her chest and the shadows of her cleavage. He let his face fall against the side of hers, the luminosity of her skin a greater draw than the lights in the sky.

He pressed his lips against her cheek and felt a knot tightening in his belly when she let her head fall to the side, baring more skin, opening up a path for him to kiss down to her pulse spot, letting his lips pause there to feel the steady thud. From there he found the sensitive spot where her neck met shoulder, letting his lips pause as she sighed, untangled a hand from his and let it come up to cup the back of his head. Her fingertips played with the short hairs at the nape of his neck, and she moaned quietly when he shivered under her fingers. When one of his hands found the soft skin of her stomach she turned in his embrace, her arms winding around his neck, pulling herself higher, pressing her body hard against his, and the fireworks ceased to exist. The sky and the moon and the stars ceased to exist. There was just Lara at the centre of his universe, and it was the first time the world had felt right.

He pulled away, breathless, and watched Lara as her breathing gradually slowed and eyes flickered open. She glanced over her shoulder. 'Fireworks have finished,' she said.

'Regatta's over.'

Untangling her arms from around his neck, she let herself fall back onto her heels, introducing just a whisper of space between them.

'Are we going to forget about this?' she asked.

'I'm not sure I can forget.' But his face was hard and

closing fast. He might not be able to forget, but that didn't mean that he thought this had been a good idea. That he wanted to repeat it.

'We pretend then,' she said, making the call for both of them. 'We go back to how things have always been and pretend that this never happened.'

'I don't want to lose you, Lara. You know how much I like—'

Like. Nice. These banalities were going to kill her one of these days. Of course they *liked* each other. If she liked him less, maybe she could countenance the idea of breaking his heart one day. But she loved him, and that meant that she couldn't be the one to hurt him. That he couldn't be the one that she hurt, trying to work out if the damage that her heart had sustained was permanent.

'I know. I don't want to lose you either,' she told him, the simplest version of what she was feeling.

'So you agree that this would be a bad idea?'

'I do. You know I do. But that doesn't mean I can't regret what I can't have.' She leant her forehead against him, because regret wasn't a strong enough word for what she was feeling. She wanted this to work. Every bone in her body ached, knowing that everything she wanted was just within reach, and she wasn't going to let herself grab it and hold it tight. She had to do this. If she wanted him in her life, she couldn't pretend to him that she wasn't damaged.

He tucked a strand of hair behind her ear. 'I'd hurt you, Lara. And I don't want to hurt you.' It was as if his heart was echoing directly from hers. But he had this all wrong. She wasn't the one that was going to hurt; it was him. She trusted him, even if he didn't trust himself.

'I'm not scared of that,' she told him, even though it didn't change where this was going.

'But—'

'I'm not scared of you hurting me, Jannes. But that doesn't mean I want a relationship any more than you do. I've never been with someone without eventually pushing them away. You know that. I don't want that to happen to us.'

He nodded, and she listened to the thump of his heart for just a few seconds longer, knowing that she was going to have to step away if they wanted to save this friendship.

'I know,' he said, his voice echoing through his chest. 'So we agree. We pretend this didn't happen.'

She nodded, and finally lifted her head. 'If we're trying to forget it, though, I think we need to stop pretending we're together. This makes it too complicated—it will be too hard to ignore this feeling if we're holding hands and kissing and pretending in front of other people.'

He let his arms drop from around her waist, and something inside her broke. Something she didn't realise could fracture any more than it already had. 'I agree. But I need to ask one last favour. A meeting with Spencer tomorrow morning. After that, you go back to London. Next time I come up it will be as if this never happened.'

He saw her swallow.

'Okay, it'll end tomorrow. And Mormor—you're going to talk to Mormor about this? Get her to stop meddling.'

'I'll deal with Mormor.'

She smiled, and he knew she was imagining how that conversation might go. 'I'm sorry I won't get to see that.'

One corner of his mouth lifted, but he couldn't bring himself to smile properly, not when he knew this was ending, when it had hardly begun. 'Come. It might help.'

She nodded thoughtfully. 'I should go to bed,' she said at last, and just the word *bed* on her lips had his heart beating faster again. If this was going to be over tomorrow anyway… No. It was going to be hard enough to forget a kiss. If they took this further there would be no going back. No way that they could pretend it had never happened. That would set him on a path that he wouldn't be able to leave until it reached its inevitable painful end.

'I'll show you to the guest room.'

At the door, she hesitated, fingers on the handle.

'Lara…'

'No, I'm not suggesting… Just…' she paused, and he couldn't help but hold his breath '…if it was going to be anyone, it would be you,' she said with a smile that managed to make her look sad.

He leaned in for a last kiss. Couldn't resist it. 'I wish things were different,' he said, leaning his forehead against hers, brushing his lips against hers. She broke the kiss, turning the door handle.

'Me too.'

CHAPTER TEN

LARA STARED AT the ceiling, wondering how long she'd been lying awake. A glance at the clock on her phone told her it was six a.m. Two hours then, since she'd woken from dreaming of Jannes and remembered how close they'd come last night to ruining their friendship. Waking frustrated and overheated, she'd wondered how bad it would really be if she padded down the corridor and knocked on Jannes's door. And in less than a heartbeat she'd known the answer. It would be bad. Really bad, when they woke up and had to undo what they had done. So she'd tried to go back to sleep at first, and then, when she'd realised that wasn't going to happen, she had resigned herself to staring at the ceiling.

The sky started to lighten and she watched the sunrise, the expanse of the sea revealed more and more by the minute. Waiting for a new day to dawn and hoping that the sunshine would wash away the memories of last night. They just had to get through this one quick meeting and she could get back to London, away from whatever strange influences the sea air had had on them.

She heard Jannes walking past her door and was

tempted to bury her head under the pillow. Maybe she should skip breakfast and just sneak back home. But they had resisted last night because they had wanted to protect one another—protect their friendship—and sneaking away at dawn wasn't going to make that happen. Would have the opposite effect, in fact. So she pulled an oversized cardigan on over her tank top and shorts and followed Jannes down the stairs.

'Morning,' she said, reaching the kitchen.

Jannes started, spinning on the spot and spilling his coffee. 'Gah,' he said, grabbing a tea towel and throwing it to the floor to mop up his spilt drink.

'I think the coffee's meant to go in your mouth,' Lara said, forcing a smile, trying to break the atmosphere.

'I'll work on that,' he said with a forced smile. 'I'll make another. Do you want one?'

'Of course,' Lara said, wondering what they had to do to break this awkwardness and get back to normal. That had been the whole point of stopping last night, when it had been the last thing she had wanted. If they had ruined their friendship anyway, she wished that she'd had less self-control.

'You going for a run?' she asked, eyes dropping to his shorts and running vest.

'Yeah. I thought I'd pick up breakfast on the way back. Pancakes? Waffles?'

'You're such a dreamboat.'

It was the sort of thing she'd been saying their whole friendship. A throwaway comment that would normally have raised a laugh and a frisson of sexual tension and which was forgotten a second later. This morning, it nearly made him drop a second cup of coffee. Whatever they had both said about not letting that kiss change things, it wasn't going to be as easy as just saying it and that making it true. They were going to have to work at it, she realised. Their friendship wasn't out of danger yet. It would be easy to let this awkwardness fester. To avoid one another for the next few weeks and have that turn into months and then years. They couldn't let that happen.

'Pancakes,' she said decisively. 'At least a dozen. Bacon, berries, syrup—the works. And whatever you're having.'

'You really know how to order. It's one of the best things about you.'

'Don't you forget it. Now, go for your run. I'll have coffee waiting when you get back.'

He hesitated at the door, and she knew that he was going to mention what had happened. But this conversation would be so much easier with coffee and pancakes in their bellies.

'Go. We'll talk when you get back. We're fine.' And she forced herself to give him a kiss on the cheek to prove it, though she wasn't sure which of them she was trying to convince more.

While he was out, she set the table with a pot of strong black coffee, a carton of orange juice she found at the back of the fridge, and plates and cutlery.

When Jannes returned, skin shining with sweat, she kept her gaze safely somewhere above his left ear.

'Shower!' she said, taking the takeaway boxes from

him, inhaling the scent of pancakes, bacon and maple syrup.

Jannes reappeared five minutes later, hair damp but less skin on show, and she forced a smile in his direction. 'Good run?' she asked, looking for a safe topic of conversation.

'Yeah,' Jannes replied. 'It's easier to think when I'm moving, you know.'

She took a deep breath. 'So we should talk about this, huh?'

'I'm not sure there's much to add from last night,' Jannes said, sitting at the table and opening the take-away carton. 'You know how much I care about you. And you know how I feel about relationships. It's part of the reason this hasn't happened before, yes? And maybe we were stupid to think that we could just ignore it. But I don't think anything has changed to make this a good idea. I want you in my life. I don't want to hurt you.'

'I want that too. You know I don't do relationships either. But I don't agree that you would hurt me. And I'm not saying that because I want us to change our minds. I'm saying it because I'm your friend and it's upsetting that you would think that about yourself.'

'Then you have to trust me to know myself. I always leave. I don't know how to stay. Maybe if I wanted to change…'

She frowned at him. 'Don't you want to?'

'No. I'm sorry,' he added, and she knew her face must have fallen. 'Maybe I should, but it doesn't matter because I've tried before and I can't do it. It's just what happens—the minute I get too close to someone, the way I feel about them changes, and I just have to get away. I won't do that to you.'

Lara shook her head. 'I'm not asking you to. I just wonder if it's what you *want*.'

'Of course I don't want to be this broken, but that's beside the point.'

'Okay, well, I wasn't suggesting you should change, Jan. I just want you to be happy.'

'I *am* happy.'

'Fine.'

'Fine.'

They glared at each other for a moment, and then Jannes turned away, and she felt something fragile between them tear away. The fireworks of the night before suddenly felt like a distant memory.

'I have some emails I need to send before this meeting,' he said, standing and clearing the table. 'If you'd rather go straight back to London, I'd understand.'

'Jannes, no. You asked for my help. Of course I'll still come.'

He sighed, a long, sad sound. 'See? I'm doing it already. I'm messing things up in the process of trying to not mess things up.'

Lara fought for composure. 'Nothing's messed up, Jannes. We're a little awkward but we'll be fine. If I race off now, we'll only be saving up the awkwardness for the next time.'

'I'm sorry, Lara.' She thought for a moment that he was going to reach for her, but then that tension in his arms and his shoulders was gone, and they were further apart than ever.

'Don't be sorry. You seem to think you're denying me something that I want. You're not. You know that.'

'I do. But I still feel terrible.'

'I know. Me too.'

Jannes ordered them both coffee and glanced at his watch. Should he be worried that Spencer was ten minutes late? There was no point trying to second-guess it. Either he would sponsor him or he wouldn't. It was probably already too late to change his mind either way.

'Deep breaths,' Lara said, brushing her hand across his shoulder as she passed him on the way back from the bathroom. 'You're nervous,' she observed, sitting beside him and resting her arms on the table.

'Hmm...'

She pushed coffee in his direction, but he wasn't sure that more caffeine would help him feel more relaxed. Selfish though he knew it was, he just wanted her hand back on his shoulder. On any part of him, come to think of it. He'd woken up knowing that they had to set new boundaries after what had happened the night before. But that didn't mean that he wanted to.

Spencer turned up before he had a chance to worry about it further, and shook his hand with so much enthusiasm that for the first time Jannes let himself get his hopes up.

'Jannes, good to see you again. And Lara too. Congratulations, you sly pair! Why didn't you mention anything yesterday?'

Jannes glanced from Spencer to Lara, wondering if

he was meant to know what he was talking about. But Lara looked as confused as Jannes felt.

'Erm, told you what, Spencer?' he asked, hoping he wasn't making a mistake that might cost him his sponsorship.

'About the engagement! I saw the notice in *The Times* this morning. Well, I'm delighted for you both; that should go without saying.'

Jannes glanced across at Lara, who was hiding her shock well. Well enough that Jannes was sure that Spencer wouldn't spot it, but Jannes knew Lara better, and could see the hardness around her mouth and the tension in the usually fluid line of her shoulders.

'Could I just…?' Lara said, indicating the paper Spencer was holding.

'"Mr Jannes Henriksson and Ms Lara Hughes are delighted to announce their engagement",' Lara read.

She stayed silent for a moment, and Jannes could barely think, never mind speak.

'We…we're just surprised that they announced it already,' Lara said, and he thanked God she was thinking better on her feet than he was right now. 'We…um…we wanted to wait until we'd picked out a ring together,' she said, glancing at her left hand, and Jannes realised she was looking for and plugging the holes in their story.

Mormor. Mormor had to be behind this. He would have to murder her. Or disown her. He couldn't believe… Actually, that wasn't strictly true. He could totally believe that she would do this. It hadn't been enough for her simply to not believe that they weren't really in a relationship—she had to up the ante and turn it into a fake engagement.

He glanced at Lara again. They had to brazen this out. He was so close to getting this funding. He took Lara's hand in his, startling her into looking up and meeting his gaze.

'I'm sorry, *älskling*,' he said, hoping that they would be able to muddle through this together, playing off each other's leads. 'I must have given them the wrong date. Good job we'd planned to choose your ring this afternoon.'

'Well, I'm delighted for you,' Spencer said, positively beaming at them. 'You're a very lucky man, Jannes. But I do hope this doesn't mean you're changing your plans for the Transat.'

'Oh, no. Trust me, nothing is going to change on that front.'

'Well, good,' Spencer said. 'Because I've decided—I'm in. I already spoke with your agent, but I wanted to let you know in person. Now I've met you—and you, Lara—I see that you're exactly the kind of person I want my business associated with. Now, I won't keep you any longer as I believe you have some very important shopping to do.'

Lara made polite goodbyes and Jannes shook Spencer's hand, not quite sure whether he was more in shock about the sponsorship or the fact that he'd suddenly found himself engaged to Lara.

They sat in silence for a few moments, watching Spencer leave.

'Jannes, what the he—?'

He returned her stare, eyebrows high. 'Mormor,' he said. 'She must have done this.'

'Why?' Lara spluttered. 'That's completely— You don't just announce someone else's engagement without even speaking to them about it. Especially when they're *not actually engaged.*'

'She's calling our bluff,' Jannes said thoughtfully.

'What bluff? We explicitly told her that we're not together. She's the one person on the entire planet who actually had all the information about what was going on with us.'

Jannes shrugged. He couldn't pretend to understand what Mormor thought she was playing at. 'Maybe she thinks this will make it harder for us to deny there's something really going on between us.'

And maybe she had an endgame of her own in mind. Because, as much as this was a completely bizarre turn of events, Mormor had been right in a way. He had been prepared to let this pretence with Lara fizzle out. Anyone could see that it had been a bad idea to torch the very careful barriers they'd erected between them right from the very start of their friendship.

'So I guess we need a ring,' Lara said at last. 'Need to stick to our story.'

'Lara, you don't have to do this.'

'You've helped me out. All the family stuff… And it's not like we have much of a choice now. Spencer thinks we're engaged. It'll put your sponsorship at risk if we change our story now. You heard him. I'm part of your squeaky-clean image.'

'Last night…' Jannes started, and she wasn't sure where that sentence was going but there was only one thing that they needed to say about what had happened, so she cut him off before he could hurt her.

'We need to forget last night,' she said. 'It was a mistake.'

'Well. That stings.' Jannes looked startled, which he had no right to, considering they'd agreed all along that this was only for show.

'You disagree?' she asked.

'No,' Jannes said quickly. 'Yes. I know we shouldn't do it again. I know that if we give in to those feelings we're going to end up hurting each other. And I don't want that to happen. But I… I don't take it back either. I don't want to pretend that I didn't have those feelings. I love you and I respect you, and it doesn't feel right to lie to you and pretend that I don't feel the way I do.'

Lara looked at him for a long moment.

'Okay,' she said at last, her shoulders set in a straight line. 'You're right; it wasn't a mistake. But it was a complication. One that we can't afford to repeat.'

Jannes nodded, and Lara breathed out a sigh of relief. 'So, do we go ring shopping?' he asked.

Lara slumped back in her chair. 'What on earth was Mormor thinking?'

'That she knows what we want better than we do.'

'You're going to deal with this, aren't you?' she said hopefully. 'Please? Because we cannot have any more curveballs like this. We need to be in control of this.'

Jannes nodded. 'I'll talk to her. I promise. No more curveballs.'

'Then I guess we're going ring shopping. But this time we need to put an expiry date on what we're doing. Because Mormor has just complicated things exponentially. Letting a vague dating thing fizzle out is one thing. That's not going to work once everyone is expecting us to be making wedding plans. We need an exit strategy that works for the both of us.'

He nodded. 'You're right. So we tell people we're not making any plans until I'm back from the Transat.'

She felt a twist of anxiety in her gut, and spoke without thinking. 'In case you change your mind about me?'

'Christ, Lara.' She could see from the expression on Jannes's face that she'd hurt him, that she'd said the worst possible thing. But she hadn't really *thought* it; asking had been a protective instinct, one that she couldn't shake. 'Is that really what you think of me?' he asked. 'Why would you say something like that?'

She shook her head. 'I don't know. Just, I wouldn't be the first girl you changed your mind about while you were racing. I'm… I'm sorry. I shouldn't have said that.'

'No. Get it all out. Tell me what you really think of me. Better to hear it all now.'

'I didn't mean anything by it,' she tried to lie. 'It just came out.'

Jannes shook his head. 'That's not true. You meant that you can't trust me. That you think I'm the kind of person the papers paint me as. That you find their version of me more believable than the person you've known for the last three years.'

She laid her hand on his arm, which was tense under her fingers.

'Jannes, I'm sorry. I was trying to be self-deprecating and I screwed up. I didn't mean to hurt you.'

He shook his head, twitched his arm from under her hand. 'I can't believe you think I'd do that, even to a fake engagement. Like you weren't the most important—'

He cut himself off, and she thought that that was probably for the best.

'It's just that…it's not like I'm not easy to leave, is it? It was a terrible joke about the terrible men in my life who have found me all too easy to disappoint.'

Jannes's hand came up to cup her jaw and she drew in a sharp breath, the feel of his calloused hands on her soft skin sparking a hundred memories of the night before.

'Lara. No one should treat you like that. I'm sorry that you could even joke about that. You deserve better. So much better. Which is why I won't let myself hurt you.'

She met his gaze and held it for a moment, before leaning back and breaking the contact.

'Come on,' Lara said. 'We should go buy a ring if we're going to go through with this.'

CHAPTER ELEVEN

Jannes walked beside Lara down the main street of the town, his hair damp from the sea mist that had rolled in that morning. They drew to a halt outside a jewellery store on the corner of one of the side streets and looked at the diamonds sparkling under the bright spotlights.

He glanced across at Lara. 'What do you think?' he asked, looking along the rows of ice-white diamonds. Lara's forehead was furrowed, a line appearing between her eyebrows.

'This isn't really me,' she said, and Jannes nodded. He couldn't argue with that.

'I spotted this place yesterday,' Lara said, linking her arm through his and leading them further down the road. She pulled him into a vintage store he had somehow never noticed, and they both gravitated to the glass case of jewellery in the corner by the window.

He sneaked a look at Lara, and saw a quiet smile turning up the corner of her lips.

'This more like it?' he asked.

'Yeah. Much more like…me,' she said.

'Am I a terrible fiancé for making you choose your own engagement ring?' he asked.

She bumped his hip with hers. 'As far as I'm concerned it makes you an excellent fiancé. Imagine having to wear something the rest of your life that you didn't get to choose yourself.'

In the end she chose a vintage opal, milky white with flashes of colour, set in old yellow gold. It was warm and full of character.

'Do you want to wear it now or do you want it in a box?' the shop owner asked them, snipping the thread of the price tag as Jannes handed over his credit card. Lara looked up at Jannes, a question in her eyes.

'Up to you,' Jannes said.

'Then I definitely want to wear it,' she said, holding out her left hand. Jannes felt a surge of possessiveness that he absolutely was not entitled to as he slipped the ring onto her wedding finger.

'It looks good on you,' he said, and before he knew what he was doing his fingers were brushing the nape of her neck and he was touching a gentle kiss to her lips and then to her knuckles. It was just to make their story look real, he told himself as he was doing it. If anyone was to approach the owner of the store about them buying their engagement ring, he would have no reason to think that this was more an arrangement than a relationship.

The owner cleared his throat, and Jannes realised that they were still staring at each other, their lips just an inch apart. Lara caught her bottom lip between her teeth and then turned away from him and turned to the owner of the store with a beaming smile.

'Thank you so much. I love it.'

'Well, I do like to see people fall in love,' the owner said, giving Lara a wink. 'I actually follow you on Instagram,' he continued. 'I just adore your feed.'

Lara fixed him with a radiant smile that almost made Jannes feel jealous.

'That's so nice of you to say. I'm going to follow you right back.' And she pulled her phone from the back pocket of her shorts as she was speaking. Three taps later and she turned the phone to him. 'There. Done. I'm going to tag you as soon as we make an announcement on there. But we're off the grid for the weekend...'

'Of course you are,' he said, smiling at them both. 'Now go celebrate that ring. Champagne all round.'

'Join us?' Lara asked, and Jannes had to suppress a laugh at the irrepressible way that she made friends.

'If I had someone to mind the shop I'd be there,' he said. 'But you'll just have to have one for me.'

After Lara had hugged him and snapped pictures of some pieces she wanted to feature on her feed, and had negotiated hard on the price of a pair of vintage platform sandals, they finally made it out of the store.

'Shopping with you is quite the experience,' Jannes said as they walked back on the main street. 'I never asked you how work is going.'

'It's going well,' Lara said, seizing on the safe topic of conversation and running with it. 'I've been doing some training so I can open my own social media consultancy. There's only so many brands I can partner with, but if I can train others to do what I've done, I can help more people to grow their businesses.'

'Sounds like an interesting pivot.'

She smiled. 'Well, I'm not going to stop what I'm already doing. I love the community that I've made too much for that. Actually, we probably need to talk about that. It's going to look weird if I don't post anything about the engagement. Do you mind if I post a picture of the ring?'

'You're doing it to save my sponsorship,' Jannes said. 'Of course I don't mind. I'm grateful.'

'No time like the present then,' Lara said, positioning them so that the sea was at their backs and pulling Jannes in for a kiss, her left hand up to his face so that it was facing the camera lens. He glanced at the screen when she was done, at the ring catching the light where her knuckles rested on Jannes's cheekbone, sunlight flaring at the side of the frame. Something inside him ached with wanting it to be real. They looked so happy, so right together, that he had to remind himself that it was all for show. That he could never really have the fairy tale that they were presenting to the world.

'You know,' Jannes said as they got back to his house, 'we never had a chance to talk about why you even agreed to go along with this engagement charade. I don't want to make you change your mind but I feel like I should be asking why.'

'Was I not supposed to?' Lara asked, tossing her tote back to one side as they walked through the house, heading for the deck at the back. 'I thought you wanted me to go along with it. It wasn't like I had much choice under the circumstances. I couldn't really argue with a notice in *The Times* in front of Spencer.'

'I know that,' Jannes said, pulling loungers into the sun and arranging them facing out over the water. 'But now we bought a ring and you're talking about it on your feed—'

Lara frowned, and he didn't think he'd ever seen her do that as much as he had this trip. It didn't take a genius to work out that he was already hurting her, despite every intention not to.

'I can't believe you're having a go at me for going along with it,' she said. 'Did you want me to make things harder for you?'

'Of course I don't,' Jannes said, returning from the fridge with a couple of cold cans of lemonade and sitting on the edge of one of the sun loungers. 'I'm not saying I'm not pleased you're doing it; I'm just saying that I would like to understand why. You're my friend and I guess I'm just…concerned. I don't know.'

Lara collapsed in the lounger next to him, all-out scowling now. 'You're concerned by the fact that I'm doing the thing that you want me to be doing?'

'I'm interested in why you're okay with lying to your family,' Jannes clarified. 'To your community, who you just told me mean so much to you.'

'I told you why. You would have lost your sponsorship. I didn't want that on my conscience.' She crossed her arms, and he knew he was pissing her off. He knew equally that this was a conversation they absolutely had to have.

'It wouldn't have been your fault,' he told her. She

didn't have to take responsibility for his failings, as much as he was grateful for her help.

'I don't get why you're making a big deal out of this,' Lara said, pulling her sunhat down now so that it hid her features. 'Are you going to start talking about my commitment issues again? Because this looks pretty committed to me.' She flashed him her left hand. She was right; it absolutely did. It looked committed in a way that struck him deep in his bones, making him wish that he had put a ring there for real.

'Maybe we *should* talk about them,' he said gently. 'Because—and I don't know if you know this—most people would find a fake engagement quite extreme, even as a way of helping out a friend.'

'It's convenient,' she said, shrugging, but he wasn't fooled by the casual gesture. 'It will save me a whole load of hassle with my family if I can pretend that we're together. And it doesn't cost us anything—it's not like you even have to turn up to things. But when they try and set me up with cousin Sandra's brother-in-law's son, or whoever it is this time, I just have to play the engaged card.'

He tried to stare her down, but it was impossible with the sunhat and the glasses. She knew what she was doing when it came to avoiding a deep and meaningful talk, he had to give her that. 'Some people might find it a little constraining—especially given what we've said about not doing anything that might undermine our story.'

'But it's not—it's the opposite.' Lara took off her sunglasses and finally looked him in the eye. 'We both know where we stand. We have all our cards on the table. Neither of us can do anything to hurt the other because we both know it's all fake from the start. It's safer, when I know that it's a lie. It's better than something like that taking me by surprise.'

He frowned. 'Because I can't hurt you.'

'Precisely.'

'Because you're not vulnerable,' he pressed.

'Now you're getting it.' She put her glasses back on and looked back over the water.

'But once this is over, pain-free with no surprises, aren't you going to find it hard to be with someone without being vulnerable?'

Lara still refused to look at him, so he knew he was on the right track. 'So I go back to the casual thing I was doing before. No big deal.'

Except she'd told him she was tired of that. And the reason she avoided anything serious wasn't because she didn't want it, but because she was scared of getting hurt.

'This needing the cards on the table thing. Is it to do with your dad?' he asked, knowing that this was sensitive ground.

Lara's gaze was determinedly fixed ahead. 'Why would you ask that?'

'I'm just trying to understand why you settled for this. For me. When you could have so much more.'

'I don't know. Why are you settling for me?'

'I'm not settling.'

He stared at her, knowing he should take those words back, or at least clarify what he meant, but he couldn't. Being with Lara, even temporarily, even pretending, even if he didn't have her for real, could never be settling.

'We should drop this,' Lara said at last, and he could

tell from the stiffness of her shoulders that they'd crossed the line and got too close to the truth of what was going on between them.

'So you're going back to London today,' Jannes said, and then bristled at his own words. It sounded too much as if he was trying to get rid of her. 'I think I should come too. I need to talk to Mormor.'

Lara laughed, and he was relieved at the familiar sound. 'Because that worked so well the last time that we tried it.'

His eyes crinkled into a smile. 'She doubled down so I guess now I have to as well. You don't have to come with me.'

'Oh, no, I have a few things I want to say to Mormor.'

'Excellent. More fireworks.'

Lara drove them back to London—it seemed stupid to take two cars—and he'd deal with how to get back to Harbourside later. With her eyes fixed on the road in the exodus of cars following the regatta, he could sneak glances across at her.

'What?' she asked, her eyes never leaving the road.

'*What* what?'

'Why do you keep looking at me?'

He could lie, but what would be the point when she could so clearly read him like a book?

'Just reflecting on how strange this is. How we got here.'

'Bad life choices, I suppose,' she said with a wry grin. 'And Mormor,' she added, with a glance at the ring on her finger.

'Bad life choices and my Swedish grandmother. I wonder how many other people out there can so accurately pinpoint the source of all their problems.'

'I think mine could be summed up as "daddy issues",' Lara said. 'I hate being a cliché.'

Jannes nodded. It was hard not to agree with that. 'We should probably have a lot of therapy.'

'Probably,' she said, but the humour had gone from her voice.

'Hey.' Jannes reached over, his hand just brushing over hers where it rested on the gear stick before she pulled it away. 'I'm sorry. Too far?'

'No, it's fine. I just think you're probably right.'

'I am?'

She nodded, her lip caught between her teeth, her eyes fixed ahead. 'I don't know, but I'm pretty angry, and some of the things you said maybe make me wonder if I'm letting that old cheating, lying bastard have more influence over my decisions than he deserves.'

'Decisions like agreeing to this?' He gestured between them and noted her knuckles were white on the steering wheel.

'Possibly.'

'Well, you know I support you, don't you? I always will.'

Lara glanced over at him and gave him a smile he couldn't quite interpret. 'I know. Maybe we should go together. Is fake couple therapy a thing?'

'I think it's best to keep to one set of daddy issues per session.'

She gave a wicked smile that for some reason set

him on edge. 'So we *are* going to talk about how being sent to boarding school at seven is at the root of your commitment issues.'

He shook his head. 'Nope, we definitely aren't going to talk about that.' He threw her a sharp look. 'What could have given you that idea?'

'So it's just me who has to do the soul-searching? God forbid we both work through our issues so we can form healthy adult relationships.'

'Hey, maybe we should save this conversation for when we've had a screaming row with my grandmother,' Jannes said, letting his head fall back against the headrest.

'She scares you.'

'She doesn't scare me; she's just…immovable. It's exhausting.'

'Exhausting and immovable. I can't imagine how difficult that must be for you,' she said pointedly.

He rolled his eyes at the sarcasm in her voice, but had to concede that she had a point. He couldn't support her decision to get therapy without thinking that he probably needed a healthy dose of it himself. It wasn't right that he'd torched every relationship that he had been in. It was one thing not to want a romantic relationship. It was another to want one as desperately as he wanted Lara, and be certain that he couldn't even try without hurting her.

CHAPTER TWELVE

LARA REACHED ACROSS and squeezed his hand as they climbed the steps to Mormor's apartment building. 'Remember,' she said, 'she can't actually force us to get married.'

Jannes nodded, and she recognised the tensing of the muscles in his game face. 'We go in there, explain that she's out of line. She's gone too far and she has to stop interfering in our lives like this.'

'Right. And then we run away.'

He laughed. A little weakly. 'I wouldn't blame you. This thing has got entirely too weird. You had no idea what you were signing up for.'

Lara shook her head. 'I knew I was signing up for you. Mormor's a part of that. Now.' She squeezed his hand again before letting it drop. 'Let's do this.'

But, before they had a chance to knock, the door flew open in front of them.

'Ah, there you are, *älskling*. I wondered when you would get here.' She pulled Jannes in by the elbow and planted a kiss on his cheek.

'We didn't tell you we were coming.'

'I announced your engagement in *The Times* without telling you. Of course you were coming.'

Jannes rolled his eyes. 'So you're not even going to deny it?'

She looked amazed. 'Why would I deny it? It was a stroke of brilliance. I'm rather proud of it.'

'It was manipulative and inappropriate—' Jannes started.

'And yet Lara seems to be wearing an engagement ring.' Mormor interrupted him with a pointed look. 'So it can't have been that terrible an idea.'

Lara could see a muscle twitching in Jannes's jaw as he struggled to keep calm. 'We found out in a business meeting. You didn't give us a choice but to play along.'

'Oh, we always have a choice, *älskling*,' Mormor said, walking down the hallway to the kitchen and speaking to them over her shoulder as she went. 'And you two chose to be engaged. So, congratulations. I'm sure that you're going to be very happy.'

Jannes leaned in the doorway of the kitchen while Mormor bustled around, making them all a drink. Lara looked from grandmother to grandson, amused by the clash of wills, or she would have been amused if she had been an innocent bystander rather than caught up in Mormor's little scheme. 'Mormor, you do know that the ring isn't legally binding, yes? We're going to break this off when the timing is right.'

She threw her hands in the air, and Jannes grabbed for the milk jug she was about to fill. 'Yes, yes, well, you can explain all of that to the vicar if you want.'

'Excuse me, the vicar? What vicar?' Jannes slammed

the jug down so hard on the worktop that Lara feared for its safety, but even with the roiling anxiety of the fake engagement it was impossible not to be charmed by the clearly well-rehearsed ballet of Mormor trying to make tea but getting distracted, and Jannes trying to minimise damage but only getting in the way.

'The vicar from the Swedish church, of course,' Mormor said, as if Jannes was the idiot for not knowing which vicar she was talking about. 'Did you know you can't get married in church until you've had the banns read three times? And I told the vicar to start this Sunday, but she absolutely insisted that she had to meet you first. I don't see why she couldn't just take my word for it, as I am your grandmother after all, and why she thinks that she would know better than—'

Jannes came to an absolute standstill. 'Let me get this right,' he said very slowly, choosing his words with care. 'You spoke to the vicar and you tried to have our banns read? Without asking us?'

'Yes, well, if you're going to have the wedding there then you have to book it well in advance.' Mormor carried on setting cups and saucers on a tray, either not noticing or not caring about the storm cloud expression on Jannes's face. 'There's only one Swedish church in the whole of London, you know that. So unless you want this to be one of those depressingly long engagements—'

'But we're not getting married!'

Mormor finally stopped what she was doing, turned to look at him with narrowed eyes. She fixed Jannes with a look that could make flowers wilt. 'Then why are you engaged?'

Jannes's jaw clenched so hard that Lara worried that he might crack a tooth. She should probably intervene, but there wasn't anything she could say that Jannes hadn't already, and really it was quite amusing, seeing Jannes pushed so close to the breaking point.

'Mormor. We are not engaged,' Jannes ground out. 'We are simply playing along because you've given us no choice. You can cancel the appointment with the vicar—'

'No, well, I can't do that.'

Jannes sighed and pinched the bridge of his nose. 'I don't think I even have the strength to ask why not.'

'Well, because I've told all of my friends at church that you're getting married there. I'd simply be too mortified.'

Which meant that word had probably spread across half the Swedish population of London. Which also meant that trying to deny it would probably spread just as fast, and hit the tabloids before the week was out.

'Mormor, *please.*'

For the first time, the older woman's expression softened, and she reached to cover his hand with hers.

'Look, *älskling*, I've spent a long time watching you be unhappy without saying anything. And now I see how you two are together—' she glanced across at Lara, who felt herself blush '—and I just think, give it a go! I can see how fond you both are of one another. And I know you like to pretend that there are reasons why you can't do this. I'm never going to forgive your parents for the way they treated you. I thought I'd clear the way for you. Show you that it can be that simple if you just decide it's what you both want.'

'But it's not,' Lara said gently, stepping into the kitchen for the first time, and coming to stand beside Jannes. 'We've talked about it, because you're right. We are very fond of each other. But not about the rest of it. I appreciate that you're trying to help, but we don't want this. We're friends, and that's all it's ever going to be.'

Mormor compressed her mouth into a thin line, but didn't argue. 'You'll see I'm right,' she said eventually. 'The appointment with the vicar isn't for a month. I'm not cancelling it.'

Jannes shook his head. 'We won't be needing it.'

'We'll see, won't we?'

'I should be going,' Lara said, looking between them, her heart aching slightly at the way Mormor looked at Jannes, as if he were still a little boy, crying after his parents had left him alone at school.

'I'll let you say goodbye,' Mormor said with a meaningful look before sweeping out of the kitchen.

'So that went…'

'Pretty much as expected,' Jannes finished. 'Don't worry, I'll speak to the vicar. Tell her that Mormor was jumping the gun and we want to wait a bit longer.'

Lara nodded. Then couldn't resist. 'Interesting that Mormor brought up your parents, after what we were talking about in the car.'

'Lara, can we not?' Jannes snapped, and she took a step back, surprised by his tone. 'I'm sorry. But just… not now, okay?'

She wrapped her arms around herself and moved towards the front door.

'Okay, I guess I'll see you next time you're in London then,' she said. 'It's the twins' christening in two weeks. Are you still…?'

'I'll be there.'

'Fine. Great. So I'll see you then.'

She slipped through the front door and leaned against the wall in the corridor, the cool paint soothing against her flushed cheeks. She hadn't imagined that things could fall apart so quickly. She'd never felt closer to another human being than she had to Jannes last night. And now—now she was running away from him because she didn't know how to talk to him any more.

Back in her apartment later that day, she pulled out her planner and looked at her schedule for the week. She was going to have to move things around now that she had an engagement to announce out of nowhere. There were a couple of posts she'd worked on with partner brands that she couldn't move. A post later in the week she'd already bumped twice. If she didn't run it soon she'd end up having to scrap it completely. Which meant that the only good slot for the picture of her engagement ring was…tonight.

She sighed and rested her head on her hand as she scribbled notes to herself. She really wasn't in the mood to come up with a caption that would make sense of her and Jannes's whirlwind romance and sudden engagement. Not least because her online following was based on her authenticity and honesty. When she'd joined Instagram, her shots of London's quiet backstreets, her vintage fashion finds and adventures in upcycling to furnish her flat had only been to entertain her friends.

With her friend Jess as her partner in crime, she'd upped her photography game and spilled her guts in her captions, constitutionally unable to stop herself oversharing. But for some reason it had struck a chord and her followers had gone from the hundreds to the thousands to the hundreds of thousands. Until she'd had enough clout that she'd been able to partner with brands that she loved and turned her hobby into a business.

The thought of lying to her followers turned her stomach. So she started writing, trying to focus on hers and Jannes's friendship and put her feelings for him into words in a way that was truthful.

He was a dear friend. She cared for him deeply. Their relationship *had* changed recently, though not necessarily in the way that people might assume. These were all things that she could say truthfully. As for the 'engagement'…well, she didn't have to say anything, did she. She could just post the picture of the ring and let people make their own conclusions.

It wasn't *honest*, but it wasn't an outright lie either. And she supposed that was the best that she could hope for. She tagged Jannes in the photo—her stomach lurching as she caught sight of his profile picture, that same shot of him they had used at the awards ceremony, a magazine shoot for a menswear brand, with Jannes hanging half off a yacht in a shirt that had once been white but had been rendered transparent by virtue of being dripping wet. She really shouldn't be driven to biting her lip over someone who she was meant to think of as just a friend. She'd been suppressing these thoughts and these feelings for Jannes since the day that she had met him—you'd think that she'd be better at it by now. But her trip to Harbourside, the fireworks, had changed all that, and she wasn't sure how they were meant to get back to normal. Not while they were meant to be engaged.

She hit post, and almost instantly the comments started flooding in, full of love hearts and bride emojis and the occasional aubergine.

She shut down her laptop—normally she interacted as much as she could in the comments, but she couldn't for this post. Even accepting the congratulations would make her stomach twist with guilt. Would make her melancholy for what she couldn't have.

She had never thought that she could lie about something so important. She had spent half her life wondering how that bastard of a father had come home to her and her mother every night—or every night he wasn't with his other family—and now she had some insight. All it needed was high enough emotional stakes, and intense enough feelings, and you found yourself making choices that you couldn't have imagined making just a few weeks before. Was this how it had been for her dad? One choice leading to another to another, until the lies got away from you and you had no choice but to stick to your story or see your life fall apart.

The big difference, of course, was that no one else's feelings were at stake. Everyone who was emotionally invested knew the truth. But Lara's online community was just that—a community. Full of people who she had never met in person but nonetheless considered to be friends. Was she hurting them, by bending the truth about her and Jannes's relationship? Or was it their business and nobody else's what was going on behind closed doors? She didn't even know that *she* understood what was going on. Okay, they had no intention of getting married, that much was clear. But what about the kisses that they'd shared? The night that she'd spent wishing that she was in Jannes's bed instead of her own? That wasn't exactly platonic, was it?

What they were doing in public was acting out what would have been happening in private if it weren't for the scars they were both carrying that made a romance between them impossible. It was an alternate version of her future playing out before her, and her and Jannes were the only ones who knew that she wouldn't be able to keep it.

Her phone rang, and she hesitated when she saw Jannes's name on the screen. She really didn't want to speak to him just now, when her feelings were so jumbled from having written that caption, and then looked at that picture on his profile. But the longer they went without speaking, the more awkward it was going to get. She hit answer and tried for an easy breezy, 'Hey.'

'Hey. My notifications just blew up. Do I take it we're official?'

'As of about five minutes ago. Everything okay at Mormor's?'

He sighed. 'She's singing. Absolutely delighted with herself as far as I can see. Not a smidge of remorse.'

'She's a monster.'

Jannes laughed out loud. 'That might be a little harsh considering all she wants is for us to be happy.'

'Hmm. Are you going back to Harbourside?' she asked, telling herself it was just friendly chitchat rather than her wanting to know how much longer he was going to be in town.

'My agent organised a couple of meetings for me here tomorrow now that Spencer is on board. Then back to Harbourside and a training camp in Norway. I don't know how contactable I'll be...' His voice trailed off and she realised that this was a 'couple' sort of conversation. Checking in and warning of radio silence. Was this where they were with one another now? Explaining your whereabouts like you would with a real-life fiancé?

She felt a familiar twinge of discomfort at this. That they were becoming more to each other than just a lie. This was where she usually started a subtle freak-out. Because when the person she was with started telling her where they were going to be, making plans to see her, she had to decide whether she was going to believe them. Or whether they were just telling her what she needed to hear, covering their tracks so that they could do what they wanted without getting caught. This was the part where trust came in. When it started to matter to her whether the other person was telling the truth. And, invariably, it was where she threw up her walls, ensuring that no one would be able to hurt her.

She had to remind herself that it didn't matter whether Jannes was telling the truth. That their relationship was a pretence. That even if he did lie to her, she wouldn't get hurt because he didn't owe her the truth. He didn't owe her anything. That was what made this safe—a relationship that she *knew* was based on a lie could never hurt her. That was what made this different.

'Well, have fun,' she said, at what she hoped was an appropriate place in the conversation. She didn't want to admit that she'd got distracted wondering whether she should care if he was telling her the truth. By wondering what their relationship might be like if she wasn't so…damaged.

'Are you sure you're okay?' Jannes asked, and she guessed she hadn't pitched her voice quite right, that he'd heard something of her doubts.

'Yeah, I'm sure,' she lied, before hanging up with a rushed goodbye.

CHAPTER THIRTEEN

TWO WEEKS LATER, and Lara had to conclude that her followers were so in love with Jannes on her behalf that it made up for the fact that they were faking the whole relationship. She'd posted some pictures from early in their friendship, focusing on the truths in their relationship—that shared history—rather than the fictional future that they were meant to be planning. She'd declined all requests to partner or advertise anything wedding-related, pleading for the moment her intention to enjoy her engagement before starting wedding planning. She might be doing something morally dubious in not revealing the full truth about her engagement, but she wasn't so morally bankrupt that she would use her fake engagement to make money.

She concentrated on the coursework for her MBA—life would be so much simpler with a consultancy business, which didn't rely on snapshots of her personal life. Jannes had been away at his training camp in Norway for the past two weeks. And should have been on her doorstep an hour ago to go with her to the twins' christening.

But there was no sign of him. His phone wasn't ring-ing and her messaging app said he hadn't logged in since yesterday. And every time she thought to herself that she'd throttle him if he made her go to this thing alone after she'd told people that he'd be there, she won-dered if it was something worse than him letting her down going on. Whether something had happened to him out on the water. That maybe he wasn't coming back to her at all.

Her stomach gave a lurch of fear. Thinking about how he was letting her down was at least a distraction from worse thoughts. She glanced at the time on her phone. If he wasn't here in the next fifteen minutes then she was going to be late to the church—and showing up solo. This whole thing with Jannes was meant to be sparing her intrusive questions—if she showed up with-out him after they'd RSVP'd that he would be there it would be bound to prompt faux sympathetic looks and whispers behind her back, entirely defeating the object of this whole charade.

Eventually she fired off a text, letting Jannes know that she was leaving without him. Maybe if he got it in time he would be able to meet her at the church.

She made sure her phone was synced with her car, just in case he called or messaged while she was on the road to the country church. More floral shift dresses and pashminas. More florid uncles backslapping one another in the hotel bar at the reception afterwards.

If they staged another intervention like the last one, she was certain that she would either die or explode with rage. Which didn't really seem fair to them, considering the rage was mainly directed at the man who had screwed over their lives as much as hers.

And, speaking of the devil incarnate, if she wasn't mistaken, she was going to have to spend the afternoon dodging that loser of a sperm donor. Pip hadn't invited him to her wedding, but she knew this branch of the family were still on speaking terms with him. Thinking about her father was more uncomfortable than ever now that she was living her own version of his lie. She didn't want to see what he had done to her in a different light. She'd spent her whole adult life trying to come to terms with the damage that he had done, and thinking of him as human again, rather than a monster, only made things more complicated.

Jannes would have been the perfect person to have her back, to keep her safe—God knew he'd proved as much at Pip's wedding. All of which was an excellent distraction from worrying that something might be seriously wrong.

She had always been slightly ill at ease when Jannes was out at sea and incommunicado. When he was on land they would text a few times a day—just mundane stuff about what they were doing, work, mutual friends. So when her phone went silent, nothing felt quite right until that message pinged letting her know that he was back.

But it had never felt like this before, this gnawing feeling that something must be seriously wrong. If he hadn't just decided that this event—that she—wasn't important enough for him to show up—or even let her know that he could be late. Her hand itched with the urge to check her phone, even though she knew that if he'd called or messaged she would have got a notification on the car's screen. But the anxiety was making her rational brain more annoying than helpful.

As the mileage countdown on her satnav reached single figures, she gripped the steering wheel tighter. So tense that when she reached the church, and Jannes was parked right outside, hands in his pockets and sunlight bouncing off the blinding white cotton of his shirt and the lenses of his sunglasses, she wasn't sure whether to kiss him, hit him or throw up on him.

Relief flooded her body like a drug as she threw open the door of her car and marched across the car park, only stopping when she had two handfuls of Jannes's shirt in her clenched fists.

'Where the hell have you been?' she managed to say through clenched teeth.

'Um…hi to you too?' Jannes said, his voice low and amused as he glanced down at her white-knuckled fingers still grasping at his shirt.

She could barely breathe with the relief of seeing him, and had to force in a breath to be able to yell at him. 'You were meant to be at my place two hours ago!'

'We…have an audience,' he said, looking past her shoulder, and she could imagine the eyes of a couple of dozen relatives fixed on her and Jannes.

They both had parts to play, she remembered. The fact that she didn't even know if she was angry with him or relieved, or delighted, didn't really matter.

'Oh, we should…' She tried to kick her brain into gear, but Jannes was already on the case. His hands came up to cup her cheeks and she shuddered as he dipped his head and pressed his lips to hers. She pulled him closer with the fists still clenched against his chest and it wasn't until she opened her mouth under his that she remembered that they were at a family event. At church.

'I'm so angry with you right now,' she said softly, pulling away though every cell in her body was protesting at the loss of him.

'Funny way of showing it,' Jannes retorted, his hands falling to rest on her hips.

'Yeah, well, we'll talk about that later,' she said, uncurling her fists and grabbing his hand instead. Adrenaline was leaching from her system and she suddenly felt limp, as if she just wanted to lean into him and soak in the fact that he was here and whole. She practically dragged him into the church and down beside her onto a pew.

'I thought you'd been eaten by sharks,' she said, keeping her face deadly serious, although it was tucked firmly into his shoulder, so the effort was probably wasted on him.

'And this is the sympathy I get?'

She glanced at his face to see that a corner of his mouth had quirked up, which only made her more angry. 'I swear, if you get yourself eaten by sharks I'll be furious with you.'

'I'm sorry I worried you,' he said, tucking a piece of hair that had escaped her messy bun behind her ear. Why did he have to be so impossibly reasonable all the time? 'My phone died and I didn't have your number.

I didn't have time to get to your apartment so I figured the best thing to do was to meet you here.'

'Your phone died?' she asked him. Why had abandoning her and being eaten by sharks featured higher on her list of possibilities than the more reasonable dead phone explanation?

'Sank, actually. Occupational hazard.'

She shoved at his shoulder with her chin. 'I was *worried*.'

'I know. And I truly am sorry.' He pulled her tighter to him with an arm around her shoulder and kissed the side of her head. 'I'll make sure the whole crew have your number next time, just in case. No more risk of complete radio silence unless I've warned you beforehand. I promise.'

'Good,' Lara replied, relaxing gently against his side. 'Now. How much of an exhibition did we just make of ourselves on consecrated ground?'

He grinned. 'I'd say an appropriate amount for a newly engaged couple who have been separated for a fortnight. Do you want to go and say hi to your family?'

She looked towards the door of the church, but more and more people were coming in, and they'd only be fighting against the flow of people if they tried to leave now.

'No, let's stay here. We'll catch up with people after the ceremony. Tell me about your training camp. How was it?'

She listened as he filled her in on what he had been up to for the last couple of weeks, and she tried to keep her eyes and her mind on him, rather than the people entering the church.

Eventually, she heard a squeal and Pip was climbing over people in the pew behind to try and reach her. She dragged first Lara and then Jannes into a hug, then grabbed Lara's hand to look at her engagement ring. 'Congratulations, you guys!' she said. 'Why didn't you tell us? Another wedding!'

'Oh, we didn't want to steal your thunder,' Lara said, throwing a quick look at Jannes. 'How was your honeymoon?' she asked, looking for a quick change of subject.

'Oh, you know, decadent, idyllic—you'll find out soon enough,' she added with a wink.

She was spared having to think of a reply by the vicar clearing his throat at the front of the church.

'I'll talk to you later,' she whispered to Pip, who hurried back to her seat.

Lara kept her gaze fixed forward throughout the ceremony, resisting the twin urges to look around to see if her father had shown up, or to get her fill of Jannes's face, to assuage that anxious feeling in her belly that persisted even though she knew he was sitting beside her. It wasn't until the adrenaline started to wear off that she realised how worried she had been, and now that he was here beside her it was as if she was finally free to imagine every terrible way she might have lost him. A huge wave of fear and relief hit her at once, and she felt for his fingers with her own, nudged his pinkie and then tangled their fingers together.

In her peripheral vision she saw him glance across at her, worried, then he squeezed her hand and lifted their linked fingers to his lips.

That simple kiss shouldn't have stirred her and stilled

her all at once. It should have been either one or the other—the comfort of a friend or the spark of a hookup. The two together? Well, it was unprecedented, and that meant it couldn't be trusted. That was what she had fought to stay away from all these years, because she knew that it could lead to nothing but heartache.

But also it felt…right. In a way that should have her running from it, while simultaneously making even the thought of doing so completely impossible. Because if she didn't, one or both of them was going to get hurt. But…wasn't that going to happen either way? Walking away from this wasn't a pain-free option any more. Not after Harbourside. She compromised by pulling her hand back and having it rest in her lap, in a demure fashion she was certain she had never attempted before.

Jannes glanced across at her, but she refused to make eye contact. She should at least try to look as if she was paying attention if she was going to convince Pip and her mother that family therapy wasn't really a thing that she needed because she was perfectly fine and had a perfectly fine boyfriend thank you very much.

The service ended with the twins in tears, the godparents looking traumatised and the vicar shouting valiantly, if not terribly successfully, over the racket. The combination of crying babies and organised religion could hardly be a more perfect storm for guaranteeing that she wanted a drink. She dodged relatives in the churchyard and headed straight for the hotel over the road where the reception was being held. At some point during her manoeuvres for the exit, Jannes must have worried about losing her in the crowd because his hand had found its way back into hers.

She didn't even bother shaking him off. It was easier if they stuck together. That was definitely the reason she let her hand disappear into his palm. Nothing to do with feeling anchored and secure in a situation that would normally make her flighty and adrift. Would normally be sneaking off to her car rather than risk having to make conversation with her father. She'd seen him there in the church, near the back, as if he couldn't be sure of his welcome. And so he should, because she couldn't understand how any of them could even stand to look at him. Some people were sentimental about family, she supposed, congratulating herself for not being one of them.

'Are you thirsty?' Jannes asked as they entered the cooler air of the hotel lobby, the door swishing closed after them, shutting out the sound of the christening party not far behind.

'A tactical retreat,' she said. 'Nothing worse than being ambushed in a churchyard.'

'I'll have to take your word on that one. Your dad?' he added gently. 'Or are the mums worse?'

'Dad. He was at the church. Don't know if he's coming here, but if he does I want to see him before he sees me.' Especially given the thoughts that she'd been having recently. The ones where she compared her behaviour to his and started to realise that he probably hadn't wanted to hurt her. That her pain over the years had come from his failings, but not necessarily his malice. Did it matter, that she could see more clearly what had happened now? Should it make a difference to her, knowing that maybe he had still loved her, even while he was hurting her? That things weren't as clear-cut and simple as she had made them when she was a teenager.

'When was the last time you spoke to him?' Jannes asked.

She tried to keep her voice matter-of-fact. 'The night we left home and went to live with Pip and her mum. He tried, for a while, to get me to speak to him, but he gave up eventually. I'm sure he won't even care that I'm here today but I don't want to risk it.'

'Okay, well, I'm here. Just tell me what you need.'

It was only as she squeezed his hand that she realised that she was still holding it, though there was no risk of losing one another here, and no one they were trying to convince they were a couple either. She should pull away, she knew, keep straight what they were to each other—what was pretence and what was real—but she didn't want to. And Jannes wasn't pulling away either.

'So what's the play if we see him? Offence or defence?' Jannes asked.

She wished she was relaxed enough to feel grateful to him, but she couldn't yet. Couldn't think much beyond the fact that her father was going to be in the same room any minute now, and she hadn't decided what she was going to do when she saw him. 'Which is the one where I down my G&T?'

'Defence, then,' Jannes clarified, scanning the room behind them.

'Keep at least five people between us at all times,

please?' Lara said. 'And if you block my view of him with your big manly shoulders then even better.'

'You think my shoulders are big and manly?'

She rolled her eyes. 'Is that really what you're taking away from this conversation?'

'Yes, I'm your distraction, remember? Let me distract you.' She smiled at the way that he always seemed to know how to get through to her. Knew exactly what she needed.

'You're definitely that,' she said. 'Have you spoken to Mormor while you've been away?' It had taken her two weeks to get her head around the last spanner that Mormor had thrown in the works. She needed to know that there weren't going to be any others heading in their direction.

Jannes shook his head. 'No, and I dread to think what she's been up to since I've been gone.'

'Well, you can put "aggressively liking my posts on Instagram" on the list,' Lara said.

'Oh, no, tell me she hasn't. She's never liked one of my posts.'

Lara gave a tight smile. 'Ah, well, you've got a treat ahead of you. Anything remotely regarding the two of us and she is *very* enthusiastic with the emojis.'

'Stop it. No. I can't…' Jannes wheezed, desperately trying to hold in a laugh, the bastard. She could see his shoulders shake, and realised how much she loved that. Making him lose control, even like this. Even when it was pissing her off at the same time.

'Don't say I didn't warn you,' she said with a smug smile.

But then a buzzing started in her ears, and she lost the sense of what Jannes was saying until his hand cupped her cheek and her eyes snapped back to him.

'Dad alert?' he asked.

'Yes. Just arrived. Get your shoulders over here.'

She pulled him into position so that she was shielded from view for most of the room, and tried to track her dad's progress as he made small talk with various relatives.

'So your mum and Gloria still think you need therapy, huh,' Jannes said quietly, so only she could hear.

'Something like that,' she replied, still peering around his shoulders, trying to keep an eye on her dad without him seeing her.

'And you're resistant to this idea because…' Jannes prompted.

'Because I'm fine.'

He raised an eyebrow. 'Says the woman hiding behind the man she's fake agreed to marry.'

Lara rolled her eyes. 'Family therapy would be worse. They wanted him to be there. They think I need to have it out with him.'

'And do you think that maybe they have a point?'

'I'd rather stick swords in my eyes.'

Someone cleared their throat behind Jannes and she felt ice-cold in her chest.

Jannes made eye contact with her. She knew that if she needed him to, he would stand in front of her, blocking her from view and protecting her in their corner of the bar, even while her dad stood there watching them. But she wouldn't make him ridiculous for her sake. This was her own fault for letting herself get distracted and not seeing him approaching. For forgetting that avoiding her father should have been her number one priority.

'Yes, it's okay,' she said, moving him gently aside with a hand on his chest. 'What do you want?' she said to her father in a low voice, making her face neutral and blank. The only thing worse than having to see him would be showing him how much it hurt. She wouldn't let him think that he *mattered*.

'Hello, Lara. I've missed you so much. Do you think we could go somewhere and…?'

'And what?' she demanded, anger welling up inside her from she didn't know where. 'I don't want to talk to you. I want nothing to do with you.'

'Lara, please, can we just…?'

'No!' she said, and realised too late that she was shouting and didn't seem able to stop. '*You* "just"—just listen to me. I don't want you in my life. Why won't you respect my decision?'

'I'm getting married,' her father said, and she felt something hollow out inside her. Another family. Another try at having a family. She could be replaced, again, just like that. 'I really want you to be there,' he said. 'Or just back in my life, however you want.'

'I'm not interested,' Lara spat, her anger burning hot and white in her chest. 'I pity your fiancée!'

'Lara, please,' he said, his face reddening, a prickle of sweat at his hairline as he glanced over his shoulder at the room. 'I'm your father.'

'No! You're not!' She could feel her control slipping even further, could feel the walls closing in on her and the friendly hum of conversation in the bar became an oppressive buzz in her ears. 'Jannes, let's go.'

She slotted her fingers through his and stalked from the bar, studiously ignoring the stares of her assorted family as she did so. Let them look—she was hardly the one at fault here. That honour went to the feckless excuse for a father that she was currently walking away from. She dragged Jannes away from the front of the hotel, across the car park and through a gate beside the church that led to a small area of woodland.

'Lara? What's going on? Are we digging a g—? *Oh.*'

He stopping speaking as Lara smashed her mouth against his, sliding her hands into his back pockets and dragging him closer. She turned them both, pulling until her back was against a tree, the rough bark biting into her skin between her shoulder blades. But with a gentle hand on her cheek, Jannes eased himself away, looking down at her, panting and flushed.

'Not that this isn't…you know,' he said, a little breathless, pulling her closer by the hips for a second. 'But I'm not sure that being angry at your dad is a good reason to do this.'

'Can't you just shut up and kiss me? It's a lot easier to not think about it when we're doing that.'

Jannes groaned. 'And while it's *extremely* flattering that you're using me that way, I'm not sure I want to be your human stress ball.'

She leaned away from him, her hands still wedged in his back pockets. 'You're turning me down.'

'I'm not turning you down,' he said, through a jaw so

tight she was surprised he could get the words out. 'You don't really want me. You're just working out your issues on me and I think things are complicated enough.'

'None of which would matter if you actually wanted me,' she insisted. Of all the times to turn her down... Normally, she could take it. But now she just needed him to need her as much as she did him. She needed what they had not to be a lie. She needed to not be her father, with a web of complicated relationships confusing the people around her. She loved Jannes, and she needed him to love her back.

'This isn't about wanting,' Jannes said, maddeningly calm in the face of her panic. 'I don't know how you could possibly believe that I don't want you after the last couple of months. This is about us making good choices, for good reasons. I don't think you can know what you want while you're mad at your dad.'

'Well, screw you then, Jannes,' she said, pushing him away. Because if she shoved hard enough, put enough distance between them, she could make herself believe that he couldn't hurt her any more. That the fact that she loved him and he didn't love her back didn't flay her and leave her raw. Her hands came up and she clenched them in front of her chest. Jannes took half a step back and then pulled her to him, her forehead against his chest and her shoulders shaking as he wrapped his arms around them.

'Jannes, no, you can't. You can't make this better. I'm... I'm broken. There's something wrong with me, and as much as I want you—us—to fix it, it isn't going to happen. You should get away from me. I'm going to hurt you if you do this.'

'You're angry. As you have every right to be,' Jannes said, letting his arms fall away as she pulled her shoulders back and sucked in a long breath, her arms crossing back over her body. Her gaze darted past him, back towards the churchyard and the car park. 'But I don't think you're angry at me, and I don't think this is the time to be changing what we are to one another.'

'You drove here, right?' Lara asked. 'You don't need me to give you a ride home.'

'I have my car,' he said, his voice wary. 'You're leaving?'

'I have to. I can't go back in there—I'm not going to humiliate myself any more.'

'And you're leaving without me?' She knew that she was hurting him. Knew that she shouldn't walk away from him. But she needed to be away from here, and she needed to be alone.

'You should stay. It's an open bar. And apparently the buffet is going to be excellent.'

'Lara.' He turned her face up to his. 'You know full well that I don't care about the bloody open bar. I care about you—don't do this.'

She shook her head. She didn't have a choice. 'I'm sorry. I have to go.'

'You're walking away from me.'

She glanced past him, back towards the hotel, the party, her family.

'Yes. I'm sorry.'

And with that she walked past him, and he watched her until he heard the creak of the gate and she disappeared into the trees.

* * *

She texted him later that night, when the adrenaline and anger had deserted her, and she was left feeling limp and uncertain.

I'm sorry. Can we talk?

She watched her phone for an hour, a cup of coffee growing cold beside it, waiting for Jannes's response. She didn't even know where he was—whether he had driven back to London or Harbourside, or straight to the marina and headed out on the water. It was unsettling to feel so adrift just because she didn't know where he was. What they were to each other right now.

How had they messed this up so badly? Because *she* was messed up. She'd fought with her dad, thrown herself at her friend, been rejected, and then walked out on him.

She had messed up in the worst possible way, and she deserved every bit of anger she was sure Jannes must be feeling. She just wished he would show up and be angry in person. Or at least call her and be mad at her on the phone, because this silence was killing her. She just needed to know that they were going to be okay. That they could pretend the last six weeks hadn't happened and go back to being friends who stridently ignored the chemistry between them, because they knew the massive disaster that would ensue if they ever decided to cross that boundary.

She checked her phone again, even though she knew she would have heard it buzz if he'd messaged back.

She cycled through her social media apps—turned out someone had shared a picture of them kissing before the christening, when she'd been so relieved to see that he was safe.

And then she remembered that he'd lost his phone, and she'd been waiting for a call that was never going to come. She dropped her head into her hands. What had she done?

CHAPTER FOURTEEN

LARA SNAPPED AWAKE the next morning as a message pinged, sitting up suddenly in bed and scrambling to read it, her hands shaking.

It was from Jannes.

Hey, sorry, just got a new phone. Want to talk now?

She replied before he could change his mind.

Yes. Please. Are you in London?

Maybe she should have worried about looking too eager, but she was desperate and there was no point hiding it.

Yeah. London Fields? Ten?

Meet you in our usual spot.

She showered and dressed quickly, running through conversations and arguments in her head, rehearsing what she could say to bring him back to her. To apologise for the way she had thrown herself at him and then run away when he'd quite understandably turned her down. And before any of that they had to decide what they wanted. What *she* wanted. Because she knew that until she'd done that there was no point talking at all.

Yes, she was angry at her dad. And yes, she had every right to be. But maybe her mum and Pip's mum and Jannes all had a point—maybe she was letting that anger make decisions for her when she should be making them for herself. She'd had more of an insight into her dad's life than she cared for, faking this thing with Jannes, and maybe she hadn't dealt with her feelings about him in the healthiest possible way. Was she going to carry on like that—avoiding the things that she was afraid of, rather than choosing the things that she wanted? How long had her choices really been just a reaction against a man who had lied to her and broken her heart before it was fully formed?

She pulled a comb through her hair and pulled on a floral jumpsuit and her vintage gold sandals. Slipping earrings into her lobes, she hesitated over the gold and opal ring sitting in the jewellery dish on her dresser. Whether she chose to put it on or not sent a message. In the end, she wore it. It was just keeping the status quo, she rationalised to herself, and being photographed without it would be a hassle until she and Jannes had had a chance to talk and decide whether they were keeping this pretence of an engagement going, and if they weren't, how they were going to get out of it.

She slipped the ring onto her finger and breathed out a sigh at the reassuring weight of it over her knuckle.

She wouldn't think too much about how attached she was to it already.

Eventually, she would have to. She'd been avoiding thinking about how she was feeling since the day her dad had left her, and maybe that wasn't the right thing to be doing. At some point, maybe she should look a little deeper, at the wounds that she was carrying around, and whether they were affecting the choices that she made.

She didn't have to do it with her family there—she wasn't ready for family therapy yet—but she had been carrying this anger for so long. And it had pushed her to the edge of control, and risked ruining her...whatever it was she and Jannes were...because she couldn't be in the same room as her father.

She pulled the door closed behind her and walked quickly down the sun-dappled pavements to the corner of Broadway Market, where she and Jannes had been meeting for weekend brunches for years. Where she had met him just a few weeks ago and concocted this plan which had soon spiralled way out of her control.

She spotted Jannes before he saw her, and she watched him approach, watched the subtle glances directed his way from men and women alike. He saw her at last, and attempted a smile that turned into a grimace, and she knew that things were very different from the last time that they'd walked here.

'Hi,' she said as he drew close, and one corner of his mouth turned up in a smile that didn't reach his eyes.

'Hey,' he replied, with such a sad tone deep in his voice that she knew she had broken something that couldn't be fixed. Whatever happened next, things could never go back to how they'd been before she had brought him into that glade and acted out her fear and anger and sadness on him, until he'd had no choice but to push her away.

'Do you want to eat or walk?' Jannes asked, and Lara turned towards the park.

'Walk?' she said. She couldn't eat, not the way she felt right now. She'd be sick.

They set out on the path that took a wide circle around the park. It was still quiet this morning, and they didn't have to worry about being overheard.

'You're still wearing the ring,' Jannes said as an opening gambit and she was relieved beyond measure that she had decided to wear it.

'I didn't want to presume…' she started, picking her words in a way she'd never had to with Jannes before. Something between them had broken, and she didn't know how to fix it.

They walked on in silence, and she didn't know where to start trying to reach out to him.

'I'm sorry,' she said at last, because it was the most important part of what she had to say. 'I shouldn't have walked away from you like that. I knew it would hurt you and I did it anyway and I'm so sorry for that. And I'm sorry for the way that I threw myself at you too. I really messed up, and I want to make it right again.'

'I want that too,' Jannes said, his voice full of regret. 'So much. But I think we're wrong, trying to go back to how we were before. I don't think we can do that. Too much has happened. Too much has changed.'

'But I care about you, Jannes. I really do. Can't we just keep hold of that?'

* * *

He wasn't sure if they could. He'd watched Lara walk away from him at the church, and it wasn't until then that he'd realised that it was his every worst nightmare come true. This was exactly why he'd avoided getting involved with her in the first place. They'd thought that they were so clever, with their rationalisations and their fake dating, and their 'just going along with it, nothing to do with us' when Mormor had upped the stakes. And in fact what they'd been doing was walking blindfolded into exactly the situation they had both sworn that they were going to avoid. When she'd hurt him, he'd realised it was exactly what he'd been scared of all along.

'I think we have to stop this,' he said as they reached the end of a path.

'Stop here?' she asked, her forehead wrinkling in confusion.

'No,' he said, turning to face her. 'Stop this—' He gestured to himself, to her. 'I can't pretend to be with you and want to be with you, and then…not be,' he said, feeling his stomach swoop as he admitted how he felt about her.

'You want to be with me?' Of course that was the part she heard, not the breaking up part. She wouldn't be Lara if she'd heard anything else.

'Of course I do,' he said, reaching for her hand, and then reminding himself. 'You must know that. You know what I would want if things were different.'

She shook her head, and he knew that she wasn't going to take being broken up with without a fight—the fact that the whole thing had been fake from the start didn't make a difference to that.

'What things?' Lara asked. 'All we have to do is decide if we're doing this—if we want it. There's nothing stopping us other than being afraid.'

'Then that's what's stopping me,' Jannes conceded. It didn't make him feel very masculine, to admit that fear. He'd made a career of pushing his limits, conquering his perception of what he thought he could do. How little sleep he could survive with. How long he could spend at sea. How fast he could keep moving. But this? He didn't want this challenge. Not when he knew he had no chance of winning. 'I'm stopping myself because I can't handle getting hurt the way I know that I will,' he told her.

She shook her head, taking off her sunglasses so she could look him properly in the eye. 'Jannes, I'm not going to hurt you. I know why you think that, after I walked away.'

'But you don't know, Lara. Because if you did know how much that hurt me, you would never have done it.' This time, she reached for his hands, both of them, and he had to take a step away.

'I've apologised for that. I want to make it right.'

'But this isn't something that you can make right. Because it's not about what you did; it's about how I reacted. There's something wrong with me, and I've accepted that.'

Her face was suddenly so full of pity that he had to look away. 'You can't believe that, Jannes. Please. There's nothing wrong with you.'

He shook his head. 'There is. I promise you. I felt something physically break when you walked away from me. And I understand why you did it—you were upset and hurting, it was a completely normal way for someone to behave in that situation. I'm not angry with you. But none of that changes how I felt watching you leave.

'There's only so many times I can do that to myself, Lara. And I know what will happen—I know who I am. If I'm scared of you leaving me, I'll leave instead. I won't want to, and I'll tell myself that this time it'll be different, but I'll find excuses to be away longer and longer and eventually just never come home. And it will be everything you've ever feared coming true. Just like yesterday was for me.'

She dragged him over to a bench and sat looking at him until he was uncomfortable under her scrutiny. 'I don't think you'd do that to me,' she said, her voice so sincere that he nearly believed her.

'I know that I will.'

'Well, I know you better than anyone else on this planet and I say that you're wrong. And I'm not saying this because I want to be with you. I'm putting that aside and being completely objective here.'

He had to laugh at that; whether it was true or not, it was a bold claim.

'I appreciate your faith in me, Lara, but you can't know me better than I know myself.'

'I can trust you more than you trust yourself. That much is clear. I already do.'

She folded her arms, and he knew that he wasn't

going to persuade her that she was wrong. Well, that was fine. He didn't need to persuade her. A relationship didn't exist without both parties being in it, and he had already decided he was out.

'I'm not negotiating here, Lara. I'm telling you. I'm sorry to be blunt, but I think we both need that. No more fake dating. No more fake engagement.'

'And your sponsorship? Spencer?' Of course her first thought was his career.

'They've already signed the contract; the launch is in a month. They can't take it back now. I'll be a disappointment to them, of course, but that can't be helped.'

Her expression turned hard, determined. 'You are not a disappointment, Jannes,' she said. 'I'm going to the launch. You can pretend to date me or marry me or not to know me, if you want, but I'm going to be there to support you either way.'

'I want us to still be friends,' he said, and Lara nodded, because what else could she do? She didn't want to lose him completely, but she knew that their friendship was never going back to what it had been before. How could it possibly, when her feelings had changed so much?

'I can't not have you in my life, Lara. I can't look at you and wonder what will happen if I mess up. If you want something and I'm not able to give it to you and you walk away again. You mean too much to me to take a risk like that.'

'But think about if it worked, Jannes. I can't promise that it will. We both know that. But just…what if it did? Because I love you—that's not a secret, and I know that you love me too. But there are all these other ways of loving each other that we've only just begun to explore, and I think that if we were brave, and decided to go for it, there's something really special there. Something that I don't know if we would ever find with anyone else.'

'I'm not saying no because I think I'm going to find something better with someone else.'

'But you are saying no?'

'I'm saying that I feel the same way. But the risks are too great, Lara. These last couple of days with things not being right between us—it's been awful. I don't want to go through that again.'

'So we make a commitment to each other—we promise that, whatever happens, we stay in one another's lives.'

'And what happens when we can't keep our promises?' Jannes asked, his voice gravelly.

She didn't have an answer to that and, honestly, she didn't know whether she was relieved or sad. Because he had made up his mind, that much was clear. And she had only just started to sort through her own issues, the things that had been stopping her from committing. She couldn't solve Jannes's problems as well.

She squeezed his hand for a second, before letting it drop. Just for a minute there, she'd been able to imagine her life if this had all worked out, and it was something shining and brilliant, and now completely out of reach.

CHAPTER FIFTEEN

JANNES SAT ON the deck of his yacht, the water calm as a millpond around him. If there had been even a breath of wind then there would be something for him to do, but still and calm like this, there was nothing to do for now but sit and think.

It was meant to be easier out here: that was why he'd come. He'd thought he would suddenly feel a whole lot better than he had when he'd walked away from Lara in the park at London Fields. But he didn't. He didn't feel better on land. Being on the water didn't help either. Which meant he had only one idea left, and he'd been putting that off for as long as he could.

Even as he was walking up the steps to Mormor's apartment, after she buzzed him in from the street, he knew that he was walking into a nightmare. There was no way she was going to look at his miserable face—and there was no way that his face wasn't miserable, given that that was how he felt—and not tell him that he had made an enormous mistake in letting Lara go. They'd said that they were just going to go back to how they were before. That they'd pretend that the dating thing had never happened. But he couldn't. She couldn't. Too much had changed in the last few weeks.

'*Älskling,*' Mormor said as soon as she answered the door. 'Come in and tell me why you are being so stupid.'

He smiled. This was going to go exactly how he'd expected. But something told him that Mormor's tough love was going to be the only thing that helped.

'So you're not getting married any more,' Mormor said, a cup of black coffee steaming in front of her crossed arms.

He sighed melodramatically, thinking that that might get through to her, and shook his head. 'We were never getting married, Mormor. You know that. We *told* you that. Repeatedly. Don't pretend that you've forgotten.'

She huffed in his face, which was precisely the reaction that he'd expected. 'Of course I haven't forgotten, Jannes. Just because I am in my nineties doesn't mean I am an idiot, you know. Anyone with any sense could see that you and Lara were falling in love and going to get married. It's not my fault if you couldn't.'

'Well, we've broken up,' he said, regretting the air of certainty and finality. 'Real us and fake us. It's all over, so you were wrong.'

Her eyes softened as she passed him a cup of coffee and a cinnamon bun. 'I don't know about that. But come on, tell me why you broke up.'

'We weren't right for each other,' he lied.

'Pfft! You're perfect for one another. Try again.'

'I'll end up hurting her,' he said, which was the truth. But he didn't think that Mormor would accept it.

'Closer. Not true, but closer to what you're really scared about.'

He shook his head, feeling the words—the fear—bubbling up and not able to stop it. 'She'll leave me. Of course she will. Even my own parents would drive away from me twice a year without a backwards glance. I know they never looked back because I watched, every time, to see if they would. Or even glance in a mirror. And they never did. I decided a long time ago that I was never going to let that happen again.'

Mormor laid a hand on his shoulder and made a soothing noise. 'And you think Lara would do that to you?' she asked.

'I know that she wouldn't mean to,' Jannes said, looking down at his clenched hands. 'But eventually the novelty would wear off. We'd fight. She'd walk away. I know how these things go. But what's worse is that I won't be content to wait for it to happen. At the first sign of something being wrong I'll be out of there, and I'll hurt her in the process.'

Mormor looked up, tried to catch his eye, but he kept his eyes down, because he didn't need her to see how far down this sadness went.

'I don't think that you do know everything, *sötnos*. I see how much she loves you.'

'Then I'll hurt her, trying to protect myself,' he argued.

Mormor smiled. 'You know, you can just choose not to do that. I'm not saying it's an easy choice. But you *can* choose it. You just have to decide how brave you want to be. I think you have it in you to make this work.

I think you deserve to be happy with Lara. I think she deserves to be happy with you. But that's not going to happen until you decide to make a change. You have to let go of what your parents did to you and decide that you're going to do better than they did. I know at least one person who would never walk away from you. Who has never thought twice about how important you are. Who knows that you would never, ever hurt her. If you can trust yourself to love me, *älskling*, you can trust yourself to love Lara. She deserves it. And you deserve to be happy.'

'I think I need to go for a walk.'

He headed out of the apartment with no idea where he was going, only that he needed to be moving to think about what his grandmother had said. She was right— he'd loved his grandmother since before he could remember, and he'd never once wondered whether she loved him back. Whether it was safe to love her. So whatever damage his parents had done when they'd dumped him in that school, it hadn't touched every part of him. There was a part of his heart that was still undamaged, and he wondered if he knew how to find it. To tap into it. To make it grow.

Because that was what he wanted—he had to admit that now, if nothing else. They might not be able to make it work, but he wanted Lara in his heart. Or wanted to give her more of it, because he really was as stupid as Mormor liked to tell him he was if he thought that she didn't have a place in there already. He'd loved her as a friend for three years, and in that time he had never doubted that she shared his feelings, that she wouldn't want to hurt him. So why did he think that would change if the way that they loved each other changed? Either he trusted her, or he didn't. He trusted himself to be there for her, or he didn't. And if he couldn't trust himself to do those things in a romantic relationship, then he had no right claiming a place in her life at all. Because she deserved better than that.

She deserved someone who would love her wholly, and he did.

He loved her, he trusted her, and he trusted himself to always feel that way.

He half sprinted back to Mormor's apartment with this revelation, a new fear sinking in.

'I don't know if she'll even take me back,' he said, the minute that he was through the door.

'And I can't promise that she will,' Mormor said, waiting for him as if she already knew this was exactly where their earlier conversation had been leading. 'Only you two can work this out. But I can promise you that she loves you. Any old fool can see that much. And I can promise you that, however it goes, I will still be here for you.'

He wrapped his arms around her and rested his chin on the top of her head.

'Thank you, Mormor. I don't know what I'd do without you.'

'You'd do fine,' she answered from somewhere below his chin. 'And you will do, when I'm not here any more to look out for you. But I'd be a lot happier knowing that you had someone else who loves you and trusts you as much as I do.'

He smiled over the top of her head. 'How do I do it? Any ideas?'

'Oh, *älskling*,' she said with a sigh. 'You know her the best. What does she like? What's important to her?'

Well, he knew the answer to that, of course. Her community, the friends and family she had made for herself, when she couldn't rely on one of the people who should always have her back.

'I follow her on Instagram, you know,' Mormor said.

'I had heard something along those lines.'

'And she follows me back. So if there was something that you wanted to say, if there was a grand gesture you wanted to make, for instance…'

But he was already ahead of her, thinking about how quickly he could make it happen, how many people he would have to contact to make it work. He opened his app and checked Lara's account. Okay. A lot. But he could do it, he was sure. He wasn't giving up on her, or on himself. It was time to bring out the big guns.

He pulled up the software that he'd seen Lara use sometimes. Downloaded the picture of them with her engagement ring from the regatta and set to work.

An hour later his hands were hurting from the copying and pasting, and he had a complicated spreadsheet on the go, logging responses from everyone that Lara followed from her feed. If he was going to take it over completely, he needed buy-in from every single person that she followed. Anything other than perfect just wasn't going to fly here. He'd colour-coded everyone's responses, and as soon as he got to the bottom of the list he circled back to the top, making a note of time zones and response time to chase most effectively.

Finally he was *doing* something. He didn't know if it would work. Even if it did, he couldn't be sure that Lara would have him back, but he was finally ready to be brave and he just had to hope that it wasn't going to be too late. He would find out soon enough. This was a one shot deal.

CHAPTER SIXTEEN

LARA SAT AT her keyboard a week later, hoping for inspiration to strike. She'd just spent an hour on the phone with Jess, hoping that it would lift her out of this funk that was leaving her unable to think of a single word to say to the friends she had made online.

Jess was still determinedly in the honeymoon phase, and as much as she had sympathised with Lara over Jannes, there had been no way to keep the treacly sound of happiness out of her voice. And Lara knew precisely what, or who, had put it there. She could hardly begrudge Jess her happiness; it was everything she wanted for her friend and more. But she couldn't help but think that she'd be able to enjoy it with her friend more if her own recent attempts at having a love life hadn't turned out quite so dismally.

She turned back to her scheduling, tried moving some posts around to see if it helped inspiration strike. But since she'd stopped lying to her followers, and Jannes had disappeared from her feed, she found that she had little to say. Not when she couldn't share her heartbreak with her followers. It was easier to concentrate on her studying, on her consulting clients, anything to take her mind off her own life.

They'd done their best to keep their breakup quiet, trying to avoid the publicity that had prompted the fake dating in the first place, and led to everything that had come after. But that was only viable for so long. It had been over a week now since she and Jannes had been in public together. And though she couldn't bring herself to take off the ring they had picked out together, every time she saw it, it made her just a little sadder that they hadn't been brave enough or bold enough to make this work.

When she closed her eyes she could smell the woodland glade where it had all gone wrong. Could feel the speckled sunlight on her closed eyelids, feel Jannes's shirt beneath her hands and her mouth hard on his. And when she opened her eyes, and knew that it was all an impossibility, it hurt more every time. She'd thought that it would be getting better, that she would be learning to live with this hole in her chest. But it wasn't.

And she knew better now than to think that those sort of emotional wounds just healed themselves. Which was why she'd finally agreed to a session of family therapy, just with her mum to start with. Perhaps she'd work with the rest of the family in future too, but she figured that her and her mum, and the spectre of her dad, had quite enough work to be going on with. The therapist had been really quite insistent that it wasn't her fault that her father had left. Which, intellectually, Lara was sure that she already knew. It turned out it was harder to believe it than to know it. But she was working on that.

She turned to her feed, scrolling through, hoping to find some solace or inspiration in the posts of one of her followers. She'd so often drawn comfort from the community on here. But as she scrolled she frowned and drew back, because something was wrong. Every post was the same—and it was one of hers. The shot of her with Jannes in Harbourside, showing off her engagement ring for the first time. Had *she* done this somehow? She checked her profile, but no. It had been weeks since she'd posted that picture, and there were plenty of posts since. She clicked back onto the main feed and opened the caption.

Just a hashtag.

#Janneslovesyou

Okay, that was weird. She clicked the next post. The same hashtag. Oh, this had Mormor's fingerprints all over it. It had to be her. She was up to something and she was the only person she knew who could wreak this sort of mischief. She searched for her profile and—surprise, surprise—she found the same post.

Her hands shaking, she clicked through to Jannes's profile and found the same picture, but this one had a caption.

I love you, I need you, I want to marry you. Come to church with me tomorrow?

She closed the laptop, drawing in a shaky breath. Her first guess had been that this was Mormor's doing. Was this him…trying to win her back? For real, or just for some publicity thing? She couldn't get her thoughts straight. Was that what *she* wanted? She had thrown herself at him twice now, and had had to recover from the fallout of him turning her down. Was she really going to put herself out there only to get knocked back again?

No. She couldn't let herself think like that. Couldn't let herself hope, because she was only going to end up disappointed.

But she had been doing the work, hadn't she? She had been to therapy and heard that everything that she told herself about herself was flawed. That the people who had hurt her had made her scared, and she had spent her whole adult life letting that fear win. Well, she had a choice now, didn't she? She could let fear win again, like Jannes had, she recognised, when he had pushed her away. Or she could accept that they were both imperfect and still learning, and still in love with each other, and see what happened when they were both brave at the same time.

She texted him, because the things that she had to say to him didn't belong in church.

I saw your messages. I think we need to talk. My place? An hour?

I'll be there.

She glanced at the clock. She couldn't decide whether that was going to go by in a heartbeat or an eternity. She decided to throw herself into the shower and worry about it from there.

The last time she'd seen Jannes, he'd been walking away from her in London Fields. Walking away because he was afraid that she would leave him. Because he couldn't trust that someone could love him enough to stay. What had changed in the last week? she wondered. Had anything? Because if this was just because he missed her, and not because he had realised that they needed to do things differently, then it was all going to end in tears.

She was never going to find out, though, if she didn't talk to him.

She mused it over in the shower, wondering how he had managed to make sure that she'd seen those posts. It was only when she got out of the shower and checked her feed again, scrolling and scrolling and scrolling, that she realised what he had done. Every single person. He had managed to get every single person that she followed to post that picture of them, of that moment when they had been so happy, so excited, those emotions real, even under the falsities that surrounded them.

They couldn't just keep taking it in turns to freak out and run away each time that one of them had a breakthrough—eventually one of them was going to have to break the pattern so that they could talk about this— that was the only way it could ever work. And Jannes had hit the ball straight into her court. He knew how she felt about him. She'd *told* him how she felt about him.

Her heart stuttered when the doorbell rang, and she knew that this was her last chance to back out. She could carry on being afraid. She could pretend that she hadn't heard the door, hide in her bedroom and wait for Jannes to go away. Or she could be brave, and go out there and talk to him, as she had been desperate to do for the last week.

She opened the door.

Jannes was standing there with his hands in his pockets, looking every inch the poster boy for wholesome Nordic health that he should be.

'Hey,' he said with a hopeful smile, and she reached out a hand and pulled him into the apartment.

'You're here,' she said.

'Yeah, I mean you texted me and... I can go.'

'Don't go, come in,' she said, leading him through to the kitchen, wondering how things could be so awkward when they'd been friends for so long. 'How did you do that to my feed?' she asked, sticking with professional curiosity because that seemed like the safest of all the questions buzzing around her head right now. 'Did you befriend a computer hacker? Break into the algorithm? Because if you did I want your superpowers.'

'No,' Jannes said with a laugh that sounded a little forced. Good, so she wasn't the only nervous one here. 'It was a little less hi tech than that. I befriended everyone that you follow. It wasn't hard, to be honest. They all love you, were happy to do anything I asked if it was for you.'

'But that's hundreds of people,' Lara said, her mouth falling open.

'A little over a thousand, actually. But, like I said, they were happy to do it.'

'I can't believe you did that,' she said, shaking her head, still trying to avoid looking at the big picture, be-cause—frankly—it scared the bejesus out of her.

'Lara, I would do anything for you. I thought you knew that.' Okay, so that was the big picture. Harder to avoid it now that he had said it out loud.

'Last time we talked,' she started, cringing at the memory. 'I asked you… Well, we both know how that conversation went. I put myself out there and…'

'I'm not proud of that. I wish I could go back and change it.'

Lara shook her head. 'But you shouldn't. I've had time to think and I'm sure you were right. I walked away and I hurt you. And I'm working on my own stuff, I even went to therapy with Mum, but the things you said were right—we both hurt each other, and if we try this again we'll end up making the same mistakes and it's not worth losing you over. This last week… God, I've *missed* you, Jannes. So much. And I can't bear the thought that we might do something that means I spend the whole of the rest of my life feeling like that. I mean, marriage! We messed up fake dating. How are we meant to make a real relationship work?'

'We will get things wrong. We'll make mistakes, and we'll argue. But that doesn't have to break us. People make mistakes all the time, and then they apologise and they talk and they figure things out. I know that you love me. And you should know that I love you. I love you a lot. So much, Lara. I want us to take a risk, if it means that we can be happy together.'

'You love me?' she asked, her mind sticking on those three words. 'Even though I don't know if I can do this?'

'Even though you don't know if you can do this,' Jannes said, reaching for her hand, threading their fingers together. 'If anything, that makes me want it more. And even if we decide that it's too big a risk, it's not going to change how I feel about you. You can knock me back and know that you'll still have me in your life. You won't lose me if you don't feel the same way. It's not all or nothing—I'm not giving you an ultimatum. I just want you to know how I feel. That I'm here, offering you my heart, everything, if you decide that that's what you want too.'

'Of course it's what I want,' she said, not able to resist the grin that was spreading across her face. 'It's what I've always wanted. I was just too scared before.'

'Then we're doing this?' Jannes asked.

Lara lifted her shoulders and let them drop. 'I don't even know what this is. Is *this* getting married? Because that still feels like a bit of a leap.'

Jannes shrugged. 'I'm ready to leap. I'm at least ready to talk to the vicar about leaping. But you don't have to be just because I am. We can take this as slow as you want to, or as fast as I want to. We will work out what we need together.'

He pulled her closer with their linked fingers and let his hands fall gently on her hips. She took that as the invitation she hoped it was intended as, and took a step closer until her body was warming against his and she had to tip her head up to see his expression.

'Jannes?'

'Lara?'

'Are you asking me to marry you?'

Creases appeared at the corners of his eyes, and she wanted to kiss every one of them. 'I thought I had already done that,' he said.

'Not properly.'

One corner of his mouth quirked, and she knew that he was suppressing a smile.

'Well, then.' He took her left hand in his and slid off the gold and opal ring, before dropping to one knee.

'Lara, you're already my best friend, and the person I love most in the world. I was wondering if you'd also do me the honour of being my wife.'

She kept her smile small, not wanting to make this too easy, not after all they'd been through to get to this moment. She wanted to make it last. Leaning down, she brushed a kiss against Jannes's lips, but drew away when his hands came to her hair, before he could deepen the kiss.

'I think that sounds like everything I've ever hoped for,' she said at last, her voice barely more than a whisper, Jannes close enough that it didn't matter.

'That's a yes?'

'Of course it's a yes.'

Jannes's arms clamped around her hips as he stood and spun her around; her dress caught on his jeans as he lowered her, so that her mouth was level with his, her legs locked around his waist. 'You really mean it?'

he asked between kisses, as they stumbled their way back onto the couch, Jannes landing on her so heavily that it knocked the air from her chest.

'I really mean it,' she said, one hand on his cheek. 'I love you, I'm going to marry you, and you're going to be mine for ever.'

* * * * *

REDEMPTION ON RIVERS RANCH

KATHY DOUGLASS

This book is dedicated to Heather G., who named a character after her beloved mother, Vicki.

It's also dedicated with appreciation to my editor, Charles Griemsman. Thank you for making this book better than I imagined it could be.

It is also dedicated to anyone who has ever needed a second chance.

Finally, this book is dedicated with love to my husband and sons. Thank you for your consistent support and love.

Chapter One

"How much longer?"

Gabriella Tucker sighed and swallowed the impatience that mirrored her daughter's. Sophia had asked this question three times in the last thirty minutes. Gabriella understood how she felt. She, too, was tired of being cooped up in the SUV.

She'd tried to turn the drive from Ohio to North Carolina into an adventure, visiting tourist spots designed specifically for children along the way. They'd spent an afternoon at the Avampato Discovery Museum in Charleston, West Virginia. Sophia and her brother, Justin, had had a wonderful time pretending to be adults in the My Town exhibit. They'd learned how to compose music in the music studio exhibit and how to live a healthy life in the Healthy Me exhibit.

When the trio reached Virginia, they visited Fort Chiswell Animal Park, where they'd gone on a delightful guided safari that they talked about for hours in their hotel room later that night. The children had enjoyed themselves immensely on those outings, but today they'd been driving for several hours and were ready to reach their final destination.

"Not long now."

"You said that last time," Justin pointed out. For the most part, he hadn't spoken much during the drive, choosing instead to stare out the window at the passing landscape. When they'd started out on their trek three days ago, the kids had been excited by the expansive farmland and ranches that differed from the perfectly manicured lawns of their gated community back in Cedar Ridge, Ohio. They'd happily counted the cows and horses they'd seen. Now they ignored the animals they passed. They were tired, cranky and ready to reach Gabriella's great-aunt's house where they'd be spending the summer.

"So I did." And hopefully that was the last time she'd have to say it. According to the highway sign they'd just passed, Sweet Briar was twenty miles away. There were two exits before that one, one of which led to her great-aunt's small ranch, where Gabriella had spent many happy summers in her childhood. Aunt Mildred and Uncle Bob hadn't had children, but they'd loved their nieces and nephews as if they'd been their own. Gabriella's mother, Yvette, had been one of those children, and she and Gabriella had visited regularly. When Gabriella had been old enough to stay on her own, she'd spent summers there. It was where some of the best times of her life had happened, with her summertime best friend, Carson Rivers.

Gabriella smiled as she recalled meeting him for the first time when she was seven. They'd taken one look at each other and recognized a kindred spirit. From that moment on, they'd been inseparable, spending every free minute together—riding horses, paddling in the swimming hole on his father's ranch or just enjoying each other's company. Life had been simple and uncomplicated.

The summer Gabriella had turned fifteen, Carson hadn't spent as much time with her as he had in the past. His father had insisted that he learn the family business, leaving him with very little free time. The Rivers family were very successful cattle ranchers, and the Rivers Ranch was one of the largest in North Carolina. Gabriella had been disappointed that her friend had been unable to spend as much time with her as he had every other summer, but she'd contented herself with the brief moments they had shared.

It turned out that that summer would be the last one she'd spend with her great aunt and uncle. When she turned sixteen, she'd gotten a part-time job, which put an end to her vacations in Sweet Briar. Then, at nineteen, she'd fallen in love and married impetuously. She'd foolishly thought that marriage would last forever. It hadn't.

Frowning, she pushed the negative thought aside. She wasn't going to think about her unfaithful husband now. She was in Sweet Briar to come up with a new plan for her life, not rehash the past.

"So when will we be there?" Sophia pressed.

"We're getting off the highway at the next exit. The road we take will have us at Aunt Mildred's house about ten minutes later."

"Okay." Sophia looked at the dashboard clock, marking the time. Clearly she was going to hold Gabriella to her word. Although Sophia looked exactly as Gabriella had at eight years old, they had entirely different personalities. Sophia was thoughtful, considering each possible outcome before acting. Gabriella had been impulsive and flown by the seat of her pants, following wherever her heart led. Hence the marriage to a man she'd known only a few months.

"So what did you do when you were here?"

Justin asked. "The only thing here is a bunch of cows."

"There are a lot of cows," Gabriella conceded. "But there were a lot of horses, too. And a swimming hole."

"Swimming sounds fun. Especially since I'm going to miss summer season."

Gabriella heard the indignation in her son's voice. Justin had been swimming from the time he was eighteen months old. She and Reggie, her ex-husband, had taken the kids to the club for a summer party. Justin had taken one look at the pool and jumped in. He'd sunk like a stone. When she'd grabbed him, he'd shoved her away and said he was "fwimming." She'd enrolled him in swimming lessons the following Monday.

Four years ago, when Justin turned six, Reggie signed him up for the swim team. Although Justin was a good swimmer, he wasn't competitive by nature. He just enjoyed the camaraderie of the team. Consequently, he generally scored in the middle of the pack. When Reggie realized that his son wasn't going to be the next Michael Phelps, he'd stopped attending the meets. Justin was a smart kid who'd connected his father's absence to his performance. He was determined to improve his times in an effort to regain his father's attention. Sadly, it wasn't going to be that easy.

"I know. But not all the kids swim every season.

Coach was fine with you taking the summer off. In fact, he said that you could try another sport." Unlike many coaches who wanted their team to practice twelve months a year and swim exclusively, Coach Mike encouraged his charges to play other sports.

"What sports are there on a ranch? And are there any other kids here? Where do they live?"

"There were when I visited."

"That was a hundred years ago."

"Wrong. It was only ninety."

They laughed together and the tension faded. Once her kids had begun to understand the basics of time, they'd joked about it—especially about her age. Little did they know that it often seemed like a hundred years had passed since those happy summers she'd spent on the ranch.

"It's been ten minutes," Sophia piped up. She raised an eyebrow, looking more like a twenty-eight-year-old than an eight-year-old.

"And here we are." Gabriella slowed the car as she drove along the deserted road. Halfway down, she turned into the driveway. The sun had begun to set, casting an orange glow around the white brick house. The grass was freshly mowed, but the flower beds on either side of the wide stairs and running along the edges of the front porch were bare. Aunt Mildred hadn't mentioned hiring anyone to maintain the property, so Gabriella could only assume one of the neighbors had been caring for the house and grounds since her aunt had moved away. That was the thing she'd appreciated about ranch life. People looked out for each other.

Gabriella half expected her aunt to come charging out the house, her arms wide open for a hug, something she could really use right now. But the house was empty. Uncle Bob had died unexpectedly three years ago. The ranch had been too much for Aunt Mildred to handle on her own, so two years ago she'd sold off most of it, holding on to the house and four acres. Then seven months ago Aunt Mildred had moved into a senior community in Willow Creek, a town about an hour from here. She'd said the house had become too big. Too empty. Too lonely. Two of her friends lived in the community and Aunt Mildred quickly made friends with several other women, as well. She was enjoying herself immensely and claimed she was too busy to be lonely. Right now she and her friends were in Florida, enjoying what Aunt Mildred had referred to as a grown folks Disney adventure.

Justin and Sophia burst from the vehicle and ran around the massive lawn, enjoying the freedom. When they spotted the front porch swing, they dashed up the stairs and hopped on, banging the swing against the concrete windowsill.

"Get your backpacks out of the car and let's go

inside. We can bring in the suitcases and boxes once we turn on the lights and look around."

"Okay," Sophia said, jumping from the swing. Justin sighed and followed his sister down the stairs.

They grabbed their stuff and then trekked back up onto the porch. Gabriella used the key her aunt had overnighted to her a week ago to unlock the front door. Reaching to her right, she switched on the overhead light in the large front parlor. A feeling of nostalgia gripped her as she looked around. The furniture was draped with sheets, but Gabriella could make out the shape of the sofa where'd she'd lain to watch the only television in the house on Sunday evenings. She'd been too busy during the week to laze around, but on Sunday nights, she and her great aunt and uncle had watched movies or Uncle Bob's beloved sitcoms.

"It's like a ghost house," Sophia whispered. Her earlier enthusiasm had seeped out of her, and she stepped closer to Gabriella.

"Boo!" Justin yelled, then burst out laughing when Sophia jumped.

"Stop it," Gabriella said. Justin had always been a sweet boy, but ever since Reggie stopped coming around, Justin had begun to take out his unhappiness on his sister. He didn't do it a lot, but he did it often enough for Gabriella to notice.

"Sorry," Justin muttered, chastised.

"The sheets are to keep the dust from settling into the furniture," Gabriella explained. She yanked a sheet off the nearest chair, revealing an orange-and-brown-patterned fabric. The fall colors somehow worked although it was only the second week of June.

It must have looked like fun because Sophia and Justin dropped their backpacks and began racing from room to room, pulling the fabric from furniture. Their laughter floated through the house, warming Gabriella's heart. There hadn't been much for them to laugh about these past two years.

The ink on her divorce papers hadn't even dried before Reggie and Natalie had gotten married. The ceremony had been an elaborate affair, attended by everyone in their exclusive social circle, so Gabriella knew they'd been planning it for a while. When Reggie had come to pick up the kids for their weekend visits, he'd been happier than she'd ever seen him. His smile, which had gone missing during the latter years of their marriage, had been ever present. Gabriella was a romantic at heart and believed in happy endings. Still, it had been difficult to see the man who'd sworn to love her until death parted them finding his happily-ever-after with another woman. Especially since she'd thought she and Reggie had already found their happy ending together.

Of course that was before Reggie confessed

that he'd always been in love with Natalie. When she'd married someone else, he'd tried to move on with Gabriella. When Natalie's marriage fell apart, she'd contacted Reggie, despite the fact that he was married with children. The rest, as the saying went, was horrible history.

Natalie had gotten pregnant immediately and the baby had been born six months ago. After his son's birth, Reggie stopped taking the kids for the weekend, choosing to pick them up early Saturday morning and bring them back after dinner. When he'd had the kids, he hadn't paid much attention to them. Instead, he'd spent his time marveling at the wonders of his new child. He'd tried to get the kids interested in their new sibling, but even Sophia had gotten bored with the baby after a while. They wanted their father's attention. After a while Reggie had requested to reduce his visitation to one weekend a month. Even then, he often canceled at the last minute or just plain didn't show.

The kids had been confused and heartbroken. Gabriella had been furious. If Reggie no longer wanted her, fine. She was an adult and could get over it. But Justin and Sophia were children. *His* children. When Reggie had told her that he wouldn't be taking the kids for his three weeks in the summer as they'd agreed, she'd known it was time for a change. The kids didn't need to be reminded every day that their father preferred his son and his precious new wife to them. When Aunt Mildred had offered up her house, Gabriella had jumped at the opportunity to leave their troubles behind. The children would enjoy their new surroundings and Gabriella could use the time here to develop a plan for the future, one that would include putting her hard-earned psychology degree to use.

Gabriella followed the kids, picking up the discarded sheets as she went and bundling them in her arms. The kids had turned on the lights before they entered a room, so the entire house was lit up like a Christmas tree. She recognized some of the furniture from her visits, but new pieces had been added. All in all, the house felt familiar and Gabriella was optimistic. The kids were laughing and happy. Gabriella might not have everything worked out, but right now things were good. For now, that was enough.

Carson Rivers drove down the solitary road to his ranch and heaved a sigh of relief. He always timed his visits to Sweet Briar so that he didn't encounter many people, but it was stressful nonetheless. A part of him knew he was being a little sensitive and more than a bit paranoid, but he couldn't help himself. Being the son of a murderer came with heavy baggage. The fact that the murder had happened over a decade ago and that Carson was the one who'd brought it to light so justice could be done didn't change things. Karl Rivers had been a powerful man who'd thrown his weight around. A few people had resented and feared him in equal measure, so they took out their anger on Carson, gloating over his unhappiness.

When Karl had died suddenly last year, Carson's childhood friend and former neighbor Donovan Cordero had returned to town after a ten-year absence when he'd been presumed dead. He had revealed a horrible truth to Carson. Donovan had witnessed Carson's father commit murder. Karl had let Donovan live, but only if he left town immediately and never came back. But as soon as Donovan learned of Karl's death, he returned. It wasn't long before Donovan renewed his relationship with Raven Reynolds—Carson's fiancée at the time—who'd borne Donovan's son in his absence.

Once Carson had learned the truth, he'd been determined to discover the murdered man's identity. Somewhere out there, a family was wondering what had happened to their loved one. Carson wouldn't be able to rest until he gave them closure. So he'd gone to the newly elected county sheriff, who'd opened an investigation. And Carson had hired a private investigator to locate the man's family. Once they'd been found, Carson had paid to have the remains, which were located after an investigation, shipped to the man's hometown in Tennessee and paid for the funeral.

Carson hadn't tried to hide what he'd discovered from his friends and neighbors. His father had hidden his crimes, and he was the last person Carson wanted to emulate. But he hadn't expected the backlash. People he hadn't necessarily counted among his friends, but whom he'd never considered enemies, began talking about him behind his back. Some of the bolder ones had even told him he shouldn't show his face in town. Carson's friends had rallied around him, but the words still stung. He couldn't help but wonder if others felt the same way but just didn't say anything.

Thank goodness, his mother had moved to Atlanta to stay with her sister shortly after his father's funeral. She was a gentle yet proud soul who would never have been able to deal with being ostracized. The gossip would have killed her. She shouldn't have to deal with this. No woman should.

Discovering the truth about his father had been a shock, one Carson had only begun to get over. He couldn't believe the father he'd idolized as a child, the father who'd held Carson in front of him on a horse as a toddler and who'd taught Carson everything he knew about ranching, had taken another man's life. It was impossible to reconcile the two sides of his father. Losing Raven had been another staggering blow, knocking him off his center.

Before all of this came to light, Carson had been a successful horse trainer. He'd worked with previously abused animals as well as teaching horses to accept the saddle. He'd branched out and begun giving riding lessons to local kids. He'd enjoyed it as much as they had and business had begun to take off. But then a whisper campaign had started. Rather than wait for his students to back out, he'd closed the school. Besides, dealing with the fallout from his father's actions and running the family's cattle ranch had left him little time for anything else.

Luckily a forensic audit revealed that the business operations were 100 percent legal and aboveboard, so Carson had been able to keep running it with a clear conscience. Which was good, considering the ranch employed over two dozen people, many of whom supported families.

Lately he'd been toying with the idea of restarting his riding school, but something held him back. Would people really trust him to teach their kids? His reputation had been impeccable before, but being the son of a killer scuffed up the shine. At least to hear some people tell it.

Did he need the pain and aggravation? He had plenty to keep him busy.

He passed his neighbor's house and automatically glanced at it. He'd promised Mrs. Johnson that he'd keep an eye on it when she moved to Willow Creek. She'd been considering putting it on the market but hadn't made up her mind yet. She said she liked knowing the house was there in case she got tired of her new lifestyle. It wasn't a problem for him. Mowing her lawn was easy enough and oddly soothing. She only had a handful of acres and he had a riding mower, so it didn't take much time.

He slowed. Lights were blazing in the house. No one was supposed to be there.

Carson considered calling the sheriff but decided against it. Only the world's worst criminal would turn on every light in the house and hope nobody noticed. He'd assess the situation and go from there.

Pulling into the driveway, he noticed an SUV with out-of-state license plates. He peered inside. Empty. Mrs. Johnson had given him a key to the house, so he headed up onto the porch, opened the door and stepped inside.

Apparently whoever was inside had made themselves at home. They'd uncovered the furniture and dropped suitcases and backpacks by the stairs leading to the upstairs bedrooms. Loud music was blaring from the back of the house. Someone was singing a popular song at the top of her lungs. The fact that she was nowhere in the vicinity of the right key didn't stop her from singing with gusto. Her attempt to hit a high note pierced his ears and propelled him forward if only to save his hearing.

A child laughed.

What in the world was going on here?

Mrs. Johnson would have told him if she'd sold or rented the house. She hadn't mentioned it when they'd spoken a couple of weeks ago. And the gossips of Sweet Briar would have said something. He might not hang out in town any longer, but his employees did. One of them would have told him if they'd heard anything about his closest neighbor.

Carson stepped into the kitchen. A woman and girl of about seven or eight were dancing around the old Formica table, trying to convince a boy who looked about ten to join them. The boy was leaning against the sink, his arms folded over his chest. Clearly he wasn't interested in participating in the revelry.

The woman laughed and the sound struck a chord inside Carson. Something about the sound stirred a distant memory inside him, awakening a long-forgotten feeling. He silenced the echo, focusing on the matter at hand.

The intruders were so wrapped up in each other that they hadn't noticed him yet. He twisted the knob on Mrs. Johnson's ancient radio, silencing the music, and then cleared his throat.

The woman spun around, then pushed herself in front of the girl, whose eyes were wide with shock. The boy looked around as if searching for a weapon to use to protect the others. Luckily there wasn't anything available for him to grab.

"Who are you and what are you doing here?" the woman asked.

The boy pulled a phone from his pocket and began punching in numbers. No doubt he was getting ready to call the police. Although by rights Carson should be the one asking questions, he chose to de-escalate the situation.

"I'm the owner's neighbor. Now who are you?"

The woman stepped closer, sizing him up. She peered at him, studying his face for so long that she could have been searching for an answer to life's mysteries. He refused to flinch under her intense scrutiny. After an uncomfortably long moment, she smiled. "Carson?"

He nodded and looked at her more carefully. The coffee-colored eyes danced with mischief. It couldn't be. Fifteen years had passed since his old friend had visited. But looking closer at her astonishingly beautiful face with clear light brown skin, high cheekbones and full lips, he knew it was her. "Gabriella?"

The woman laughed and launched herself at him, squeezing him in a tight hug. "Oh, my goodness. It has been years."

"Yes, it has." He and his parents had been invited to her wedding some years ago, but they hadn't been able to attend. Carson hugged her briefly, then stepped back and forced himself to ignore the way his body reacted to the contact. It had been a long time since he'd held a woman in his arms. More than a year since he and Raven had ended their engagement. Last November and December, he'd had a brief entanglement with a woman who'd spent a few weeks in Sweet Briar. They'd enjoyed themselves, but neither of them had expected it to be any more than it turned out to be. And when she'd left town, it ended.

Holding Gabriella that brief moment had felt like sticking his finger into a live electric socket. And when they ended the hug, his blood was still humming from the aftereffects. He did his best to smother the response. He might be the son of a killer, but he had never hit on married women, no matter how beautiful they were or how good they smelled. He wouldn't start with his childhood friend.

"You know him?" the boy asked, his hand hovering over the phone as if unsure whether or not to call for help.

"Yes." Gabriella beamed at Carson again, making his heart lurch before she turned to the boy who he assumed was her son. "We were best friends when I was your age. We hung out all day every day for many summers. He lives on the ranch right across the road."

The boy looked from Carson to Gabriella. Was

he trying to imagine them being kids his own age, or was he seeing something more? That was ridiculous. There was nothing more. And that strange tingling sensation that shot through Carson every time Gabriella touched him? That had to be the result of his long drought.

"So, what are you doing here?" Carson asked the question he'd wanted answered since he'd entered the house. Now suspicion was replaced by curiosity.

She turned to her kids before answering. "Why don't the two of you go choose your rooms? Then we can make up the beds."

"Aren't you going to introduce me, Mommy?" the little girl asked, looking all kinds of offended.

"I'm sorry, sweetie." Gabriella held out her hand. When the little girl reached her, Gabriella dropped an affectionate arm around her shoulder and pulled the child close to her side. "This is my daughter, Sophia. And as you might have guessed, that is my son, Justin. This is Mr. Rivers."

Justin crossed the room and held out his hand, looking quite serious and mature. "It's very nice to meet you, sir."

Carson shook the boy's hand. "It's nice to meet you, too. And no need to call me sir. Just call me Carson."

The kids glanced at Gabriella for permission, which she gave with a slight nod. Apparently calling an adult by his first name was not something they ordinarily did.

"Go on upstairs," Gabriella repeated.

"Okay," Justin said as the kids raced from the room.

Gabriella didn't speak again until the sounds of the kids pounding up the stairs receded. Then she turned to him, and the smile that had lit her face faded. Her shoulders slumped, and the carefree air she'd had when the kids were present vanished. "Do you want to sit down?"

He shook his head. This wasn't a social visit and he wasn't planning on staying long. It had been a tiring day, and he was ready to get home, microwave a frozen meal and vegetate in front of the TV for a couple hours of mindless entertainment. Besides, it would be too easy to fall into the habit of spending time with her. And since as far as he knew she wasn't free, that would be a worse idea than getting involved with Raven had been. "What are you doing here, Gabriella?"

She inhaled and then blew out the breath. "I'm divorced. My ex-husband remarried and his new wife had a baby a few months ago. Now Reggie doesn't have time for Sophia and Justin. He cast them aside like… I don't know like what. They're beginning to feel the sting of his rejection. School is out for the summer so I thought a change of scenery might do us all some good. I loved spending time here when I was a kid and thought they might like it, too. And they won't have to listen to another one of their father's lame excuses about why he can't pick them up for their visit. If he even bothered to call at all."

Although she spoke in a matter-of-fact manner, he heard the pain in her voice. Maybe the kids weren't the only ones suffering from being replaced. Perhaps she hadn't wanted her marriage to end. Maybe Reggie's new wife and child were too much for Gabriella to bear.

Carson sympathized. But if that was the case, after the way his body had responded to a simple hug, he'd be wise to avoid her. He'd already traveled down that road with a woman who was in love with another man. There was no winning the heart of a woman if it wasn't available. He'd learned that lesson with Raven. Not that Gabriella had even hinted at any such thing. It was just good to plan in advance to avoid confusion in the future.

He glanced up. Gabriella was staring at him expectantly while awaiting his reply. "That makes sense. I'm surprised your aunt didn't mention your visit to me."

"It was a spur-of-the-moment decision. She was already on her vacation when I called her. Lucky for me, she still keeps the key to this place on her key chain so she sent it to me."

That explained it. Now that he knew that Gabriella had a right to be in the house, there was no reason for him to remain. They could discuss whether she wanted him to continue caring for the lawn another time. But his feet didn't move toward the door. Instead, he stood there staring at her, mesmerized by her beauty.

Time had been good to her. She'd been fifteen the last time he'd seen her. Though she'd shown promise of the beauty she had become, she'd been what his mother had referred to as a late bloomer. The tall willowy body she now possessed had been skin and bones back then. Since he hadn't been interested in her romantically, her looks hadn't mattered to him. It was only when the other boys pointed out her shortcomings that he'd realized others had viewed her as lacking. But then, he'd been a late bloomer himself and a target for bullies. If it hadn't been for Donovan Cordero's protection and Carson's father's wealth and power, life for Carson would have been torture.

He turned his thoughts back to the present. He was still standing in Mrs. Johnson—and now Gabriella's—kitchen.

"Okay," he said abruptly. "I'll get out of your hair so you and the kids can get settled."

Gabriella frowned and he realized he could have been more gracious. She had come a long way. If he read the situation right, for all intents and purposes, she and her kids were all alone. If he appeared unfriendly, she might not call on him if she needed help.

He pulled out his cell phone. "Let's exchange numbers. That way if you need anything you can give me a call."

She gave him a relieved smile and he knew he'd done the right thing. "Thanks."

Once he'd entered her phone number into his contacts and called her phone so she'd have his number too, he headed for the front door. She walked beside him.

"I'm glad to know that my best summertime friend is still around. Things will definitely be better now," Gabriella said as she opened the door for him.

He stepped onto the porch and quickly made his way to his pickup. If she thought having him around would make her life better, she was sadly mistaken. As the son of a murderer, he was the town pariah and the last person she and her kids needed in their lives.

Chapter Two

"Can we go outside for a little while?" Sophia used her best smile to try to wheedle a yes from Gabriella. Justin stood behind his sister, holding his breath, waiting for the answer.

Gabriella sighed. There was so much to do and they'd barely made a dent. After Carson had left last night, she and the kids had put clean linen on their beds. This was a five-bedroom house so there had been no arguing over rooms. Justin had wanted the room in the back, overlooking the huge yard. The room wasn't particularly big, in fact it was only a third the size of the room he had back home, but he liked the slanted ceiling and the hidden staircase that led directly to the kitchen. Sophia had chosen a sun-drenched room at the front of the house. She'd been enchanted by the padded window seat with storage beneath where she could keep her puzzles, books and dolls.

Although Aunt Mildred had told Gabriella to feel free to use the master bedroom, she'd chosen the room she'd used as a child. There was something comforting about sleeping in the same bed that she'd slept in when her life had been carefree. She knew she couldn't go back to that time, but she hoped the familiar surroundings would provide her with the peaceful slumber that had eluded her ever since Reggie had told her he no longer wanted to be married to her. And they had. For the first time in nearly two years, she'd slept without tossing or turning.

"Are your rooms clean?" The floors needed to be mopped and the area rugs could use a good vacuum.

The kids exchanged looks and then sighed in unison. Gabriella knew she should insist that they complete their chores before playing, but she was tired of being the disciplinarian. "Did you at least make up your beds?"

"Yes."

"All right. Don't wander off. We'll be going to town in a little while." They needed groceries if they were going to eat again today. This morning they'd polished off the takeout they'd gotten on the road. The kids hadn't minded having leftover chicken and mashed potatoes for dinner and again for breakfast, but Gabriella's stomach hadn't been pleased. She preferred to start her morning with sausage and eggs. Not to mention she really missed her morning cup of coffee.

"Thanks, Mom," Justin called over his shoulder. They raced out of the house as if they expected her to change her mind.

She nodded and headed for the screened-in back porch. The washer and dryer were in the far corner, hidden behind gray bifold doors. Last night she'd washed and dried the sheets that had been covering the furniture, but she'd been too tired to get the last load out of the dryer, so she did that now.

As Gabriella folded the laundry, she gazed out the window. The old willow tree that she used to climb was still there, looking as tempting as ever. Of course, her days of tree climbing had come and gone, but sitting in a chair in the shade of the tree, sipping on a cool glass of lemonade, was just her speed.

She put the stack of folded sheets into the linen closet and returned to the kitchen. She'd already cleaned the front room and the dining room. They'd eaten off paper plates last night and this morning, but she didn't intend to do that every day. Gabriella had brought pots, pans and dishes with her, so she unpacked the boxes and quickly washed everything. Aunt Mildred had left some dishes behind, taking only what she'd needed to her smaller place, so Gabriella washed them, too.

Smiling, Gabriella put away the last of the silverware. She hadn't accomplished everything on her extensive to-do list, but she'd done enough to make their stay comfortable. And really, what was the rush? They'd be here all summer. Brushing a hand over her hair, she went out the back door. As was the case at the front of the house, the flower beds were barren here, too. It was sad to see them standing empty.

As a child, she'd helped her aunt and uncle plant countless flats of annuals early each summer. Gabriella wondered if the nursery on the outskirts of town was still in business. If so, she'd stop there and buy some flowers, and she and the kids would plant them together. She'd always enjoyed digging in the dirt and then watching as the plants grew bigger and more beautiful with each passing day.

They employed a gardener back home, so Justin and Sophia hadn't had that opportunity. Not that Gabriella was complaining. Her children had had advantages that she'd never imagined she'd be able to give them. Her ex-husband was one of two children born to a successful television station owner. The Tucker family owned three hundred television stations in ninety markets across the country. Additionally, Reggie, his brother and parents owned a minority share of a professional football team. Her children had been born into a life of extreme privilege, and it had taken effort to keep them grounded and not let their paternal grandparents spoil them. Luckily Reggie had felt the same way, although his idea of what constituted a necessity and what was an extravagance differed from hers.

He'd been more than generous in the divorce settlement and she didn't have to worry about money. Their futures were financially secure. Yet no amount of money would alter the fact that he'd abandoned his kids and betrayed her.

She felt herself going down a dark path and ordered herself to snap out of it. The past was over and done. Nothing could change that or make Reggie love her.

Her children's laughter floated to her on the breeze and she paused. They were fine. Although she knew they were still hurt and confused by their father's rejection, they were happy in the moment. If she joined them now, she'd only make them sad, too. She had always kept her misery from them, but she didn't have the energy to put on a happy face now. So she'd sit on the back stairs until her mood improved. After all, the grocery store would be there twenty minutes from now.

She needed a moment to gather herself and regain control of her thoughts. She needed to stop thinking about her ex-husband. Reggie was living his best life with his new wife and baby. It was time for her to do the same. If only she knew what that life looked like.

"Hey!"

Carson looked up. Justin and Sophia were sitting on the top rail of the white fence surrounding his corral. He'd been hired to train a mare, something he enjoyed immensely. He'd been so involved in his task that he hadn't realized he had an audience. He had no idea how long they'd been watching him, but clearly it was long enough for them to make themselves at home.

He removed the hat from his head and wiped his damp forehead with the back of his arm. "Hey yourselves."

"What are you doing?" Justin asked.

"I'm training this horse. The owner wants her to be able to work with cattle. Right now I'm trying to get her used to having a saddle on her back. Then I'll get her used to having a rider. After that, I'll teach her how to follow commands."

"What's her name?" Sophia asked.

"Can I help?" Justin asked, before Carson could reply to Sophia's question.

"Her name is Summer Smoke," Carson replied

to the little girl, who smiled in return. "And no, thanks for the offer, but you can't help, Justin."

The boy looked disappointed and the light faded from his eyes. The expression on his face reminded Carson of how Gabriella's joy had slipped away last night, and Carson was filled with remorse. That didn't make sense. He wasn't responsible for the boy's pleasure. And training horses could be risky. Although Summer Smoke was a good horse, she and Carson were still getting to know each other. The mare could react unexpectedly and injure Justin. That would be pain the kid didn't need to endure and one more worry Gabriella didn't need. She already had enough on her plate.

Carson looked around. Where was she? He couldn't imagine that she'd allow her kids to wander over to his ranch alone on their first day here.

"Why not?" Justin asked.

This was so not the way he'd planned for his day to go. He'd gotten up early as usual and watched the sunrise while eating a bowl of cereal and a couple of pieces of buttered toast. He would have preferred something more substantial, but he wasn't a good cook. Probably because he hated cooking. In the good old days, before his father's crime was revealed, the Rivers family employed a cook/housekeeper. After everything became public, Gladys had retired and moved away. At his lowest, Carson wondered if her retirement had had less to do with living closer to her daughter and more to do with no longer feeling safe alone with him in this house. Perhaps she'd thought he was a criminal like his father. Some people did.

That was why he hadn't advertised for another housekeeper. He didn't want to have his suspicion confirmed.

"I don't want to take a chance on you getting hurt."

"I won't."

Carson really didn't want to have a long drawn out discussion with the kid, but it was too late for that. Justin wasn't going to be easily deterred. "Have you been around horses before? Do you know how to ride?"

Justin shook his head.

"That's why." Instead of feeling victorious for proving his point, Carson felt small. Guilty, which was ridiculous. The kids weren't his responsibility, and he was under no obligation to entertain them. "Where's your mom?"

"She's in the house," Sophia piped up. She swung her legs back and forth, hitting the fence rhythmically. "She was cleaning up, but we got tired of working and she said we could come outside and play for a while."

That sounded like a good plan. But how did they end up here?

"Do you have a lot of horses?" Justin asked.

"Yep."

"Are they already trained so people can ride them?"

"Yep."

"Then maybe you can teach me to ride one of them so I can help you train Summer Smoke."

Carson huffed out a laugh. He should have seen that coming, but instead he'd walked right into the trap. Carson was about to tell Justin that he no longer taught kids to ride, but the beseeching expression on the boy's face stopped him in his tracks. What had Gabriella said about their father? Their dad no longer spent time with them because he had a new baby with his new wife.

Carson didn't have to think hard to know how that kind of rejection felt. He and his father hadn't had a lot in common, yet Carson had still believed that his father loved him in his own way. Even been proud of him. That is, until he'd read his father's journals. Then he'd learned his father had considered him a loser. It had hurt to find out that he hadn't been the kind of son his father wanted. He'd wanted a son who was athletic with a magnetic personality. A son with a gift for gab and the ability to persuade people to follow him. A kid who was popular with the girls.

A son who was everything Carson wasn't.

Even so, it wasn't his job to make the kid's life right. He wasn't the one who'd blown it to smithereens. He sighed. What would it hurt to teach Justin how to ride? He might not owe the kid anything, but he could do it as a favor to his old friend. Gabriella didn't know it, but she'd been more than his summertime best friend. She'd been his best friend, period. He'd counted the days until she'd arrive in the summer and dreaded the day she'd leave.

"You'd have to ask your mom to be sure it's okay with her."

"Me, too?" Sophia asked. "You'll teach me, too?"

What had he gotten himself into? He liked being alone—or at least he'd gotten used to being on his own. Once he'd planned to be a stepfather. He and Elias, Raven's son, had begun to bond. That relationship had ended when Raven got back together with Elias's father. Of course, since Carson's father had been the reason Raven and Donovan had been apart, he couldn't blame them for reuniting and creating a new family. Sadly, his heart had been collateral damage. He wouldn't set himself up for that kind of hurt and disappointment again. If Gabriella agreed to the lessons, Justin and Sophia would simply be his students. Nothing more. Nothing less.

"Sure. But you need to ask your mom."

"I'll do that now," Justin said, scrambling down

from the fence with ease and then racing across the lawn.

Sophia twisted on the rail, struggling to get down on her own. Her sandaled foot slipped, and Carson watched in horror as she began tumbling to the ground. He jerked himself out of his stupor and grabbed her before she hit the dirt. He stood her on her feet and then checked her for scrapes or bruises.

When his eyes reached her face, she gave him a snaggletoothed grin. "That was close."

No kidding. And wasn't this what he'd been worried about? One of Gabriella's kids getting hurt on his ranch? They were city kids who had no idea how to act around animals. Even though he had taught kids from Sweet Briar how to ride, they lived near ranches and had some exposure to horses. Justin and Sophia had been born and raised in the city. But since they lived so close to him and obviously had no qualms about coming on to his land, teaching them how to ride was important.

"What's going on?"

Carson turned at the sound of Gabriella's voice. Justin had her by the hand, pulling her toward the fence. Despite the confused expression on her face, she looked absolutely beautiful. Carson had convinced himself that he'd exaggerated just how gorgeous she'd become, but if anything, he'd undersold it. She took his breath away.

"I told Mom you wanted to teach us how to ride horses, but she wanted to make sure you meant it. I guess she thinks I made it up."

Gabriella laughed, a sweet sound that warmed Carson's chilled heart.

He shook his head. "That's not exactly how things happened, but yes. I told the kids that I would teach them how to ride."

"Are you sure? I remember how busy the ranch gets in the summer."

"Mom," Justin said, unwilling to risk the possibility that Gabriella might talk Carson out of it. "He wants to teach us."

"That's right, Mommy," Sophia chimed in. She slipped her hand inside Carson's as if proving how close they'd become, and some of the ice around his heart melted. Oh, no. He wasn't going to allow this little girl to steal his heart.

"Well," Gabriella said, "we'll see."

"I really don't mind. In fact, if you're going to be here all summer, they should know how to ride. It'll give them something to do. And given the fact that my horses are nearby and can be a temptation to even the most well behaved kid, it would be good for them to have supervised access to the horses."

"Please, Mom," Justin said.

"Remember how much fun we used to have," Carson cajoled. Wait a minute. Was he really trying to convince Gabriella to agree? Apparently so. But everything he said was true. The kids really did need to know how to ride. And they would enjoy it. There were a couple of riding schools in the area, but he wouldn't trust anyone else with Gabriella's kids.

She seemed surprised by his argument, as if she'd expected him to try to wiggle out of his offer. "If you really don't mind, I'm all for it."

"Yay," Justin cheered, and started to climb over the fence. "What do we do first?"

"Not so fast there," Gabriella said. "We're going to town. We have to get groceries."

"Aw. Do we have to go to go with you?"

"Yes. Besides if you're going to be riding horses, you each need a pair of boots."

"Can I get a cowboy hat, too?" Justin asked.

"If we can find one."

"There's a Western shop in Sweet Briar," Carson volunteered. "They'll have hats."

"Do they have cowboy hats for girls?" Sophia asked. "Because I really want a pink one."

"Yep," Carson said. Something about the little girl warmed his heart. Perhaps because she was the spitting image of her mother. Just looking at Sophia brought back memories of the fun he and Gabriella used to have when they were Sophia's age.

"Thanks," Gabriella said. "Now let's get going.

And you, Sophia, need to get on this side of the fence."

Worried that the girl would slip while climbing, Carson picked her up and lowered her over the fence, then hopped over himself.

"So can we ride a horse when we get back from the store?" Justin asked.

Carson shook his head. He hated to disappoint the kid, but he did have work to do. There was a rancher in South Carolina who was paying him to train this horse. "How about Saturday?"

"That's two days away," the boy complained.

"The time will go fast," Gabriella said. "We have some work to do to get the house in shape."

Justin groaned and Carson had mercy on him. No kid wanted to do housework, especially on a nice summer day. "I won't have time for lessons until Saturday, but you can come over and get acquainted with the horses before then."

"Today?"

"Or tomorrow. Let's play it by ear."

Justin inhaled, and Carson had a feeling he was going to try to pin him down to a specific time when Gabriella interrupted. "We won't be able to meet the horses until we get the shopping and other chores done. If you stand here talking for much longer, the stores will be closed."

Justin's mouth slammed shut immediately.

"I'm ready now. Bye, Carson," Sophia said before turning and running across the grass. Justin waved before following her, leaving Carson alone with Gabriella.

"Look before you cross the road," Gabriella called to her children before she turned back and gave him a rueful smile. "Sorry about the intrusion. I didn't know they'd come over here. And I certainly didn't expect them to harass you into giving them riding lessons."

"Don't worry about it. I like your kids and I really don't mind."

"You aren't just saying that to make me feel better, are you?"

"Why would I do that?"

She shrugged, leaving him with questions he wouldn't ask now. They were still getting to know each other. Besides, he wasn't sure how close he wanted to get to her. "No reason. So what time do you want them here Saturday?"

He smiled. Justin and Sophia were so excited about riding they'd probably show up at the crack of dawn. He remembered being excited about something as a kid and how time seemed to crawl. "How about we say after breakfast? I get up early, so no matter when you show up I'll have been up for hours."

"You always were an early riser," she said slowly.

"And you preferred sleeping in. You loved the

nightlife," he joked. There was nothing remotely resembling nightlife in Sweet Briar and even less on the ranch.

"I still like to sleep late, although with two kids I don't get to do that much these days."

He didn't have anything to add so he simply stood there. The horse neighed, and Gabriella sighed and shook her head. "I'll let you get back to work. See you later."

"See you." Carson should have turned back to the horse, but instead he watched Gabriella cross the field to the road, her round hips swaying gently with each step. Once she was out of sight, he turned to get back to work.

She was his friend and off-limits. Besides, she was only here for the summer. And if recent history was anything to go by, she might not return for another fifteen years. Not only that, once the town gossips filled her in on his father's crimes, she might turn her back on him, too. Still, though his life was in shambles, he was glad his best friend had returned.

Chapter Three

Sweet Briar looked different than Gabriella remembered. The town had grown and appeared more prosperous than the last time she'd been here. When she was a kid, she, her aunt and uncle had come to town on the occasional Saturday afternoon to pick up items at the local five-and-dime. Afterward, they'd go to Mabel's Diner for an early dinner of burgers, fries and vanilla shakes. There'd been one or two other stores back then, but they'd appeared to be on their last legs. Clearly Sweet Briar had enjoyed a renaissance.

There were numerous shops lining the pristine streets, each of which appeared to be doing brisk business. Instead of deserted sidewalks, the town bustled with people. Baskets overflowing with colorful flowers and iron benches gave the small town a quaint appearance.

"It's so pretty," Sophia whispered. "It looks like a movie."

"It's all right," Justin said, obviously not impressed by the picturesque scene. "Do you see the boot and hat store? I want a black hat like Carson's."

Justin had been going on and on about riding lessons and how he was going to jump over the fence on his horse. Gabriella didn't want to burst his bubble by telling him the first lesson would probably consist of him being led around the corral on horseback. It had been so long since Justin had been this enthused about anything. True, he was dedicated to his swim practice and liked being on the team, but sometimes he appeared to swim more out of duty than fun.

"We should be able to find the color of hats you want," Gabriella said, hoping that was true.

"Can we go there first?"

Getting the hats and boots first seemed the practical thing to do. After all, she had no idea how long it would take for them to make up their minds. She didn't want to leave food in the car to possibly spoil. Besides, grocery shopping would be less stressful if they weren't rushing her.

"That sounds like a plan. All I have to do is find the store."

As she'd driven down the street, she'd noticed that there were very few free parking spots. When she spied an empty space, she pulled into it. She had no idea where they were going, but given the compact size of the town, they had to be within walking distance of the store.

Once she parked, the kids hopped from the car and leaped onto the sidewalk. They seemed delighted by the old-fashioned light pole by the curb, and each grabbed on by one hand, then swung around it several times. Luckily, in addition to the street signs, there were signs with names of the various shops and arrows beneath pointing the direction they should go. The Western wear store was one block away.

"Ready?" she asked the kids, and they instantly stopped circling the pole and ran over to her. Sophia took her hand and smiled at her. Justin had decided that holding his mom's hand wasn't cool, so he shoved his hands into the pockets of his cargo shorts just in case Gabriella tried to take his hand, too. She experienced a slight twinge of sorrow at her son's rejection.

"Which way?" Justin asked.

She pointed in front of her. "It should be on the next block."

Although it was a weekday morning, there were

many people about. Not enough to make the streets crowded, but sufficient people to make business owners happy. In one of their more recent conversations, Aunt Mildred had mentioned that the Sweet Briar mayor had created a two-pronged plan to revitalize the town. He'd worked hard to attract new businesses and to shore up existing ones. Then he'd begun to market the town as a year-round tourist destination. Cleary he'd been successful.

Despite all of the changes, Sweet Briar retained the friendly feeling she recalled from days gone by. They passed a barbershop where several older gentlemen watched as two others played a game of checkers. One player moved a piece, and the spectators groaned in unison. One of the men was smoking a cigar, and the pungent odor brought back memories of her uncle Bob. He hadn't been a regular smoker, but every once in a while he'd sit on the front porch swing and puff on a cigar.

They passed Mabel's Diner and Gabriella was pleased to see the old restaurant was still around. She couldn't wait to take the kids there for arguably the best burger and fries they would ever taste.

When they reached the Western wear shop, Justin hurried to open the door. Sophia released Gabriella's hand and ran the final few steps to the store, and they all stepped inside.

The smell of leather surrounded Gabriella, and

she immediately had no doubt that the products sold here were authentic and made to last. Clearly, some of the boots, hats and accessories were designed to appeal to vacationers who were shopping for souvenirs, but the majority of the items were geared toward the ranchers who lived in the area.

The store consisted of one large room divided into several departments. The front was decked out in pretty hats and boots, some of which had sequins and feathers. Sophia instantly gravitated toward the colorful hats, all of which were adult size and much too big for her small head.

A smiling middle-aged man approached them. "Hi. I'm Travis. How can I help you?"

"We need cowboy hats and boots," Justin said. "Real ones, though. Not like these."

"I like these," Sophia piped up, and Justin shook his head.

"I see. Are these to wear around town or to take back home as souvenirs?"

Clearly, the salesman thought they were tourists. And in a way, they were. They were only going to be here for the summer. But while they were in North Carolina, they were going to be living on a ranch. They weren't typical vacationers; nor were they locals. They were somewhere in between, not fitting in either category.

"We're staying on my aunt's ranch for the summer," Gabriella said. "They'll be doing some riding, so they'll need proper boots and hats."

He nodded. "And will you be riding, too?"

Although the notion appealed to her, Gabriella shook her head. She'd loved riding with Carson as a kid, racing across the vast acres of his ranch on sunny days without a care in the world. But those days, as wonderful as they'd been, were over now. Now she was a mother with kids to raise. More than that, she needed to come up with a plan for the rest of her life. She couldn't do that by trying to relive her youth. Besides, Carson's offer had been limited to teaching her kids and hadn't included her.

"Why not?" Sophia asked. "It's going to be fun."

"And you said you used to ride horses with Carson when you were a kid," Justin added. "If you forgot how, I'm sure he'll teach you, too."

"Are you talking about Carson Rivers?" asked a man who looked a little bit older than Gabriella. He'd been trying on boots and obviously listening to their conversation. Now he dropped the new boots into the box. Eyes narrowed, he frowned and his face and neck turned beet red.

"That's right," Gabriella said. "He's a neighbor and a friend."

"And he's going to teach us how to ride horses," Sophia added.

The man shoved his feet into well-worn boots, grabbed the box and then stood. He looked pointedly at Gabriella. "Nice kids you have there. If I were you, I'd be careful who I let them be around. Not everyone can be trusted."

"Don't start that again, Rusty," Travis warned. "You know you can't judge him by his father's actions."

"The apple don't fall far from the tree."

The salesman grunted and his eyes turned stony. The smile he'd shown to Gabriella and her kids had been replaced with a hard look. He pointed at the box in Rusty's hands. "Do you want anything besides those boots?"

Rusty glared, apparently annoyed at being shut down. "No. This is all."

"Then let's get you checked out." Travis took Rusty's box, walked to the front of the store and set the box in front of a young cashier.

Rusty walked over to Gabriella. "Remember what I said. Don't trust him." His final warning issued, he went to the cash register and slapped his credit card down on the counter.

The cashier rung up the sale with impressive speed. Even so, Gabriella didn't move a muscle until Rusty had left the store, slamming the glass door behind him. Then she blew out a pent-up breath.

"Ignore Rusty," Travis said. "He's a bitter man,

disappointed that life didn't work out the way he wanted it to. Of course, his own actions played a major part in that."

Gabriella nodded. The entire conversation confused her. Why had the man spoken so badly about Carson? And what had Carson's father done? Gabriella hadn't known Karl Rivers well, but he'd been nice enough to her whenever she'd come over to hang out with Carson.

"I don't like that man," Justin said.

"Me, either," Sophia added. "He's mean."

"Our children's section is in the back," Travis said, as if trying to put an end to the uncomfortable moment and bring the focus back to the reason they'd come to the store in the first place.

Gabriella and her children followed him to the smaller room. In addition to boots and hats, there were jeans, shirts, belts, jewelry and buckles in a wide array of styles. The boys and girls sections were separated by a row of chairs. Justin picked up a black hat that was a miniature version of the one Carson wore, and Sophia made a beeline for the earrings. She quickly picked up a silver pair shaped like horses and held them up to her ears. "Aren't these pretty, Mommy?"

"They are, indeed."

Sophia had gotten her ears pierced this past Christmas. Ever since then, she'd been enamored of earrings. She spent several minutes each night before bed selecting the ones she wanted to wear the next day.

"Do you suppose I could have them?"

Gabriella nodded. Although they weren't necessarily shopping for souvenirs, the earrings were pretty and would give Sophia a happy reminder of days spent on the ranch. As an added bonus, she'd actually get some use out of them, unlike most souvenirs from vacations past that had become dust magnets. "I'll hold them while you try on boots and hats."

Justin had placed a hat on his head and was standing in front of a rack of boots. He frowned at the dark brown boots he held in his hands. "I want some like Carson's, but they don't have any in the right color."

Gabriella studied the options and then pulled out a pair of tan boots. "They were like these."

"Those are too light," Justin countered. "His were darker."

"Trust me, they started out this color. That was a lot of dirt and other things on his boots."

"Are you sure?"

"Yep." Gabriella didn't want to think too hard about how she'd noticed what color boots Carson was wearing that morning. Truth be told, she'd been aware of everything about him, from the faded gray T-shirt with long sleeves pushed up to his elbows that had a slight tear near the collar, to the well-worn denims that showcased his muscular thighs. She'd always thought Carson was handsome—if a little on the skinny side—though she'd never been attracted to him when they were younger. When it came to Carson, romance had never crossed her mind. He'd been like the brother she'd never had.

Now, though, feelings she'd never imagined she'd have for Carson were starting to take root inside her. That was unacceptable. She needed to get rid of them before they began to sprout. She was only here for the summer, so there was no way a relationship between them could ever work. More importantly, she wasn't ready to trust her heart with any man. Even Carson.

Oh sure, as a boy, Carson had been completely honorable. She'd never met anyone with quite as much integrity as he had. If he said he was going to be somewhere at a certain time, he'd be there, no matter what. If he promised to do something, he did it. Although time and experience changed people, she didn't believe they had the ability to alter a person's true nature. A good person remained good no matter the trials life threw at him.

But she could be wrong. After all, Reggie had once appeared to be an honest man, vowing to forsake all others for her. That hadn't happened. Once the woman he'd actually loved for his entire life was free to marry him, those words had proved empty. He'd left Gabriella behind without a second thought. If he'd been forthcoming about why he'd proposed to her in the first place, Gabriella would have been able to make an informed decision. She never would have married him if she'd known he was truly in love with someone else. Which, no doubt, was why he'd kept that information to himself.

She shoved the troubling thoughts out of her mind. She'd never be able to move forward with her life if she kept reliving the past. And more than anything else, she needed to get on with her life. She shifted focus back to the gear she'd come to buy for her kids.

After thirty minutes of trying on boots and debating the perfect shade of pink for Sophia's hat, they finally made their selections. Predictably, although they'd brought jeans with them to Sweet Briar, the kids wanted real cowboy and cowgirl jeans. They'd convinced Gabriela to buy a pair of boots for herself, but she'd drawn the line at a hat or jeans. Although she didn't intend to ride a horse, the gray boots she'd tried on had been too cute to leave behind.

Once they gathered their gear, they took everything to the checkout. The cashier smiled at Sophia and Justin, then met Gabriella's eyes. "Remember, don't pay any attention to what Rusty said about Carson. Carson is a nice guy. One of the best around. It's a shame that a few small-minded people want to ruin a good man's reputation."

The cashier's comment reminded Gabriella of the earlier incident. She'd been busy with her kids and had put the whole thing behind her. She wondered just what was going on, but she didn't ask. She didn't want to gossip. Carson deserved better than that. If there was something he wanted her to know, he'd tell her.

"I'll keep that in mind," Gabriella said as she and the kids grabbed their purchases and left.

After the events at the Western wear shop, the rest of their shopping trip was blessedly uneventful. The grocery store wasn't as big as the warehouse club back home where she held a membership, but it carried a surprisingly wide variety of items. And if it wasn't on the shelves, the manager said she could order anything Gabriella wanted. That was good to know even though she doubted she'd do it.

While Gabriella enjoyed fancy meals and possessed an adventurous palate, the kids preferred simple foods. They'd happily live on macaroni and cheese and bologna sandwiches if she'd let them. Since it was just the three of them, she imagined they'd be eating the same simple meals here that they ate at home.

Once they were inside the vehicle, Gabriella decided to drive around the town to see just how much it had changed in her absence. After fifteen or so minutes, she came upon a three-story brick building with a dynamic mural painted on the outside. A prominent sign welcomed them to the Rachel Shields Youth Center. About thirty children were playing in a fenced-in playground on the side of the building while adults supervised.

"What's this place?" Justin asked, leaning out the window for a better look.

"It's a youth center."

"Do you think we can come and play here one day?" Sophia asked.

"I don't know. I'll ask Carson about it later," Gabriella said as she drove away. It would be nice to find a place where Sophia and Justin could make new friends while they were here. They generally got along well with each other—Justin's recent behavior notwithstanding—but they needed friends. Gabriella hoped that some of the nearby ranch families had kids around their age, but if they didn't, the youth center would be a nice alternative.

Satisfied that she'd gotten a good feel for the town, Gabriella headed for the highway and home. Traffic was light and before long she was pulling into her driveway. She glanced across the road to Carson's place, hoping to catch a glimpse of him, but he was nowhere in sight. Telling herself that wasn't disappointment she felt, she opened the back of the SUV so she and the kids could unload the groceries.

It took several trips between the kitchen and the car, but eventually all of the bags were inside, covering the table, the limited counter space and the floor. As expected, the kids toed off their gym shoes and immediately put on their boots. The salesman had suggested that they break them in. Not that they needed encouragement. They'd be clomping around the house in them for the foreseeable future.

Although a lot of groceries had to be to put away, once they put the cold food into the refrigerator, Gabriella told the kids to drop their jeans in the laundry room and then go outside to play. If they helped put the food away, she'd never be able to find it. Better to do it alone now and save time later when she wanted to cook.

The kids dashed out the back door and into the yard. Their happy laughter filled her with unspeakable joy. Reggie might have lost interest in them, but they still had each other. The three of them were their own little family.

Once the groceries were put away, she went and sat on the back porch. The breeze wafted through the screens, cooling her skin. Early evening was her favorite time of day. The sun was low in the sky, so it wasn't quite dusk, and there was the promise of a beautiful starlit night. But as much as she was enjoying the quiet, she couldn't sit here much longer. Any minute now the kids would be hungry and cranky.

She went into the kitchen and whipped up a quick meal. Once dinner was ready, she called the kids in to wash their hands. Although she didn't like the kids wearing shoes in the house, she gave them a pass with their new boots. They were still so excited about what the boots represented—horseback riding—that she didn't want to steal their joy. Besides, she had to mop the floor after the kids had gone to bed anyway. Given the way they were drooping now, that wouldn't be long.

While they ate, the kids told her about their day as if she hadn't been there with them the entire time. As they swallowed their pork chops, rice and steamed broccoli, they began to pepper her with questions about her childhood and her summers spent here. After she'd told them a few stories, they asked why they hadn't been allowed to stay with Aunt Mildred like she'd been.

That was the sixty-four-million-dollar question. Though her former in-laws were basically good people who'd welcomed her with open arms, they could be snobs at times. To them, summers were to be spent at their Martha's Vineyard compound, not on a dusty ranch in North Carolina. That was the way they'd raised Reggie and his younger brother, and they'd wanted the same for their only grandchildren. And Reggie had always agreed with them. The one time Gabriella had gone to her parents for backup, they'd sided with Reggie and his family. Gabriella's parents had been happy that she had married into money and that her future was assured, and they hadn't wanted her rocking the boat. She'd been young and foolish back then, and rather than cause a rift she'd gone along with the program.

Well, her future hadn't turned out the way she'd hoped it would. Still, one good thing had resulted from her divorce. Her kids would get to enjoy a carefree summer in North Carolina just like she had growing up. Of course, most of the ranch was gone, Aunt Mildred having sold the bulk of her land to her neighbor a few years ago. But there was still plenty of space for the kids to run around.

As Gabriella regaled them with tales of her childhood, she realized just how many of her stories included Carson. They'd had the best times together. She wondered if he'd be interested in making more memories with her this summer.

She didn't know much about his life now. She hadn't noticed a ring and he hadn't mentioned a wife. There hadn't been any evidence of a Mrs. Carson Rivers when she'd been at the ranch. But even if he wasn't married, that didn't mean there wasn't a special woman in his life. Carson was a great catch. He was kind, honest, loyal and gorgeous. Surely the women in town and on the nearby ranches had noticed that. He probably had women chasing after him day and night like it was their job.

A strange emotion that felt suspiciously like jealousy churned her stomach, and she quickly squashed it. She wasn't looking for romance, or even a short-time affair, which was all they could have since she and the kids were returning to Ohio at summer's end. There was no sense in starting something that had an expiration date. If she decided to fall in love again, and that was a big *if*, it would have to be with someone who lived in Ohio, where she and the kids had made their lives. Justin and Sophia had already endured too much upheaval and she wouldn't add to it. This was simply a break from reality. A much-needed vacation.

After dinner, the kids put their dishes in the sink, then went upstairs to take their baths. When they were done, they snuggled together in Sophia's bed and Gabriella read them a story. Story time was something she'd started when the children were little, and they all enjoyed it. Every once in a while Justin tried to back out saying he was too big, but tonight he joined in happily. Sophia conked out just as Gabriella read the last word, and Justin's head was bobbing.

Gabriella tried to pick him up and carry him to his bed, but he pulled away.

"I'm a big boy. I can walk." He pushed to his feet and wobbled.

"Okay." She stood beside him, steadying him, and then steered him to his bedroom and into his bed. He was snoring softly as she covered him with the thin blanket. She watched him sleep for a moment before heading back to the kitchen, where she mopped the floor. When that was done, she went and sat on the front porch.

The night was country dark. With no streetlights, the only illumination came from the moon and stars overhead and the sliver of light from the lamp in the front room that peeked through the sheer curtains.

"Hey. I'm surprised you're still awake." Gabriella smiled at the sound of Carson's voice. She'd been drifting away on dreams and hadn't noticed him crossing the darkened road and walking up the driveway. Now, though, she made out his muscular body. He jogged the rest of the way to the house and stood at the bottom of the steps, his hand on the rail. "You want some company?"

She smiled. "I'd love some."

He climbed the stairs and then sat beside her on the porch swing, setting it into motion. "I thought I'd have to throw rocks at your window, but I didn't know which room you were sleeping in."

"I'm using the same one."

"That's good to know. I wouldn't want to wake up one of the kids by mistake."

"I appreciate that. But I'm the adult now, so I don't need to sneak outside any longer."

"Also good to know."

They sat in companionable silence for a few minutes, the only sound the chirping of the crickets and the occasional hoot of an owl. A feeling of rightness swept through Gabriella. She didn't poke and probe it to try to figure out why she felt that way; rather, she simply accepted it.

It was as if the years hadn't passed and they were picking up where they'd left off. That wasn't true, of course. Fifteen years had passed. Fifteen years of living. If they were going to be friends, she needed to know a few basic things about his life, such as his marital status. "You know I'm divorced. What about you? Is there a Mrs. Carson Rivers? Or someone hoping to gain the title?"

"Nope."

Though it was only one quietly spoken word, it created conflicting emotions inside Gabriella. On the one hand, she felt bad that her friend hadn't found love. On the other, she was glad that his heart was still free. But that seemed selfish and guilt churned her stomach. She should want Carson to find true love. And she did. She was just glad that he was available to spend time with her this summer.

That is, if he was interested in renewing their friendship. Only time would tell that.

Chapter Four

"Hurry up, Mom," Justin said, urging Gabriella to walk faster. He and Sophia had been awake since six o'clock, something that was nothing short of a miracle. During the school year, Gabriella had needed to be Mean Mom in order to get them up on time. Even then, they'd dragged through breakfast and hadn't perked up until they were sitting in the parent drop-off line at their private school. But when she'd stepped into the living room this morning, the kids had looked at her with bright smiles and eager eyes.

They'd wanted to go over to Carson's ranch the minute they swallowed their bacon, eggs and grits, but she made them cool their heels until seven thirty. Carson might be an early riser, but he couldn't possibly want to deal with two boisterous children this early in the day.

"I'm coming." She couldn't help but smile. The kids looked so cute. Dressed in their new jeans, boots and hats, they could have passed for miniature ranchers. She made them hold still while she took several pictures of them. She'd email copies to her aunt and her parents later. Although Reggie didn't deserve them, she'd send him copies, too. After all, he was their father, and she knew how valuable that relationship was even if he'd temporarily forgotten.

They crossed the road together and started down Carson's driveway. When they spotted him in the distance, Sophia and Tucker took off running. Gabriella chose to follow at a more leisurely pace, taking her time to study Carson. Dressed in jeans that fit his muscular butt just perfectly, and a pinegreen T-shirt advertising the local feed and grain that hugged his barrel chest and six-pack abs, he looked better than a man had the right to look.

When Gabriella had been married to Reggie, her social obligations had included countless white-tie and black-tie events. She had become accustomed to seeing men dressed in tailored tuxedoes. None of them had looked anywhere near as good as Carson did in his casual clothes. He didn't have an inch of fat on his over-six-foot frame. He was all sexy, lean muscle. Deciding there was nothing wrong with looking as long as she didn't take it any further, she let herself enjoy the view.

The kids were chattering a mile a minute and Carson laughed at something Justin said. The sound of his deep baritone voice reached inside her and her heart skipped a beat. Her skin tingled and goosebumps popped out on her arms. Oh, that was trouble. Friendship was good and desirable. Even admiring his sexy body and gorgeous face was acceptable. But she wasn't supposed to be attracted to him. That could lead down a very dangerous road. At least for her. Unrestrained attraction could easily turn into desire and, if she wasn't careful, love. She wasn't willing to risk having her heart broken yet again.

"Good morning," Carson said as she closed the distance between them. He touched the brim of his ever-present black hat and smiled. A deep dimple flashed in his left cheek, and his dark brown eyes sparkled with mischief, sending blood racing through her veins. Apparently, her good sense had sailed up to the sky and was hiding behind one of the puffy white clouds scattered across the mostly blue sky. He was just too charming and sexy for her to resist.

"Good morning," she replied, pleased that she sounded natural. If her common sense and body were conspiring against her, it was comforting to know her voice was still on her side. "I hope we're not too early."

"You're right on time."

"See, we told you. Mom was trying to make us wait even longer," Justin complained.

"We've been ready for hours," Sophia added.

"Well, I won't make you wait a minute longer," Carson said. "Let's meet the horses."

Sophia and Justin skipped along beside Carson, leaving Gabriella to trail behind them. When they reached the corral she noticed that four horses were inside. Each had been saddled, and they were now standing around nibbling on the green grass.

"I want to ride the big black one," Justin said.

Carson laughed. "Sorry. Excalibur is my horse. I'm the only one who gets to ride him."

"Okay. Which horse can I ride?"

"You'll be riding Peanut Butter. Can you guess which one that is?"

Justin laughed. "The kind of brown one?"

"Yep."

"He is the same color as peanut butter."

"I thought so when I named him," Carson agreed.

"Which one will I be riding?" Sophia asked.

"You'll be riding Angel. That should suit you since you have an angel face."

Sophia beamed at the compliment, ignoring her brother's groan. "What's Mommy's horse's name?"

"I'm not dressed for riding," Gabriella said quickly. "I'm just going to watch."

"We told you to wear your boots and jeans," Sophia said, slipping into little mama mode.

"You look fine to me," Carson said, his eyes sweeping from her toes to her head. She was wearing a pair of cutoff denim shorts and a cropped T-shirt she'd bought in a moment of rebellion. As a member of the upper-class Tucker family and wife of the oldest son, it had been incumbent upon her to be dressed appropriately at all times. Cutoffs and other revealing clothes had been forbidden. Of course she'd been unceremoniously dumped, and the role of Mrs. Reginald Tucker was now being played by Natalie Carter-Tucker, so Gabriella was free to wear whatever she chose.

"I'm not dressed to sit on a horse." That wasn't entirely true. She'd worn shorts many times when she and Carson had gone riding, especially when they'd ridden to the swimming hole. It had been too hard to pull her jeans over her damp skin after a day spent in the water, so she'd worn her bikini under her cutoffs and T-shirt.

"Well, if you change your mind, Beauty will be waiting for you."

"Is Beauty the name of Mommy's horse?" Sophia asked.

Carson nodded and his eyes bored into Gabriella's. "It fits. Don't you think?"

Gabriella's cheeks warmed under Carson's stare, and her toes curled in her gym shoes. Did he think she was beautiful?

Sophia nodded. "Mommy's the most beautiful mom in the whole wide world."

"Can we get on now?" Justin asked, clearly bored by the conversation.

Carson broke eye contact with Gabriella and turned his attention to her son. "In a minute. We'll meet the horses first and go over a few safety guidelines. Riding won't be fun if you get hurt."

"We'll be real careful," Justin promised, and Sophia nodded in agreement.

"I'm sure you will. Now the first thing we have to do is take off those hats and put on helmets."

"What?" Justin squawked. "But I want to be a real cowboy like you."

"Well, being a cowboy is more than wearing a hat. It's more a code of behavior."

"A what?"

Carson grinned and Gabriella's heart lurched. He was so magnetic. She couldn't believe a woman hadn't already swooped in and claimed him. There had to be something wrong with the women in this town.

"It means treating everyone fairly. You know, like not taking advantage of a younger kid. It means helping people who are in need. Being honest and keeping your word. That's the cowboy code."

"Is it the cowgirl code, too?" Sophia asked.

"Absolutely." Carson gestured to the hat on Justin's head.

Justin sighed, reluctantly removed his hat and handed it to Gabriella for safekeeping. Sophia did the same. Carson grabbed two black helmets from the top rail of the fence surrounding the corral and handed one to each of them. After they'd strapped them beneath their chins, Carson checked to be sure that they'd fastened them securely before nodding in approval.

He opened the gate, stepped inside and held it for them. After the children had stepped inside, Carson glanced at Gabriella. "Last chance."

She smiled and shook her head. "I'm the keeper of the hats."

"Okay. Feel free to set them anywhere and join us if you like."

"No, thanks. I'll just watch."

"Suit yourself."

Carson led the kids to the horses, his long-legged stride loose and relaxed. He looked just as good from behind as he had from the front. The wind carried his baritone to her, but he wasn't talking loudly enough for her to make out his words. Gabriella climbed on the fence and sat on the top rail. She'd spent many summer days on this ranch, sitting beside Carson and watching as his father trained horses. Back then, they'd sit for hours without speaking, barely moving, awed by the power of the beautiful animals and his father's skill. Now she found herself once more in awe, this time of Carson.

He instructed each child on how to tighten the girth, guiding their hands as he made slight adjustments to be sure it had been done correctly. Next, he helped Justin mount his horse, then measured the stirrups to his ankles.

Fascinated by what she was seeing but wanting to listen as well, Gabriella jumped down and circled the fence until she was close enough to hear. She didn't climb on again, choosing instead to lean against the rail, her arms stretched across the top, her chin on her forearms.

"Lean over and touch your left foot with your right hand," Carson said. Laughing, Justin did. "Good. Now stretch out your right foot." When her son complied, Carson made slight adjustments to the right stirrup.

Once Justin was set, Carson went through the same procedure with Sophia, who followed his instructions to the letter. Carson then had them lean forward in the proper riding form.

"You guys are naturals," Carson said, earning broad smiles from them. Gabriella found herself smiling as well. "Grab hold of the reins. Not too tight."

The kids picked up the leather straps and then sat there, eagerly awaiting their next instructions.

Carson picked up the leads and held out one to Gabriella. "Since you're not going to ride, you might as well make yourself useful."

Gabriella pushed away from fence and climbed over. Carson's eyes never left her, and she wondered what had possessed her to wear this outfit. It hadn't felt too revealing in the privacy of her bedroom. Now, though, she wanted to tug the denim shorts lower and cover her thighs. Since she couldn't change clothes and pulling on her shorts would only draw attention to her, she simply lifted her chin and strutted over to where Carson awaited.

As she took the lead to Sophia's horse, her hand brushed Carson's and she felt a jolt of electricity. He must have felt the same shock because he sucked in a breath. He released his hold on the lead and turned his focus to the space in front of them. "Take it slow."

That sounded like good advice for her unruly emotions. Unsure if she would be able to speak normally, Gabriella only nodded. Carson made a clicking sound and tugged on the lead. Justin let out a whoop as his horse began to walk. Gabriella pulled on Sophia's horse and Angel began walking, too.

Sophia giggled. "I'm riding a horse, Mommy."

"Yes, you are. Are you having fun?"

"Yes. You should be riding, too. Then you could be having fun."

"I'm having a great time," Gabriella replied honestly. As a mother, if her kids were happy, she was happy. But the pleasure filling her was more than a result of knowing her children were having the time of their lives. It was being outside on such a beautiful day. It was the sunshine warming her skin, managing to touch her soul. It was the breeze that stirred the trees and grass, perfuming the air with a sweet summer fragrance.

But mostly, it was Carson. Being close to him revived feelings she'd believed died with Reggie's betrayal. There was something so calming about Carson. So comforting. It came from knowing that he truly lived by the cowboy code. He didn't lie or cheat. Didn't deceive or mislead. He treated everyone fairly and with kindness. As a woman who'd been lied to and cheated on, betrayed by the one person she should have been able to trust, she appreciated those qualities now more than ever.

"How are you two feeling?" Carson asked after they'd walked around the corral once, his voice breaking into her musings. And not a moment too soon. She didn't need to start thinking of him as some perfect man. He had his flaws. Everyone did.

"Great," Justin said.

"Me, too," Sophia replied.

"Good. Let's walk a little bit faster." He picked up the pace, but not so much that Gabriella had difficulty matching his stride.

They walked around the corral twice more before coming to a stop. "Okay. That's enough for today."

"Can't we ride a little longer?" Justin asked. "I'm not tired."

"Trust me, forty-five minutes is plenty of time. You don't want to end up sore."

"Okay. When can we ride again?"

"Maybe in a couple of days. We'll see how you feel tomorrow."

Carson instructed them on how to dismount, then stood by, ready to assist if they needed help. When they were back standing on the ground, Justin rubbed his horse's neck. "Bye, Peanut Butter."

"Why are you saying bye?" Carson asked. "There's more to riding horses than what you've done. You need to take care of your horse."

"How do we do that?" Sophia asked.

"You mean we get to hang around here longer?" Justin asked, his eyes brightening.

"I'll show you," Carson replied to Sophia before turning to Justin. "And yes, you get to hang around longer."

He handed each child the lead rope for their horse and then grabbed the leads for the other two animals. He gave one to Gabriella and kept the other for himself. They led the horses into the stables, where Carson showed the children how to remove the saddles. Neither Sophia nor Justin was strong enough to lift the saddles on their own, so Carson provided the necessary assistance. Gabriella was distracted by the way Carson's muscles bulged beneath his cotton shirt and she nearly dropped Beauty's saddle.

He glanced up, caught her staring and lifted his eyebrows. Although she felt her cheeks heating and knew her face was decidedly redder, Gabriella held his gaze. It couldn't possibly be the first time he'd noticed a woman gawking at him. Looking like he did, he had to be used to it by now. Gabriella turned her attention back to her task. Once they'd put the saddles and blankets away, Carson showed the kids how to brush their horses. The kids tackled the chore with enthusiasm, and Gabriella had a feeling the horses were about to get the brushing of a lifetime.

Carson sidled up to her. "Your kids really are great."

"Thanks. And thank you for spending so much time with them. Riding horses has been the highlight of their year." In truth, it had probably been the highlight of their past two years.

Reggie had done a number on them when he'd moved out. Gabriella hadn't been the only one taken by surprise when he'd announced he wanted a divorce. The kids had been shocked and cried when he'd left, asking over and over what they'd done wrong. It had to be something terrible if their daddy no longer wanted to live with them. Gabriella had done her best to assure them that they weren't at fault, but she'd been reeling herself, so no doubt she hadn't been very convincing. But since she'd been asking herself the same questions, she'd understood where they'd been coming from.

It was only when Reggie had admitted that he'd never loved her that she'd stopped wondering what she could have done differently. In that moment she'd stopped hoping for a reconciliation. She wouldn't waste her love on someone who'd never loved her. Her kids had been brokenhearted and she'd focused on healing them. In moments like these, when they were so happy, she felt like she had made some progress.

"I've had a good time myself. It's been a while since I taught riding lessons."

"You gave lessons?"

He nodded.

"No wonder you're so good at it." She glanced at her kids. They were brushing the horses inch by inch. Justin's brow was furrowed in concentration and Sophia was nibbling her bottom lip, a sign that she was completely involved in her task.

"Would you be interested in giving my kids regular lessons?"

"I don't know."

"I'll pay you, of course."

He looked shocked and slightly offended, which surprised her. "I don't want your money, Gabriella."

"Did you charge other people?"

"Of course. It was a school."

"Then you can charge me, too. I have money."

"We're friends."

"Exactly. Friends don't take advantage of each other."

"The thing is, I'm not sure about restarting lessons. I'd gotten away from it. Let's keep it casual for the time being. That way I can discover if I want to get back into teaching, and Sophia and Justin can discover if they really want to learn to ride. The novelty might wear off. Or they might decide that taking care of horses is too much work."

She thought for a second. "That makes sense."

"I'm glad you agree." He playfully poked her shoulder. "I'd hate to have to tickle you until you saw things my way."

"You wouldn't dare."

When they'd been kids, Carson had been incredibly ticklish. They'd never argued, but on the rare occasion when she hadn't been able to get him to go along with her plans, she would tickle him into submission. It was only after he'd discovered that she was even more ticklish than he was that he'd had a chance of getting his way.

Grinning devilishly, he wiggled his fingers and took a step in her direction.

She knew that look all too well. Letting out a squeal, she ducked under his arm and then ran for the relative safety her kids provided. Laughing and calling her a chicken, Carson followed.

Carson inspected the horses and then looked at the kids. "I don't think they've ever been brushed this well before. Good job."

"It was fun," Sophia said.

"We can do it every day if you need us to," Justin said. "We can brush all of your horses. Plus, we know how to do lots of other stuff, too."

Gabriella's heart pinched at her son's eagerness. He longed for a man's attention. Clearly he hoped Carson would fill the hole Reggie's absence had created.

"I'll keep that in mind." Carson led the horses to their stalls. Justin and Sophia were right behind him, never taking their eyes off him for a moment. When he checked the horses' hooves for rocks, they were standing so close that Gabriella worried they might get injured if the animal made a sudden move.

"So what are we going to do now?" Justin asked, once the horses were secure and everyone was standing outside in the sunshine once more. Apparently, he planned to make a day of it.

"We're going home so Carson can get to work," Gabriella announced. She didn't want Carson to think they intended to monopolize his time. It might be Saturday, but she knew work on the ranch didn't stop for the weekend.

"Aw," Sophia and Justin moaned in unison. "But we're having fun."

"You can still have fun. You're just going to have to do it at home. Now say thank you."

"Thanks, Carson," they replied dutifully. They looked mournful, but Gabriella held her ground. She didn't want to overstay their welcome.

"You're welcome," Carson replied. He glanced at their sad faces and then continued, "If you're not too busy tomorrow, you can come over and ride again."

"We're not too busy," Justin said.

"Then I'll see you all tomorrow."

"Tomorrow," Gabriella echoed, feeling as hopeful as Justin and Sophia. Though she tried not to read too much into his offer, the word held such promise.

The decision to come to Sweet Briar was looking better by the minute.

Carson stood still, watching as Gabriella and her kids walked home. He didn't look away until he could no longer see them.

Why had he invited them to come back to-morrow? Hadn't he decided that he wasn't going to involve anyone else in his life? But there was something about Gabriella and her kids that he couldn't resist. Today he'd felt happier than he'd been in a long time. Gabriella was just as easy to be around now as when they'd been kids. He'd come to grips with being all alone and had accepted that he was going to live the rest of his life that way. But being with Gabriella had him reconsidering. Maybe he wouldn't have to live a solitary life. At least not this summer.

It wasn't just losing Raven, since she hadn't really been his to begin with. Even when he'd proposed to her, he'd known that her heart belonged to another. But Donovan had disappeared years before and hadn't been heard from. Carson had been convinced that once they married Raven would come to love him. Then Donovan returned, only days after Carson's father had died. Once the truth was out, it was only a matter of time before Donovan and Raven had reconciled.

Carson had been hurt at the time, but once it had become common knowledge that his father was a murderer, he'd had other things to worry about. Carson had become a pariah. Or so it seemed to him. His friends had stood by him. But even if only a handful of people had decided he was persona non grata, that had been enough to make him rule out bringing a woman into his life to share in his ostracism. That had been true then and it was still true now. Especially a woman with kids. They didn't need to endure the pain that would come from being associated with him.

He accepted that intellectually, but, judging from the way his body reacted whenever Gabriella came near and the warmth that filled him just thinking of her, his heart hadn't gotten the message.

Carson shook himself. Gabriella hadn't expressed an interest in being anything other than friends. Hell, she'd even wanted to pay him to teach her kids to ride, as if he were nothing more to her than an employee. But he couldn't focus on that now. He had jobs that needed to be completed before sunset. He intended to work so hard that the sound of Gabriella's laughter, the sight of her smile, the feel of her hand beneath his and her sweet scent were no longer even distant memories. With any luck, that would kill the intense longing she'd awakened in him.

If not, he was in for a long summer.

Chapter Five

The next two weeks passed quickly. The kids were enjoying their time in North Carolina, especially the time they spent with Carson and his horses. They were still as thrilled to learn to ride as they'd said they would be.

When it became clear that the children were committed, Carson scheduled their lessons for midmorning several days a week. Gabriella had no doubt that he was interrupting his regular activities, but since he didn't complain she wouldn't mention it. After the first few lessons, the kids were able to guide their horses without assistance. As a precaution, Carson walked between them.

Justin hadn't mentioned missing swim practice once. He was too busy learning how to ride or taking care of Peanut Butter. After the first day, he'd asked to give his horse water and lay hay in the stall. Carson had employees whose job it was to do that, but Justin had been so enthusiastic that Carson had let him do it. Not wanting to be left behind, Sophia took on the extra chores, too. Her kids were turning into ranch kids, right before her eyes.

Today she was sitting in her usual spot on the top rail where she could see everything without being a distraction. She'd dressed in jeans, a cotton shirt and her new boots. It looked like she was turning into a ranch mom, too. After they'd made one circuit, Carson called over to her, "I'm going to ride beside the kids now. Do you want to give Beauty a try?"

She hopped down from the fence, and joined him and the kids. Riding sounded more fun than watching. Truthfully, she'd been aching to ride. "Why not?"

"Give me a minute." He disappeared into the barn and returned with two saddles. He quickly put one on the horse. After getting on, Gabriella adjusted her stirrups and rode over to the children. Carson followed.

"I thought you said you were riding."

"I am." He let out a loud, long whistle. Excalibur lifted his head and trotted over. Carson put the remaining saddle on his stallion.

"Wow. He's trained," Justin said.

"Yes." Carson swung into the saddle in one graceful move.

"Impressive," Gabriella said. Seeing man and horse together, Gabriella was filled with an emotion that she couldn't name and wasn't sure she wanted to.

"Will he come if I whistle for him?" Justin asked.

Carson shook his head. "He only comes for me."

If Justin was disappointed, he shook it off. "Are you and Mom riding with us?"

"Yes. And since you guys are such fast learners, I thought we'd see a little bit of the ranch. But remember everything I taught you. You have to be calm and keep control of your horses."

"We can do that," Justin said, and Sophia nodded.

"Your mother can lead. Justin, you follow her. Sophia, follow your brother. And I'll be last."

Sophia grinned. "You're the caboose of the horse train."

"I guess that's one way of looking at it."

"Where are we riding?" Gabriella asked.

"How about to the old double tree? Do you still remember the way?"

"Of course." It had been years since she'd been

riding on Rivers Ranch, but much like the memories she and Carson had created together, the layout was etched in her mind. Emblazoned on her soul.

Gabriella had observed her children's lessons and knew their abilities and limitations, so she set a moderate pace. It would be slightly challenging, but they would be able to keep up. Given the length of time since she'd been on a horse, she was surprised at how natural she felt. A sense of freedom filled her, and she yearned to let Beauty race across the open land. She wouldn't, though, because her kids didn't ride well enough to keep up with her.

She lifted her face to the sky, letting the sun warm her skin. Memories of other rides she and Carson had taken over the years filled her mind, and she smiled. Those days had been so happy. So carefree. Days when her only worry had been whether Aunt Mildred would make her favorite dessert.

After about twenty minutes, the double tree came into sight. What had started off as two trees growing separately had turned into two trees growing together. The branches wrapped around each other, making each tree stronger. She and Carson had spent many lovely afternoons sitting under that tree, eating sandwiches and cookies and scheming about ways for him to get out of doing his chores. Sometimes they'd run around, but mostly they'd talked. And talked. They'd never run out of things to say. She'd shared her deepest secrets with him without ever worrying that he'd betray her confidence. Only now, when she didn't have a confidante, did she realize how valuable his friendship had been.

They reached the trees, and she slid from Beauty's back. Sophia and Justin had learned how to properly dismount, but she still watched until they were standing firmly on the ground.

"It really is a double tree," Justin said, removing his helmet. He freed his cowboy hat from the satchel attached to the saddle, checked its shape and then placed it on his head.

"It looks like the trees are hugging," Sophia said.

"Yep," Carson said, joining them. "Your mother and I used to ride out here all the time when we were only a little bit older than you."

"What would you do out here?"

"Talk. Play."

"Weren't there any other boys around here?" Justin asked. Clearly he couldn't understand why Carson would want to hang out with a girl unless he'd had no other option. His question also made it apparent to Gabriella that Sophia and Justin needed other kids to play with.

Carson slung his arm around Gabriella's shoulder and pulled her to his side. His enticing scent encircled her, and she had to remind herself that they were just friends. Buddies. Pals. Even so, she fought back a sigh when Carson released her and stepped away. "Sure, but your mother was my best friend. At least in the summertime."

"Speaking of kids," Gabriella interrupted. "We drove by the youth center when we were in Sweet Briar. Do you know anything about it?"

"Yes. I know the director. Joni's a nice woman and very popular with the kids. They adore her. The whole town does."

The little green monster poked Gabriella in the side at the admiration in Carson's voice. She shoved it down. So what if Carson admired the other woman. If she was thinking of entrusting her children to Joni's care, she should be someone who was thought highly of. Besides, she could be sixty years old. Or better yet, the mirror image of a troll.

"Would you introduce us? I know we can probably just walk into the center, but I would feel better having a friend with me. And as a reward, I'll cook dinner for you."

Carson hesitated and Gabriella worried that she'd overstepped. It had been so easy to fall back into the close relationship she and Carson had enjoyed as children that she'd thought he felt the same. Maybe he didn't share her sense of familiarity. Perhaps he was only being polite to her and her kids.

"When were you planning on going?"

"Anytime that works for you."

"We can go this afternoon. I have a couple of things to do, but they shouldn't take more than forty-five minutes or so."

"And dinner? Surely you must be tired of eating frozen meals."

He laughed and a shiver danced down her spine. "You have no idea."

The kids had wandered off and were now chasing butterflies, so Gabriella called them back over. When she told them that they were going to visit the youth center they cheered, evidently delighted at the prospect of making new friends.

They went back to Carson's house in the same order as they'd ridden to the tree. Once they were back, they bypassed the corral and went straight to the stables. The kids knew how to care for the horses and did so carefully. Carson had told them that if they treated Angel and Peanut Butter with love, the horses would feel it and love them in return. Sophia had taken his words to heart and she lavished Angel with attention, talking to the horse as she brushed her.

"I'll drop by your house in an hour or so," Carson said when they were finished.

"We'll be ready."

Gabriella and the kids took quick showers, ate a small snack and were sitting on the front porch when Carson walked into view. The kids ran to greet him and grabbed him by his hands, pulling him across the long driveway and up the stairs.

"Carson is here," Justin said as if she could miss six-foot-plus of good-looking male standing right in front of her.

"I see. Let me grab my purse and lock the door."

Carson and the kids were waiting by her SUV, so Gabriella clicked the key fob and unlocked the doors. The kids immediately climbed in back, sitting in their normal spots—Justin right behind her and Sophia behind the front passenger seat. The middle seat had been removed and in its place was a crate filled with toys and books, which came in handy on long rides.

Carson walked to the driver's side and opened her door for her. "Thanks."

"You're welcome," he said, circling the front of the vehicle. He'd taken a shower and was now wearing black denims and a white button-down shirt. His woodsy aftershave smelled exactly how she imagined heaven would smell. She was glad she'd taken the time to apply a bit of mascara, spray herself with a light perfume and put on a short floral denim skirt and cute pink top.

Once they were all strapped in, Gabriella drove down the road and turned onto the highway to town. Normally, the kids grabbed toys or books from the crate to keep themselves entertained while she listened to music on the radio. Today their toys remained untouched as they asked Carson questions about his horses and what it was like being a rancher. While they talked, Gabriella's mind wandered and the kids' voices faded to the background. But her attention flew back to the conversation the second she heard Sophia ask Carson if he had a girlfriend.

"Sophia. That's a personal question," Gabriella said, catching her daughter's eye in the rearview mirror and shaking her head before glancing over at Carson. "You don't have to answer that."

He flashed her a dimpled grin. He was so gorgeous. Probably always had been. But until this visit she hadn't really cared. They'd only been friends so his looks hadn't mattered. Now she found herself wondering what it would be like to be kissed by those full lips of his. The ecstasy she would feel if he wrapped those strong arms around her and held her against his muscular body. Just as her daughter's question was off-limits, so were her imaginings. Gabriella didn't have friends to spare. She valued Carson's friendship too much to risk ruining it by trying to turn it into something it wasn't.

"I don't mind answering Sophia's question. It's not as if it's a state secret or anything." Carson spun around in his seat in an attempt to meet her daughter's eyes. His voice was filled with mischief. "I don't have a girlfriend. Do you have a boyfriend?"

Sophia giggled. "No. I don't like boys. Except for Justin."

"Mom doesn't have a boyfriend, either," Justin volunteered. "So if you want, Mom can be your girlfriend."

Yikes. Talk about making her sound pathetic and desperate. And delivered with such matter-of-fact innocence.

"I'll keep that in mind," Carson said with a laugh.

"No need to do that," Gabriella muttered. More loudly she added, "We're in town now. I'm not sure I remember the way to the youth center. Which way should I go?"

Carson grinned at her abrupt change of subject. "Turn right at the corner. Then go two blocks and make a left."

She followed his instructions, and within min-utes they were pulling into the parking lot in front of the building. As before, she was captivated by the colorful mural that wrapped around the build-ing.

Kids swarmed the playground, laughing as they swung on swings, went up and down on seesaws, or just chased each other. A few girls jumped rope while others played hopscotch. Several boys were playing kickball. As before, all of the action oc-curred under the watchful eye of adults.

Gabriella approached the nearest chaperone while Carson and the kids hung back. "Hi. I'm

Gabriella Tucker. Those are my kids. We're staying on my aunt's ranch this summer and are interested in joining the youth center if possible."

"Of course. Go on inside. There's someone at the desk who'll be able to give you information and show you around. I'm sure your kids will have a great time here."

"Thank you."

Gabriella returned to where she'd left Carson and the kids. Sophia and Justin weren't ordinarily shy, but being the new kid was never easy. When they stepped inside the building, Gabriella instantly felt welcome.

"Look at that," Justin said, pointing at a colorful mural on the far wall. "It's so cool."

"Yes, it is," said a woman seated at a reception desk just inside the large entry. "It's one of several in the building. Do you like art?"

Justin shrugged. "It's okay."

"Well, we have more than art. Whatever your favorite thing to do, I'm sure you'll find it here." She stood, circled the desk and approached Gabriella. "I'm Madison."

Gabriella introduced herself, Carson and the kids.

Madison looked at Sophia. "I have a daughter about your age. She's playing outside with some of the other kids. If you want, I can introduce you to her later."

"Okay," Sophia said.

"What about boys my age?" Justin said.

Madison laughed. "I don't have a son, but there are plenty of boys your age around. I'll introduce you to some that I know."

"Okay."

"Let's look around the center," Madison said.

The building was bigger than Gabriella had expected. There were numerous rooms where kids were engaged in a variety of activities. Teenage girls were making jewelry in one room, preteen girls and boys were rehearsing for what appeared to be a musical in another. Teenage boys were playing basketball in the gym, and a group of toddlers, decked out in plastic smocks, were finger painting. The activities were varied, but one thing was consistent. Everyone appeared to be having a great time.

The tour ended outside a small office. Madison knocked on the open door, and the woman inside looked up, smiled and stood.

"Hey, Joni. I've just been giving this new family a tour. They're interested in summer activities."

"Thanks. I'll take it from here."

"Nice meeting you," Madison said before walking away.

"Hey, you," Joni said. She rose, walked around the desk and gave Carson a kiss on the cheek. "I didn't know you had friends visiting."

When Gabriella saw that kiss, jealousy once

more reared its ugly head. Joni was gorgeous and didn't bear the slightest resemblance to a troll. Gabriella was definitely going to have to work on ridding herself of that emotion.

Carson returned Joni's smile with a rueful one of his own. "They aren't staying with me. Gabriella is Mildred Johnson's niece. Sophia and Justin are her children."

"Mrs. Johnson is one of our favorite volunteers. She talks a great deal about her favorite niece and her children, which must be you. I've heard so much about you, so it's nice to finally meet you in person."

Gabriella smiled. "Nice to meet you, too."

Joni grabbed a folder from her desk and handed Gabriella a few papers to fill out. "I need a little information about you so your family can use the center."

"Can we play outside now?" Justin asked.

"Please," Sophia added with a winning smile.

"I can introduce them around if you want," Joni offered.

Gabriella nodded. "Thanks. I'll fill out the forms now."

Joni led them to the lobby, where Gabriella and Carson sat down on a bench while Joni took the kids outside.

"She seems nice," Gabriella said, trying to keep her voice neutral. The lingering jealousy she felt made it harder than it should have been. After all, Gabriella didn't have dibs on Carson.

"She is." Carson gave her a long look, then continued, "Her husband is nice, too. So is their son."

"You're making fun of me." Even though she'd never admit it, she felt a bit of relief knowing that the other woman was married.

"Maybe a little. You're just so easy to tease." He flashed a dimpled grin that made her pulse race. "You're my summer best friend, remember? And it is summer."

"Does that mean we're going to be hanging out together like we used to? Because I have to tell you that I really enjoyed riding Beauty today. If not for the kids, I would have gone racing across the ranch."

"You could have taken her for a ride before."

"I know." She didn't understand why she'd deprived herself of a good time before.

"If the kids like hanging out here, we can ride to our favorite spots."

"I'm going to hold you to that."

Gabriella completed the papers and gave them to Madison before she and Carson went outside. Standing side by side, they watched the kids play. All of Sophia and Justin's earlier shyness had vanished. Justin had joined the group of boys playing kickball and was shouting encouragement to a younger kid standing at the plate. Sophia was playing a hand-clapping game with several other girls. They seemed happy—much happier than they'd been in Ohio. There they'd been their father's forgotten kids, reminded daily that they no longer mattered to him. He hadn't been a part of their lives in Sweet Briar, so they didn't notice his absence. He wasn't hovering over them like a ghost, casting a pall on their joy. Or hers.

"Do you need to get back to the ranch right away?" she asked.

"No. Why?"

"I was hoping we could stop in at Mabel's Diner. I could really go for a burger, some onion rings and a shake."

"That sounds like a plan."

Gabriella called the kids. They raced over, big grins on their faces.

"This place is so much fun. Can we come back tomorrow?"

"I don't see why not. But right now, we're going to get something to eat. How do burgers and fries sound to you?"

"Sounds good."

Once they were all in the SUV, Gabriella drove the short distance to the diner. The moment they went inside she smiled. It was like stepping back in time. Nothing had changed. Red vinyl booths lined the walls, while table and chairs filled the space in between. It was midafternoon and the lunch rush had passed, so there were several available tables and booths.

A uniformed waitress was gathering dishes from an empty table and loading them into a bin. She looked up and called to them, "Have a seat anywhere. Menus are on the table. Someone will be over to take your order in a minute or two."

Justin and Sophia made a beeline for a booth near the large front window where they could see people pass by. Justin sat by the window and Sophia scooted next to him, leaving Gabriella and Carson to share the other seat.

Carson looked at Gabriella. "Do you want the inside or the outside?"

"The inside," she said, sliding across the bench.

Carson sat down beside her and the warmth from his body wrapped around her. Each time she inhaled she was treated to his wonderful scent. It had been a long time since she'd had romantic thoughts about a man other than her husband. When her marriage ended, the last thing she'd wanted was another man in her life. The determination to keep her heart safely locked away was being tested with each moment she shared with Carson.

A waitress approached their booth and set down four glasses of ice water. "Are you ready to order or do you need more time?"

"We're ready now," Justin said before anyone else could reply.

Once the waitress had taken their orders, she walked away. While they waited on their food, the children told Gabriella and Carson about the friends they'd made at the youth center. Gabriella tried to pay close attention, but Carson's nearness made it difficult for her to focus.

Carson laughed at something Justin said and shifted slightly in the seat. His denim-clad leg brushed against the bare skin of her calf and her awareness of him reached new heights. This was ridiculous. Was she really reacting this way to Carson? Growing up, he'd been the closest thing she'd had to a sibling. But there was nothing sisterly about her imaginings. She glanced out the side of her eye at him. He was sipping from his ice water, unfazed by the contact. To him, she was still his childhood friend, not a woman he was attracted to. Clearly this attraction was a one-sided thing, the result of the lack of male attention for too long.

She wasn't vain, but she thought the years had been good to her. She worked hard to stay in shape. Back home, she'd had a standing twice-a-week tennis match with the club pro, and she ran at least two miles three days a week. True, she hadn't been as consistent lately as she'd once been, but she'd done her best to not let herself go. But attraction involved more than outward appearances. It also required compatibility. They'd always gotten along as kids. If their latest interactions were anything to go by, time apart hadn't changed that.

Gabriella frowned. She had no idea why she was thinking that way. She wasn't looking for a man. And even if she was, Carson wasn't the one for her. He lived in Sweet Briar and she lived in Ohio. Long-distance relationships could work if one party was considering moving at some point, but that wasn't the case in this instance. Carson had grown up on his ranch and was happy here. Although Gabriella felt comfortable in Sweet Briar, she and her kids had lives back in Ohio. Their father was there. Reggie might be besotted by his new child now, but despite all evidence to the contrary, she knew he loved Sophia and Justin. They deserved to have their father in their lives. The time would come when he'd want to play an active role again. Gabriella wouldn't create a barrier between them by moving here.

The waitress brought their lunches, and Gabriella and Carson exchanged amused smiles as the kids marveled at the enormous size of the burgers and the huge pile of fries on their plates. Although they'd dined at some nice restaurants and had eaten fast food on many occasions in their lives, nothing had prepared them for Mabel's food.

The kids added ketchup and mustard, and then Gabriella cut their burgers in half. They'd each just taken a first delicious bite when a woman approached their table.

"Carson. It's good to see you. How are you?"

Carson froze, then forced himself to swallow the bite of burger. Raven Reynolds. Or rather Raven Reynolds-*Cordero*. His former fiancée was the last person he'd expected to run into in Mabel's Diner in the middle of the afternoon. After all, she and her husband, Donovan, were ranchers and were ordinarily hard at work at this time of day.

He stood up as he'd been raised to do, and said, "Raven. I'm surprised to see you in town." *Shocked* was more like it.

She shrugged and then gestured to her son, Elias, and her husband, who were standing slightly behind her. "We had dentist appointments in Willow Creek and decided to grab food here before heading home."

Raven glanced past him to Gabriella and her kids. Interest sparked in her eyes, and he could tell she was putting two and two together and coming up with a romance. Ever since she'd married Donovan, Raven had been on a mission to find a woman for Carson. She had tried to set him up with every available woman within a fifty-mile radius. He'd tried to get her to quit matchmaking, and she would for a while, but then she'd start up again. It was as if she felt guilty for not loving him and wouldn't be completely happy until he was one half of a blissful couple.

Raven wasn't a bad person. Neither was Donovan, as far as that went. He knew neither of them had wanted to hurt him. They were simply two people whose love for each other had been too strong to ignore. Since Carson's father had played a role in keeping them apart, he shouldn't resent them. And he didn't. But he didn't want to go back to being friends with them, either.

But not introducing Gabriella and her children would be rude. Gabriella might get the impression that she wasn't important to him, which was the farthest thing from the truth. He wasn't exactly sure what their relationship was—it was evolving daily—but he knew that she mattered to him. So he smiled and then motioned to Gabriella, who had a curious expression on her face. "This is Gabriella Tucker and her children, Justin and Sophia. Gabriella is Mrs. Johnson's niece. Gabriella, this is Raven Reynolds-Cordero, her husband Donovan, and their son, Elias. Their ranch adjoins mine."

Donovan and Elias said hello, but Raven's brow wrinkled. "Are you the same niece who used to visit in the summer when we were kids?"

Gabriella smiled and Carson's heart lurched. *Whoa.* Just where had that reaction come from? "Yes. But I don't remember you."

"We never officially met. But I do remember

seeing you from a distance a couple of times one summer. I should have come over and introduced myself, but I was having too much fun annoying my older brothers or hanging out with Donovan and some of the other boys."

Carson remembered those days. Even as ten-year-olds, Donovan and his friends had been the cool kids. They'd hung out together at a clubhouse they'd built on Jericho Jones's ranch. Carson had only been a year or so younger, but he'd been light-years behind them in all the ways that counted. He'd been a short, scrawny kid who had never been invited to join the club.

His status as an outsider had followed him to high school, where he'd been the target of bullies. For a reason known only to himself, Donovan, the most popular kid in school, had protected him. He'd made it clear that anyone who bothered Carson would have to answer to him. And just like that, the bullying stopped. From then on, Donovan and his friends had included him on occasion, but for the most part Carson's circle of friends hadn't increased.

"Well, it's nice to meet you now," Gabriella said.

"Hey, do you know about the youth center?" Elias asked.

"We just came from there. It's cool," Justin said.

"Do you know about the sleepover party?"

"No."

"It's a lot of fun. I don't know when it is but be sure to ask your mom to let you come. And the summer Olympics are really fun. And there's a basketball tournament and a cookout at the beach."

Laughing, Raven put an arm around Elias's shoulder, stopping him when he looked like he would continue extolling the virtues of the youth center for a while. "And on that note, we'll let you enjoy your meal. It was nice meeting all of you. Gabriella, if you need anything or just want some female company, give me a call. Carson has my number."

"Will do."

Carson sat down as the trio walked away. Running into his former fiancée and her family hadn't been on his to-do list, but he had to admit that it hadn't been as horrible as he'd imagined.

"Can we go to the sleepover?" Justin asked.

"We'll see," Gabriella replied. "We need to find out when it is."

That answer satisfied Justin and he resumed eating.

"Are you okay?" Gabriella asked, leaning close to him. Her soft hair brushed against his cheek and her sweet scent floated around him. Tempting him. When had he started reacting to Gabriella like this? They were friends. That's all they'd ever been. And he wasn't in the market for a relationship now. Or ever. So why did the possibility suddenly sound so enticing?

It wasn't just because Gabriella was so beautiful, although she was.

His eyes had nearly popped out of his head that first day she'd brought the kids over for their riding lesson. No one had ever looked as sexy as Gabriella had in those shorts and the cropped T-shirt. Her shapely legs had gone on forever. It had taken every ounce of his self-control to focus on the kids instead of staring at her. But on more occasions than he cared to admit, his eyes had drifted over to where she sat, ankles crossed, on the top rail. When he'd become so distracted he couldn't concentrate, he'd invited her to help. Her nearness had been more tempting than he'd expected, but he'd extend the invitation again in a heartbeat. Which just proved that he was a glutton for punishment.

"Yes. I'm fine." He wasn't going to allow anything to ruin this perfect moment. True, he and Gabriella didn't have a future as a romantic couple, but they were good friends. He was going to enjoy her presence as long as she was here. And when she and her kids left, and he was once more alone? He'd deal with that when the time came.

Chapter Six

Something was bothering Carson. Gabriella couldn't put her finger on what exactly, but his mood had definitely changed. He laughed with the kids, but the mirth never reached his eyes. The children were too young to notice, and the shift was so subtle she might have missed it too if she didn't know him as well as she did. But they'd been friends for years. True, time had passed since they'd seen each other, but that absence hadn't changed the essence of their relationship. She knew him at his core, and she knew when something was wrong. Like now. He was masking his pain with jokes, but she wasn't fooled.

He'd been fine until the Corderos had come

over to their table. She replayed the brief conversation in her mind. Nothing untoward had been said. Quite the contrary. They'd been very friendly. Over time, Gabriella had become a good judge of character—her ex-husband being the exception that made the rule. Raven and Donovan had seemed to sincerely like Carson. Their son had been delightful. But something about seeing the three of them had upset Carson. She just wished she knew what it was.

"Mom," Justin said, yanking Gabriella out of her musings. "Can we have dessert?"

"You can't possibly have room for dessert. You didn't even finish your burgers and fries," Carson said, grinning.

"I have room," Justin countered.

"So do I," Sophia chimed in.

"Neither one of you ate all of your food," Gabriella said.

"That's because we were saving room for dessert," Justin shot back.

Carson and Gabriella laughed. There was no arguing with that kind of logic. "Sure. What do you want?"

The kids decided on brownies with a scoop of ice cream. Carson agreed that it sounded great, and he got the same with two scoops of ice cream. Gabriella passed on dessert. While the others had ordered colas with their meals, she'd gotten a large vanilla shake. That was enough ice cream for one day.

When the waitress brought dessert, she also brought cardboard containers so Gabriella could pack up the kids' leftovers. Although they hadn't finished their lunches, they managed to eat all of their desserts.

Carson pulled a few bills out of his wallet.

"Just what do you think you're doing?" Gabriella said.

"Paying for lunch."

"You're our guest. I'll pay."

"Gabriella."

"Don't make a fuss. You can pay next time."

He nodded and put the money back into his wallet.

The ride home was much quieter than the one to town. Once they'd reached the highway, Gabriella glanced in the rearview mirror. The kids were dozing. They didn't generally nap, but they'd been getting up earlier than usual. It was bound to catch up with them sooner or later. A short snooze in the car wouldn't hurt anything, and it would give her a chance to talk to Carson without interruption.

"So, what's wrong?" she asked, getting right to the point.

"What do you mean?"

"There's something bothering you."

He blew out a breath, and for a moment she

thought he wasn't going to answer. Had she crossed a line? She hoped not.

"Raven and I used to be engaged. But she was still in love with Donovan. He'd been gone for years, but he came back a few weeks before our scheduled wedding day. It was only a matter of time before things ended between us and they got married."

Wow. She didn't know what she'd expected him to say, but it wasn't that. Raven was exceptionally beautiful and friendly, so it was easy to see how Carson and Donovan had both fallen in love with her. And not to knock Donovan—he was handsome enough and probably had some great qualities—but Raven must have been out of her mind to choose him over Carson.

Carson was not only gorgeous, he was one of the best people Gabriella had ever met. In addition to being kind and generous with his time, he was a great listener. Plus, he had a great sense of humor. Given the opportunity, Gabriella would choose Carson over any other man. But she wouldn't be given the chance. Perhaps that was for the best. Their friendship was too valuable to risk. Now she needed to figure out how to control her attraction to him.

"Oh," she finally responded. It certainly explained the change in his mood.

"Yeah. Oh."

Gabriella couldn't decipher the emotion in his voice. Was it sorrow? Resignation? Something else entirely? He'd done a good job of camouflaging his feelings. Too good. Perhaps she didn't know him as well as she'd believed.

"Where'd Donovan go?" Gabriella asked.

"Oh, that's right. You'd stopped visiting by then, so you weren't around." He frowned. "It's a long story and one I don't feel like going into right now."

"Are you still in love with her?"

Carson shrugged. "It doesn't really matter, does it?"

She took that as a yes and her heart sank, which was foolish. They were friends. Carson's feelings for Raven wouldn't change that. In fact, they guaranteed that Gabriella wouldn't let her attraction grow into something more when she knew he wouldn't return those feelings. Been there. Done that. Still, she felt sorry for him. It hurt to be in love with someone whose heart belonged to another. But she knew that it was possible to get over it.

There had been a time when she'd tried to convince herself that she'd stopped loving Reggie the moment he'd told her he wanted a divorce so he could marry the love of his life. But that hadn't been true. She'd still loved him as much as ever and would have given anything for him to stay. Her heart had been ripped to shreds when he left.

She'd been devastated when she signed the divorce papers. She'd known rationally that ending the marriage had been the right thing to do for her well-being. But even so, it had taken time and distance to kill the residual love in her heart. She didn't know if Carson still loved Raven, but if he truly wanted to get over her, he could.

"No, I guess not," she agreed. Because if he didn't want to get over Raven, then everything else was immaterial. That was the most compelling reason—as if she needed another—she and Carson could never be more than friends. She'd already had her heart incinerated by a man who'd been in love with another woman. She wasn't going to make that mistake again.

She turned onto the road that separated their properties, pulled into her driveway and shut off the engine.

"The kids are still sleep. Do you need help carrying them into the house?" Carson asked.

She shook her head. "I'm waking them up. Once the air hits them their sleepiness will pass. Thanks again for today. Are we still on for dinner?"

He shook his head. "Can I get a rain check? I'm not all that hungry now."

"Sure. See you later."

Gabriella waited until Carson had hopped from her SUV and crossed the road before waking up the kids. They grumbled a bit, but eventually she got them into the house. She unpacked a large jig-saw puzzle and they worked on that for a while.

The kids were happy to polish off the remains of their lunches for dinner, so Gabriella warmed their leftovers in the microwave and heated herself a can of soup. Once the kids were in bed, she sat on the front porch. She hoped Carson would come over again, but as it grew later, she knew she was going to be disappointed.

It was for the best, she told herself as she put on her nightgown. The more she was around him the more she liked him. Keeping her distance would help her keep her feelings under control and thus protect her heart.

She almost convinced herself that was true.

The next morning Gabriella found herself thinking more about Carson and his feelings for Raven. Just once she would like to be attracted to a man who wasn't hung up on someone else. Not that she was convinced Carson was still in love with Raven. But there was definitely some-thing between the two—or three of them if you included Raven's husband—that had made Carson uncomfortable.

Whatever it was, it had occurred after Gabri-ella had stopped coming to visit. Aunt Mildred had never been one to gossip, so if she'd known anything, she hadn't told Gabriella. And, really, did it matter now? Whatever had happened was over now, and Raven and Donovan were married.

After breakfast she sent the kids outside to play while she cleaned the kitchen. As she put a load of clothes in the washing machine, she realized that she no longer heard their voices. That could only mean one thing.

They'd wandered over to Carson's ranch.

He hadn't seemed bothered by the way her kids kept coming around, but she didn't want them to wear out their welcome. She knew he had work to do, something the kids didn't understand. Or perhaps they didn't realize that training horses was actually his job. But she did.

Sighing, she turned on the machine and went to get the children. She took a minute to run a comb through her hair and check her appearance before leaving. She and Carson might not have a future as anything other than friends, but it didn't hurt to look her best.

As expected, Justin and Sophia were sitting on the top rail, watching as Carson worked with a horse. Rather than pull them away, Gabriella leaned against the fence to watch.

The horse bucked, and her breath caught in her throat when it looked like Carson would be tossed to the ground. With practiced ease, he adjusted himself in the saddle. The kids clapped and cheered, clearly not the least bit worried for Carson's well-being.

Justin glanced at Gabriella, his eyes lit up with admiration. "He's really good. He never falls." Gabriella doubted that was true, but she nodded anyway. Not that Justin noticed. He'd already turned back to the ring.

Carson sitting on a horse was sight to behold. He was such a commanding presence. The horse bucked again and Carson leaned forward, murmuring to the animal and rubbing its neck. Gabriella had no idea what he'd said, but the bucking slowed, though it didn't stop. Yet Carson was still kind and patient with the animal.

That was Carson in a nutshell. Although he was bigger and stronger than most, he was endlessly kind. His body was perfection and his face was exceedingly handsome, but his attitude was the single sexiest thing about him. She'd choose a nice guy over a bad boy every time.

He rubbed his hand down the horse's mane, calming it, and Gabriella imagined him caressing her hair in the same manner. When she realized her thoughts had taken a turn for the forbidden, she ordered herself to snap out of it. Their relationship was strictly platonic. He wasn't going to be running his hands over her hair or any part of her body.

After a few more minutes, Carson dismounted

and handed the reins to an employee who'd been watching from the sidelines.

"Hey," Carson called as he ambled closer to them.

"Hey, Carson. I want to be a horse trainer like you. Can I help you next time?" Justin asked.

"Not next time. Let's stay focused on becoming a good rider first. Then you can become a trainer."

"I'm getting good, aren't I?"

"You sure are. Both of you are," Carson said as if anticipating Sophia's inevitable question.

Gabriella loved the way he interacted with her kids, especially the way he listened to them. Encouraged them. Things their father should have done but couldn't be bothered to do now. But she couldn't let her appreciation lead her down the path she'd just decided she wasn't going to take. She had to do better at keeping her imagination under control.

"I hope you don't mind us coming over uninvited," Gabriella said.

"Nope. I don't mind at all. I enjoy the company."

"What are you going to do now?" Justin asked.

Carson grinned. "I had planned to do some paperwork, but I can just as easily do that tonight. What do you say about taking the horses out for a short ride? That is, if you have the time."

He'd addressed that last comment to Gabriella, but Justin took it upon himself to answer. "We have plenty of time. Come on, Sophia. Let's get our horses."

He climbed down from the fence and then held out his hand to help his sister. Sophia brushed his hand away and got down on her own. Chivalry might not be dead, but Sophia was an independent girl and wanted to do things on her own. When she was on the ground, she and Justin ran into the barn.

"Thanks. I'm sorry about disrupting your day," Gabriella said as they followed the kids.

"No worries. I'm not a big fan of paperwork. Accounting is the worst. I'd rather be riding any day. My mother used to keep the books, but now she lives out of state. In a pinch, I know she'll pitch in, but I don't want to keep asking her."

"So why don't you just hire an accountant to do it?"

"I'm actually in the process of hiring someone. Hopefully, I'll be able to do that soon and I won't have the headache for much longer. But in the meantime, I'm stuck with the chore."

They stepped inside the stable and the sweet scent of hay surrounded Gabriella, bringing back happy memories. How many days had she and Carson spent in this very place? How many hours had she spent sweeping floors and cleaning out stalls, helping Carson to complete his chores so they could spend the rest of the day together?

The stable had appeared so much bigger back then, and it had taken what seemed like hours to clean tack and get the stable clean enough to satisfy Carson's father. But once the job was done, they'd hopped on horses and raced away, the wind in their faces, the taste of freedom sweet in their mouths.

Sophia and Justin had already saddled and mounted Angel and Peanut Butter. After Carson checked to make sure they'd done everything properly, he and Gabriella climbed on their horses and they headed out. Gabriella led them across the vast fields to one of her favorite spots on the ranch—a grassy hill overlooking a valley filled with wildflowers. A stream crisscrossed the valley and if you waited long enough and were quiet enough, you might spot deer coming to get a drink.

It took about forty minutes to reach her destination. She dismounted and looked around. It was just as breathtaking as she remembered. When the others joined her, she looked at the kids. "What do you think?"

"It's so pretty. I like all the flowers," Sophia said.

"And guess what? Sometimes deer come to get a drink."

"Really? Will some come today?"

"I don't know. We'll have to wait and see. But we need to be very quiet."

"We can do that," Justin said. "What do we do?"

"We just need to watch and wait."

Her kids were city kids, so seeing deer up close and personal would create a treasured memory they could share. They all sprawled out on their stomachs—Justin and Sophia lying between Gabriella and Carson—and watched, their anticipation growing with each passing minute.

"Look, Mommy," Sophia whispered after they'd been lying there for about ten minutes. "There are the deer."

"I see. We need to stay quiet so they don't get scared and run away."

The four of them watched as the family drank from the stream. There were two large deer and two small deer. The smallest was a baby and absolutely adorable. He took his time sipping the water as if delighting in each swallow. When they were finished drinking, they walked around for a while as if enjoying their outing. But then Justin sneezed loudly, startling the deer, and they raced away, disappearing into the trees.

"Sorry," Justin said as they all sat up. "I didn't mean to scare them away."

"They were probably going to leave anyway," Gabriella said. "Just like we need to."

The kids groaned and then headed back to their horses. Carson caught Gabriella's eye and smiled at her. Feeling happy, she reached out and grabbed his hand, intertwining their fingers. They swung their hands back and forth as they walked, only releasing their hold in order to mount their rides.

She didn't know why she'd taken his hand. There hadn't been any thought behind it. It had seemed a natural thing to do in the moment. As they rode across the ranch to the stables, her fingers tingled and she wondered if she would be able to control her feelings.

When they reached the stables, they took care of the horses as usual and then went back outside. The day had started out warm, but it was hot now and on its way to becoming a scorcher.

"What are we going to do now?" Sophia asked.

"We're going to have lunch." Gabriella had started the slow cooker at the crack of dawn that morning. "Pulled pork sandwiches."

"You should eat lunch with us," Justin said to Carson.

"Thanks, but that's not necessary." His stomach growled, so Gabriella knew he was hungry. And she knew he liked pulled pork sandwiches because he'd eaten them often enough at her aunt's table.

"I made plenty," Gabriella said.

"In that case, yes."

"Let's eat on your patio," Sophia said. "After we eat we can go swimming in your pool."

"It's not polite to invite yourself to someone's house," Gabriella hastened to say, then laughed at herself. They had been wandering onto Carson's ranch just about every day. But there was something different about inviting themselves to use his pool, although Gabriella couldn't say exactly what it was.

"But he won't know we want to swim in his pool if I don't tell him."

"Sophia is absolutely right. I wouldn't know. So let's just put it out there. You are invited to use my pool anytime you want. Just make sure that either I or your mother is with you. Agreed?"

"Yes!" Justin joined Sophia in her cheer.

"In that case, I'll go home and grab the food," Gabriella interjected. "You kids come with me to get your swimsuits."

"You put on yours, too," Carson said, a grin on his gorgeous face. "That is, if you have one."

"Don't you worry about me, cowboy," she said, putting a swing in her hips. "I have a suit that will knock your eyes out."

He laughed. "I can't wait to see it."

Actually, Gabriella's swimsuit was nothing special. It was a one-piece racer-back suit that she wore to swim laps. But it was red, which was her favorite color.

Fifteen minutes later, they were sitting around a table on Carson's patio. Lemonade and potato chips were his contribution, complementing the sandwich fixings and carrot sticks with dressing she'd prepared for lunch. They laughed and talked while they ate, and Gabriella couldn't help but notice how happy her kids were around Carson. They were more talkative than they'd been since Reggie moved out. Horseback riding had become the highlight of their lives. But it was more than learning about horses that gave them pleasure. Carson was providing them with the male attention they'd been craving for the longest time.

Gabriella had mixed feelings about that. On the one hand, she was thrilled they had someone willing to fill the void their father's absence had created. They were thriving. On the other hand, she worried that she was setting them up for more disappointment and heartbreak. They were going back home at the end of summer. The more attached they became to Carson, the more it would hurt when the time came to sever those ties. She had no doubt that Carson liked them, but she didn't expect him to keep in touch with them—or her—when summer was over.

Their relationship—although special—had always been a seasonal one. Just because she was beginning to wish that it could be more didn't mean that Carson felt the same way. He seemed perfectly content with his life and their temporary place in it.

"This is so good," Carson said, scooping more pulled pork onto a bun and setting it on his plate.

Her heart burst with pride at his words although she didn't know why. It wasn't as if she'd done anything special. And it wasn't even her own recipe.

"Thanks," Gabriella said.

"Mom is the best cook," Justin bragged.

"You should eat with us every day," Sophia said.

Carson laughed and Gabriella's heart skipped a beat. "Your mom might not want to cook for me every day."

"She won't mind," Sophia insisted. "Mommy's nice."

"Consider this a standing invitation. You're welcome to eat with us anytime you want."

"Thanks." His voice sounded huskier than normal. Why would a friendly invitation make him emotional? It had to have something to do with his mysterious past. If only she knew what it was.

"Can we swim now?" Sophia asked, yanking her T-shirt over her head. She unfastened her shorts and started to wiggle out of them.

"Please stop undressing at the table," Gabriella said. "And no. You can't swim now. You have to wait at least twenty minutes for your food to digest."

"You know that's an old wives' tale," Carson said.

"Maybe. But I don't want to take any chances. They can help me clear the table and then walk around for a while."

The kids started to complain, but Gabriella silenced them with a look. They picked up their paper plates and napkins, marched into the kitchen and threw everything into the trash. There was a little bit of pulled pork left over and Gabriella insisted that Carson keep it. He didn't put up even a token argument when she put the remaining meat into a storage container and placed it in his refrigerator.

Every two minutes one of the kids asked whether it was time to swim yet. Although time was apparently dragging for them, it was flying by for Gabriella.

"Yes," Gabriella said the last time Justin asked. She didn't know whether twenty minutes had passed or not, but she was a mixed bag of emotions. She was dreading the time when she would have to strip down to her swimming suit, revealing her body. At the same time, she was anticipating the minute Carson put on his swim trunks, revealing what she expected was a muscular chest and powerful thighs.

The kids let out loud whoops while pulling off their T-shirts and shorts. A few seconds later water splashed Gabriella and she jumped.

"You don't intend to go swimming in your clothes, do you?" Carson asked. He gave her a once-over, running his gaze over her breasts before continuing down to her hips, where he hesitated before moving down to her feet. She'd been restless last night so she'd given herself a pedicure, for which she would be eternally grateful.

"You haven't changed yet," Gabriella replied, looking him over from head to toe. Turnabout was fair play. As her eyes moved over his broad shoulders, muscular chest and flat abs, her stomach fluttered and she felt the stirrings of something stronger than attraction. Longing. Desire. Her face heated, but she steadfastly continued her assessment until her eyes reached his boots. "I know you don't intend to swim in jeans and boots."

"Nah." He pulled the T-shirt over his head and dropped it onto the arm of a nearby chair. Then he sat down and began toeing off his boots. Unlike her, he didn't appear hesitant about revealing his body. But then, why should he be? He hadn't given birth to two children in twenty-two months. His body was perfection and he knew it. Well, she was no slug if she said so herself. Her stretch marks were the result of two children she loved.

When his feet were bare, he stood and began unfastening his jeans. Did he intend to swim in his underwear? Her confusion must have shown on her face because he laughed. "I put on my suit when you guys went home to change and then put my jeans back on so you wouldn't be too distracted by my body to eat." He winked and she knew he was joking, but he was nearer to the truth than she cared to admit.

He stepped out of his jeans, revealing a pair of blue-and-white-patterned swim trunks. Without hesitating, he stepped to the edge of the pool and executed a perfect cannonball, making the kids laugh. His lighthearted manner chased away Gabriella's self-consciousness and she quickly stripped down to her suit. Following his lead, she walked to the edge of the pool and then bellowed "cannonball!" as loudly as she could before jumping into the water.

Sophia and Justin stared at her in surprise. She'd never goofed off in the pool with them. When they'd swum at the club, she'd always behaved in the dignified manner befitting a Tucker wife. Had they come to believe she didn't know how to have fun? Had she tried so hard to be the perfect wife that she'd forgotten how to be spontaneous? Well, it was time to change that.

She swam to where the others were bobbing in the water and began splashing them mercilessly. They blinked in amazement and then began to splash her in return. That quickly morphed into dunking each other. Before long they were all laughing and playing.

After a while, they called a truce and started to tread water.

Justin pointed to a basketball hoop at the shallow end of the pool. "Do you have a ball, Carson?"

He nodded. "Let me get it."

Carson swam to the edge of the pool with strong strokes, then pulled himself onto the patio. Water sluiced down his muscular back and dripped from his trunks, but he didn't seem to notice. Gabriella did, and heat bloomed inside her stomach. She couldn't pull her eyes away to save her life. Lucky for her, he was focused on getting a ball from the storage container near the edge of the patio and didn't see her expression. He turned around, and she sank under the water in a futile attempt to cool off. When she couldn't hold her breath any longer, she pushed her head above the water and took a deep breath.

When she opened her eyes, Carson was right in front of her, close enough to touch. The children were at the other end of the pool taking turns shooting baskets.

His hands never touched her, yet she could practically feel when his eyes caressed her bare shoulders, and goose bumps popped up on her skin. She wasn't sure who moved first, but suddenly their bodies were mere inches apart. It was as if an invisible band had drawn them together and a magnetic force was holding them in place.

His lips parted slightly and he blew out a soft breath. The need inside her grew, becoming more demanding with each passing second. Suddenly her face and body were splashed with water and she jumped. Carson did the same.

The kids laughed uproariously as they shot Carson and Gabriella with huge water guns. Apparently they'd gotten tired of playing basketball and had taken the water guns from the storage bin.

"You guys look so goofy staring at each other," Justin said, dodging the water Carson splashed in his direction.

"You really did," Sophia added. "You guys looked just like statues. This is how you looked, Mommy." She froze, her hands stretched out in front of her as she mimicked Gabriella. Had she been reaching out to touch Carson? She remembered thinking how smooth his skin looked, how muscular his body was, how much she'd longed to caress him, but she hadn't known she'd been about to act on it. Yikes. What else would she have done if she hadn't been interrupted?

She wouldn't think about that now. Or ever.

Carson went to the bin and returned with two more water guns. He filled one, gave it to Gabriella and then filled his. "This is war."

He aimed at the kids and then fired. They squirted water at each other until their guns were empty. Dropping his empty water gun, Carson grabbed Justin by the waist and tossed him across the water. Justin landed with a splash and laughed.

"Do me next," Sophia begged, swimming over to Carson.

"You don't have to ask me twice," Carson said. "I need to pay you back for splashing me."

He tossed each child three times and then declared that they were much too heavy for him to throw again.

"But you didn't do Mommy," Sophia said. "It's not fair if Mommy doesn't get a turn."

"Oh, that's all right," Gabriella said, backing away as she saw the mischievous gleam in Carson's eyes. "I don't need a turn."

"Oh, I insist," Carson said. Gabriella began to swim to the other end of the pool, but he was faster and he caught her before she could escape. His hands wrapped around her waist, slowing her progress. He pulled her against his body and she gasped. Her playfulness was replaced by intense desire. She could get used to being held against his hard chest. Too used to it. If she knew what was good for her she'd slide from his grip, climb out of the pool and run home as fast as she could. The fact that she didn't only confirmed the power of the need he awakened in her.

Carson turned her so that they were face-to-face. Then he lifted her into his arms. When he held her over his head, he swung her out and then released her. Laughing, she sailed a short distance and then landed with a great splash, submerging slightly before pushing herself to the surface.

"You're in for it now, cowboy. Come on, kids, let's get him."

She and the children surrounded Carson, tugging his arms and shoving his back. When they'd pulled him under the water Justin and Sophia applauded and declared themselves the victors. Gabriella knew that he'd let them win. He was too strong for them to have dunked him without his cooperation. She appreciated him for being a good sport.

"On that note, I'm calling it a day," Carson said. "I need to get back to work."

"Oh, but we're having fun," Sophia whined.

He tugged on one of her wet braids. "And you can keep having fun. You're welcome to stay in the pool for as long as you want."

Gabriella cleared her throat dramatically.

"What I meant to say is as long as your mother *says* you can stay."

Gabriella tried not to stare as Carson climbed from the pool, gathered his clothes and went inside. Once he'd vanished, she released a long sigh. That man was hot. And he definitely made her hot in return.

"Can we keep playing, Mom?" Justin asked.

"For about thirty more minutes." That should be long enough for her heart rate to return to normal.

* * *

Carson shivered as the cold water pounded against his body, yet he didn't turn up the temperature. Whew. That had been close. Being around Gabriella had awakened feelings he'd forgotten he possessed. But touching her, feeling her soft body pressed against his, had ignited desires inside him with a force he'd never felt before. With each touch, he'd become more aroused, and his resolve to keep her at arm's length had been tested. He'd won this battle, but he didn't want to test his willpower too often.

After everything that had happened with Raven, he'd managed to ignore his longing for companionship, keeping his heart protected. He'd never once let his desires get the best of him. But his need for Gabriella had blown past every blockade he'd erected. Even the chilly temperature of the pool had done little to cool him off. This ice-cold shower wasn't much better. Especially whenever he pictured Gabriella as he was doing now.

She'd looked so sexy in her swimsuit. Although it hadn't been nearly as revealing as suits he'd seen women sporting at the beach, it hadn't needed to be. He'd been practically salivating and wondering what delights it kept hidden. Gabriella possessed the sexiest legs he'd ever seen. Long and shapely, with lean muscles, they'd seemed to go on forever.

She couldn't be more than five foot seven, but she was five foot seven inches of tantalizing woman.

Just thinking of her made him grow aroused again, and he forced himself to face the reality of their situation as he got out of the shower and toweled off. First, she was only here for the summer. In a handful of weeks she would be returning to her regularly scheduled life. He'd never ventured to Ohio so he knew nothing of her life there. She could be an entirely different person there than she was here. After all, environment had the ability to change people. Or if not change them, emphasize different characteristics as the situation dictated.

Second, he thought as he pulled on his jeans, he had no idea if she was still in love with her former husband. For all he knew, she could be hoping for a reconciliation. After the disaster with Raven, he knew nothing was beyond the realm of possibility. Donovan had been gone and presumed dead for years, yet Raven had continued to love him. He was not going to become involved with another woman who was hung up on someone else.

Frowning, he fastened the buttons on his shirt, stopping his thoughts before they became too morose. It was futile to keep reliving the past. Truth be told, he hadn't thought of Raven in a long time. His feelings for her had gradually diminished until they were a distant memory. It was only now that he found himself becoming attracted to Gabriella that he thought of Raven at all. And then only as a warning of what could go wrong between them.

He needed to stop letting his thoughts get ahead of him. No matter how strongly he was attracted to Gabriella, the reality was he was just a friend to her. For both their sakes, it needed to remain that way. His life was too big of a mess to have a romantic relationship with her or anyone else.

With that all decided, he stood. He was halfway down the stairs before he realized he no longer heard voices coming from his backyard. Gabriella and her kids had gone home while he'd been showering and getting dressed. And honestly, hadn't that been his plan? Wasn't that why he'd taken as long as he had, staying in the freezing shower until he was at risk for hypothermia? Because he hadn't trusted himself to be around Gabriella again. Despite the fact that the children had been nearby, he'd nearly kissed her earlier. In that brief moment, it had felt as if only the two of them were in the pool. *In the world.* Nothing and no one else had existed for him. All he'd wanted to do was kiss those soft, full lips, wrap her in his arms and feel those firm breasts pressed against his chest.

But her children had interrupted them in the nick of time, providing the reminder he'd needed. There were more than two people involved. Sophia and Justin mattered. Their feelings needed to be taken into consideration. They were at a vulnerable point in life and didn't need an added complication.

No matter how he wanted to deny it, there were still people in this area who disliked him because of his father's actions. Carson avoided confrontation whenever possible, but he didn't know how he would respond if someone mistreated Gabriella or her kids. He blew out a breath. That was a lie. He knew exactly how he would react and it wasn't pretty.

Maybe he wasn't as different from his father as he wanted to believe. And that scary thought was one more reason to keep Gabriella at a distance.

Chapter Seven

Gabriella stood in front of the window, staring across the road toward Rivers Ranch. The view was beautiful, but she wasn't entranced by the clear blue sky or the leafy trees swaying in the gentle breeze. She was too preoccupied with trying to catch a glimpse of Carson to appreciate the scene in front of her.

It had been three days since they'd swum together in his pool. Three days since she'd seen or talked to him. Three long days of wondering what was going on between them. Wondering if their friendship had changed. And if so, to what? Were they going to have a closer relationship? Or were they going to be uncomfortable in each other's presence?

The insecure part of her worried that he was avoiding her. But that was ridiculous. He had no reason to avoid her. Unless... Had he somehow figured out that her feelings for him were changing and were no longer purely platonic? Perhaps he'd sensed that she longed for him to kiss her that day in the pool. Maybe he knew what she'd been thinking and was now trying to give her a hint by staying away from her. Perhaps he was hoping that he wouldn't have to come out and tell her directly that he wasn't interested. Could he be trying to let her down easy? After being let down the hard way—Reggie had all but run over her in his Mercedes in his rush to get to Natalie—she appreciated the consideration. But it still hurt.

But then, Carson could simply be busy. He had a cattle ranch to run as well as his horse training business. She was lucky he'd spent as much time with her and the kids as he had.

"We're ready," Justin said, charging into the room, Sophia on his heels.

"Great." They were on their way to the youth center. The kids had spent a few hours there yesterday and had a great time. They had quickly made friends and planned to see them again today. Gabriella wanted her children to have other kids to play with, so she was happy for them.

Once the seat belts were all fastened in the SUV, Gabriella steered down the driveway and tried to put thoughts of Carson behind her. She hadn't come here looking for romance. Her plan was to give her kids a happy summer while she found a new direction for her life. She was on track for the first, but sadly nowhere near making progress on the second. Honestly, she hadn't given much thought to her future. She needed to focus more on that and less on Carson.

When they arrived at the youth center, they joined the line of vehicles pulling into the lot. She found a parking spot and they got out of the SUV. They'd taken a few steps when Justin and Sophia spotted their new best friends—a brother and sister duo who were their ages—and ran to greet them. Gabriella followed.

"Hi. I'm Vicki," the other kids' mother said as they walked together to the entrance.

"Gabriella. I'm Sophia and Justin's mother."

"I know. Jessica and Jason told me about them last night. I know all about the horseback riding lessons and going swimming in the biggest pool around. Now my kids want to take horseback riding lessons. And suddenly the ocean isn't as cool as an Olympic-sized pool with a basketball hoop."

Gabriella laughed. Apparently, her kids hadn't left out a single detail about their activities. She hoped they'd been a little more discreet when it came to discussing hers. "Well, if you're interested in horseback riding lessons, let me know. Carson used to give lessons in the past and is thinking about giving them again."

"Is he expensive?"

Gabriella shrugged. "I have no idea. We've been friends since we were kids, so he refused to let me pay. Plus, we're neighbors, and I think he might have been worried about the kids taking it upon themselves to hop on one of his horses unsupervised. Not that they would," she hastened to add. She didn't want Vicki to get the wrong idea about her kids.

"Well, if he's interested and not too expensive, I'd like to sign up my kids."

"Give me your number. I'll check with him and get back to you." And though she loathed to admit it, she liked having a reason to contact Carson.

They stepped inside the building and joined the line in front of the reception desk.

"I need to get to work now," Vicki said after signing in her kids, "but maybe we can get together for coffee one day next week."

"That sounds good."

"I'll call you tonight," Vicki said. She hugged her kids and then dashed out the door.

Gabriella signed in Sophia and Justin. They ran down the hall the second she said goodbye, and she stood in the entry feeling ridiculously bereft and alone.

"You look lost."

Gabriella turned and looked into Raven's smiling face.

"Maybe a little bit. I didn't quite expect my kids to just dart away like that without even saying goodbye."

"It's not you. It's this place. All the kids act the same way. Once they step inside the door all parents cease to exist."

"I guess."

Raven gestured to a woman who was coming to join them. "Do you know Roz Martin?"

"No."

Raven quickly introduced them. "We were on our way to get a cup of coffee at Mabel's Diner. Do you want to join us?"

"I'd love to."

Ten minutes later they were sitting at a table near the back of the restaurant.

"I still can't get over how much the diner looks the same as it did when I was a kid," Gabriella said.

"Did you grow up here?" Roz asked.

"No. My aunt and uncle had a ranch outside of town. I visited them every summer for about ten years. It's been a while since I've been back, but I always loved it here."

"So do I. I moved to Sweet Briar a couple of years ago. I had a bit of a rough time for a while, but things are looking up." She twisted a large princess cut diamond engagement ring on her left hand.

"I take it you're getting married soon."

"In three weeks."

"Congratulations. You must be so happy."

"Very." Roz's smile was so bright it illuminated her entire face. "Paul is a great guy. And he and my kids love each other. They're just as excited about the wedding as we are."

"Did you meet him here?"

"No. We were high school sweethearts and later in-laws."

Gabriella had been adding sugar to her coffee, but her hand froze at Roz's words. She had so many questions but wouldn't ask a single one. "Sounds complicated."

"You don't know the half of it. For a while we were estranged. Miraculously, everything worked out and now we're getting married."

"I love a happy ending."

"You and me both."

After that, conversation turned to the details of Roz's wedding. Neither she nor her fiancé had wanted anything big or formal, but her daughters had begged to wear fancy dresses, shiny shoes and crowns. So the affair would be a little ritzier and bigger than their initial plan. Roz confided that she was looking forward to wearing her glamorous new wedding dress.

As they talked, Gabriella's mind wandered back to her wedding. It had been an over-the-top affair that had cost a fortune. Her parents hadn't been able to afford such an elaborate event, but the Tuckers had insisted their oldest child have a wedding and reception befitting their status. So they'd paid for it. Gabriella had gotten swept away in the fantasy and romance of it all.

Looking back, Reggie hadn't been involved in the planning. At the time she hadn't thought much of it. After all, most men didn't care about fabric swatches, table runners or the cardstock used in invitations. Now she knew that his indifference stemmed from his true feelings for her more than the wedding. He wasn't going to be marrying the woman his heart longed for, so nothing else mattered. They could have gotten married in a garbage dump for all he'd cared.

The next time she got married—if she remarried—her groom was going to be just as invested as she was. She wasn't going to be the only one who was completely in love. She was going to be his first—and only—choice.

"So how are you keeping busy?" Raven asked, returning Gabriella's attention to the present.

"Pretty much the same way I did as a kid."

"Hanging out with Carson?"

"Yes. My kids sort of glommed onto him. The fact that he has horses and the biggest swimming pool known to man is a plus. They'd spend every waking moment with him if I let them."

Raven grinned impishly, and in that moment Gabriella knew that they could become good friends. That is, if the whole used-to-be-engaged-to-Carson-who-might-still-be-in-love-with-her thing didn't get in the way. "There's that. Not to mention that he's great to look at, which would make it that much easier for *you* to hang around all day."

"He didn't look like that when we were kids. The last time I saw him we were fifteen. I left behind a lanky kid, and a gorgeous hunk of a man took his place. I swear if he didn't have the same easy way about him, I wouldn't even know it was him."

Raven and Roz exchanged a glance.

"What did I say?"

"He's not the same easygoing person you remember," Raven said. "At least not around town and definitely not around me. I don't know if he told you or not, but we were engaged."

Gabriella nodded, glad to have it out in the open. Hopefully, they could talk about it without it becoming weird. "He told me you ended it."

"I didn't end it. He did."

"Oh. I thought..." Gabriella sputtered. Why had she thought Raven had ended it and broken Carson's heart?

"Oh, he was right to end it. I was in love with someone else although I was in complete denial about my feelings. If Carson hadn't broken up with me, I might have married him, making all of us miserable. He saved all of us a lot of needless pain, for which I'll always be grateful."

Sadly Gabriella knew firsthand what that pain felt like.

"Didn't he tell you anything about what happened with his father?"

"No." Gabriella wanted to know. It would probably explain so much. But she wanted Carson to be the one to tell her. Otherwise, it felt like she was gossiping about him behind his back. It was one thing to say how gorgeous he'd become over the years. It was another thing entirely to hear about whatever it was that happened with his father. And given the surprise in Raven's voice, Gabriella knew it couldn't be good. "I suppose he'll tell me later if he wants me to know."

"I hope so. It's good that he has you in his life. He and Donovan were friendly in high school, but as you can imagine, our marriage put a strain on that. It did the same to my friendship with Carson, which is sad even though it's completely understandable. Carson supported me through the worst time of my life. Yet no matter how stoic he acts or how much he's distanced himself, he needs friends the same as everyone else."

Gabriella nodded her agreement, effectively bringing the topic to a close. They'd finished their coffee while they talked so they paid the bill and left the restaurant. Promising to get together soon, they went their separate ways.

Rather than return home, Gabriella strolled around town. Today was the perfect day to visit the interesting shops she'd spotted on earlier visits.

The weather was gorgeous, and she smiled as she walked down the picturesque street. The wind blew the sweet scents of the flowers overflowing the large pots on the sidewalk into the air. Cedar Ridge, was an exclusive community with an equally well maintained shopping district. But in Gabriella's estimation, Sweet Briar had a certain je ne sais quoi that elevated it above Cedar Ridge. Perhaps because she associated Sweet Briar with happy times, and Cedar Ridge reminded her of deceit and betrayal.

Her first stop was Louanne's Homemade Chocolate Shoppe. Gabriella stepped up to the store and stared at the window display. Trays of chocolate-covered nuts, pretzels, candies and every delight known to woman surrounded a flowing chocolate fountain. Just looking at it made Gabriella's mouth water. Filled with anticipation, she stepped inside and looked around. Glass-fronted cases lined three walls, forming a perfect U of temptation.

"Welcome," a smiling woman said as she slid a tray of chocolate-covered strawberries into a glass-fronted refrigerator. "Look around. If you don't see what you want, just ask."

Gabriella returned the other woman's smile. "You have more in here than I could imagine. If I don't see what I want, it doesn't exist."

"Is this your first time visiting us?"

"Yes. And if I had known what I was missing, I would have been here sooner."

"I'm Stephanie," the woman said, coming from behind the counter.

"Gabriella."

"Let me give you a little tour. The cases on the right of the door contain our covered fruit. On the left we have covered nuts and candies. And in the tray facing the window, we have our covered salty treats. Pretzels, popcorn, potato chips and such."

"Chocolate-covered potato chips?"

"Yes. They're quite delicious if I do say so myself. I'll give you a sample. In fact, feel free to ask for a sample of anything that interests you."

"Really? Thanks."

Stephanie nodded at Gabriella's appreciation. "We make everything on-site using only the finest ingredients."

"Do you create gift boxes?"

"Of course."

"My aunt loves chocolate. She's on vacation now, but I'd love to send her a present when she gets home." That was the least Gabriella could do for her aunt who'd done so much for her.

"Just stop by when you need it and I'll put it together."

"Thanks."

"Do you want anything now?"

"Oh, yeah." There was no way she was leaving empty-handed.

"Let me know when you're ready."

Gabriella took her time, looking at everything and requesting several samples. The chocolate-covered chips were unique, but they weren't for her. She decided to stick with her favorites: chocolate-covered almonds and chocolate-covered strawberries.

Once she'd paid for her purchases, she visited a couple more businesses before going to the grocery store for a few staples she needed.

When she got home, she completed her chores and then wandered around the house at loose ends. She'd promised the kids that she wouldn't pick them up before four o'clock, so she had lots of time to kill. She grabbed a book she'd been planning to read and sat on the front porch. After a few minutes spent rereading the same page, she closed the book. She wasn't in the mood to read. There was only thing she wanted to do. One person she wanted to spend the day with.

Carson. It was senseless to deny it. Even though

she knew that he was probably busy, she couldn't convince herself to stay home. Rivers Ranch beckoned to her. The ranch was enormous, and Carson could be anywhere, so the odds of actually running into him were slim, but she would take her chances. If he was around and not too busy, they could hang out together. If she didn't see him, she would find a way to occupy herself.

Gabriella combed her hair and spritzed on a bit of her favorite perfume, stopping herself before she could put on makeup. This wasn't a date.

After checking her appearance in the mirror, she headed for the ranch. Her heart beat faster the closer she got to the corral, and it was practically pounding by the time she was standing beside the fence. To her disappointment, Carson was nowhere to be found. She leaned against the top rail and watched the horses milling around. She stood there for a long moment before deciding to walk back home.

"Hey."

Gabriella spun around. Carson was astride Excalibur, riding in her direction. As usual, he was dressed in a casual shirt and faded jeans that teased her by hinting at the muscular thighs they covered. His black hat dipped low on his head, but she could still see his smiling face.

"Hey."

"What are you doing here? We didn't schedule a lesson for today, did we?"

She shook her head, suddenly feeling foolish. She hadn't considered how desperate she would look showing up out of the blue like this. "The kids are at the youth center today."

"And you're bored? Lonely?"

He knew her so well. Too well for her to deny the truth. "I had some time on my hands and thought I'd say hi. But I can see that you're busy, so I'll let you get back to whatever it is you're doing."

"I'm just riding out to check some fence. You can come with me if you want."

"How long will we be gone?"

"Just a couple of hours."

"Well…"

"You know you want to come. I'll saddle Beauty for you."

She smiled. "You just want another pair of hands."

He laughed. "You discovered my devious plan."

He saddled her horse, and soon they were riding across the ranch. Carson started at a moderate pace and she urged her horse to go faster, leaving him behind. He quickly sped up, and they went flying over the grass in an exhilarating ride. After twenty or so minutes, they reached the fence line and slowed.

"That was fun," Gabriella said.

"I take it that our rides with the kids don't satisfy your need for speed."

"No. But this hit the spot."

He dismounted and knelt before the fence. There was a hole that needed to be repaired. Gabriella slid from Beauty's back and knelt beside Carson. It had been years since she'd helped him fix fence, but she still knew how. Suddenly she was anxious to get to work. Although there were none around today, cattle roamed in this area of the ranch, so the fence was made out of wire, which provided both a physical and visual barrier. They spliced two feet of new wire into the hole and used the hammer to tighten it. The two of them worked as one and it didn't take long to complete the task.

"I'm surprised you still know how to do that."

"Why? We must have done it a hundred times over the years." Carson had often followed Avery McAllister, one of his father's ranch hands, around. The older man had never married and didn't have kids, so he hadn't minded the company. Over time, he'd taught Carson how to do lots of jobs around the ranch. When Gabriella had started hanging around, he'd let her help, too. When Carson was old enough to do repairs on his own, Gabriella had assisted. The two had made a great team. Even Mr. Rivers hadn't complained that Gabriella was interfering with Carson's chores since he completed the tasks twice as fast with her help.

"But it's been years. Unless you're working as a ranch hand in Ohio." Carson put the hammer in his saddlebag.

Gabriella sighed. "Sadly, no. I haven't even been on a horse in years."

"Why not?"

"It's complicated."

"Isn't everything?"

"Yep." She inhaled deeply, breathing in the smell of grass. In that moment, she was filled with peace. She didn't want to ruin that feeling by talking about anything unpleasant.

They got back on their horses and continued to ride the fence line. As they went, they talked about everything except her disastrous marriage and his broken engagement. They made a few more minor repairs before turning around and heading for the house. Gabriella couldn't think of the last time she'd enjoyed herself this much, and she was sorry for the moment to end. There was so much she wanted to say to Carson. So much she wanted him to say to her.

Had he felt the same attraction she had? And if so, did he want to act on it and see where things led? She wished the answer to those questions was yes, but she couldn't ignore the fact that she hadn't seen or heard from him in days. He might be busy, but he could have taken a moment to seek her out if he wanted. He could have wandered over any night if he had wanted to. But he hadn't. If she hadn't sought him out today, he would have been content to let another day pass without contact.

For as well as they got along, things were complicated between them. Were they two people renewing their friendship or were they two people starting a romance? What did Carson want? She recalled Raven's words. The other woman was right. Carson needed friends. People in his life who cared about him. She definitely fit the bill. That was what he needed, so for now it would have to be enough.

And what had happened with his father? She desperately wanted to know—and not just to satisfy her curiosity but to be a better friend to him. He might not want to tell her yet, but there was something she needed to say regarding his father. Once they were in the stables, brushing the horses, Gabriella spoke.

"You know, I want to apologize to you."

"For what?" He paused and looked at her.

"When your father died, I could have called but I didn't. I only sent a card and some flowers, which in retrospect seems kind of cold. I was so wrapped up in my own problems that I didn't consider what you and your mother were going through. I should have done more to reach out."

Carson gave a bitter laugh. "You did enough. More than was necessary."

Gabriella thought the response was odd, but

she didn't comment on it. Who knew what kind
of relationship Carson and his father had? When
they were kids, Carson's dad had seemed to dote
on him. But as Carson had gotten older, his father's attitude had changed He'd become more
demanding of Carson, setting what appeared to
Gabriella to be impossibly high standards. And
if Carson failed to reach those expectations, his
father seemed incredibly disappointed. But over
a decade had passed since she'd spent time here.
Their relationship could have improved. Or it could
have gotten worse. But it wasn't her business so
she wouldn't ask now. Perhaps he was no more
interested in discussing his father than she was in
discussing her marriage.

The happy mood that they'd enjoyed on the ride
faded away and Gabriella knew her comment was
the cause. Sadly, she didn't know how to restore
their earlier easy communication.

Once they finished grooming the horses, she
thanked Carson for letting her ride with him and
returned home to shower before she picked up the
kids. As she drove down the road, she became
more convinced that something was hurting Carson. As his friend, she was going to do what she
could to help him.

Carson felt Gabriella's absence the minute she
was gone. As she'd walked away, he'd wanted to

call her back and beg her to stay a little bit longer. Of course he didn't. He couldn't. It was best for everyone if they didn't get too close. How would she feel about him once she learned that his father had killed a man in cold blood? And what would she think about him if she knew that he still missed his father sometimes?

According to the journal Carson had found, Karl had thought Carson was a loser. Although his father had often been hard on him, Karl had never once spoken the word "loser" to Carson. And he'd never suspected that his father had felt that way. Sometimes Carson wished he'd never found those journals and discovered the truth.

That was the good thing about Gabriella. She hadn't been around for years and didn't know what his father had done. He wasn't constantly bombarded by the truth when she was around. Unlike when he was with other people, he didn't have to wonder if she was trying too hard to act normal. She didn't have a clue about his past, and he wanted to keep it that way.

If he kept her in the dark, their relationship wouldn't grow closer or become deeper. They couldn't truly be best friends with a giant secret between them. If he held back from her, he couldn't ask her what had happened to send her running back to her aunt's ranch. He wanted to know what had gone wrong in her marriage and whether or not she was still in love with her ex-husband. But since he wasn't willing to talk about difficult topics pertaining to his personal life, he wasn't entitled to ask her about anything hard for her to discuss, either. Fair was fair.

When Carson finished with the horses, he went inside the house to his mother's office. He'd been avoiding her office as well as his father's for months. But being around Gabriella had awakened feelings of nostalgia and a longing for the good old days.

He pulled several dusty photo albums from a bookcase and then sat down in a chair near the window. He opened one and came face-to-face with himself as an hours-old newborn. Though he'd been a cute baby—all babies were—he was looking for memories. He flipped a few pages and landed on a picture of himself as a toddler. He was dressed in cowboy boots and hat, clinging to his father's hand. Karl was smiling from ear to ear, his pride apparent. Carson reached out and touched his father's face. When he realized what he was doing, he snatched his hand back and turned the page.

How many times did he have to remind himself before it stuck—his father had been a murderer? Karl Rivers didn't deserve to be remembered fondly. Cherishing his memory would be like condoning his father's actions. Or forgiving him. Karl had never sought forgiveness; nor did he deserve it.

Carson flipped through a few more pages, and his heart ached each time he saw a picture of his father and him together. He soon discovered that the volumes were organized by year, so he ignored the really old ones, focusing instead on the albums that included Gabriella.

His mother had taken pictures of everything, determined not to miss a second of his childhood, so there were hundreds of photographs of him and Gabriella together. A few of the images had him laughing out loud. Although Carson had been a quiet, self-contained child, he'd been bolder and taken risks when Gabriella was around.

He came upon a picture of the two of them standing arm in arm beside the corral fence. Gabriella's shirt was covered with dirt and her shorts had a tear in them. Her knees were covered with drying mud and there was a huge smear of mud on her face. He'd been just as dirty, with clumps of mud in his hair. Despite their appearance, the two of them were grinning from ear to ear.

They'd been ten years old and two decades had passed, but he could remember that day as clearly as if it was yesterday. They'd decided to walk on top of the fence circling the corral. It had rained earlier that morning, so the painted wood was slippery. He'd only taken two steps before he'd fallen off. Gabriella had teased him mercilessly. He'd tried to warn her that the wood was slick, but she'd ignored him. Pushing him aside, she'd climbed on the rail and done a crazy spin in attempt to prove how much more graceful she was than him. Seconds later she'd gone sailing through the air, her arms flailing wildly. She'd crashed to the ground, landing in a huge mud puddle. She'd screeched and then burst into laughter.

He'd laughed and offered her a hand to help her to her feet. Before he knew what she'd planned, she'd pulled him into the mud with her. They'd been rolling around, wiping mud on each other when his mother had come along. She'd snapped a few pictures before telling them to hose off. Normally his mother hadn't liked him to get so dirty, but that day she hadn't chastised him. His joy had mattered more than upholding the image of a perfect family.

Carson slipped that picture out from behind the protective plastic and set it on the arm of the chair. He thought Gabriella would enjoy seeing pictures from their past. And he knew her kids would get a kick out of seeing their mother as a child. He flipped through the rest of the books, and over the next hour he amassed a stack of photos filled with memories to share with his good friend.

Reliving the past had made him feel better than he had felt in a while. Whistling, he rose and went to his office, intent on getting the ranch's books in some semblance of order. He needed to ready them for his appointment with Roz Martin, one of Sweet Briar's newest residents. She'd recently opened her own accounting office in town. Hopefully, things would go well, and he could hand over the books to her and dedicate himself to the tasks on the ranch he preferred.

When he'd done all he could, he headed to the kitchen. He was hungry, but nothing appealed to him. Then he remembered Gabriella's open invitation for dinner. Hopefully, it still stood and he wouldn't have to suffer through another frozen meal. More than that, he'd get to see her again. Despite his common sense warning against it, she was coming to mean a lot to him. He just hoped getting close wasn't a mistake they'd both regret.

Chapter Eight

"Okay, let's go," Gabriella called up the stairs. When there was no response she shook her head, went upstairs and checked the bedrooms. Justin and Sophia were nowhere to be found. It didn't take much guessing to figure out where they were. They had to be at Carson's. They'd decided he was their best friend and went over there every chance they got. She'd reminded them repeatedly that although they were on vacation, he wasn't. Working with horses was his job. Lucky for them, he never complained about them constantly showing up and following him around.

Even so, she hadn't expected them to go to Carson's today. The sleepover at the youth center was tonight. They'd talked about it for days. Joni had requested that families who were able bring treats to share with the other kids. Sophia and Justin had run amok in the candy aisle of the Walmart near the highway. They'd each selected three large bags of individually wrapped candy. Since it was for sharing, Gabriella had let them get it all. Her children had benefited from their time at the youth center and Gabriella was grateful for the opportunity to show her appreciation.

Gabriella went outside to wait for the kids to return. In a couple of minutes, they ran up the driveway.

"We went to tell Carson goodbye," Justin said.

"He told us to have a good time. He wants us to tell him all about it when we see him again," Sophia added. "I told him we would."

"Good idea. You can tell him tomorrow."

"I don't know if he'll be back. He said he had to go out of town to deliver a horse today."

Really? He hadn't mentioned that to her. Not that he needed to keep her abreast of his plans. "Okay. Well tell him the next time you see him. Now, let's get your stuff into the car. You don't want to be late."

They grabbed their brand-new sleeping bags, backpacks and bags of candy and then scrambled into the SUV. As they drove down the highway, they talked about which of their friends they hoped to see and the games they wanted to play. Their enthusiasm was heartwarming. Coming here had been the right decision.

We could live here permanently.

The idea came out of nowhere, and although the prospect held a great deal of appeal, Gabriella didn't allow herself to entertain it for long. They couldn't stay here. The children's father was in Ohio, and she couldn't move them so far away from him. Reggie had called them the other night out of the blue, something she took as a good sign. She'd been surprised to hear his voice and had nearly dropped the phone. Clearly, he missed them and wanted to know about their lives.

She'd pushed down the anger that had sprung up out of nowhere and handed the phone to Justin. She'd tried not to eavesdrop, but since they were all in the kitchen eating a snack, that had proved impossible.

Justin had talked a lot about riding horses on Rivers Ranch and swimming in Carson's pool. After a while he'd handed the phone over to his sister. Sophia hadn't talked as much, but Gabriella heard her mention Carson and her horse. She'd told him about the fun she was having at the youth center, too, but Carson had definitely dominated their conversation.

When Sophia had handed the phone back to

her, Reggie's first question had been about Carson. "Who is this man that you and the kids are spending so much time with?"

She'd been startled by the fury in his voice. He hadn't shown the least bit of interest in the kids for over a year. He'd barely acknowledged their last birthdays. *Now* he was all concerned about who they were spending time with? He had to be kidding her. Sure, she wanted him to be a part of Sophia and Justin's lives, but he had lost the right to question who Gabriella spent time with.

She'd never thought of Reggie as a selfish person before, but now she was seeing him in a different light. Perhaps he liked thinking that she was sitting alone in this house pining over him. Maybe he liked believing there was a woman out there who'd never gotten over him the way he'd never gotten over Natalie. She had no intention of living her life that way. She deserved better than to be an afterthought. And so did her kids.

"Are you listening, Mommy?" Sophia's voice cut through her musings.

"Sorry. What did you say?"

"I said that Jessica and Jason are having a party and we're invited."

"Okay. We can go shopping for gifts."

The kids looked at each other and laughed.

"It's not a *birthday* party. It's a fun-in-the-summer party. Kids here have those, you know,"

Justin said as if he'd become an authority on the kids in Sweet Briar.

She didn't know that, but she made a point to ask Vicki for details.

Gabriella pulled into the youth center parking lot. It was jammed with cars, and she circled it twice before lucking upon a spot. Every parent in the vicinity seemed to be taking the opportunity to have a night to themselves. Seeing the number of kids running to the front of the building, Gabriella felt a moment's hesitation. Had they planned on this many kids showing up? Would there be enough adult supervision? Her kids were little and basically newcomers. Would they feel comfortable? Before she could ask them if they were sure they wanted to stay all night, they'd hopped from the car and grabbed their gear.

"Hey. There's Ms. Joni and the mayor," Sophia said, pointing across the lot.

"The mayor is here?" That was something Gabriella hadn't expected. Maybe this event was a bigger deal than she'd thought. But how did Sophia know what he looked like?

"Yes. He's married to Ms. Joni and they have a baby. The mayor comes here a lot to say hi." Well, that explained that. Sophia spotted a friend and dashed away. The two little girls squealed and then admired each other's sleeping bags.

Justin walked beside Gabriella, looking for a

friend. She was hoping they'd run into a kid he knew when she heard Justin's name being called. His face lit up as a boy ran up to him. Forgetting all about her, her kids went inside the building with their friends.

"It's sad the way we become unnecessary when they see their friends," a woman said as she and another woman came up beside her.

Gabriella smiled at the women. "Yes. Or maybe they're embarrassed to be seen with me. I'm definitely not the coolest mom."

"Oh, they're too young for that. You have a couple of years before they want to be let out of the car before their friends can see you together. I'm Carmen Knight, by the way, and this is my sister, Charlotte Tyler."

Gabriella introduced herself. "It's nice to meet you. Are your kids inside?"

Carmen nodded. "My oldest daughter, Alyssa, is a teenager, so she's volunteering to help with the younger kids. My other daughter, Robyn, is participating, and I have strict orders not to do anything to embarrass her. I also have twin boys, who unfortunately are too young to spend the night."

"My son, Bobby, has been looking forward to this all year," Charlotte said. "He's already inside."

"How are they able to keep up with all of the kids?" Gabriella asked.

"Organization," Carmen said without hesitation.

"And a ton of volunteers. In addition to the teenagers, they have college students who help out. Our husbands will be here, too. My husband is the chief of police and Charlotte's husband is the town doctor. Trust me, the kids are in great hands."

Knowing that a doctor would be around did ease Gabriella's concern, and she relaxed as she stepped inside. The single reception desk had been replaced by a line of tables. Check-in was alphabetical. She found Justin and Sophia and strapped their colored wristbands around their wrists. She hugged them each goodbye and told them to have a great time.

They nodded absently before racing to join a group of kids their age who marched down the hall and out of sight. Waving goodbye to Charlotte and Carmen, Gabriella got back into her SUV and headed home.

She spent the day catching up on tasks that she'd let slide and then ate a quick dinner. Before she knew it, the sun had set and evening was making an appearance. She stood on her front porch and thought about Carson's hot tub. He'd said that she had an open invitation to use it.

Before she could think better of it, she changed into her swimsuit and covered it with a loose dress. Since there wouldn't be anyone around to see her, she put on a tiny orange bikini. She shoved her feet into a pair of old sandals and crossed the road to the Rivers Ranch.

The horses were in the stable and all was quiet.

Gabriella turned on the hot tub, stepped out of her shoes and pulled her dress over her head. Exhaling a soft sigh, got into the hot tub and sank into the warm, bubbling water. She leaned back and closed her eyes. "I should have brought a bottle of wine," she murmured to herself.

"I'm having a beer, but I can get a glass of wine for you."

Her eyes flew open. Carson was standing in front of her dressed only in his swim trunks.

"What are you doing here?" she asked.

"I live here."

"You know what I mean. You're not supposed to be here."

His eyebrows rose and he gave her a crooked grin. "Where am I supposed to be?"

"The kids told me you were out of town delivering a horse."

"I was. But it was only a couple of hours away." His eyes glowed with mischief. "So, what are you doing here?"

"You said I had an open invitation to use your hot tub. The kids are spending the night at the youth center, so I decided to take advantage of a night to myself."

"I see. Do you want that wine?"

"I'll take a beer if you have another."

He nodded and then went inside. Gabriella used

those few moments alone to take several deep breaths in a desperate attempt to calm down. Her heart was pounding and the blood rushed through her veins. Though she and Carson were only friends, she was incredibly attracted to him. Standing there in nothing but his swim trunks, his muscular torso bare, he was a tempting sight. She'd seen him like this before, but, unlike the other time, her kids weren't around to chaperone.

She and Carson were completely alone. This time she was wearing a tiny bikini. Thank goodness, she hadn't removed the top as she'd planned to do.

Carson returned and stepped into the hot tub. After sitting down, he handed her the cool bottle of beer. She twisted off the top and took a long swig of liquid courage before daring to look at him. He was staring at her. Even though the night and the water were warm, she shivered.

They were silent for a while.

"The kids get off okay?" he asked finally.

"Oh, yeah. They forgot about me as soon as they spotted their friends."

He grinned and patted her shoulder. "You know they still need you, though. Right?"

"I know. And I'm happy that they're enjoying themselves without me. After the divorce, they clung to me as if they were afraid that I was going to leave, too."

* * *

Carson took a long pull from his beer and then leaned against the back of the hot tub. Questions about Gabriella's marriage and her husband swirled around his mind. He'd reminded himself repeatedly that her divorce was none of his business, so he hadn't asked her about it. Now he wondered if he'd been wrong about that. He and Gabriella were friends. Their friendship had survived both time and distance. Over the past weeks they'd grown closer although he wasn't sure how much closer they could—or should—become.

He didn't know how to label their relationship. They were more than friends and less than lovers. Potential lovers? Who knew? The night was young. Maybe their relationship didn't need a label. Perhaps simply being Gabriella and Carson—summer friends—was enough for now.

"So what happened? Why did you get a divorce?"

She inhaled and then blew out a long breath. She toyed with her beer bottle, picking at the edges of the label as if organizing her thoughts. "Where to begin?"

"The beginning?"

She lifted one corner of her mouth in a sad imitation of a smile, and he felt a twinge of pain in his heart. She laughed humorlessly. "The beginning. The start of our relationship was actually the end of another one for him. Or rather, it was the middle."

"I have no idea what that means."

"I met Reggie my first year of college. I was waitressing part-time at a restaurant and he came in. He seemed so sad. I know it sounds ridiculous, but I actually tried to cheer him up by giving him a free slice of pie."

"That sounds like something you would do."

"Yeah. It didn't work, and he was just as sad when he left as he'd been when he came in. But he left me a nice tip. A few days later he came back and sat in my section. He didn't seem as down. We talked for a few minutes while he decided what to order. A lot of guys I served tried to hit on me, but he didn't. He was a perfect gentleman. He came back three more times. The last time, he asked me to go to this affair at the museum. I was reluctant to say yes at first because it sounded so fancy and not something that I would ordinarily do. I mentioned it to my mother and she encouraged me to go. So I did.

"It was a bit stuffy and a lot of the people were really old, but it wasn't that bad. Reggie introduced me to his friends. They were nice and I ended up having a good time. When he asked me to go out again, I said yes and we started dating. He was always a gentleman and we always had fun. My parents adored him. Before I knew it, we were engaged. Not long after that, we were married."

She sighed. Carson couldn't tell if it was sadness or resignation that he heard. Though the events she'd described had occurred over a decade ago, he wanted to know what it was she'd felt at the time and how those feelings affected her now.

"Reggie's thirteen years older than I am, but he always said age was just a number." She shrugged. "And truly, he was right. The difference in age didn't have anything to do with the problems in our marriage."

She swallowed more beer before continuing. "He wanted kids right away so when I got pregnant with Justin, I quit school. Sophia was born two years later. When she started kindergarten, I went back to school and got my degree in child psychology."

"You're a psychologist?"

"Yep. I never worked, though. Tucker wives get college degrees, but they don't get jobs. They volunteer at worthy charities." There was a self-disgust in her voice Carson had never before heard. A tone that he hoped never to hear again.

"What does your husband do?"

"Ex-husband. His family owns a bunch of television stations across the country. Reggie is a vice president of the corporation. They're also minority shareholders in a professional football team, but I think that's more a status thing."

"I see." Spoiled rich kid.

"It's not like that," she said, in a rush to correct any bad impression he might have of her ex-husband. Interesting. Why would she care what he thought about the other man? Did she still have feelings for him? "Reggie's really smart and works hard. His father might own the company, but he earned his position."

"Okay. He sounds like a great guy. So what was the problem?" He heard the bitterness in his voice. Apparently she did, too, because she gave him a startled look. He grabbed his bottle and chugged more beer. The last thing he wanted to hear from Gabriella was how great another man was. From where he sat, Gabriella was still hung up on her ex. He'd been there and done that once before. The ride hadn't been fun the first time around, and he wasn't anxious to repeat the experience.

"He didn't love me. Oh, he liked me well enough and seemed content enough to be married to me. But that was before."

"Before what?"

"Remember when I said that our beginning was really the middle of his story. The day we'd met was the day after the love of his life married someone else. Reggie had asked her to marry him, but for some reason she'd said no. Up until the moment that she'd said *I do to the other man*, he'd held out hope that she'd end her engagement and come to him. Once the deed was done, Reggie faced reality. Since he couldn't have her, he decided to move on with his life.

"And there I was. All young and innocent. And stupid."

"You weren't stupid."

She snorted. "What do you call it?"

"You said it yourself. You were young and innocent. And he was a jerk who took advantage of you. You were honest about your feelings. He was a liar. He let you believe his heart was available all the while knowing he was in love with someone else."

Her eyes filled with tears. She blinked and one fell. She brushed it away before he could. "Thank you for saying that. For the longest time I thought that I'd done something to make him stop loving me. The truth is, he'd never started. I couldn't lose his love because I never had it."

Sadly, Carson could relate. He knew that story all too well. He'd lived it. But, unlike Gabriella, he'd always known that Raven was still in love with Donovan. But he'd believed that Donovan was dead. Carson had hoped that with enough time Raven would come to love him. Now he was wiser. He knew that love didn't work that way.

"Anyway, a couple of years ago, Natalie's marriage ended. She called Reggie and he went running. The next day he asked for a divorce and I gave him one."

"Bastard. I hope you made him pay."

"I'd signed an ironclad prenup. Remember, I was young. Not that it mattered. He felt so guilty about what he'd done that he gave me a ton of money. Plus the house and my cars. Even my lawyer was shocked by the amount he offered. As if that could make up for abandoning his family." She frowned again. "Or maybe he was just so eager to be rid of me that he didn't care about the money and wanted to avoid a prolonged fight. All he wanted was to be with Natalie."

"I'm sorry."

"Why? You aren't the one who deceived me." She closed her eyes for a long moment. When she spoke again her voice was so quiet he could barely hear her. "And you know what the worst part is?"

"No." He couldn't imagine what could be worse.

"He tossed the kids aside, too. Not at first. The divorce decree gave him regular visitation. Every weekend and one day a week. But then Natalie got pregnant. Suddenly Reggie was making up reasons not to take the kids overnight for their weekend visits. He would pick them up on Saturday mornings, take them on an outing and then to lunch. They were always back home by dinnertime. At first he came back on Sundays, but that didn't last long.

"I understand if Natalie was sick and unable to care for them. But they were *his* kids. He should have been taking care of them when they were at his house. Once she had her baby, things went from bad to worse. Suddenly Reggie didn't want to spend Saturdays with them. He made up lame excuses, but I knew the truth. Unfortunately, so did the kids. Now that he had his baby with Natalie, he didn't need them. His new family was complete and there wasn't room for Justin and Sophia."

"He doesn't see them?"

"Not really. He hadn't seen them in months before we came here. I didn't know what pain was until I watched my children staring out the front window, waiting for their father to come visit them when we all knew that he wouldn't. I hated being helpless and unable to fix things.

"But it wasn't until Justin asked me what he'd done to make his father stop liking him that I knew we needed a change. We couldn't stay in that house any longer. Or in that town, for that matter. So I called Aunt Mildred. You know the rest."

He knew some. But he didn't know all. Like, was she still in love with that jerk? Had she been standing beside her children, looking out that front window and hoping her ex would show up? What about the future? The way he saw it, nothing had changed and probably wouldn't. Did Gabriella believe things would be different when the summer ended and that her ex would become a doting father? Was she counting on their absence making his heart grow fonder? And why did Carson's stomach sour at the thought?

"I stand by my earlier statement. Your ex-husband is a jerk. And a fool. Trust me, he'll regret letting you and the kids go."

"The kids? Maybe. I sure hope so. But me? I was nothing but a distraction. A placeholder."

Carson agreed with her assessment, but he kept that to himself. There was no sense adding to her pain.

"And the worst part is that I never knew. If I had known the truth, I never would have married him. But he didn't care enough about me to tell me the truth. And because of that, my kids are hurting."

Carson couldn't stand to hear the pain in her voice for a moment more. The sorrow was ripping a hole in his heart. Though he knew better than to get close to her, knew that touching her would awaken all kinds of feelings that he'd deliberately buried, he reached across the hot tub and pulled her into his arms.

She froze for a second as if uncertain of where this was leading, and he worried that he'd made a mistake. While he was contemplating a way to ease out of the situation before it became uncomfortable, she inhaled and then collapsed against him. Her soft breast pressed against his chest and he sucked in a ragged breath. She moved even closer and her sweet scent wafted around him. Fighting against the desire growing within him, he patted her back. From the strength of her sobs, it was clear that she'd never let the tears fall before. No doubt she'd been trying to remain strong for her kids.

The harder she cried, the angrier Carson became. What kind of man took advantage of a woman as sweet as Gabriella? She might not believe her ex-husband had deliberately targeted her, but Carson knew better. The guy had been looking for someone young and naive who could be easily fooled. Someone without money who'd be impressed by fancy restaurants and expensive gifts. Someone exactly like Gabriella.

Though his relationship with Raven was similar to Gabriella and Reggie's, there was one big difference. Raven had agreed to marry him, but she had never deceived him. He'd always known that her feelings for him hadn't come near to what she'd felt for Donovan.

After listening to Gabriella's tale, he also knew he had no reason to resent Raven or Donovan. He'd been holding on to his pain and anger, but he now knew those feelings were misplaced. They hadn't done him wrong. Gabriella's experience was a perfect example of what being done wrong looked like.

He wished he could take away her pain. Caressing her hair, he whispered nonsensical words to her. He found himself promising her that things would get better and that she'd find a man worthy of her love.

Gradually her sobs slowed and she lifted her face. Her eyes glistened with unshed tears. But he saw more than moisture in her eyes. He saw longing. And need. On some level he knew he was making a monumental mistake, but he couldn't resist. Her parted lips were mere inches from his. Beckoning him. Moving slowly, giving her time to stop him, he brushed his lips against hers.

The shock that swept through his body was unsurprising. He'd felt that tingling sensation often enough when their hands accidentally touched or when their eyes met. But the intensity of the electricity he experienced now had him wondering if he'd ever be the same. If he hadn't known the hot tub had been expertly grounded, he'd think there was a short in one of the wires. But no. The sensation came from kissing Gabriella.

Her lips moved gently beneath his and he groaned. Without breaking contact, he slipped his arms beneath her knees, lifted her onto his lap and increased the intensity of the kiss. He had kissed many women in his life, but the feelings that were currently growing within him far exceeded anything he'd ever felt in the past.

It was more than just the physical pleasure, although that was off the charts. Being with Gabriella felt right. She made him whole. Life with her was good. The pain of the past year lessened when she was around. He felt her easing away and reluctantly released her. Breathing heavily, he leaned his forehead against hers. Her breathing was just as labored and unsteady as his. After a moment, she slid from his lap and returned to the spot she'd vacated. He didn't like the distance between them and yearned to pull her back into his arms, but he resisted the urge. She'd made her wish clear and deserved to have it respected.

"Uh." She blinked as if she were as startled and amazed by the kiss as he was. It had been an earth-shattering kiss and he was gratified to know that he hadn't been the only one who'd been struck speechless.

"Yeah."

She blew out a breath. "I didn't expect that. I certainly didn't plan on it." She looked at him and he saw the concern in her eyes. Was she worried that he'd think she'd set out to seduce him? He wasn't that lucky. Besides, he remembered how surprised she'd been when he'd stepped onto the deck. She'd believed she was alone.

"I know. Neither did I."

"I guess it's no secret that I'm really attracted to you. I mean, who wouldn't be?"

The excitement that had been building inside him began to dissipate, replaced by dread. He knew where this was going. "But."

"I'm not in a place to get involved with anyone. The kids and I are finally getting used to being just us. But more than that, you live here in Sweet Briar and our lives are in Ohio. Their friends and family are there."

What she was saying sounded reasonable, but it was what she didn't say that made him doubt that she was being entirely truthful about her feelings. She might deny it, but he believed she was still in love with her ex-husband. Why else would she insist upon being near someone she'd just said had no interest in maintaining a relationship with the kids.

Not that Carson thought she should uproot herself and her children for him. Especially right now. They weren't involved romantically. Before tonight, they'd never even kissed. One kiss, no matter how earth-shattering, didn't make a relationship. They were still in the process of getting to know each other again, as adults instead of as children.

He wished he was in a position to see how things could evolve. But with the shape his life was in, bringing Gabriella and her kids into it would be wrong. Her reluctance to get involved only convinced him of that fact. He hated the idea, but he cared about her too much to do anything else.

"I know. And you're right. We should remain just friends. You're the best friend I ever had and I don't want to lose that. Besides, I'm not looking for love either."

"Friends for life?" she asked as if looking for confirmation.

"Yes. We're friends for life."

He thought the light in her eyes dimmed, but knew he had to be imagining it. After all, she was the one who'd said that she wasn't in a position to get involved with anyone. There was no reason for her to be disappointed. And given everything that was going on in his life, he shouldn't be disappointed, either.

And yet he was.

Chapter Nine

"Who is Aunt Mildred again?" Sophia asked as Gabriella pulled the SUV up to the gate leading to the senior community. Exquisite landscaping created a border separating the entry and exit lanes. A manned guard shack was centrally located in front of the decorative yet functional iron gate. Before answering, Gabriella rolled down her window and handed over her driver's license to the uniformed man, who checked her identification before returning it and opening the gate.

Gabriella was pleased that her aunt lived in a subdivision that took security seriously. Of course, that guard was probably hired to keep out peddlers and trespassers as opposed to hardened criminals.

"She's my mother's aunt. So she's my great-aunt and your great-great-aunt. We're staying in her house."

Sophia nodded. Ever since the divorce, she'd been trying to figure out how people were related to her. Or more accurately, where she fit into the family. She'd had a hard time when her father left, and she had been so confused by everything. How could Daddy get another wife when he already had one? Over and over she'd stated that she had a mother and didn't want another one. As time passed she'd come to understand the situation better, but she still liked to keep relationships straight in her mind.

"Why haven't we met her before?"

"You have. You were just too little to remember."

Sophia nodded, apparently content with the answer.

Not for the first time, Gabriella wished that she'd brought the kids to visit Aunt Mildred before now. She'd been such an integral part of Gabriella's formative years. Her aunt had understood her in a way that her parents hadn't. Gabriella's parents had grown up in a small town in rural Georgia, but neither of them had liked country living. They'd moved to Cleveland as soon as they'd been able to afford a house and hadn't been back to their hometown since. Thankfully, they hadn't been opposed to Gabriella spending time with her aunt and uncle in a place that she'd loved.

Reggie and his family hadn't felt the same way about the ranch. They'd been so subtle and clever in their manipulation that Gabriella hadn't caught on. There were always so many activities keeping her and the kids busy that visiting Aunt Mildred had never been possible. Now Gabriella was furious with herself for not insisting that the kids visit her aunt.

For her part, Aunt Mildred had never complained. She'd called often and sent gifts for the kids at Christmas and for their birthdays. But phone calls were poor substitutes for time spent together. Gabriella didn't know how much she'd missed her aunt until she pulled in front of the town house and parked. Tears filled her eyes, and she blinked them away before the kids could see them.

She grabbed the box of chocolates that she'd purchased at Louanne's, and she and the kids got out of the car. Aunt Mildred had been peering through her front window, and she opened the door before they reached it.

Although she'd celebrated her annual fortieth birthday more times than Gabriella could count, Aunt Mildred was ageless. Dressed in faded jeans and a colorful top, she radiated energy. Her brown face was smooth and unlined and Gabriella hoped like heck that she'd inherited those genes.

"Hello. Welcome. It's so good to see you," Aunt Mildred said. "You didn't have to bring me gifts," she added, taking the candy and setting it on a table in the entry, "but I'm glad you did."

She gave Gabriella a hug that felt like coming home. All the pain of the past two years lifted from her shoulders, and she felt like everything would be okay. Why hadn't she come back sooner? Aunt Mildred rubbed her back and murmured, "It's going to be all right. You just have to give it time."

Gabriella nodded. She remained in that comforting embrace a few moments before stepping back. The kids were watching with worried eyes and she gestured to them. "You remember Justin and Sophia, don't you?"

"Of course I do. But they were a lot smaller the last time I saw them." She smiled at each of the kids, who were suddenly shy. But Aunt Mildred was an expert at dealing with bashful kids. "And I hope you like presents as much as I do, because I brought you back souvenirs from Disney World."

"We love presents," Justin said, and Sophia hastened to second him.

"Good. Then look on the chairs by the window and see what packages have your names on them."

The kids dashed into the living room and

straight to the two chairs piled high with gaily wrapped boxes. Even more boxes were propped against the chair legs. Aunt Mildred had gone overboard with the souvenirs.

"Wow," Sophia said as she ripped the paper off a box and then turned it around so Gabriella could see. It was the Disney princess doll she'd been longing for. "This is just the one I want."

"I know," Gabriella said.

Sophia hugged the doll to her chest before running across the room to give her aunt a hug. "Thank you so much."

"You're welcome. But there's more."

Gabriella and her aunt exchanged glances as Sophia went back to her packages. She opened another box and gasped. "My own princess dress." She held the dress up to her body. It wasn't the cheap costume that was mass produced and sold in stores across the country. This dress was made of good-quality fabric and sewn with tight stitches. "Can I try it on?"

"Of course," Gabriella said. "Then we'll take your picture."

"And what about you, Justin?" Aunt Mildred asked. He hadn't said a word. But he'd placed his Mickey Mouse ears on top of his ever-present cowboy hat.

"This is just like Christmas." He swung an

authentic-looking lightsaber around. "I can't wait to show Carson everything."

"So, they've met Carson," Aunt Mildred said, sotto voce.

"He's our neighbor," Gabriella said, trying to sound normal. She didn't want her aunt to get the wrong impression. Aunt Mildred was all for taking chances and living life to the fullest. She took risks and let the chips fall where they may. Gabriella had once shared that philosophy. Of course, it was easier to live that way when you didn't have children's hearts to worry about. Gabriella couldn't make a mistake that would end up hurting Justin and Sophia, so she had to play it safe. Despite how attracted she was to Carson, given all that needed to be resolved in her life, getting involved with him was too risky.

Aunt Mildred raised an eyebrow, and Gabriella wondered what her voice had betrayed. What she'd said had been true, but she'd sounded defensive. "I was glad to see that he was still around," she added.

"Yes. To be honest, for a while there I thought he might sell the ranch and start over somewhere else. I certainly wouldn't have blamed him."

There it was again. A comment that piqued Gabriella's curiosity and made her wonder what Carson was hiding. She wouldn't ask her aunt. Carson had to be the one to tell her. She needed him to trust her enough to be honest and vulnerable with her. And if he wasn't? Then their friendship wasn't as close as she believed.

She'd already dealt with one man who'd kept secrets from her. True, Reggie's secret—he was madly in love with another woman—far exceeded anything Carson could be keeping from her. Still, a secret was a secret. The result was the same. She was in the dark. As long as he kept her at arm's length, they wouldn't get any closer.

Knowing all that, why couldn't she keep her feelings under control? Why was she longing to be closer to him? Why couldn't she forget the way his kiss felt? Even now, days later, her lips tingled as she recalled how wonderful it had felt when they kissed. It had been like floating off to heaven. When he'd lifted her in his arms and settled her on his lap, she'd experienced a level of desire that she'd never felt before. His touch had awakened feelings that had been slumbering her entire life. Emotions that she hadn't known she'd possessed had run wild through her.

She'd thought she'd known passion, but apparently she'd been wrong. Not once had she felt the depth of desire with Reggie that she'd felt with Carson. What she'd shared with her husband paled in comparison to the feelings Carson had aroused in her. Feelings that she wanted to experience again. And again.

But she wasn't ready to be vulnerable with a man who was holding back part of his life. Perhaps he didn't feel as close to her as she felt to him. Or maybe he was being cautious. He might be waiting for the right time to share his deepest secrets with her. It was possible that they were simply on different timetables. Her feelings for him were unexpected, and she was trying to find her footing. She shouldn't judge him too harshly, because he might be trying to do the same in his own way.

But not knowing what he felt was driving her out of her mind. If she knew what he felt... If he thought of her as more than a friend, she would... She would what? Uproot her kids? Tear them away from their family and friends so that she could be happy?

"Have you worked it out yet?" Aunt Mildred asked with a smile.

Gabriella frowned. "I'm not sure."

"Well, the kids and I are ready to go to lunch, so you're going to have to figure it out later. Of course, if you need an ear, my two are available."

"Thanks."

They tossed the wrapping paper into the trash, piled the gifts into the back of the SUV and then drove to Mabel's Diner.

Aunt Mildred definitely hadn't lost her touch with kids. By the time they arrived at the restaurant and took their seats, Aunt Mildred was Justin and Sophia's new best friend and they were telling her their entire life stories. Gabriella managed to get them on track long enough for them to order their lunches. That done, they were back talking nonstop until their food arrived.

Gabriella craved her aunt's ear and her opinion, but she knew she wouldn't be able to talk candidly with the kids around. She could barely get a word in edgewise as it was.

"It sounds like you're enjoying yourselves," Aunt Mildred said after the kids had taken bites of their burgers.

"This is the best place in the world," Justin said.

"I like the youth center. We have fun there. Plus, we have horses," Sophia added. "Angel is my horse and Peanut Butter is Justin's."

"You have horses?" Aunt Mildred looked from the kids to Gabriella.

"Carson's horses," Gabriella clarified. "He's been teaching them to ride."

"I heard that part. Several times," Aunt Mildred said with a smile.

They finished their lunch and after getting doggie bags for the kids, they went outside. Gabriella had intended for them to stroll along the beach, letting the kids gather shells while she and Aunt Mildred talked. But the day was dreary. Heavy clouds hung overhead, and rain threatened to fall any minute. Apparently, she wasn't going to get that time alone with her aunt today. The conversation would have to wait.

"What are we going to do now?" Sophia asked.

Good question. "What do you want to do?" Gabriella countered.

"Can we go to the youth center for a little while?" Justin asked.

Gabriella glanced at her aunt, who nodded. "Sounds good to me."

Maybe she'd get to pick her aunt's brain after all.

They made the short drive to the youth center. Aunt Mildred stayed in the car while Gabriella signed the kids in.

"So what do you want to talk about?" Aunt Mildred said, once Gabriella was behind the wheel again.

"Oh, you know. Life. Love. The future."

"In that case I'm going to need some tea. There's a new teahouse in town. Have you been there yet?"

"I didn't even know it existed until you mentioned it."

The older woman gave directions. It was on a side street, a ways from the beaten path. Apparently, word had reached everyone but Gabriella because there were quite a few people inside.

They'd eaten a delicious lunch, but the cherry tortes looked too good to pass up, so they decided to share one. They talked a bit about Aunt Mildred's vacation until their beverages and dessert arrived. Gabriella took a sip of her raspberry tea. Perfect. After setting the delicate china cup on the saucer, she looked up at her aunt. "I don't know where to start."

"Anywhere works for me. You can start at the beginning. Middle or end. I'm smart enough to follow along."

Gabriella sighed. "I don't know what to do with the rest of my life. I feel like a kid, you know? Except with adult responsibilities. Reggie has been ignoring Justin and Sophia. When I told him we were coming here for the summer, he seemed relieved. It's as if he knows what he's doing is wrong, but he doesn't care enough to change."

"Is he worried about upsetting his new wife?"

"Who knows? And does it matter?"

"Not to me. But knowing all the facts will make it easier to come up with the best strategy."

"I don't follow."

"If he wants to be with the kids and is afraid to get on the wrong side of his new wife, you can compromise and find a way to make it happen."

"I shouldn't have to convince him to spend time with his own kids."

"You're right. He should move heaven and earth to be with them. But if he's not going to do that, you have to deal with the situation as it exists. Now, if it turns out that he isn't coming around because he doesn't care about them, that's a horse of a different color. Then you don't try to work things out. You just move on and do your best to protect your kids."

"He called them last week."

"That's good."

"Yeah. But he had the nerve to be bothered about how much time they're spending with Carson."

"How does he know anything about Carson?"

"You heard them. Every conversation begins and ends with him. Now that they go to the youth center, they talk about the friends they've made there, but Carson is still a big part of their lives."

"And yours?"

Gabriella sipped more of her tea. There wasn't any use trying to fool Aunt Mildred. She'd always known Gabriella better than anyone, and she didn't tolerate nonsense. "Right now? Yes. It's almost as if fifteen years haven't passed. He's the same now as he was then."

Aunt Mildred laughed and then cut into her half of the torte. "That's not true. He's different. And so are you. You were kids before. Now you're both adults who've experienced some things. Good and bad."

"I guess I should have said that being with Carson feels the same." Gabriella sighed. "It's still so easy being with him. He's easy to talk to. It feels…"

"Right?"

"Yes. And natural. We didn't quite take up where we left off, but it didn't take long for us to become friends again. At least I thought we were becoming friends."

"Why do you have doubts?"

"He's keeping something from me. Everyone else in town knows, but I haven't got a clue. I think you know it, too."

"I do. But it is more to do with his father than with him."

Gabriella nodded. "I've gathered that much."

"I can tell you if you want."

"It has to come from him."

"I agree. And, given time, he will tell you." Aunt Mildred sipped her tea and then looked back at Gabriella, her eyes serious and all seeing. "What are your plans for the future? What if Reggie doesn't want to be a father to Justin and Sophia? Then what? What if things progress between you and Carson?"

"I don't know. I told myself that coming here would help me to figure out things. I thought I would have space to think. Instead, I added one more complication to my life and I'm running out of time."

"Well, you know you're welcome to stay in the house as long as you want."

"I take it you aren't moving back."

Aunt Mildred laughed. "Not a chance. I held on to it because I wasn't sure if I would be happy living in Willow Creek. I didn't want to be hasty. I wanted to get my feet wet, so to speak, before diving into water. But I love my town house. It's the perfect size for me. And I like living closer to my friends."

Even though Gabriella was happy for her aunt and glad that she had a fulfilling life, she still felt a sense of dread. "So are you selling the house?"

"Why? Do you want to buy it?"

Did she? She had the money. And the property was a size she could easily manage. But still… Could she make a move like that? It would be difficult to do under normal circumstances, but now that Reggie was showing an interest in her kids, did she have a right to get in between them? Would staying in Sweet Briar benefit the kids? Or would it hurt them?

"I'm not sure. I need to think about it."

Aunt Mildred raised her eyebrows as if surprised by Gabriella's answer. Heck, she was surprised herself. Moving here would mean a massive lifestyle change for herself and the kids. But being different didn't make it wrong. It didn't make it right, either. Still, it was an idea that deserved consideration.

How much of her decision-making was based on her hope for a future with Carson? Would she even consider making this move if he told her that they would never be more than friends? How would Reggie react if she moved to Sweet Briar?

"I see. Well, take your time and think about it. I don't need to sell right away. When I sold off the land, I paid the remainder of the mortgage, which wasn't all that much. I also paid cash for my town house, and I have plenty of money left over." She smiled broadly. "I'm not as rich as you, but I'm not hurting either."

"Thanks. It helps to know that I'm not costing you money."

"I didn't say that," Aunt Mildred said, her eyes twinkling with humor. "I just said that I'm not desperate for money so I don't need yours. Nor do you need to make a hasty decision."

"Okay."

"So now, tell me more about you and Carson. What kind of trouble have you two gotten into?"

Gabriella knew her aunt was thinking about all of the mischief she and Carson had gotten into over the years, but her mind instantly flashed back to the other night's kiss and her cheeks warmed.

"Oh, I see."

"Do you? I wish I did. My life is a mess, and I have a feeling his isn't much better. Yet there is something about him that makes my heart happy, which, given his secret, has me worried. I'm not even sure if he's thinking of me that way. For all I know he's still stuck on Raven."

"I don't think so. In my opinion they were just two lonely people reaching out who happened to find each other."

"They were engaged."

"I know. But Donovan was always the only one for Raven."

That addressed Raven's feelings, but not Carson's. "But Carson still wanted to marry her."

"Perhaps he thought it was time to settle down and she was available. And you'd already gotten married. Was he supposed to live the rest of his life waiting for you to come back?"

"It wasn't like that between us. We were always good friends. Only good friends."

"Friends who spent every waking minute together. Who knows what would have happened between the two of you if you hadn't been pressured to marry Reggie."

"I wasn't pressured."

Aunt Mildred snorted. "You were too young to have been involved with that man. Your parents should have slowed things down. Instead, they had dollar signs in their eyes. I'm not saying I don't understand where they were coming from. They wanted you to have a more secure future than they'd had. But still, the cost was too high."

Hearing Aunt Mildred voice thoughts Gabriella had recently begun to entertain made her emotional, and she could only nod as a lump materialized in her throat. Her aunt must have sensed that Gabriella had reached her emotional limit, because she turned the conversation to lighter topics.

When they finished their tea, they drove back to the youth center to pick up the kids. This time Aunt Mildred accompanied Gabriella inside. She signed out the kids and waited for a volunteer to bring them to the entry.

A group of preschoolers passed by. One of them spotted Aunt Mildred and let out a happy squeal. "It's the book lady."

As one, the kids charged Aunt Mildred, wrapping her in their arms. "Are you here to read to us? Do you have your puppets?"

"Not today. But I'll be back soon."

Gabriella smiled as she watched her aunt give each child a hug and then help them get back in line. Once they'd been corralled, the teen leader led them back down the hall. One little one waved to Aunt Mildred before disappearing into a room.

"I see you're just as popular as ever."

"With some. With others?" She shrugged. "Who cares?"

That was a strange answer. Before Gabriella could ask her aunt what she meant, she heard her name being called. Turning, she saw Justin barreling toward her, Sophia behind him. Whereas Justin was running, Sophia was walking slowly, carrying a clay sculpture in her hands.

"Is it time to go home already?" Justin asked.

"Yep. Did you have a good time?"

"I always have fun here."

Sophia reached them and held out her artwork. "Look what I made in art class."

"It's beautiful." And that was the truth. The horse sculpture looked exactly like Angel. Sophia had captured the likeness perfectly, from the shades of brown to the white socks. The horse seemed to be in motion.

"Mrs. Knight said that I have an artist's eye. I didn't know what that meant, so she told me that I am talented."

"You certainly are."

The children greeted their aunt, and then they all climbed into the SUV. When they pulled up in front of Aunt Mildred's town house twenty minutes later, the children got out and gave her big hugs.

"I'll come and see you very soon," Aunt Mildred promised. Then she blew a kiss to Gabriella. "And you. Be brave. The answers are inside you. All you have to do is listen."

Gabriella laughed. "I wish it was that simple."

"It is. Just trust yourself."

Aunt Mildred's words repeated in Gabriella's

mind all the way home. Was it possible that the answers to her questions were inside her? Maybe. But unless they revealed themselves, they weren't doing her a bit of good.

Chapter Ten

Finally. He was home. Carson had spent three of the past four days on the road, taking two previously abused horses to their new homes. He could have had the owners pick them up, but he'd wanted to help them get the horses acclimated to their surroundings. And truth be told, he needed some time away from Gabriella to clear his head. It was impossible to think clearly when she was around. He needed to come up with answers to some pressing questions, and soon. He'd planned to use his time on the road to think, but he'd been too preoccupied with the way she'd felt in his arms to think of anything else. Now he was back on the ranch, and the questions still remained unanswered.

Did he want a more intimate relationship with her or was he satisfied with just being friends? If things worked out between them, would she be willing to relocate here? Was he willing to move to Ohio if she wasn't?

Rivers Ranch had been in his family for four generations. He was connected to every acre and couldn't imagine living anywhere else. Despite all that had happened here, his life was here. Gabriella and her children were enjoying their time in North Carolina. But he knew that everything was fun on vacation. Could they be happy living here all year round? Though he loved ranch living and the small town of Sweet Briar, he knew that the town didn't have the amenities that were available in a larger city. There weren't any big-box stores or fast-food restaurants. To him, that was part of the charm, but when you'd grown up with conveniences, their absence could be a problem. It was a matter of perspective.

But Carson had spent so much time in his own head mulling over these questions and a dozen others that he'd only confused himself. He needed someone to talk to. Someone who wasn't so close to the situation and who could give him some guidance.

Once he'd had close friends he could have contacted, but over the past year he'd drifted away from them. At the time he'd thought they'd been trying too hard to convince him that nothing had changed. That he still fit in. He hadn't believed them. The foundation of his life had been rocked and everything he'd once believed had turned out to be lies. Consequently, he'd thought of himself differently. He'd believed they must have, too.

But maybe they'd been telling him the truth. They'd continued to call him and attempted to include him in their activities. He'd been the one to shut the door on their friendship. Maybe to them he *was* the same Carson Rivers. Just today he'd received a text reminding him of the Thursday night basketball game. For the past few years, a group of men and teenagers met up at the youth center for a few games. Before things had fallen apart Carson hadn't played every week, but he'd attended more times than he'd missed. And he had enjoyed the camaraderie.

He checked his watch. There was enough time to wash off the dirt from the road, grab a sandwich and still get to the center in time to play.

He parked his truck in the barn, and then unhooked the horse trailer and cleaned it. He took a shower and made a ham sandwich, which he ate standing up at the kitchen counter. After brushing the crumbs from his shirt, he grabbed his keys and headed for town.

He recognized a couple of the cars in the lot as belonging to his teammates, and his excitement built. Until this very moment, he hadn't realized how much he'd missed hanging out with the other guys.

He parked and then went inside the building. He was walking down the hall to the gym when someone called his name. Turning, he smiled at Joni.

"Hey, Carson. Long time no see."

"Hi, Joni." She was holding the hand of her young son, Joshua, who was toddling beside her. Carson waited for them to catch up.

When she reached his side, she smiled. "I take it that you're here for another dose of humiliation at the hands of the teenagers."

He laughed. "So the team hasn't gotten better in my absence."

"Did you think it would? Surely you don't think you were the cause of their abysmal record."

"Not solely." Carson was actually one of the better players. The adult team was composed of players whose best days—if those days ever truly existed—were behind them.

"Father Time is to blame for that."

"Are you giving us an out? That wouldn't be because you're married to a player on our team, would it?"

She laughed but didn't deny it.

They reached the gym and stepped inside. The familiar sounds of basketballs pounding the floor reached him, and he began to feel at home. Why had he stayed away from his friends for so long?

"Heads up."

Carson grabbed the ball that had been bounced in his direction. Man, he hoped that wasn't supposed to be a pass. John Howard was a great mechanic, but he couldn't play basketball to save his life.

"Good catch," John said, before jogging back to the bench and picking up another ball. He aimed at the basket and missed by a mile. Yep. Looked like his team was going to be beaten again tonight.

"Hey." Lex Devlin jogged over and picked up his son, lifting him over his head. Joshua let out a long laugh, squealing as Lex released him and then caught him a second later.

"Again, Daddy. Do it again."

"Sure thing, bud."

Carson watched as father and son played for a minute, his heart suddenly filled with unexpected longing. Since when did he want to have a child? Over the past year he'd convinced himself that he didn't want to be a father. After discovering what his own father had done, he didn't want to risk bringing a child into the world. Who knew what evil lurked in his genes?

Before long he'd convinced himself that he didn't deserve a family. What woman would willingly take on the baggage that he carried? It would be unfair to ask. Now he wondered if he'd been mistaken. Maybe talking with Lex would help him clarify things. Carson had never been one for spilling his guts—the exception being with Gabriella when they'd been kids—but desperate times called for desperate measures.

Lex kissed his son's cheek before handing the little boy back to Joni. He gave her a hug, and then turned to Carson and slapped him on the shoulder. "It's good to see you, man. I was beginning to think you'd put us down."

"It's good to see you, too."

"Everything all right?"

Carson shrugged. As a child, he'd often longed for a big brother. Although Lex had lived an entirely different life than Carson had—Lex's family owned one of the most successful cosmetic companies in the country and he'd been raised in a tony New York suburb before becoming mayor of Sweet Briar—Carson had come to think of Lex as an older brother. Lex shared his wisdom as well as a dose of razzing that had always made their relationship comfortable. At least until Carson had decided he was unworthy of friends.

"We're taking the teens out for pizza after the game," Lex said. "We'll talk then."

"Okay."

"Are you guys ready?" one of the teens called, dribbling the ball between his legs.

"Yeah, Benji. I'm surprised you're so anxious to get beat," Rick Tyler replied. Rick was the town doctor and the best player on the team. He also talked the most trash.

The teenager laughed as if that was the funniest thing he'd heard.

"How long has it been since we won the night?" Carson asked as he and Lex joined their teammates. Tonight there were ten players on each team. Three college girls were officiating. At first, the players had called their own fouls, but that hadn't lasted long. The adults had thought everything was a foul and the teenagers had thought that if it didn't draw blood it was allowed. It was good having referees to settle that debate.

The games had started as an informal way of building relationships between the adults and youth in town, but had soon become an attraction. Tonight there was a group of teenage girls in the bleachers, as well as several wives with their children. Carson wished he'd invited Gabriella and her kids to come and watch, but that would have made a statement he wasn't sure he was ready to make.

"Longer than I can recall. We're lucky if we win one game."

The teams played three twenty-minute games each night: two ten-minute halves separated by a five-minute halftime. Best two out of three won the night and bragging rights for the week.

"Well, tonight we're going to win," Carson said.

"Yeah," Rick said, coming beside Carson. "You old guys just let us young guys have the ball."

"You do realize that you're trash-talking your own teammates," Trent Knight, the chief of police, said.

"No offense to the over-forty crowd, Chief," Rick said, grinning. "All I'm saying is let us twenty- and thirtysomethings take the lead. We have more stamina."

"Oh, I have stamina," Trent said with a wicked grin.

They all laughed. Carson had missed this.

"Are you guys ready yet?" a teen called again. "All that stretching isn't going to make you any faster or help you make baskets."

The other kids hooted.

Carson joined four of his teammates on the floor. The two teams nodded as Melanie, the referee, told them to play fair and have a good game. The youth were bigger and stronger than Carson remembered. Melanie threw the ball up and Lex and Benji battled for it. But only for a second. Benji tipped it to a teammate, who took off down the floor. Two quick passes later and the teens had scored.

Oh, boy. They were faster than Carson remembered, too.

The adults took possession of the ball and ran

down court. Unless things had changed in Carson's absence, they didn't have set plays. They just passed the ball until someone got open and took a shot. Or until one of the teens stole the ball.

After five times up and down the floor, the adults had yet to score and the teens hadn't missed. Two older guys were huffing and puffing, looking like they would keel over any second. Rick might not have been diplomatic, but he wasn't wrong when he said that the over-forty crowd should take a back seat. With the exception of Lex and Trent, the older guys had definitely lost a step, and that was being generous. There were a couple of fathers on the team who were taking the opportunity to spend time with their sons. Carson appreciated the desire for father-son bonding, but they were dooming the adult team to certain defeat. Carson looked at Rick, who nodded. It was time for the under-forties to take over.

Carson stole the ball and passed it to Rick. Rick dribbled down the court and made a basket. Finally. At least they weren't going to get shut out. The teens took offense to being shown up and upped their level of play. At halftime, the teens were leading thirty-eight to six.

"It's a good thing you younger guys are here," John said as he mopped sweat from his brow. "Otherwise we might be losing. Oh, that's right. We are."

Carson laughed. "Tell that to Rick, not me."

"I'm not the one getting posterized," Rick said to John.

"Benji is good," Lex said. "He's got offers from colleges all over the country. And a couple of NBA teams have been sniffing around."

"What's he going to do?" Carson asked.

"Your guess is as good as mine. His mom's a widow with kids to support. From what I hear, she's been trying to convince him to go to school. But he might go for the money so he can help her out."

Carson couldn't imagine the pressure the kid was under. He'd grown up financially stable and as a teenager hadn't given money a second thought. Karl Rivers might have been many things, but he'd provided well for his family. Carson frowned. He hated even thinking something positive about his father. Karl had killed someone, depriving other children of their father. A woman of her husband. Carson didn't want to give his father a free pass, but at the same time he couldn't alter the past, even if his outlook had changed. It was so much easier to not think of his father than to try to sort out his complicated feelings.

At times like this he understood why his mother had moved away. She was doing her best to put his father and the place he'd held in her life behind her. She could live her life without risk of running into someone who'd known what her husband had done. She'd chosen to relocate while he'd chosen to isolate himself on the ranch. Until now.

Ever since Gabriella and her children had moved across the road from him, isolation had lost its appeal. He wanted to be around them and had a hard time picturing his life without them.

"Why are you frowning?" Rick asked. He was the most carefree of all the guys. But then, he had the perfect life. He had a beautiful wife and a great son.

"Just a passing thought. Nothing serious."

Rick nodded. They'd been friends long enough to know when the other wasn't in the mood to talk.

Melanie blew the whistle. "One minute."

Carson swallowed some water and, shoving aside his troubling thoughts, jogged to center court for the jump ball.

The second half went much the same way as the first. Carson had believed he was a fairly good player, but playing against these kids disabused him of that notion. The teenagers won by a score of sixty-five to fourteen. The second and third games were as lopsided as the first two. Carson was in good shape, but after an hour of playing with these kids, he was panting as hard as the over-forties and every muscle in his body ached. As the clock wound down on the third and final game, he dropped into a chair beside his visibly exhausted teammates.

"Those kids are fierce," he managed to say.

"Surely they weren't too much for you under-forties with all of your stamina," Trent said, smirking.

"That was Rick who said that, not me," Carson corrected with a grin.

"How about one more game? We'll spot you thirty points just to make it interesting," Benji said before running to the other end of the gym and dunking. The other teens began shooting hoops with spare balls, never missing once.

"We've got reservations at Marconi's. That is, if you still want pizza," Lex said.

"Oh, yeah."

The players gathered up the balls and returned them to the storage closet at the far end of the gym. Most of the spectators had gone home after the second game, so only a few parents remained. Rick and Trent assured them that they'd make sure the teens got home safely.

Once the gym was restored to order and the lights were turned out, they piled into their cars and drove to the pizza parlor. Marconi's was a popular restaurant, and there were a few people finishing their meals or lingering over dessert. The players were quiet as they walked through the dining room and into the large party room at the back of the restaurant. Lex had called in their order ahead of time, so once they were seated, the waitresses set the food on a long table at the head of the room.

There was orderly chaos as the youth charged the table, piling slices of pizza on plates and filling glasses with soda. Once they'd sat down, the adults took their turn. There was a bowl of salad on the table, which remained pretty much untouched.

Adults and teens shared tables, and laughter quickly filled the room. There was lots of good-natured teasing and trash-talking, and Carson joined in between bites of cheese-and-sausage pizza.

Time passed, and one by one people began to leave. Rick and Trent lingered by the door while the teens they were driving home dropped the last of the pizza into paper napkins to eat later. When they were done, they waved and exited the room, leaving Lex and Carson alone.

"So, what's going on?" Lex asked as he sat in a recently vacated chair at Carson's table.

Carson should have prepared an answer over the past hour, but he hadn't. Now he had no choice but to give an unrehearsed answer. "It's Gabriella."

He was surprised that of all the things on his mind, Gabriella's name tumbled out of his mouth.

"Gabriella?"

"You might not know her. Her aunt, Mildred Johnson, owns the house across from my ranch."

"Ah, the book lady."

"Who?"

"Mrs. Johnson reads to the kids at the youth center. Joshua loves her and Joni sings her praises."

"Yes. Well, anyway Gabriella used to visit every summer when we were kids."

"I take it you were close."

"Close" didn't come near to describing their relationship back then. And it was becoming insufficient in describing their current relationship. But since Carson couldn't find an adequate word, he nodded.

"And now?"

"Now our friendship has picked up from where we left off. To be honest, I'm thinking that our relationship could become something deeper. Something more personal."

"So what's the problem? Why do you sound so depressed?"

"Because. How can I bring her into the mess that is my life?"

"You lost me. What part of your life is a mess?"

"Are you kidding?"

"Not at all."

"Every part of my life. My father was a killer. He murdered a man and got away with it for years. He threatened Donovan and made him leave town. That's my life."

"No. That's your father's life. He did those

things, not you. Nobody holds you responsible for his actions."

Carson thought about his run-ins with Rusty Danvers and his friends. The angry, hateful words. The way he'd tried to ruin Carson's reputation. Rusty had worked for Carson's father for a hot minute and had bounced from ranch to ranch over the past decade. And though Rusty was the only one of a handful of people who'd said anything, Carson couldn't believe others didn't also harbor a negative opinion of him. "Some do."

"You can't let what some misguided and, dare I say it, jealous people think control you. Live your life and ignore the fools. Stop hiding out on your ranch. Reclaim your life."

"That's easier said than done."

"I know. But what does that have to do with Gabriella?"

Carson picked up his cup and drank the remainder of his soda. The ice had melted and the flavor left something to be desired. "If I take things with her to the next level, then I risk making her a part of this. She also has two young children. I don't want them being mistreated."

"I don't think anyone would do that."

"But should I even take the risk? Gabriella and I are really good friends. We could keep on being just friends."

Lex laughed. "You know Joni and I were good friends before we got married, right?"

Carson nodded. Everyone in town had known that they'd belonged together long before they'd gotten married.

"Well, I almost blew it with her. I wasn't ready to face the depth of my feelings. When she got pregnant, I suggested we should get married for the sake of the baby."

"Yikes." Carson laughed. "You seem so much smarter than that."

"I thought I was being smart. The way I saw it, I would get to be with Joni and our son without having to deal with my feelings."

"I think you're trying to tell me something, but I'm not getting the message."

"Don't worry about protecting your feelings."

"It's not my feelings I'm worried about. It's Gabriella and her kids."

"If you say so. But either way, my advice to you is going to be the same. Figure out how you feel. Talk to Gabriella. Be honest about everything, and let her decide what's best for her and the kids."

"It might be a moot point anyway."

"How do you figure?"

"Her ex still lives in Ohio. From what she told me, he hasn't been a part of Justin and Sophia's lives for a while, but she doesn't want to get in the way of them having a relationship with him in the future. She's planning to go home at the end of summer."

"That does complicate things, but it's not an impossible hurdle. Figure out how you feel. Then make your move. You won't regret it."

They stood and walked to their vehicles. Carson pondered Lex's words as he drove back to the ranch. Was he more concerned about his own feelings than he was about Gabriella's safety? Was her safety simply an excuse he was using in order to protect his heart? He didn't know. But he needed to figure that out soon. Time was running out.

Chapter Eleven

Gabriella smiled as she and the kids walked across the road to Carson's house for their horseback riding lessons. When he'd called her last night to confirm the time, he'd told her that he wanted her to ride with them. The lesson would be thirty minutes earlier than usual because the kids were going to attend a sleepover party with their friends. When she'd told Carson that the kids would be gone for the night, he'd invited her out to dinner. She'd immediately said yes, and her mind had been swirling with excitement ever since.

She'd visualized the limited wardrobe that she'd brought with her from Ohio—jeans, shorts and casual skirts—and knew there was nothing in her closet that she could wear to the swanky restaurant Carson was taking her to. She'd have to stop by the boutique in town and buy something stylish. Something that would knock Carson's socks off. She smiled at the thought. Who would have believed her feelings for Carson would change from friendship into something that felt suspiciously like love?

That just showed you how life could change in a minute. Of course, she'd learned that lesson when her marriage imploded. Change was so much better when it was positive.

The kids spotted Carson and as usual ran to him. When they reached him, they hugged him around his waist. Her heart squeezed at the sight. The three of them looked so good together. Almost like a family.

Seeing the kids with Carson only emphasized how much more attention they'd needed from Reggie. If he wasn't willing to change and give them time and attention, then she needed to act. But what should she do? She couldn't just slot Carson into the place that Reggie had vacated. They weren't interchangeable pieces. Carson was his own man. But what if he wanted that place in her kids' lives? Would that change things?

When she reached the happy trio, Carson smiled at her and all her worries vanished.

"We were telling Carson about the presents Aunt Mildred brought us and about lunch with her," Sophia said.

"I'm sorry I missed it," Carson said, leading them to the horses.

"You can come next time," Justin pronounced.

"I'd like that."

Gabriella trailed behind them, her eyes drawn to Carson's firm bottom. The jeans he wore fit his body perfectly. Not too tight, not too loose. He turned around and caught her staring. Blushing, she trotted over to the fence. His laughter reached her, but she wasn't sure whether he was laughing at her reaction or something one of the kids had said.

"I thought we could ride out to the watering hole this morning," Carson said, coming up beside her. He was standing so close his hand brushed against hers and tingles danced down her spine.

"What's a watering hole?" Sophia asked.

"It's a place your mom and I used to swim when we were kids."

"Why didn't you just use the swimming pool?" Justin asked. "It's right there."

"I didn't have a pool until I was about thirteen. I was happy when my mother had it put in, but we still liked going to the swimming hole."

"Half of the fun was getting there," Gabriella added. Those had been the days, racing across the seemingly endless acres of green grass and the occasional hill to reach the pool created by Mother Nature. The cool water had felt so good on her skin in the hot summer months, and they'd swum and splashed for hours.

When they'd been young, they'd lain together on a blanket, letting the sun dry their suits. When they were older, they'd swum well past sunset. They would often build a fire and sit close together on that same blanket, sharing their innermost secrets.

They had been so innocent back then. There hadn't been a hint of anything sexual between them. Now, though, the thought of lying beside Carson aroused her, and she struggled to control her imagination.

"We aren't going to swim now, are we? The party is today and I don't want to mess up my hair," Sophia said.

"No, we're just going to ride there and come back," Carson confirmed. They mounted their horses and Carson approached Gabriella, who was astride Beauty. "Sophia is pretty excited about that party."

"They both are. That's all they've been talking about for days. They're supposed to be there around three o'clock. Apparently there's going to be a magician and a bounce house. But naturally the highlight of the event is sleeping on someone else's living room floor." She shook her head. "Go figure."

Carson laughed. "Come on. Surely you remember how much fun we had at our sleepovers as kids."

"Yeah. I admit there was something magical about spending the night under the stars in your backyard. Of course I was so much younger then, and the ground didn't feel quite as hard."

"You're forgetting my stellar company."

"That goes without saying. Still, I can't imagine willingly doing so today no matter how wonderful the company."

"So you're saying I need to provide you with a comfortable bed if I expect to enjoy your company overnight."

Gabriella choked, and Carson's eyes widened as he realized what he'd just said. Obviously he hadn't meant to be provocative, but the idea did hold appeal. And just like that, she pictured herself lying in his bed. But truth be told, the way she felt right now, she wouldn't complain about making a bed on the ground, as long as he was beside her, his arms holding her close.

"Are you and Mommy having a sleepover?" Sophia asked, riding up beside them. Gabriella had been so involved in her daydream that she'd forgotten that little kids had big ears.

"Not tonight," Gabriella said, avoiding Carson's eyes.

"Too bad," Sophia answered.

"Are you guys ready yet?" Justin asked.

"Yep." Gabriella didn't wait for Carson to assign riding order. Instead, she turned and headed toward the watering hole at a pretty steady clip. Beauty had a smooth gait and liked the quicker pace. The kids had no trouble keeping up with her, and she was pleased that they were becoming such good riders. Carson was an excellent teacher.

As she rode, her mind replayed the earlier conversation. Did he want to have a sleepover? Or was she making too much out of an innocent comment? There was no sense in denying that she wanted one. Heck, she was beginning to want more than just one night of shared passion. She enjoyed his company. She was happier with him than she'd been in years. The more time she spent with him, the more time she wanted to spend with him.

She wondered just how much of this newfound attraction was based on happy memories of times they'd spent together and how much was based on the man he was now. Was she falling for him because she was tired of being alone, or did she actually care for him? Was she trying to prove that she was still a desirable woman, despite the fact that her husband had dumped her?

She stopped that thought in its tracks. Reggie had nothing to do with her feelings for Carson. She might not know everything, but of that she was certain. And in that moment, she knew her feelings were not based on the past, either. At least not entirely. It was impossible to separate her current emotions from what she'd felt all those years ago. But, back then, they'd been friends. Only friends. When she'd returned to Sweet Briar, all she'd felt for him had been friendship, and barely that. But it hadn't taken long for them to renew their friendship.

The relationship had grown over these past weeks and turned into something deeper. Something that touched her heart, awakening strong emotions. Did he feel the same shift in their relationship? That was the crucial question. And one she intended to get an answer to.

If her divorce had taught her one thing, it was the importance of honesty. She could have avoided so much pain and disappointment if she had known the score with Reggie from the beginning. Time had made her wiser and bolder. She wasn't going to wait to find out how Carson felt. Nor would she try to interpret his actions or decipher the meaning of his every word. No more wondering. She was going to be direct and ask him. Tonight. She inhaled a peaceful breath. By the end of the night she would have her answer.

She reached the watering hole and dismounted, then waited as the others did the same.

The kids took one look around and then ran to the water as Gabriella had known they would.

She'd reacted the same way the first time she'd come here.

"It has a waterfall," Sophia exclaimed. "It looks like a big shower."

"Why didn't we go on that side?" Justin asked, scrambling atop a boulder.

"Because this is the side we always came to," Gabriella said, and then laughed. There really hadn't been a reason. Only habit. "We usually just got in over here and swam to the waterfall."

"It's really big," Justin said. "It's even bigger than your pool."

Sophia giggled. "I thought it was going to be a big puddle. Or just water in a hole."

"Well, we did call it a watering hole, so I can see how you thought that," Carson said.

"We should come out here to swim one day," Justin said.

"And bring lunch, too. Like a picnic," Sophia said, warming to the idea.

Gabriella didn't bother telling the kids yet again that it was impolite to invite themselves over to Carson's ranch and make big plans. They were just so comfortable with him and felt at home. She felt the same way.

"That would be fun," Carson added. "We'll put it on the list of things to do before you go back home at the end of summer."

Where had that come from? They were going

to be here for a few more weeks. Was he already thinking about the time she and the kids would leave? Was he reminding her that their relationship had an expiration date? Hearing him talk about the end took some of the wind from her sails. Was she the only one considering a possible future for them? She knew it wouldn't be easy, but with each passing day she was becoming more willing to take the risk.

She thought about the life she'd left behind. Justin and Sophia had lived in the same house all of their lives. Moving here would make it more difficult for them to spend time with their father. But, realistically, how much time had he spent with them in the past year? Not much. As painful as it was to admit, he didn't care as much for their children as he did for his child with Natalie. So he wouldn't be a factor when she decided where she and the kids lived in the future. If he wanted to be a part of their lives, she wouldn't stop him, but he was going to have to put in more effort. She was through accommodating him.

The most important thing was the kids' happiness. She wouldn't forget that. But her happiness mattered, too. Thankfully, they weren't mutually exclusive. They were all happy here now. They could be happy here later.

The children climbed over more rocks and then walked along the water's edge.

"Be careful," Gabriella called.

Justin waved an exasperated hand in reply and Gabriella smiled. She'd crawled over these very same rocks when she'd been their age. Somehow she'd turned into an overprotective mother when she hadn't been paying attention.

Gabriella knew from experience that it would take about thirty minutes for the kids to make it around the watering hole. It might take them longer if they kept stopping to look at things they spotted on the ground, which would give her more time to talk with Carson.

"I haven't told you this before, but I think you're an excellent mother."

"Thanks," she replied, surprised by how much his compliment meant to her. Sometimes she doubted herself and the moves she'd made, so it felt good to know that at least one person believed she was doing it right. Especially when that person was someone she admired as much as she did Carson. "I'm making it up as I go along."

"I think that's what most parents do."

"I guess. But somehow it seems like everyone else has it together." She glanced at the kids, who were looking at something Justin held in the palm of his hand. "For a while there I was second-guessing every decision I made, and how it would impact them and everyone in our lives."

"And now?"

"Now, I'm trying hard to trust myself. To extend myself a little bit of grace. They're such good kids. I don't want to do something to mess them up."

"It'll take more than one wrong decision to do that. It takes a lifestyle of consistent bad behaviors—unless that one decision is a huge, life-altering, horrible one. Then all bets are off."

He sounded bitter, and she had the feeling that he was no longer talking about her but someone else. If she had to guess, she'd say it was his father. Just what had he done that impacted Carson so much? She could find out by asking any number of people, but doing so would have a terrible effect on their relationship. Besides, she had a feeling he was close to telling her. She was going to have faith in him for a while longer. Hopefully, he trusted her enough to tell her the truth.

Maybe he was waiting for the right time to tell her. They would be alone tonight. If he didn't bring it up, she would. The time for keeping secrets—if there was one—was over.

"We're back," Justin announced.

"I see. It's time to get back to the ranch and take care of the horses."

"When will we be able to race?" Justin asked Carson. "We want to go really fast."

"We'll build up to that. Right now you're going about as fast as you can and still be able to control the horse."

Justin didn't look particularly happy with that answer, but he nodded.

Gabriella led the group back to the stables, where they brushed the horses and gave them water.

Sophia gave her horse a hug. "I'm going to a sleepover party. I'll tell you all about it when I see you next time."

Justin rolled his eyes, but he gave his horse an extra pat before closing the bottom half of the stall's door and walking beside Carson into the sunshine.

Even though Justin and Sophia said it was unnecessary, Gabriella insisted that they take showers and wash off the smell of horses. Then she fed them lunch and helped them pack. Finally it was time to go to the party. The kids were bursting with excitement, and she had to admit she felt the same although for an entirely different reason.

The children chattered excitedly on the drive to Jessica and Jason's house and gave a quiet cheer when she parked the car. She recognized several parents from the youth center dropping off their kids. Apparently, this was going to be quite the shindig.

"Vicki is way braver than I am," Elisabeth, another mother Gabriella had met at the youth center, said, coming alongside her.

"Than me, too. I can't imagine having a sleepover party. I'm doing good getting my own two kids to bed," Gabriella said.

"Vicki and her husband, Scott, do this every

year. They have it down to a science. They grill hot dogs and burgers, and let the kids run around all day until they wear themselves out. When it gets dark, they sit around a campfire and sing songs."

"Really? I guess I'd better up my game if I ever let my kids have a sleepover. I was picturing pizza and a few Disney movies for the girls and video games for the boys."

"Trust me, after tonight your kids won't be satisfied with a regular sleepover. Between this and the youth center, the sleepovers of our childhood are a thing of the past."

"Apparently," Gabriella agreed. Perhaps she would ask Carson if they could use his pool or horses. Though she kept walking, inside she stilled. Her kids' birthdays were in the fall. She and the kids would be in Ohio by then. Or would they? Perhaps, while her brain was still mulling things over, her heart had reached its conclusion. Maybe this was where they belonged. In Sweet Briar. With Carson.

Sweet Briar was beginning to feel like home. From the way her kids greeted their friends, she wasn't the only one making connections here. Maybe there wouldn't be as much upheaval as she'd worried about.

She went inside and greeted Vicki, thanking her for inviting Justin and Sophia to the party.

"No worries. Our kids have become good friends quickly. Justin and Sophia fit in here."

"What time should I pick them up tomorrow?"

"About ten o'clock works for me. The kids will stay up pretty late and sleep longer than normal. I'll feed them breakfast, too."

"You are a saint."

Vicki just laughed. "The kids all enjoy themselves. And tomorrow my two will be happy and exhausted. They'll be too tired to bicker. Instead, they'll spend the day talking about how much fun they had. I'll have time to relax and read. I count that as a win."

After saying goodbye and reminding her kids to behave themselves and earning matching eye rolls, Gabriella hurried to her car. She needed to get something sexy for tonight. She'd passed Hannah's Boutique on one of her trips to Sweet Briar, but she hadn't done anything other than peer through the window. The clothes she'd seen had been gorgeous, and she had planned to return. At the time she hadn't thought she'd need anything fancy for a while, so a visit had fallen low on her list of things to do. Now, though, she was counting the seconds until she could step inside.

There were only a few other customers in the shop, and Gabriella took the opportunity to look around. This was clearly a high-end establishment, catering to those with money. The hardwood floors gleamed, and the clothes on the racks were organized by color, item and size. There were skirts and dresses, as well as shorts and pants. The clothes ranged from casual to after-five to formal. Everything was very well-made. Gabriella had no doubt she would find something wonderful to wear tonight.

"Hi," the saleswoman said, coming to greet Gabriella. "I'm Hannah. Are you looking for anything in particular?"

"Hi. Yes. I'm going to dinner tonight and need something nice to wear."

"Are we talking a date or a business meeting?"

"Date," Gabriella said, and then smiled.

Hannah grinned and steered Gabriella to the dresses near the wall. "From the smile on your face I take it that this date is with a special someone, so we can look at something a little more…enticing."

"Oh, yes." She definitely hoped she could entice Carson tonight.

Hannah quickly looked at Gabriella from head to toe, and then reached onto a rack and pulled out two different dresses. "You have a great shape and would look good in anything. I think you'll blow his mind in either one of these."

"Thanks." Hannah could have been flattering her, but Gabriella thought the other woman was being sincere. It wouldn't be good business for Hannah to sell clothes that didn't flatter her customers. Word would get around soon, and before long her clientele would vanish.

"If you want to look through some of the other dresses, I can get a room started for you."

"Thanks." Gabriella sorted through the rest of the items on the rack and picked up three other dresses. Folding them over her forearm, she headed to the dressing rooms. She slipped off her clothes and then pulled on the first dress that Hannah had selected. The green silk sheath felt so good on her skin. Gabriella fastened the zipper and then looked at herself in the mirror. The dress clung to her, emphasizing her curves. Although she no longer had the tiny waist she'd possessed before she'd had her kids, she still had a nice figure.

Green wasn't a color she generally wore, but the emerald shade made her skin glow. This dress was definitely a keeper even if she didn't wear it tonight.

Taking the dress off, she rehung it on the hanger, and tried on a red-and-orange-patterned dress. It hugged her torso and flared out at the hips. She shimmied in the mirror and smiled, pleased at the way the fabric moved with her. Another keeper. She tried on the other three dresses, one purple, one black and the other silver. Each of them looked great. After putting on her own clothes, she stared at the dresses, trying to make a decision.

"How's it going?" Hannah asked from outside the door.

"Great. And terrible."

"Yikes. Great I like, but terrible, not so much."

Gabriella opened the door. "They're all beautiful and I love the way I look in all of them. The hard part is deciding which one I'm going to wear tonight."

"Well, you can always use the process of elimination. Knock out your least favorite color or fabric. Things like that. Then I'll put those back. Eventually you'll be left with the *one*. It's kind of like weeding out the wrong men."

Gabriella laughed. "Where were you when I was getting married? I could have used your help then."

"Probably choosing the wrong guy to get involved with."

Gabriella pointed to the enormous diamond on Hannah's left ring finger. "Apparently, you figured it out."

Hannah smiled and her entire face lit up. "Thankfully."

"When is the big day?"

"New Year's Eve. We want to ring in our new year as husband and wife."

"That's so romantic. Congratulations. I wish you and your fiancé the best."

"Thanks. I can't believe I met a man as wonderful as Russell Danielson."

"Danielson? Is he related to Joni who runs the youth center?"

"He's her brother."

"Wow. I've only met her a few times, but I think she's wonderful. You're marrying into a great family." And from her own experience, Gabriella knew that in-laws mattered.

"They're the best," Hannah agreed, "but we need to get back to the task at hand. Which dress can you live without?"

"Oh, they're all coming with me," Gabriella hastened to correct her. "I just don't know which one to wear tonight."

"Oh. Well, then let's talk shoes. Which dress works best with shoes you already have?"

"Of course," Gabriella said, slapping a hand on her forehead. "The red and orange. That was easy."

They walked to the cash register, where Hannah quickly rang up Gabriella's dresses and expertly placed them inside a garment bag. Gabriella paid, and, after wishing Hannah all the best at her wedding, she drove home.

Carson would be picking her up in about an hour, so that didn't leave much time. She turned on soft music, took a warm bath and, after drying off, smoothed scented lotion onto her body. After spraying on perfume, she dressed and took extra care with her hair and makeup. She was taking a final glance at her reflection when the doorbell rang.

She looked at the clock. Right on time. The fact that Carson was prompt made her smile. It was a small thing, but it showed that she mattered to him. She hurried down the stairs, unwilling to make him wait. After all, he was important to her, too.

Swinging open the front door, she took one look at Carson and sucked in a breath. She'd seen him in his swim trunks, so she knew he had a great body. Heck, she'd caressed his muscular shoulders and chest. Her fingers still tingled at the memory that she'd played over and over in her mind. But there was something about the way he looked in his navy suit that made her mouth water. The jacket had been tailored to fit his broad shoulders and massive chest, and was tapered to fit his trim waist. The pants fell perfectly over his powerful thighs and brushed over his shined shoes. She couldn't decide if he was an angel from heaven or a devil sent to tempt her. Either way, he looked like each of her dreams wrapped into one perfect man.

He cleared his throat, and she realized she'd been gawking at him. Stepping back, she waved him inside. "Come on in. I just need to grab my purse."

"Take your time. And might I say you look gorgeous tonight."

His voice sounded deeper than normal, and butterflies began fluttering in her stomach at the admiration she heard there. "Thank you."

He wasn't the only one who sounded different. There was a breathless quality to her voice. "You don't look too shabby yourself," she added, trying both to lighten the mood and to control her voice.

"Thanks." He'd followed her across the room

and now was standing mere inches from her. The heat from his body wrapped around her bare shoulders, warming her. She inhaled and his scent tantalized her. His cologne was subtle yet woodsy. When combined with his unique scent, it made her weak in the knees.

She looked into his deep brown eyes and saw warmth and affection. And something else. Desire. Perhaps he was feeling the same longing for her that she felt for him.

After Gabriella grabbed her purse, they crossed the room side by side and then stepped onto the porch. Surprisingly, his truck was nowhere in sight. In its place was an expensive late-model sedan. She glanced at him, letting her eyes ask the question. He grinned. "I couldn't take you to the best restaurant in the state in a pickup."

"I didn't know you owned a car."

He shrugged. "I keep it in the garage. I only bring it out for special occasions. Like this."

He held out his arm and she took it, and they walked down the stairs together. When they reached the car, he opened her door for her and then circled the vehicle.

They made small talk on the way to the restaurant, but Gabriella didn't find it mundane. On the contrary, it was comforting. She was a bundle of nerves, which was ridiculous, given the fact that she and Carson were old friends. Yet she didn't think she would be able to talk about anything deeper right now. Besides, it was soothing to discuss things of little consequence to either of them when she knew the serious conversation that was looming.

The night was warm and they drove with the windows open. The scent of wildflowers floated on the summer breeze and the leaves rustled in the trees. An owl hooted in the distance and crickets chirped. She loved the sounds of the country. Or perhaps it was the lack of sound that appealed to her, harkening back to the carefree days of her youth.

When they reached the restaurant, Carson parked and helped her from the car. It was a small courtesy, but one she appreciated. He'd offered his hand when he assisted her, but rather than release her hand as she'd expected, he held it as they walked the short distance to the entrance of Heaven on Earth. It felt natural to hold hands. Perhaps their lives could be joined as easily.

There were more people out and about than Gabriella had expected. Several other couples strolled down the walk, nodding and smiling as they passed by. A few teenage boys sat on the iron benches lining the street, laughing and talking.

When Gabriella and Carson reached the restaurant, the door swung open and a young man stepped outside, holding it for them. Carson nodded. "Thank you."

They were ushered inside and Gabriella looked around. Although she'd been to many upscale restaurants and clubs, she was still impressed by the graciously expensive decor. The lighting was exquisite in its subtlety. Uniformed waitstaff walked silently over the carpeted floors while elegantly dressed patrons dined at tables covered by pristine white tablecloths.

The maître d' led them to their table and promised that a waitress would be by soon to take their orders.

The beauty of the room was nothing compared to the aromas floating on the air. Every time she inhaled, she got a whiff of the most delectable scents. If the food smelled this good, the taste had to be heavenly. She laughed quietly.

"What's so funny?" Carson asked.

"It just occurred to me how the restaurant got its name."

"Do tell." He leaned forward as if expecting her to tell him a secret.

She leaned in as well, looking into his eyes. They sparkled with amusement. "It's because the experience is going to be heavenly. And we're on earth. Hence heaven on earth."

"Well, that's one type of heaven we can experience together. Of course, there are others."

She'd picked up her glass of water to take a sip. Her hand froze halfway to her mouth. What? Had he really said that? He picked up his glass and swallowed some water as if he hadn't just deliberately shocked her. If he was going to flirt or tease, she'd do the same. Smiling mischievously, she repeated his words. "Do tell."

His mouth dropped open and she laughed. She'd always had fun with him when they were kids. She was still enjoying herself now although this was a different kind of fun. As she batted her eyes in faux innocence, she wondered just how far she was willing to take things tonight. Would she do more than flirt? That depended on just how well the conversation went.

A waitress stepped up to the table, pen and paper in hand, ready to take their orders. As neither of them had even glanced at the menu, they asked for a few more minutes.

Gabriella perused the menu. There were so many tempting offerings. She glanced at Carson. "What's good?"

"Besides me?"

"Yes. Besides you."

"I like the crab cakes. But you might like the seafood crepes."

"I was totally thinking about getting those."

The waitress returned and they placed their orders. Once the woman returned with their wine,

Carson leaned back in his chair. He looked casual enough, but Gabriella was discovering that she could read the adult version of Carson nearly as well as she'd read him as a kid. There was something on his mind.

"So, Gabriella, the summer will be coming to an end soon," he began without preamble. "Have you made up your mind about your future? As I recall, when you came here, you said something about needing this time to think and come up with a plan. Have you?"

Chapter Twelve

Carson sipped his wine and tried to maintain a calm facade as he waited for Gabriella to answer. This was the moment he'd been anticipating while simultaneously dreading it. When they'd agreed to have dinner tonight, he'd mentally planned everything down to the last second. He'd pick her up and then they'd listen to the radio on the way to town. They'd discuss inconsequential matters as they enjoyed dinner. After lingering over coffee and dessert they'd stroll around town, ending up at the beach. Then, under the starlit sky, he'd gently steer the conversation around to the future.

That was before he'd seen her in that dress. He'd

known that she was sexy—some things couldn't
be camouflaged by jeans and T-shirts. Besides,
he'd seen her in a swimsuit. But even that sight
hadn't prepared him for the vision that had nearly
knocked him off his feet. It had taken all of his
willpower not to sweep her into his arms, carry her
upstairs to her bedroom, remove that sexy dress
and make love to her.

But that was short-term thinking, and he was
playing the long game. He wanted more than one
night of passion with Gabriella. Creating a pleasant
memory he could pull out on a cold winter night
and hug close wasn't enough. He wanted to build
a future with her. After spending time in town, he
was starting to believe that people didn't associ-
ate him with his father. When he'd played basketball the other night, his friends had treated him
the same as they always had. None of the teens
had appeared afraid of him. They'd talked just as
much trash to him that night as they had before
his father's crime had become public.

Most importantly, Gabriella and her kids had
been made to feel at home. No one treated them
poorly because of their association with him, something he'd dreaded. Sophia and Justin had been em-
braced by the kids and now had a circle of friends.
But one question remained, and it would determine
whether they could truly have a future. How would
Gabriella react when he told her the truth about his

father? Sweet Briar was a small town, so he was surprised that nobody had told her yet. But maybe he shouldn't be. He'd been well liked before, and the people were generally nice. Most of them anyway. Maybe they were giving him the opportunity to tell her in his own time. Or maybe over time his father had simply become old news. Whatever the case, he needed to tell Gabriella. Tonight.

"I'm working some things out," she said slowly. "I'm starting to see things more clearly."

"Anything I can do to help?"

"Maybe."

The waitress chose that moment to place their food in front of them, interrupting the conversation. Perhaps that was for the best. That way he could get back on schedule. There was a reason he'd wanted to have the more serious conversation after a leisurely dinner. He wanted Gabriella to see how good things could be between them.

Gabriella picked up her fork and cut into a crepe. He watched as she placed the morsel into her mouth. Her eyes widened in surprise at the taste and then closed in bliss. She groaned softly, and sudden desire pulsed through his veins. "Wow."

"I take it that you like it."

"It's the best thing I've ever eaten in my life."

Carson took a bite of his own food. It was delicious but, unlike Gabriella, he managed to control his reaction. "Brandon knows his way around the kitchen."

"That's an understatement." She took another bite and sighed. "I think I'm in love."

Carson knew she was joking, but jealousy sliced through him like a knife. Gabriella was *his*. Whoa. He'd never been the possessive caveman type. Even when he'd been engaged to Raven, he'd never reacted so viscerally to a joke about another man. Then again, he and Gabriella had a deeper connection than he'd ever had with Raven. Their relationship was built on years of shared experiences and a lifetime of confidences. In a way, she had always been his.

He blew out a breath. "From what I hear, you're not alone. Sadly for you and the women of this town, there is already a Mrs. Brandon Danielson."

"Danielson. Is he related to Joni?"

"Yes. He's her brother."

"I met her other brother's fiancée today. She owns the shop where I bought this dress."

"I've met Russell once or twice. He's a good guy."

She nodded and continued to eat, making her delight obvious with each bite she took. With each contented sound she made, his desire became stronger. He didn't know how long he would be able to bear it. Luckily for him, she restarted the conversation. "The town sure has grown a lot.

There are so many new families. And new businesses. I know it's been fifteen years since I've been here, and the changes could have happened gradually, but to me the difference is staggering."

"Is it a good difference or not?"

"Well, the town is obviously more prosperous, so that's good. It never looked dirty or felt poor, but there is a definite improvement. The streets are cleaner and there are flowers everywhere, which I love. It's picture-postcard beautiful. It looks like the set of one of those movies that takes place in a small town. It's almost too good to be real. But it is."

"Don't go romanticizing us. We have our problems, just like everywhere else. Sweet Briar isn't perfect."

"I know." She sipped her drink.

"I have the feeling you were going to say that not all of the changes were good. Unless I was reading into your words."

"No. You're right. I miss some of the open space. There didn't used to be that many houses on the road to town. Now there's an entire subdivision of McMansions. I'm not sure I like that."

"No? Why not?"

"It just doesn't feel right." She shrugged one slender shoulder. "But then, I'm an outsider. I don't get to say how the town should or shouldn't develop."

"Technically, those houses aren't part of Sweet Briar. They're part of the county, if that helps restore your sense of nostalgia."

"Somewhat."

"Good."

"And I have to tell you I miss the rest of Aunt Mildred's land. Four acres is nothing to sneeze at, but she used to own fifty. I understand why she sold it. And even though I have no right to feel this way, I wish she would have held on to it."

"Would it make you feel better to know that the new owner is a good guy?"

"Maybe. Do you know him?"

"Yes. She sold the land to Jericho Jones. Do you remember him?"

She shook her head. "The name doesn't ring a bell."

"His family originally owned your aunt's ranch. One of his ancestors sold it to your aunt and uncle. When your aunt put it on the market, Jericho jumped at the opportunity. He's been buying back pieces of his heritage whenever he can."

She flashed a small smile. "I guess that does make me feel a little better, knowing that his family had been the original owners. And really, Aunt Mildred couldn't handle it and I certainly can't." Gabriella looked at him. "She offered to sell her house to me if I want it."

His heart skipped a beat. "What did you say?"

"I told her I needed to think about it."

"Are you thinking about it?" If she moved closer, they'd have more time to develop their relationship and rid her of whatever doubts she might have. He wouldn't need to make a rash declaration of feelings in the next few weeks.

"I don't know. I love it here, but is Sweet Briar the right place for us? Sure the kids like it now, they're on summer vacation. Would they want to live here year-round? And would it be right for me to rip them away from their father and the rest of their family? Everything that they know?"

"Are you still in love with your ex-husband? Do you hope that he'll come back to you if you wait long enough? Because I can tell you from experience, that won't happen. No matter how good or kind or sweet you are to him, he won't love you back."

"I'm not still in love with him. But he is the kids' father, and they deserve the chance to have a relationship with him."

"What if he doesn't want one? You can't force him or sweet-talk him into being a part of their lives if he doesn't want to be."

Her shoulders slumped and her eyes filled with sorrow. Guilt pummeled him. This was supposed to be a fun evening designed to discover if the closer relationship he wanted was possible. He'd sure killed the mood with that remark. But he was only being honest. And honesty was important. Gabriella would never be able to move forward if she didn't accept the truth about the man she'd married.

After they decided to skip dessert, the waitress returned with their bill. Carson barely perused it before adding a tip and handing over his credit card. Neither he nor Gabriella spoke until they were standing outside of the restaurant. Most of the shops had closed so there weren't many people about. Tension spiked between them, and from the set of Gabriella's shoulders he could tell she wasn't as happy as she'd been at the start of the evening. He wanted to get back those easy moments. It would make telling her about his father less difficult. He was determined to tell her the truth tonight. They couldn't have a future as long as his secret hung between them.

He lifted her chin and looked into her eyes. The sparkle was missing. "I'm sorry. I shouldn't have said that."

"It's okay. You're right. I just have a hard time believing that Reggie would turn away from his kids permanently. He loved them before. He might have been busy at work, but he always carved time out for them."

What kind of father *carved out time* for his kids as if they weren't an important part of his life? A jerk, that's who. But Carson wouldn't tell her that.

For a reason that escaped him, Gabriella needed to believe the best of her ex. And who was he to disabuse her of that notion? Reality would take care of that. It always did.

"I thought we could walk along the beach, but if you're not in the mood, I completely understand."

She smiled and some of her sadness vanished. "Actually, that sounds wonderful."

He looked at her sandals before deciding to drive the short distance to the beach. The orange shoes were cute and showed off her delicate feet and painted toenails, but they had four-inch heels. Gabriella's feet would be begging for mercy before they'd walked two blocks.

Sweet Briar might have changed over the years, but one thing had remained the same. It still had the most beautiful stretch of beach in the entire state. With the stars sparkling in the dark sky, a soft breeze blowing and the sound of waves brushing softly against the sand, it was the ideal setting for a quiet conversation.

About two dozen teenagers were sitting around a small bonfire, toasting marshmallows and singing along as a guy strummed a guitar. Another group of teens played in the water, laughing and splashing each other. Empty pizza boxes leaned against a cooler. By unspoken agreement, Carson and Gabriella skirted the area so as not to disturb the revelry.

After they'd wandered far enough from the party that they couldn't be overheard, Carson led her to the edge of the water. He'd grabbed a blanket from the car, and now he spread it on the sand for them to sit. They were close enough that the warm water splashed against their bare toes but not close enough to get their clothes wet. They stared at the water for a while watching the moon rise over the horizon.

He took a deep breath. His future rested on these next few minutes. "I have something to tell you."

She turned to him. "It sounds serious."

"It is. I should have told you a long time ago, but the time never seemed right."

"Whatever it is, it can't be as bad as you imagine." She reached out and gripped his hand, giving it a tight squeeze. "Just tell me."

"It's about my father."

"What about him?"

He'd barely opened his mouth when he heard a loud voice behind him. "Carson Rivers. I thought I saw you walking along the beach, but I told myself I had to be seeing things. By now you should know better than to show your face in public. Nobody has forgotten what your father did. But maybe this newcomer doesn't know and you somehow managed to lure her out here."

Rusty Danvers.

Carson was trying to figure out how to respond when Gabriella hopped to her feet, hands on her hips. "I don't know who you think you are, but you're not welcome here. So go away."

"You're a stranger in town. I'm just trying to help you."

Carson had shaken off his stupor by then and was standing, too. He didn't want Gabriella to defend him. Especially when he wasn't certain he deserved her defense.

"Did I ask for your help?" Gabriella snapped.

"Gabriella," Carson began. "Let it go."

"But…"

"Let it go," he said more firmly before turning back to Rusty. He would handle this.

A crowd began to gather around them. A few of the people were with Rusty, but not all of them. Apparently, they hadn't gotten as far away from the teenagers as he'd believed because several of them were running in their direction. He recognized a couple of them as kids he'd played basketball with at the youth center a couple nights ago. A girl was on her phone, giving a blow-by-blow to whomever she was talking to. Great. He was going to be the subject of another round of gossip. Just what he didn't need. He wouldn't be able to convince Gabriella that life with him would be good if she got caught up in a whirlwind of trouble.

"Let's go," a skinny woman said, tugging on Rusty's arm.

Rusty snatched his arm away and stumbled. "I'm not going anywhere. I'm trying to be a good citizen." His words were slurred, and he staggered and pointed at Gabriella. "I'm protecting this woman."

"What you're doing is making a fool of yourself," one of the teens said, surprising Carson by speaking up. He recognized him as the older brother of one of Carson's former riding students and a star player on the Sweet Briar High football team. Carson looked at the other kids. He recognized many of them as also being high school athletes. All of them were imposing.

Rusty looked at the kids and then stopped blustering.

"I appreciate all of you coming to my aid, but it's not necessary," Carson said. "He was just leaving."

Rusty looked at his two friends, who were decidedly less willing to jump into the fray when the numbers were no longer in their favor. Perhaps it was realizing that he was outnumbered or maybe it was seeing two uniformed officers sprinting across the sand, but whatever it was, Rusty thought better of continuing the confrontation. He raised his hands in surrender and took two wobbling steps backward. "Come on. Let's get out of here."

Rusty took a step toward the line of teenagers, who didn't budge. Rather than try to brush past them, Rusty turned and went back the way he'd come.

The youth watched as if making sure he was truly leaving before they jogged back down the beach to resume their party.

"Is everything okay here?" one of the officers asked when they got near Carson.

"Everything is fine," Carson said.

"Are you kidding me?" Gabriella said, still outraged on his behalf. He'd forgotten how fiery she could be.

"Gabriella. Let it go." He appreciated her loyalty, but he didn't want her to have to defend him. He didn't want to need defending. But he couldn't have what he really wanted, which was for his father to have been the man that Carson had always believed him to be. Karl Rivers wasn't an upstanding citizen. Karl Rivers had been a criminal, and no amount of wishing could change that.

The officer looked from Carson to Gabriella. When she clamped her mouth closed, the officer looked back to Carson. "We received a call that Rusty Danvers was harassing you. If you want to file a complaint now, you can do that. If you'd rather come in later, you can do that, too."

"Thanks. I'd rather just move on and forget the whole thing."

The officer nodded. If he thought Carson's behavior was unusual, he didn't say so.

"Let's go," Carson said to Gabriella. The night that had held such promise had turned into a total disaster. Had he honestly expected it to go otherwise?

Tonight had proved that he'd been right to protect Gabriella from the mess that his life had become. He didn't want her to become a target for harassment—even if indirectly—so he had to stay away from her. The mere thought made his heart ache because he knew without a doubt that he had fallen in love with her. What else could he do? He couldn't bear it if anything happened to Gabriella.

She'd come here to figure out her next move. She didn't need anything distracting her from that and complicating her life. Becoming wrapped up in his problems would definitely do that.

Gabriella frowned and he prayed that she wouldn't argue. "Fine."

They walked back to the car at a much faster pace than when they'd initially crossed the sand to the water. After they reached the pavement, they put on their shoes and got in the car. Neither of them spoke until they were driving down the quiet street.

"What's going on, Carson?"

She'd spoken softly, but he heard the concern in her voice and it was nearly his undoing. She deserved to know, but he didn't want to have this conversation while they were driving. "I'll tell you when we get back to your house."

She nodded.

Neither of them said anything else until he parked in her driveway and turned off the engine.

"Do you want to come inside?" she asked.

"No. Let's sit out here."

They got out of the car and walked up the stairs to the porch swing. She sat down and then looked at him expectantly. After hesitating, he sat beside her. If this was going to be the end, he wanted to inhale her sweet scent for as long as he could. She crossed her ankles and folded her hands in her lap.

He gave the glider a gentle push, setting it in motion. On any other occasion he would have enjoyed the intimate moment. Now, realizing it might be their last time together, he was reluctant for it to end.

The silence stretched, and he realized that she wasn't going to pressure him to talk. She was going to give him however much time he needed to gather his thoughts.

There was no way to ease into the conversation, so he just blurted it out. "My dad was a criminal."

She jerked and the swing rocked. He put his foot on the porch floor, bringing the swing to a stop. "Say that again." Her voice quavered, and he could only imagine the thoughts that were racing through her mind.

"My father was a criminal."

"Are you talking about embezzling or something?"

"I wish. No. He actually killed someone."

She sat there as if digesting what he'd just said. Or maybe she was too stunned to reply. He'd certainly been in shock when he discovered what his father had done. Even now, although he'd seen proof, he still had a hard time believing it.

"Who told you that?" she finally asked.

"Donovan Cordero."

"Your former fiancée's husband?" He heard the skepticism in her voice and knew it was only because of her loyalty to him.

"Yes." He raised a hand to forestall any argument she would make. "He saw the entire thing."

"What?" She blew out a breath and then shook her head as if she was still unable to process what he'd said. Since he'd had the same difficulty, he understood. "Start at the beginning."

"You know my father died."

She nodded.

"Donovan came back to town at the same time. Remember I told you he'd been gone for ten years. Anyway, he said that my father was the reason he'd left town and hadn't been able to raise his and Raven's son, Elias. I tried not to think about it, but it continued to nag at me.

"After the funeral I was cleaning my father's office. I discovered that he had two sets of journals. The ones he kept for posterity's sake, in case anyone ever wanted to write his biography, and a hidden set where he'd written down events that only he would know about. I started reading from that second set. They went back years and years. Most of them were pretty boring accounts of business deals or donations he'd made to politicians. Anyway, in a journal from about ten years earlier, I found a reference to Donovan. My father had written that Donovan had better keep his mouth shut but didn't say about what.

"So I went to Donovan to find out what it was that he knew. He was reluctant to tell me at first, but I was persistent." Sometimes Carson wished he hadn't been so determined to know the truth and had just let the matter go. But that was the scared little boy who'd idolized his father talking. The man he was now knew that discovering the truth, no matter how painful, was always better than believing a lie.

"What did he say?"

"He said that he'd witnessed my father shoot someone. Donovan had never seen the man before and didn't believe he was from around here. When he'd realized my father had seen him, Donovan begged for his life. My father remembered how Donovan had always been good to me, so he didn't kill him. Instead, he told him that he'd better leave town right then and never come back. And he could never contact anyone. If he didn't do exactly as my father said, he'd kill not only Donovan, but his parents and Raven, too. So Donovan left and didn't come back until he learned that my father was dead."

"Wow."

"Yeah. Wow." Carson felt himself tensing up as he always did when he thought about what his father had done, and forced himself to take a deep breath and then blow it out slowly. "You weren't here that summer, but we all wondered what had happened to Donovan. He'd disappeared without a trace. Everyone looked for him for months and months, retracing his steps in an attempt to find a clue that could help us find him. His parents put up flyers for years. The church raised money for a reward for information. My father, hypocrite that he was, contributed twenty-five-thousand-dollars."

"That's pretty…something."

"Looking back, my father had been acting strange around then. I just figured that he was worried that whatever had happened to Donovan could happen to me. You know, like a serial killer or something. The truth was he was worried that

Donovan might come back and tell someone what he'd seen."

"Oh."

"Anyway, Donovan didn't return until he saw news of my father's death on TV."

"So, did anyone ever find out who the man was that…" She waved a helpless hand in the air, and her voice trailed off as if she couldn't say the words.

"That my father killed?"

She nodded.

"Yes. Once I knew what my father had done, I was determined to get justice for his victim. I told Sheriff Leonard what I knew, which wasn't much. He interviewed Donovan, who agreed to sit down with a sketch artist, and they came up with a picture. At the same time, the sheriff contacted the FBI. They brought in cadaver dogs and scoured every inch of the ranch until they found the man's remains. Once we identified him, I contacted his family."

"Why? I mean, I get telling them what happened, but shouldn't the authorities have done that? Why were you the one to do it?"

So many people had asked him that question. Why hadn't he just let the police handle it? Why had he felt the need to face the family and apologize for his father's actions? He hadn't had an answer then and he didn't have one now. Other than it had felt like the right thing to do. Maybe he had wanted to prove that he was different from his father. He'd admired his father so much as a child and had wanted to be like him. Now he'd wanted to make it clear that they were nothing alike.

The victim's family hadn't appreciated the gesture. He'd had children who'd grown up without a father. When he'd vanished without a trace, they'd been left wondering if he'd stopped loving them.

"To give them closure," he finally said. It was the best answer he could come up with. Not that his action had given them any more peace than it had given him.

"I appreciate the need for closure. I still don't understand why you had to be the one to give it to them."

"It was a matter of honor. My father was the reason that man was dead and that his children had grown up believing he'd abandoned them. I didn't want to take the easy way out by letting someone else apologize on my behalf."

"You had nothing to apologize for."

"Well, on behalf of our family, then." He rubbed a hand across his head. "I had to do it. I can't explain it any better than that."

"Okay. How did it go over?"

"About as well as you would expect hearing from the killer's son that your father or husband had been murdered." They'd ranted and raged at him, not that he would tell Gabriella that. She'd only say the same thing the investigator and the sheriff had said. That they were wrong to blame him. He didn't need to hear more useless platitudes.

He just needed to find a way to forgive himself. Even though he knew what his father had done, a part of him still loved and missed him. And that was unforgivable.

"Okay. So what does that have to do with Rusty? He wasn't related to the man, was he?"

"No."

"Then what's his problem?"

"I have no idea." That was something he hadn't been able to figure out. They had never been friends, but they hadn't been enemies, either. But then, Rusty's life hadn't turned out the way he'd planned. He'd briefly worked for Carson's father, but that had been years ago. He hadn't lasted long and had bounced around from job to job since then.

"Well, if he knows what's good for him, he'll stay out of my way. I don't like bullies."

"About that." His heart began to race and fill with dread as he did what he had to do.

"What?" Her voice sounded wary, as if she knew what was coming.

"I don't think we should see each other any longer."

Chapter Thirteen

Gabriella sucked in an agonized breath. She tried to keep the pain from her voice, but she couldn't. "Why?"

"After what happened tonight do you really need to ask?"

"Yes."

"It's not good for us to be together. You came here to figure out how to move forward with your life, not to get entangled in my problems. You're only going to be here for a few more weeks anyway. There's no need to make them difficult."

How could such a smart man be so wrong? "Being with you isn't making my life difficult.

Being with you makes my life better. I'm happier with you than I've been in years."

"That's not me. That's Sweet Briar. You're reliving happy childhood memories. I just happen to be a part of a lot of them."

"Maybe. But I'm also creating new memories with you. Wonderful memories."

He turned his face away from hers and stared into the dark night. "We're having fun together. There's nothing wrong with that. But there's no future for us. I knew that all along. I just forgot it until tonight."

"That's not true." She closed her eyes, summoning all of her courage. It was now or never. If she let Carson walk away from her, she might not get the chance to say what she felt. If he was still determined to leave after hearing her out, so be it. But she wasn't going to let the words go unsaid. "I'm falling in love with you."

Shaking his head, he jumped to his feet and backed away from her as if she'd morphed into a two-headed monster. "No. You're not."

She stood in front of him and blocked his path to the stairs. He glanced over at the porch rail as if contemplating climbing over it before turning his eyes back to hers. Even in the pale moonlight, she could see the panic on his face. Was being loved by her so awful? Stepping closer, she reached out and touched his cheek gently so as not to spook him.

"I am. And I might be wrong, but I think you're coming to care for me and my kids, too." ·

He closed his eyes, but not before she saw the naked longing there. He blew out a long breath. "My feelings aren't the point. All that matters is you and the kids. Think about it. Do you really want to raise them in this situation knowing at any time they could be harassed? And what about their father? How would he feel about me, the son of a murderer, being a part of their lives? Think of the trouble he could make for you."

She hadn't considered that. But then, she'd only just found out what Carson had been hiding from her. Would Reggie make a big deal of this? After all, Carson hadn't done anything wrong. He was the one who'd brought his father's crime to light.

"No, he wouldn't do anything like that. Reggie is a good man."

"A good man wouldn't ignore his children. You're fooling yourself if you believe otherwise."

Gabriella opened her mouth to reply and then clapped it shut. She'd almost answered in anger but caught herself in the nick of time. She wasn't going to be distracted or drawn into a senseless argument. Reggie wasn't the issue here. "You never said whether I was right or wrong, so I'll ask you straight out. Do you love me?"

He stiffened then looked at her with tortured eyes. "Of course I love you," he said, his voice fierce with emotion. "That's why I have to stay away from you. I'm bad news. Maybe only a few people wish me harm, but that's still too many. I won't put any of you in a bad situation. I'm sorry, but it's over."

Gabriella didn't try to stop Carson as he stepped around her. She watched in silence as he descended the stairs and then all but ran to his car. She hoped that he would realize he was wrong and turn around, but with each step he took that hope diminished. By the time he'd gotten into the vehicle, no hope remained.

Of course he wouldn't turn around. Carson was an honorable man. He wouldn't do anything he thought would put her or her children at risk. In his mind, Gabriella being with him was harmful. She knew he was wrong. He was the best thing to happen to them. He was good for them and their lives were richer because of him. But he had to figure that out on his own. He said he loved her and now he knew that she felt the same way. He needed to believe their love was worth fighting for. Hopefully, in time he would.

But she didn't have time to worry about that right now. She had to focus all of her attention on her kids. They were going to be devastated when she told them that they weren't going to be spending time with Carson for a while. Justin was going to be especially disappointed. He'd come to idolize Carson and loved every minute they spent together.

Gabriella stood on the porch long after the tail-lights from Carson's car had faded from view. The night, which had started so wonderfully, had ended with her hopes and dreams dashed into dust. But she wasn't ready to throw in the towel just yet. Surely, with a little time and space, Carson would come to see that he was overreacting. She just hoped it didn't take too long.

"But why can't we go over to Carson's house today?" Justin glared at her as if she was the one standing in the way of their friendship and not Carson. When she'd picked the kids up from the sleepover party, they'd been bursting with stories and had chattered all the way home. Once she'd pulled into the driveway, Sophia and Justin had hopped from the car, ready to make a beeline to Carson's ranch. She'd stopped them and told them that Carson needed some time on his own to figure things out. They'd looked perplexed but she'd managed to distract them.

That was four days ago. Even daily visits to the youth center hadn't been enough to lessen the pain of Carson's absence. In fact, the visits had the opposite effect. When they arrived home each afternoon they'd been brimming with excitement and eager to tell Carson all about their day. She'd hated being the bad guy who made them respect his boundaries.

The separation was hard on her, too. On more than one occasion she'd found herself halfway down the driveway on her way to Rivers Ranch. When she'd realized what she was doing, she'd forced her legs to walk in a different direction.

Gabriella had told the kids that this was just temporary, and soon things would go back to normal. As yet another day passed, she was beginning to wonder if she'd lied to all of them. Maybe Carson had actually meant it when he said they were over. Perhaps he would always believe it was risky for them to be around him. If that was true, how did that affect her plans for the future?

Despite the way things looked now, she'd believed they had a future together. She had told him she was falling in love with him, but that hadn't been the entire truth. She *was* in love with him. But could she stand living near him without being a part of his life? And what about Justin and Sophia? Would they be able to cope with his rejection? They deserved better than to have another man walk out of their lives. They were hurting now, and she was to blame. She should have known better than to let them get attached to Carson. They were in the exact same situation with Carson that they'd been in with Reggie—craving the attention of a man who no longer wanted to give it to them.

"Mom," Justin said loudly when she hadn't answered. "Why can't we go to Carson's?"

"Because he needs some time to think about things. He can't do that when we're around."

"Why not? I can be quiet. Remember how quiet I was the other day when you were doing some work?"

A week ago she'd been writing down the pros and cons of buying this house and starting over in Sweet Briar. Of course, that was before her relationship with Carson had imploded, taking most of the pros away and leaving only the cons. Along with heartache and rejection.

"Yes. You were really quiet. But Carson needs the kind of quiet that only comes from being alone."

"That doesn't make any sense to me."

It didn't make sense to her, either, but it was what it was. "I know."

"Angel misses me," Sophia said. "She needs me to brush her and tell her stories."

"I'm sure someone is brushing her and caring for her like they were before we came."

"But I bet they aren't telling her stories," Sophia said. "They don't know my stories."

"You're right."

"Don't you think our horses miss us?" Justin asked, surprising her. Justin wasn't normally sentimental. But then, since he missed riding his horse—and missed Carson, too—it was probably natural for him to want to be missed in return.

"Of course. But right now we need to give Carson his space."

"We could just go to the corral and say hello to the horses without bothering Carson," Sophia said, flashing her most charming smile.

"No, you cannot," Gabriella said firmly. "We don't just go trespassing on other people's property."

"But Carson said we could come over anytime when we were swimming that day. He said we have an open invitation," Justin said. "Remember?"

Of course she remembered. She remembered everything that had happened between them. Every word that had been spoken. Every touch. Every kiss. Her heart ached at the thought that those were the last memories she and Carson would create together.

"Yes, but that was before. Now he needs some space." The kids opened their mouths, clearly not giving up the fight, so she cut them off. Talking wasn't getting her anywhere and her loneliness grew with every word. "Listen, nothing you say is going to change things. Carson wants to be alone for a while, so we're going to leave him alone. Now there's a carnival in Willow Creek. How about we go check that out today?"

They looked at each other, nodded and trudged away. Gabriella hadn't expected cheers, but she had hoped for a more enthusiastic response. Clearly they missed Carson as much as she did, which was more than anything in the world. Her heart ached with every breath she took. Her feelings hadn't diminished one bit in the time they'd been apart. But there was nothing she could do to fix things. She'd already told Carson how she felt. Now she had to wait and hope that he would come to his senses soon and realize they belonged together.

Carson pulled his truck into the driveway and shut off the engine. He'd spent the past day and a half on the road, but the feeling of happiness that normally filled him when he returned home was missing. Instead, the loneliness he'd tried to avoid by staying away was waiting to greet him, pouncing on his shoulders the minute he pulled onto the Rivers Ranch.

Though he was reluctant to admit it, he really missed Gabriella. He really missed Justin and Sophia and their constant conversation. They'd carved a place in his heart that only they could fill. But what choice did he have? He couldn't put them in a position where they were subjected to harassment.

After putting the horse trailer away, he crossed the lawn to the patio. He caught a glimpse of a shadowy figure lying on a lawn chair and he stopped. Even from ten feet away, he recognized

Justin. The little boy was dressed in his blue pajamas and sound asleep. He must have sneaked out of his house and come to see him. Carson was immediately consumed with guilt at the way he'd cut Gabriella and her kids from his life. Justin had already had his father turn his back on him. Carson didn't need to be one more man who let him down. And yet he had.

He shook Justin's shoulder, waking him. Justin's eyes fluttered and then opened. He blinked and then looked around before focusing on Carson. Then he smiled. "Hi."

"Hi." Carson pulled a chair closer and sat down.

"I guess I fell asleep."

"Looks like."

"I came over to see my horse, but the stable door was locked."

"Yes." Carson felt marginally better that he wasn't the reason the boy had left his house obviously without his mother's permission. "I do that to protect the horses. They're probably asleep this time of night anyway."

"Yeah. I figured that out. But I knocked on your door and you weren't here. I figured that you were taking a horse home, so I decided to wait until you got back."

"Was there something you wanted to talk about?"

Justin nodded and the smile disappeared from

his face. He stared into Carson's eyes. "Why don't you like me anymore?"

Although he should have expected to hear them, the words still cut deep. "Who said I don't like you?"

"Nobody."

"Good. Because I do like you."

Justin looked down at his hands. "You don't have to say that."

"I know I don't. I only said it because it's true."

"Then why don't you want me around? What did I do to make you mad at me?"

"I'm not mad at you."

"You don't want me around."

Carson huffed out a breath. That was the thing about kids. They said exactly what they thought without sugarcoating it or beating around the bush. And Justin deserved to have Carson be just as direct with him, without getting into the gritty details. "I need some time to work things out."

"I can help you," Justin said eagerly. "I'm good at that. I help Sophia with her homework all the time."

"That's because you're a good brother."

Justin nodded. "And I help my mom, too, because I'm a good son."

"You certainly are. But sometimes a person needs to do things on his own. And this is one of those times."

Justin lowered his head and his little body deflated. In that moment, Carson was angrier with his father than he'd been in a long time. Maybe ever. Even from the grave Karl Rivers was still causing pain. Because of his actions, Carson had at least one committed enemy, one he would never allow to hurt Justin. So he had to keep the child at a distance, no matter how much it hurt both of them.

"Come on. Let's take you home. I bet your mother doesn't even know you're here."

"No. I was really quiet walking down the stairs. I didn't put on my boots until I was outside. And I closed the door really soft."

Justin seemed very proud of himself, and Carson didn't tell him that his mother would be worried if she knew he'd left home, crossed the street in the dark and then waited outside for Carson to come home. It was a good thing Justin hadn't come yesterday when he would have spent the entire night alone. Carson had slept outside many times as a child, but his parents had been home to keep an eye on him. He shuddered at the thought of Justin spending the entire night alone on the patio.

Justin tucked his hand into Carson's and his heart squeezed. He loved this little boy as much as any father ever loved his son.

"Hey, Carson," the boy said hesitantly as they walked down the path. It was nearly ten o'clock and the moon and stars illuminated the way.

"Yeah."

"Can you help me with something?"

"If I can."

"Can you tell my mom that I know my dad doesn't want to be my dad anymore and that she doesn't have to pretend that he does. Me and Sophia already talked about it and we're okay."

Carson froze. "What?"

"My dad has a new baby. He likes to be with him. It's okay if he doesn't want to be with us anymore. We still love him because he's our dad, but now we have you. You're the best."

Talk about reaching inside his chest and squeezing his heart. Carson just stood there gaping, unable to think of a word to say. Luckily for him Justin wasn't done.

"When you finish doing what you need to do all by yourself, we can start coming around again. And riding our horses. Right? It can be just like it was before when we were all happy."

Carson couldn't squash the boy's hope so he only nodded. The picture Justin painted was appealing. If only it were that simple.

"Good. So how much longer do you have to think? Will you be done tomorrow? Because Sophia and I miss our horses. We want to ride to the watering hole again. And this time we want to take lunch so we can eat there and go swimming."

"You do, huh?"

"Yeah. We talked about it."

"Okay." As they started walking again, Justin talked about the things he wanted to do. His plans, which would take years to complete, all included Carson. He was now a part of Gabriella's kids' lives, whether he wanted to be or not. But he wanted to be. More than anything. That wasn't the problem. But he wasn't good for them.

They were climbing the stairs when the front door swung open. Gabriella flew down the stairs and pulled Justin into her arms. "I was so worried about you."

"Sorry, Mom. I didn't know you knew I was gone."

"I didn't until ten minutes ago when I went to your room to check on you."

"I would have been back sooner, but it took Carson a long time to come home."

Though it was subtle, Carson heard the accusation in the boy's voice and he laughed. Carson glanced at Gabriella, who clearly didn't see the humor in the situation. "Sorry."

"Let's get inside so Carson can go home." Gabriella kissed her son's cheek before standing and finally looking at Carson. "Thanks for bringing him home."

"No problem. I should have called the minute I found him, but we had some things to discuss."

"That's okay. And really, I'm the one who should be apologizing to you. I'll keep a closer eye on him so he doesn't bother you again."

She turned and with a hand on Justin's shoulder began to walk away. He wanted to call her back, but what would be the point? Nothing had changed for him. Unless you counted the ever-growing pain in his heart.

Two days later, Carson walked into the feed store. He generally sent one of his employees, but today the ranch had felt claustrophobic and he'd needed to get away. It didn't make sense to him, but then nothing had for a while. Perhaps being in town would help him think clearly.

"Be right with you," Gerald McCarthy said when he spotted Carson. "I just have to grab something from the back."

"Take your time," Carson said as the man hurried from the room.

"Well, it if isn't the killer's son. Coming to find another victim?"

Carson spun around and faced Rusty, who was standing with his arms folded over his chest. He was with a friend, of course. Rusty was only brave when he had backup.

"Come on, man. Not today," his friend urged.

"Why not today?" Rusty said. "He walks around town like he owns the place. Everybody knows his dad stole what he had. And then he killed that man to cover it up. And as you know, the apple doesn't fall far from the tree."

Carson looked at Rusty's red and bloated face. He'd been trying to avoid confrontation, hoping the whole thing with his father would eventually die down. And for the most part it had. When the majority of people looked at him, they saw Carson. They saw a friend. A rancher. A mentor. What they didn't see was a killer's son. Only Rusty saw that and made a point to remind Carson of what his father had done every time he saw him.

Then Carson remembered what Justin had said to him. He'd said Carson was the best. He thought of Sophia's trusting smile. And of Gabriella's unconditional love. Was he going to let Rusty take that from him? No.

Carson was fed up with the taunts. He didn't believe in violence, but maybe that was the only language Rusty understood. He had backed away when the teens confronted him the other night. There had been fear on his face. Maybe it was time for Carson to scare him away. After all, nothing else had worked. He looked at Rusty. "You don't really believe that."

"That you're just like your father. Of course I do. Why wouldn't I?"

"Then you're a bigger fool than I thought."

"What did you say?" Rusty stepped closer until his face was mere inches away from Carson's. His chest heaved and he breathed his rancid breath into Carson's face, trying to intimidate him. Instead of backing away, Carson moved closer, then spoke softly so that only Rusty could hear him.

"If you really thought I was like my father, the last thing you would want to do is antagonize me. Neither of us know what happened between my father and the man he killed. Perhaps the other guy threatened my father in some way. Or maybe he kept getting in his face and my father had finally had enough of it. Just like I have."

Rusty's face blanched, and he stepped back as the meaning of Carson's words struck him. Carson was nothing like his father. He would never take another person's life, but he didn't mind if Rusty wasn't as sure. Especially if that doubt would keep him out of his life. Away from Gabriella and the kids.

"Are we clear?" Carson asked.

Rusty nodded and tried to smile. "I didn't mean anything. I was just giving you a hard time."

"I suggest you stop. You know, just in case you're right about me and the apple didn't fall far from the tree."

Rusty stumbled as he ran out of the store. His friend followed slowly. Before he reached the door, the friend looked back and nodded. Apparently, there weren't even a few people who judged Carson by his father's actions. There was one.

Was he going to allow that one person to control his life? Was he going to let one person's opinion keep him from being with the woman he loved?

No. To be honest, he wasn't going to allow a million people to keep him from Gabriella.

He'd been such a fool to walk away from the best thing in his life.

He left the feed store without picking up his order and ran to his truck. His heart raced as he sped down the highway. He needed to get back to Gabriella. Now that he knew that he'd never again let anything keep them apart, he had to let her know before another moment passed. He thought of how he'd hurt her and the children, and his heart seized. They hadn't deserved his rejection. Hopefully, they'd accept his apology if he promised not to be so foolish again. If they forgave him, he'd never leave them again.

When he reached the road separating their properties, he turned into her driveway. As he parked and jumped from the truck, it occurred to him that he was showing up empty-handed. He should have stopped by Louanne's and bought a dozen of the chocolate strawberries that Gabriella liked so much. Or stopped by the florist and gotten a dozen roses. Something. He needed something to show Gabriella how sorry he was and how much she meant to him.

He was about to get into the truck when Gabriella's voice stopped him. "What are you doing? Are you coming or going?"

Good question. He stepped around the truck and

walked to the stairs. The gift would have to wait for a better time. If he played his cards right, he would have a lifetime to give her gifts. "I'm coming."

"Okay." She'd been sitting on the swing and she rose. "In that case, you should come and sit down."

She didn't have to tell him twice. He climbed the stairs two at a time. When he reached the porch, he stopped and stared at her. She was just so beautiful. Dressed in a pair of white denim shorts that showcased her shapely legs and an orange T-shirt that clung to her, she was the sexiest thing he'd ever seen. His heart thumped in his chest and he knew he would never be tired of looking at her.

But her beauty wasn't just on her outside. She was beautiful on the inside, as well. Gabriella gave her love freely and with her entire heart.

"Are you going to say anything or are you just going to stare at me?"

He shook himself and walked over to the swing. She had been sitting in the middle, so she scooted over to make room for him to sit. "As much as I would like to just look at you, I've come to speak with you."

She smiled and relief surged through him. Although she didn't need to—and he certainly didn't deserve it—she was making it easy for him.

"You're a sight for sore eyes, yourself, Carson."

"I guess I should just get to the point of my visit. I was so wrong to step away from you. I was wrong when I said that our love didn't matter. It's the only thing that does matter."

"What about your father? And Rusty?"

"Ah, my father. I hate what he did and always will. But I can't change the past. We're two different people. His actions are his and his alone. They don't define who I am as a person."

"Do you truly believe that in your heart?"

"Yes." He shook his head. "It's just…"

"What?"

"I've never told anyone this, but a part of me misses him."

"Of course you do. No matter what else he did, he was your father. Just like you can't change what he did, you can't change your relationship. And that doesn't make you a bad person to love or miss him. Nor does it make you undeserving of love. It makes you human."

"And do you still love me?"

"You have to ask?"

He knew in his heart the answer, but yes, he needed to hear it again. He nodded.

She cupped his face in her hands and looked directly into his eyes. "I love you, Carson Rivers. Now and forever."

He closed his eyes and inhaled deeply. She still loved him. Opening his eyes, he held her gaze. "And I love you, too, Gabriella Tucker."

He pulled her close and kissed her with all the

love he had inside. Although he wanted to hold her and kiss her for the foreseeable future, he had a promise to keep. Ending the kiss, he wrapped her in his arms. "I know you want the kids to have a relationship with their father, but that might not happen."

She sighed heavily. "I know."

"And the kids know, too."

"What?"

He told her about the conversation he'd had with Justin.

Frowning, Gabriella shook her head. "Reggie doesn't know what he's missing."

"His loss is my gain. I love those kids and want them in my life. I'll be the best stepfather in the history of stepfathers."

"What? Are you asking me to marry you?"

"Yes. I know it's soon and I don't have a ring, but will you marry me and make me the happiest man in the world?"

"Yes."

As he reached to kiss her, he heard footsteps pounding through the house a minute before the front door opened.

"Carson!" Justin and Sophia ran over to him. "You're here."

He stood and gave each child a hug. "I'm here."

"Are you finished thinking yet? Because we want to ride our horses. And swim in your pool."

"Absolutely." He reached out a hand to Gabriella, helping her to stand. What better way to celebrate his engagement than with a horseback ride with his new family?

He hadn't thought it was possible, but he knew he was going to get a happy ending. They all were.

* * * * *

COMING SOON!

We really hope you enjoyed reading this book.
If you're looking for more romance, be sure to
head to the shops when new books are
available on

Thursday 24th
June

To see which titles are coming soon, please visit

millsandboon.co.uk/nextmonth

LET'S TALK
Romance

For exclusive extracts, competitions
and special offers, find us online:

f facebook.com/millsandboon

🐦 @MillsandBoon

📷 @MillsandBoonUK

Get in touch on 01413 063232

For all the latest titles coming soon, visit
millsandboon.co.uk/nextmonth

MILLS & BOON
A ROMANCE FOR EVERY READER

- **FREE** delivery direct to your door

- **EXCLUSIVE** offers every month

- **SAVE** up to 25% on pre-paid subscriptions

SUBSCRIBE AND SAVE

millsandboon.co.uk/Subscribe

MILLS & BOON

THE HEART OF ROMANCE

A ROMANCE FOR EVERY READER

MODERN

Prepare to be swept off your feet by sophisticated, sexy and seductive heroes, in some of the world's most glamourous and romantic locations, where power and passion collide.

HISTORICAL

Escape with historical heroes from time gone by. Whether your passion is for wicked Regency Rakes, muscled Vikings or rugged Highlanders, awak the romance of the past.

MEDICAL

Set your pulse racing with dedicated, delectable doctors in the high-pressure world of medicine, where emotions run high and passion, comfort an love are the best medicine.

True Love

Celebrate true love with tender stories of heartfelt romance, from the rush of falling in love to the joy a new baby can bring, and a focus on the emotional heart of a relationship.

Desire

Indulge in secrets and scandal, intense drama and plenty of sizzling hot action with powerful and passionate heroes who have it all: wealth, status good looks…everything but the right woman.

HEROES

Experience all the excitement of a gripping thriller, with an intense romance at its heart. Resourceful, true-to-life women and strong, fearless m face danger and desire - a killer combination!

To see which titles are coming soon, please visit

millsandboon.co.uk/nextmonth

JOIN US ON SOCIAL MEDIA!

Stay up to date with our latest releases, author
news and gossip, special offers and discounts, and
all the behind-the-scenes action
from Mills & Boon...

 millsandboon

 millsandboonuk

 millsandboon

't might just be true love...

MILLS & BOON
MEDICAL
Pulse-Racing Passion

Set your pulse racing with dedicated, delectable doctors in the high-pressure world of medicine, where emotions run high and passion, comfort and love are the best medicine.

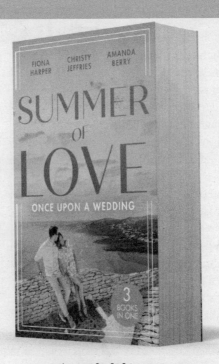